Run and Gun

Run and Gun is a novelized version of what happened to a young Professional Baseball player after he was drafted into the United States Marine Corps during World War II.

The places and events depicted in this memoir are true, only the names of some of the characters have been changed so as not to disrupt their lives in any way.

Pfc. Lee James Walewander
USMC

Table of Contents

Dedication

This book is dedicated to my wife Peggy and our four wonderful children, Robert, James, Elizabeth and John who always wanted to know what it was like for me to bea United States Marine in World War II. Well this is what it was like for me. I hope you're not disappointed.

Love Always,
Dad

All Rights Reserved

ISBN 978-0-615-22354-4

Acknowledgements

When I participated in the "Battle of the Perimeter" on Bougainville Island in the in Southwest Pacific in March of 1944 and the invasion of Luzon Island in the Philippines in January of 1945 I had no idea what was actually happening.

It wasn't until I started to write my memoirs and began to research the involvement of Marine Air Group 24 in World War II, when everything began to fall into place.

Therefore, I want to thank and acknowledge Robert Sherrod's book on the "History of Marine Corps Aviation in World War II by Combat Forces Press as my main source of factual information. I also want to thank the U.S. Marine Corps Photographers for some of the pictures I used in my memoirs.

Pfc. Lee James Walewander
USMC

*Additional copies of "Run and Gun!" may be purchased by going on line to --

http://www.grandpastories.

Run and Gun

I wonder what's to become of me, thought Lee Walewander, as he lay in his Pullman berth on his way to San Diego, California and the United States Marine Corps.

Lee Walewander a Class D Minor League baseball player who didn't expect to be drafted so soon after turning eighteen. Yet here he was on his way to Boot camp, on a military train that was picking up recruits along the way.

I was beginning to feel sorry for myself when all of a sudden a boisterous individual stuck his head into my upper Pullman berth.

"Say kid, wanna play a couple of hands of poker?

I looked around and saw a man who wprobably in his early thirties, with dark oily hair, sporting long side burns, loudly dressed and smoking a strong smelly cigar.

The names Sam Bergoni, but all my friends call me Sammy. What's your moniker kid? "

"Lee Walewander, I groggily replied.

He extended a massive hand, a hand whose nails were neatly trimmed, manicured and extremely powerful looking.

"Well Lee, whadya say, want to play a little poker?"

"I don't think so. I don't feel much like playing poker, perhaps later on."

"Okay Lee, save your pennies, but where we're going you won't need them," he laughed and with that he left me.

As I lay there in my berth, the thought of giving up a career in baseball for fighting didn't sink in as yet. I crept under the cold sheets and starred out the window. I wondered how my life was going to change, or for that matter if I do survive, will I be maimed in any way?

At least now those little old ladies won't bug me after every game.

But when you're asked, "How come a healthy young man like you isn't fighting for his country like my son is," night after night, you get tired of hearing it. I turned over and went to sleep.

I awoke early the next morning, as I was too excited to sleep. I gazed out the window at the seemingly lonely farmhouses in the distance.

The next thing I heard was the Sergeant in charge telling all the recruits to get ready for breakfast. I quickly dressed and hurried to the diner. I sat down at a nearby table and was shortly joined by Sammy the acquaintance I made last night.

"Hi Lee!" he blurted out.

"Hi Sam, did you win last night?"

"Sure! Sammy always wins," he winked as he sat down. Just then, we were joined by another recruit who asked if he could join us.

"My name's Chuck O'Leary."

"Hi Chuck, I'm Lee Walewander and this guy here is Sam Bergoni."

"Hi, are you guys as excited as I am?"

"What's exciting?" Sammy asked.

"Joining the Marine Corps"

"You're kidding aren't you? The only reason I'm here it's because I was drafted. I had it made. I had plenty of dough, lots of women and my own apartment," Sammy lamented.

"I didn't know the Marine Corps drafted anyone. I was always under the impression that you had to enlist to be in it," Chuck replied.

"Technically you're right. After I was drafted, and after I passed my physical, they gave me a choice, either the Navy or the Marines."

"What about the Army?

"Nope, No Army! Just the Navy or Marines."

"Then why in the world would you choose the Marines if you hate it so much?" Chuck inquired.

"Because I swim like a rock! Does that answer your stupid question?" Sammy fumed.

I had to laugh at Sammy's dilemma, because what happened to him also happened to me. I soon found out that this was common practice during the war. If the Navy or Marines didn't have enough men volunteering for their outfits, they picked a certain number of draftees to fill their quota.

"Well what about you guys? What were you doing before you were drafted?"

"I wasn't drafted," Chuck replied. "I enlisted for four years and if I like it I'll make the Marine Corps my career. I always wanted to be a Marine, and now that I am, I'm so thrilled that I can't believe that all this is taking place."

"Listen to him, will you," Sammy grunted, "I've heard of patriotic screwballs but nothing like this," Sammy laughed.

"Yeah and its characters like you that make this a rotten world to live in," Chuck angrily replied.

Sammy was about to get up when the waiter interrupted us. I ordered orange juice, ham and eggs, toast and milk. Chuck ordered the same while Sammy insisted on a double stack of pancakes with a side order of sausage.

After breakfast, I came back to my berth, which was now made up, and sat down next to the window.

"How about a stick of gum?" Chuck asked, as he sat down next to me.

"Thanks," I replied, as I reached out and took out a stick of gum from his pack.

"Are you from Chicago?" he asked.

"Yes I am. It's a great big city with plenty of parks, a lot of Museums, Lake Michigan, and best of all two Professional Baseball and Football teams."

"How about you Chuck, are you from Chicago too?"

"No, I'm from downstate Illinois, near the University of Illinois. My folks run a dairy farm down there."

"I take it you must like cows," I jokingly quipped.

"Can't stand them," he laughed.

"Were you in school when you were drafted?" Chuck asked.

"No, I was playing Professional baseball in Tennessee."

"Really! You're kidding aren't you?"

"No I'm not. I was playing shortstop for the Kingsport Cherokees in the Appalachian League."

"Wow! A Professional Ballplayer! I'm impressed."

"Yeah, I'll bet you are." I kiddingly, replied.

"What made you want to be a ballplayer?" Chuck asked.

"Well when I was a kid growing up in Chicago I sold newspapers near Wrigley Field and one of my customers was a ticket taker who would let me in the ballpark free after the seventh inning. I would then buy a small box of popcorn and sit in the bleachers and watch the rest of the game. As I sat there munching my popcorn, the ballplayers seemed to be having so much fun and still they were getting paid for playing.

I then began to play baseball with a purpose and found out that the Good Lord blessed me with speed and quickness. I attended Joe Stripp's school of baseball in Orlando Florida and from there I was offered a tryout with the Kingsport Cherokees. The Cherokees were in the Class D Appalachian League.

Needless to say I jumped at the offer seeing that so many of the Professional ballplayers were in the service, so I figured I had an excellent chance to make the team."

"I take it you made the team," Chuck surmised.

"I sure did, in fact they had a picture of me and my second baseman Vince Fauci in the paper which brought us celebrity status in this small town.

The only drawback that I had is that I was constantly being harassed, by little old ladies who wanted to know why I wasn't fighting for our country like their children or grandchildren.

Even though most of us were too young to be drafted, these little old ladies were determined to get us to join the Armed Forces in one way or another. I guess in a sense they succeeded because after our last road trip, I was drafted and I chose the United States Marine Corps over the Army or Navy."

"That's a bummer," Chuck shook his head in disbelief.

The next two days, Chuck and I either read or talked about home. Chuck showed me pictures of some of his girl friends, and proceeded to make cute remarks about each one, while he kept talking my thoughts were of Sue Meyers a High School cheerleader that I liked very much.

Sue was a pretty blue-eyed blond whom I met when I was trying out for the Cherokees. She approached me with five of her cheerleading girl friends and asked for my autograph while I was warming up on the sidelines.

"Hey Lee, may I have your autograph?" she shouted as she leaned over the railing.

"Sure," I smiled, as I proceeded to jaunt over to a bevy of charming, happy cheerleaders.

"Would you make it out to Sue with love," she giggled.

Her girl friends that were standing behind her and perhaps egging her on were also dressed in their cheer leading outfits. It seems they all came to our game directly from their Saturday morning practice.

The minute I laid my eyes on Sue, I knew I wanted to see more of her. She was so wholesome and bubbly so when she asked me for my autograph I made sure to include my phone number under my name.

When she saw what I had done, she looked at me with a sparkle in her eyes that suggested that she wanted to meet me as much as I wanted to meet her.

That same day, after our ball game, which we lost 4 to 1, I was leaving the ballpark with our second baseman when I heard someone tooting their car horn, trying to get our attention.

I looked around and there was Sue standing up in her red convertible waving at me furiously.

"I'll see you later Vince," I winked as I walked over to where Sue was parked. As I approached the car I couldn't help but notice how pretty she was. She was wearing a light blue blouse; a dark blue pleated skirt, white bobby socks with sneakers to match. Her long blond hair was rustling in the wind.

"How do you like my car?"

"It's great!" I replied as I walked around it, kicking a few tires to show my approval.
"My folks bought it for me as a High School graduating gift. Wasn't that nice of them?"

"It sure was!"

"Hop in, and I'll give you a tour of our town."

"Okay," and with that I hopped into the car as Sue hit the gas pedal to show me what a pick up, it had.

Kingsport Tennessee wasn't a very large city but evidently large enough to warrant a Minor League franchise. As we drove slowly through the town, Sue showed me her High School, the only movie theatre in town, and the huge Kodak Film Company where most of the people worked and where Sue's father was an executive.

As we drove along, Sue would toot her horn whenever she saw anybody she knew.

I didn't know if she was showing off her new car or her new friend.

"Do you have any trouble getting gas," I asked as we passed a small gas station.

"Yes we're all on rations, but my Dad has connections, so I have no trouble getting gas. Although I had intentions to drive my new car to College, I may just wind up taking the train. Once I'm out of Kingsport I may have trouble getting gas so why take the chance."

"You may be right. Why chance it. "

Since I haven't eaten for some time, my stomach began to growl.

"Sue do you know of a good place a hungry ballplayer can get a hamburger and fries?" I asked, as I rubbed my tummy.

"Sure do," and in a few minutes we were pulling into a Drive Inn where the waitresses were serving their customers on roller skates.

"Hi Sue, who's your friend?" one of the waitresses asked as she approached our car.

"Lee I want you to meet Dianne Woods a good friend of mine. Lee's from Chicago and playing ball for the Kingsport Cherokees."

"Oh a Yankee," she quipped as she extended her hand.

"Nice to meet you Dianne. I like your town very much, and everyone is so friendly. Now I know what is meant by Southern Hospitality."

"Oh my, are there any more like you on your team?" she winked as she took out her order pad from her pocket. '

"Sure, we have a lot of single ball players on our team. You want me to introduce you to a few of them?" I smilingly asked her.

"No I'd like Sue to meet them first. She knows my type."

Sue said she would and with that, I ordered my burger, fries, and a strawberry malt. All Sue wanted were fries and chocolate malt.

"They have the best fries in town. Wait till you taste them."

Just then Chuck snapped his fingers to get me out of my trance.

"A penny for your thoughts," he blurted out, as I half-heartedly awoke from my pleasant daydream.

The next three days were spent picking up recruits as we journeyed to San Diego and the United States Marine Corps. A journey that may be the last one for some of us.

To pass the time away, we read every newspaper and magazine we could get our hands on.

Sammy meanwhile was playing poker all the time only stopping long enough to eat, sleep or go to the bathroom.

We arrived late that night to San Diego California. I was in a deep sleep when I heard a faint cry, which I assumed was a part of my dream.

"Alright, on your feet, snap to it, you're in the Marine Corps now," someone bellowed. I looked at my watch; it was 3:10 in the morning.

"Be with you in a minute Sarg," I muttered, closing my eyes once more.

"Come on Lee," Chuck shouted. "We're at the station and everybody is off the train but us."

I quickly arose, dressed hurriedly, and bolted down the passageway. As I was descending the stairs, I heard a bunch of Marines, probably going home on their ten-day furlough, shouting, "You'll be sorry!"

Meanwhile a tall blond rugged individual with three stripes on his sleeve was waiting there to meet us.

"Where are you guys from? Chicago or New York," he bellowed as he sized us up.

"Chicago!" we proudly answered.

"What no machine guns," he chuckled, poking an old salty looking Sergeant who stood alongside of him.

"A guy would really have to be stupid if he couldn't recognize a Chicago or New York bunch of recruits when he sees them. Why look at yourselves. Some of you are wearing Zoot suits, chains, loud ties and lo and behold what do we have here?" he pondered, as he looked at our buddy, Sam Bergoni.

"Hey Bill, come over here. I think Al Capone joined the Marine Corps, cigar and all," he bellowed.

We didn't know who this character was, but we soon found out. He was our D.I. (Drill Instructor) who was to be in charge of us during Boot Camp.

As was the custom during the war, the D.I. would meet the recruits at the station. He immediately would take roll call to make sure that everyone was present and accounted for.

Once that was done, we were then escorted to the mess hall, fed, and put up for the rest of the night in temporary barracks. What a day!

****

Chapter 2

It wasn't very long before the bugler woke us up. This was the first time in my life a bugler woke me up and it seemed kind of neat. I loitered for what seemed like a minute when all of a sudden Sergeant Briles bursts into our temporary barracks ranting and raving.

"You lazy no good S. O. B's where in the world do you think you are? When you hear that bugler blow reveille I want you to get your asses out of those fart sacks and hit the deck, on the double, or I'll have you sweeping out this barrack with your toothbrush. Do you hear me?

"Yeah" we grumbled, still half asleep.

"I don't think I'm making myself clear," he raved. "You louses will address me as Sir and when a question is asked of you I want you to answer up as loudly and as clearly as you can. Do you hear me?"

"Yes Sir," we replied.

"I can't hear you! Louder!"

"Yes Sir!" we screamed.

"Louder!"

"Yes Sir!

"Louder! Louder!"

"Yes Sir! Yes Sir! " We shouted at the top of our lungs. "That's better, now listen up. The Marine Corps has certain rules about your bunks. Once made up, you never sit on them or play cards on them. They are only for sleeping purposes. Do you hear me?"

"Yes Sir! Loud and clear! "We shouted.

Sergeant Briles then proceeded to show us how to make our beds, the Marine Corps way. When he was done he took a quarter and dropped it onto the bed. The quarter bounced a few times before settling down.

"Now that's how taut your blankets are to be. Do you hear me?

"Yes Sir!" we shouted, as loud as we could.

"That's better. Now make up those sacks the way I showed you and fall out on the double. We have a very busy day ahead of us."

We soon found out what our D.I. meant by a busy day. When we left our temporary barracks we marched over to the Mess hall and fell in line with the other boots. The line was quite long, but it moved very quickly. As I approached the door, I picked up a metal tray, some silverware and slowly moved past the counter where a line of boots were busily engaged in placing food onto our trays.

"You'll be sorry!" they chanted as bacon, scrambled eggs and toast were placed on my tray.

We followed each other like sheep until we were all seated at our designated table. There was no talking during chow, if you ran out of milk or iced tea, you lifted the container over your head and one of the boots on K P (Kitchen Police) duty, would fill it for you.

The food wasn't bad, but it lacked the appeal of a home cooked meal. There were signs posted all over the Mess hall, which dealt with the wasting of food, one that I'm sure I shall never forget.

"Food is ammunition! Don't waste it!"

I felt so guilty when I couldn't eat all of my breakfast and now was embarrassed when one of the cooks chewed me out for wasting ammunition.

"Hey boot," he shouted. "If you can't eat it, don't order it! Want not! Waste not!"

"Yes Sir," I replied as I emptied the remains in a large garbage can that stood near the door. Another group of boots were busily engaged in putting the trays and silverware in an automatic washer that was there for their disposal.

As we left the Mess hall our D. I. was waiting for us. When assembled, we marched to sickbay for still another physical. During this physical we were inoculated for Tetanus and Typhoid. These shots prepared us for oversea duty.

We were also told that some us, may encounter a slight fever from these shots and if that happens we should report to sickbay.

After these shots, we went over to have our lungs X-rayed. As I waited, I couldn't help but over hear various comments:

"All right spread your cheeks."

"Cough"

"Have you had your tonsils removed?"

"This Gyrene has to be circumcised."

"All that meat and no potatoes"

"Man this bench is cold."

Just then, Chuck approached me.

"How does your arm feel? Chuck asked, as he massaged his arm quite briskly.

"Not bad, a little stiff, but it doesn't hurt."

"Mine seems to ache a lot. I hope I don't get sick from those stupid shots" Chuck winced.

"I'm sure it will work itself out."

"I hope so."

Our next stop was to have our eyes tested. As we waited our turn, we heard the unmistakable voice of Sam Bergoni;

"What chart, Doc?"

"The one that nude blond is hiding behind. Can you see it now?"

"Yeah, I can see it, but tell me Doc, are these spots I see in front of my eyes, mine or yours?"

"The Doctor looked at his aide, winked, 20-20 next."

We passed our physicals with flying colors and once more assembled outside of sickbay, where Sergeant Briles was waiting for us.

"All right you Chicago gangsters and pimps, fall in, on the double. We're going shopping!"

We quickly dressed our ranks and then were double timed to the Quartermaster Depot to do a little shopping.

As we entered the depot, the Quartermaster was there to greet us. He stood there like "God" behind the counter knowing everyone's size just by looking at them.

As we approached the counter, dungarees, skivvies, T-shirts, socks, a pith helmet and a sea bags came flying out at us. I caught most of my issue but others weren't as fortunate. If I ever saw chaos this was it! Wearing apparel was strewn all over the place. It reminded me of a Fire sale at Marshal Fields.

"Come on move on. Pick up your gear and move out. Move it! Move it!" they shouted at us.

I managed to get my gear into my sea bag and fall in line behind Sam Bergoni who was really in sad shape. He had clothes draped all over himself and underneath this mess Sam was really pissed.

"If they think they can keep me in this looney outfit they're crazy. I'll go over the hill before I put up with much more of this. Man I've had it!"

"You ain't seen nothing yet Bergoni. You'll really be sorry you joined the Marines when I get through with you," growled our beloved Sergeant Briles who was standing by and overheard Sammy complaining.

"The rest of you, stop beating your gums and get your gear into your sea bags. We're moving on to have you amphibians fitted for boon dockers."

"What the hell are boon dockers," I whispered to Chuck.

"Beats me!" he whispered under his breath.

We soon found out what boon dockers were, when our feet were X-rayed and we were issued two pairs of what the Army calls Combat boots.

Most of our clothing was now issued except for a pair of dress shoes and the blouse to our dress uniforms.

We were to be issued these in our last week of boot training. After we got "squared away" we marched over to an area, which contained hundreds of tents.

"This is "Tent City", your new home for the next two weeks," Sergeant Briles informed us.

"Do you like it?"

"Yes Sir!" we shouted.

"I can't hear you," he shrieked.

"Yes Sir!" we shouted once more, but this time, I thought my eardrums would burst.

Our beloved Sergeant was still disappointed and so we had to convince him many times over that "Tent City" was indeed a splendid place to call home.

We were assigned a certain number of tents and were told that eight of us were to occupy each one. Chuck, Sammy and I moved into one of them and as soon as we were inside, Sammy dropped his sea bag and collapsed on top of it.

"Man I've had it!" he groaned. "I haven't been this tired since the cops chased me back home in Chicago."

"Tell us about it Sam, what did you do?"

"Well I was running a private little crap game when someone blew the whistle on me. The cops were all over the place and so we all took off in different directions. I ran as fast as I possibly could but the Cops chased me with their squad cars and I was losing ground. Fortunately squad cars can't climb fences so I was able to escape. I was beat! Just the way I feel right now."

No sooner did Sammy tell us about his escapade with the Cops, five more boots moved into our tent, and busily began to unpack their sea bags and unfold their cots. We were instructed to have our cots aligned in fours, that is, four on each side. Our sea bags, with all of our gear, had to be placed at the right of our cots except the sheets, blanket and pillow, which was now a part of our sack.

"Fall out in five minutes!" Sergeant Briles bellowed, "and make sure all your gear is squared away."

Chuck and I were just about finished when we noticed that Sammy was still asleep.

"Hey Sam you better get up, we fall out in five minutes. Briles wants us to have all of our gear stowed away and as yet you haven't opened up your cot," I shouted as I shook him. When Sammy heard this, he bolted upright and speedily began to unpack his cot.

"Hey guys how about helping me, I don't think I can make it."

"Sure thing," we replied, and the seven of us got Sammy squared away in the nick of time. We fell out on the double and found two burly, weather-beaten Marines, standing alongside Sergeant Briles.

"Boots," he said. "I want you to meet Corporal Olson and Private First Class Kotowski. These two gentlemen are going to help me to either make you the best darn platoon in this here Marine Corps or the worst – nothing in between. Do you hear me?" "Yes Sir," we shouted in unison.

"As you men all know, we're in the early stages of the war. We are desperately in need of trained fighting personal and our job is to give you the best possible training in the shortest period of time. Normally, boot camp runs anywhere from fourteen to twenty weeks but in your case we have to train you in seven weeks.

Some of you won't make it, others will wish they were dead, but when done, you'll be proud of yourself and proud that you're a Marine.

Now I'm going to give you people just three minutes to go back to your tents and get rid of your civilian clothes. Put on your skivvies, T-shirt, socks, dungarees, belts, boon dockers and pit helmets. When you fall out, Pfc. Kotowski is going to march you over to the base Barbershop where you'll be sheared of your golden locks.

"Fall out!"

We quickly scrambled into our tents, tossed our civvies on our sacks put on our dungarees which not only will we train in but perhaps die in. My dungarees were a little too big in the shoulders but after noting how some of the others looked, I was perfectly happy. I just finished tying my shoelaces when the whistle blew and we literally flew out of our tents and fell in line.

"Tetch Hut" (Attention) shouted Pfc. Kotowski.

"You're looking at your new God, because what I say will be the last word as far as you're concerned, and if there's anyone in this platoon who is going to disagree with me in any way, please step forward so I can whip your ass once and for all."

Just then one of the boots stepped forward and Pfc. Kotowski winced when he saw the size of this enlistee. He stood over 6 feet tall and must have tipped the scales at about 250 pounds. His nose looked like it was broken a few times and the word was passed around that he was a professional boxer.

"Pfc. Kotowski was no slouch himself. He too was about 6 feet tall, weighed about 190 pounds, which seemed to be concentrated in his shoulders.

He also had dark curly hair, which was slightly gray at the temples. His features were of the pugnacious type, which prompted his buddies to nickname him "Bulldog."

"You men will remain in ranks until I whip this big idiot and drag his carcass back for you to observe." And with that Bulldog motioned for the boot to follow him.

They proceeded to walk behind our tent where there was a little more room for this tussle to take place. We soon heard a lot of groans and dust flying about.

"Tiny must be killing him!" we shrieked with joy. But when it ended Bulldog emerged from behind our tent and barked an order;

"O'Leary, Carson step forward and drag this idiot back into ranks, and on the double."

"That dirty bastard used Judo on me, boy I'm lucky he didn't kill me," moaned Tiny as he held his stomach.

When Tiny was back in ranks, Bulldog stood facing us with his hands on his hips.

"Anyone else?"

No reply.

"I can't hear you!"

"No Sir!" we shouted.

"Now as I was saying, before I was so rudely interrupted. You people will show me more respect than you show your Chaplains back home. You will address me as Sir, and when called upon to do a job you will do it above your capabilities. Enough isn't enough in the Marine Corps, we expect more from you people and nine times out of ten we get it, do you hear me?"

"Yes Sir!" we shouted.

"Tent City is going to be your home for the next two weeks. During this two-week period you will be rounded into shape, not only physically but also mentally.

You will be taught how to march properly, will be issued a rifle which you will take apart, and learn the name of every part, and put this rifle together while blindfolded.

You will memorize the duties of a sentry, run an obstacle course in a certain time, attend swimming classes if you can't swim, be taught Judo, bayonet fighting and learn how to defend yourself in a bar room brawl. But most of all you will be taught discipline. This here Marine Corps runs on discipline and don't you forget it. Now let's start marching!"

"Tetch Hut! Right Face, Forward March!

Your left, Your left, Your left right left. Your left, your left, your left, right left. "

As we marched along, we kept stumbling in ranks and were constantly getting out of step. This irritated our D.I. to such an extent that he would either trip us or give us a swift kick in the ass.

"You're waddling like a duck Walewander," shouted Bulldog and with that a size 12 found its mark.

As the stars faded away, I cursed under my breath, which startled me.

My God, I mused, this is only my first day and already I'm changing. So as not to get kicked again, I began to listen to Bulldog's commands and before long it was kind fun marching in step. It seemed to me like a square dance only we didn't twirl.

We soon arrived at the base barbershop and lined up near the entrance.

"When you get your hair cut, you'll fall out on the double and wait for the rest of your platoon. Is that clear?"

"Yes Sir!" we shouted.

Upon entering the barbershop, I counted eight so-called barbers busily engaged in scalping the boot. To me it looked like they were shearing sheep.

As we waited our turn, it was quite obvious that some sort of speed contest was in progress because one of the barbers shouted out, "One minute and forty seconds! Try and beat that!"

And try they did. Clippers were humming, scissors were clicking, and Sammy was complaining.

"Just take a little off the top and thin out the side burns," grumbled Sammy, knowing full well that whatever he said was falling on deaf ears. My haircut took a little over 1 minutes and it looked it! Since my hair wasn't trained to stand upright, my hair took on the appearance of a worn out scrub brush. Some members of our platoon were smart and got crew cuts before joining the Corps and consequently looked pretty good.

When done, we mustered and marched over to the parade grounds where we proceeded to learn "Close Order Drill."

"Dress up those lines! Arms length, crapheads!

Left face! Right Face! About Face! Count off, loud and clear! One, two, three, four, Column left! Column right! Right oblique! March!"

As we kept marching up and down the parade grounds our feet were beginning to hurt. Our boon Dockers weren't broken in as yet and I felt as if I was getting a blister. I figured if I was getting a blister, others in our platoon are too, but nobody complained. We marched all morning with Briles, Olson and Bulldog taking turns calling cadence.

Bulldog finally double timed us back to Tent City and allowed us 15 minutes to take care of our bodily needs. The first thing I did when we were back in our tent was to take off my boondockers.

"Oh my God! Chuck, look at the size of this blister on my heel. It's as big as a silver dollar!"

"I've got one too, but not as big as yours," Chuck replied.

"Look at this one," Sammy winced.

After comparing our blisters, we rubbed a little Vaseline on them and then put on a fresh pair of socks.

We soon fell out for Chow. I soon learned that breakfast, lunch and dinner was called Chow and it didn't make any difference what time of day it was, it was still Chow or Chow call.

We went to chow and afterwards returned to our tent to relax for a few minutes before Briles, Olson or Bulldog took over. We had to sit on the wooden deck because once our sacks were made up you were forbidden to sit on them or catch holy hell. "What good are these cots if you can't crap out in them?" Sammy replied, as he proceeded to take a little nap before the whistle blew for muster.

It was only a few minutes later, when Sergeant Briles stalked into our tent.

"Attention!" shouted one of our tent mates.

We sprang to our feet and stood rigidly at attention, but Sammy wasn't fast enough to get up in time.

"Bergoni, when I give you an order, I expect you to carry it out.

When, I tell you to stay out of that God Damn sack, I mean just that. Do you hear me?"

"Yes Sir!" Sammy shouted.

"Yet here you are calling my bluff. I don't like when somebody calls my bluff. Do you hear me?"

"Yes Sir!" Sammy shouted.

"Get down and give me 50 pushups. Right now! And count them off!"

"One, two, three, four, etc." Sammy kept pushing up and down with his arms, and as he approached 50 he was shaking like a leaf. He knew he was really out of shape.

When Sammy was done, Briles told him that he would have to find and string up 100 cigarette butts when he gets his sewing kit.

When he had 100 of them strung up, he was to drape them around his neck and report to his tent.

When Briles departed, Sammy scratched his head.

"Where in the world am I going to find 100 butts? This area is spotless, and when we do smoke we have to dismember the butt."

"Maybe you can get someone to pick up a few cartons of cigarettes from the P.X. and then you can cut them up into butt sizes. What do you think? "Chuck asked.

Just then the whistle blew, and we dashed out of our tents and aligned ourselves in columns of three.

"Tetch hut!" barked Bulldog.

This afternoon we're going to visit the dentists to see if your pearly whites are in good condition. If they're not they will be before you leave their chair.

This dental office was very similar to the barber shop, only instead of cutting your hair they clean, pull, and fill any cavity you have in one sitting. I had two cavities, drilled and filled in about fifteen minutes. After our teeth were checked out, we mustered outside the dental building until everyone was present and accounted for.

"Tetch Hut!" Bulldog shouted.

"Now that we have taken care of your teeth we want to find out how smart you are. You are going to be given a battery of tests from which we will decide if you're capable to fly a plane, cook a meal, repair a motor vehicle, etc."

"Tetch hut! Rite Face, Foward Hartch. Yo lept, Yo lept, Yo lept rite lept, Yo lept, yo lept, yo lept rite lept," chanted Bulldog, as he marched us over to a large administrative building. The first test was for general intelligence, which is commonly referred to as an I. Q. test. These tests were timed and after completing them we were interviewed to find out what our likes and dislikes are. -

"Hi Lee, how would you like to be an aerial gunner in the Marine Air Corps?" the Captain asked me.

"In the Marine Air Corps, Sir!" I blurted out. "I didn't know the Marines had an Air Corps."

"Well they sure do! And a pretty darn good one if I have to say so myself," he smiled.

"What would I do?"

"Well sometimes the Marine Air Corps has to protect the Marines fighting on the ground and give them close air support when they're pinned down. So you'd be sent to gunnery school and if you qualify you'd be a gunner on our Dive bombing planes. What do you think?"

"I guess it's alright, instead of fighting on the ground, I'd be fighting in the air."

"Okay Lee, but you know that after Boot Camp is completed, they may put you in a Marine Infantry division or in the Marine Air Corps.

It all depends on where you're needed the most. So I can't promise you anything."

I stood up, saluted, and another boot sat down to be interviewed

The next test we took was to determine if we had the ear to be able to send and read Morse code at a rapid pace. -22-

If you could interpret the dots and dashes as letters, you had a pretty good chance that you'd be sent to Radio school after Boot Camp.

After we left the building, I was hoping we would have a little free time so I could write a few letters to my loved ones, which of course would include Sue, my favorite cheerleader. But I was disappointed!

We mustered and marched over to the Quartermaster Depot, where we were issued a field jacket, a poncho and a bucket which contained a sweat shirt, towels, scrub brush, soap, razor and blades, shaving cream, sewing kit, shoe polish, stationary, pencils, etc.

The pail and its contents cost us $12.50 which was be taken out of our first month's salary.

With the bucket in one hand, and our jacket and poncho in the other, we marched over to our tent area and stood at attention.

"At Ease! Your great white father has something to tell you. You people received a pail, scrub brush and soap a few minutes ago, which you shall put to good use every day. At about 1500 (3 o'clock), you will wash the clothing that you wore that day. At 1600 there will be a clothing inspection.

If I find a speck of dirt, or fart stains on your skivvies, I'll drop them and grind them into the dirt, and have you wash them over again. Is that clear? "

'Yes Sir! " we shouted.

The wash racks were about twenty yards long and about four feet wide. In the center and running lengthwise were two pipes that carried the hot and cold water for our use. There were two faucets for every scrubbing area.

The tables were made of wood and since they were out in the open, they got very hot. Directly behind us was a large area that had clotheslines attached to wooden posts. This is where we were to hang our clothes to dry after inspection.

We washed our clothes wearing only our skivvies, boon-dockers and pith helmets.

We filled our buckets with hot water, placed the item we were to wash into it and then put it on the rack where we soaped, scrubbed, rinsed and inspected it.

Promptly at 1600 hours, the whistle blew and our beloved Bulldog began to growl –

"All right you maidens, drape your wash over your extended arms, so I can see if you did a good job."

He started with Tiny and we knew what was going to happen.

"What's this yellow stain on your skivvies?"

"Where, Sir?

"Here!" He motioned, as he dropped the skivvies onto the ground and proceeded to grind them into the dirt with his foot.

Sammy and I looked at each other knowing full well what was in store for us.

"Dirty T shirt, Walewander" and off my arm it fell.

"Bergoni, I told you to wash your clothes, not soak them," and with that he proceeded to drop Sam's wash, article by article to the ground.

Sam stood there gnashing his teeth as Bulldog proceeded to chew him out. As he left, he accidentally stepped on Sammy's wash before attacking someone else. After rewashing our clothes, we hung them up to dry. We then showered and spent the rest of the afternoon shining our boon-dockers, while Sammy stood guard over our clothes. About 1700 we fell out for chow. Sergeant Briles stood before us and took attendance.

"After you people are finished chowing down, we are going to the amphitheatre to hear Lieutenant Baker give you the inside "scoop" on guard duty.

I want you people to pay strict attention because you will be held responsible for every blessed syllable he utters. Is that clear?"

"Yes Sir!" we shouted.

"Tetch hut! Rite face! Fohward hartch ! Yo lept, Yo lept, Yo lept, Rite lept -

We aligned ourselves in single file outside the mess hall and slowly moved towards the entrance.

"What do you think of the Corps now? Chuck asked me?"

"If the rest of our training is anything like this first day, I don't know if I can make it. What do you think Sam?"

"I think that if I didn't have to put up with Bulldog and Briles it wouldn't be so bad."

"You're sounding like you're a twenty year man," I quipped, as I pulled Sammy's pit helmet over his eyes.

Just then one of guards whose job it was to see that the line kept moving and no infiltration took place bellowed out.

"Quit the gabbing and move along!"

"Yes Sir! We replied.

We quickly took up the slack in our line and in a few minutes were picking up our metal tray and cutlery. Our chow consisted of lamb, mashed potatoes and gravy, sweet peas, a jello salad, bread, butter, ice cream and milk. No coffee!

We were instructed to go back to our camp area, take care of our needs and be ready to fall out at 1800 hours. It wasn't very long before the whistle blew and we were on our way to learn about guard duty. We arrived at what looked like an out-door arena and made ourselves comfortable on the bench like seats.

When the amphitheatre was filled, Lt. Baker introduced himself and then proceeded to welcome us to the Corps. After the hissing died down he began his lecture on the "Duties of a Sentinel on Post and over Prisoners."

He started with the General Orders of a Sentinel on Post.

1. "A sentinel on post will take charge of his post and all government property in view.
2. He will walk his post in military manner, keeping always on the alert and observing everything that takes place within sight or hearing.
3. He will report all violations of orders, that he is instructed to enforce.
4. He is to repeat calls from posts more distant from the guardhouse than his own.
5. He is to quit his post only when properly relieved.
6. He is to receive, obey, and pass on to the sentinel who relieves him all the orders from the Commanding Officer, the Field Officer of the day, and all Officers and Non–Commissioned officers of the guard company only.
7. He is to talk to no one except in the line of duty.
8. He is to give an alarm in case of fire or disorder.
9. He is to call the Corporal of the Guard in any case not covered by instructions.
10. He is to salute all officers, and all colors.
11. He is to be especially watchful at night, and during the time for challenging, and to challenge all persons on or near his post, and to allow no one to pass without proper authority. "

As Lt. Baker continued his lecture, I was becoming uneasy. Sporadic chills crept over me. Chuck kept looking at me, sensing something was wrong.

"You look feverish Lee! Aren't you feeling well?"

"I don't know what's happening to me Chuck. I felt good all day and all of a sudden I'm getting these hot and cold flashes."

"Sounds like you have "Cat Fever" Lee."

"What the hell is Cat fever?"

"It's a reaction or mild fever you get when your body is adjusting to the shots we got this morning."

"How long does it last?"

"I really don't know Lee, but if you turn in to sick bay they'll probably keep you there for a week or so.

"What about the training that I would miss?"

"You'd be assigned to a new platoon, one that is just beginning its boot training."

I had mixed emotions about my dilemma. I'd like to go to sickbay and feel better but at the same time I want to stay with my platoon.

As I sat there listening to Lt. Baker, I decided to stick with my platoon at any cost.

No sooner did I make my decision, the chills became un-bearable; Lt. Baker just as vociferous and I just as miserable

"If you pull interior guard duty your purpose as a guard is to preserve order, protect property, and enforce orders and regulations. And furthermore if you should become ill while on Guard Duty, you will call on the Corporal of the Guard to relieve you."

He continued for what seemed like another hour and when he finally finished we filed out of the Amphitheatre and fell into ranks.

It was quite late so Sergeant Briles marched us directly back to our camp area.

"At ease men," yawned Briles. "Tomorrow morning, when you're awakened by the bugler at 0530, you will have exactly three minutes to make up your sacks before roll call. After roll call you will have exactly fifteen minutes to take care of your needs.

You will then fall out for chow and upon your return, you will police the area (clean up), and be ready to fall out for a very busy day. Is that clear? "

"Yes Sir!" we responded. "Ten Hut ! Fall out ! "

As soon as we were dismissed, I spread my blanket, field jacket and seabag over my cot and climbed into my sack.

"What are you doing?" Sam asked.

"I'm trying to keep warm, I'm freezing to death!"

Before I knew what was happening, everyone in our tent covered me with their blanket.

I now had eight blankets over my shivering body and I was still freezing.

"Hey guys don't say anything to our D.I.'s. I don't want to go to sickbay tonight. If I don't feel better in a little while you can tell Briles but not as yet," I chattered.

"Okay, we'll give you an hour," Chuck replied.

As I lay there freezing, I couldn't help but think of home and the attention I would be receiving at a time like this. Yet here I was over two thousand miles away, alone and ill. I was really feeling sorry for myself when I overheard Sammy whispering.

"Lee and I were to report to Briles at 1900 hours but since we attended that lecture on guard duty, maybe he doesn't want to see us tonight, or maybe he forgot.

On the other hand, if I did report, he'd tell me to fetch Lee, which I couldn't do, so I better leave well enough alone. I'm sure he'll blow a gasket tomorrow but I don't have much of a choice, do I."

"No you don't!"

"I think the fever is breaking, look how he's perspiring."

"Gee I hope so," replied Sam. "I'd sure hate to see him leave our platoon."

The bugler blew taps and our first day of Boot Camp came to an end.

****

Chapter 3

As the bugler announced the dawn of a new day, we promptly bounced out of our sacks. It was 0530.

"Lee, how do you feel this morning?"Chuck inquired, as he speedily removed the extra blankets from my sack and began to return them to our tent mates.

"A hundred percent better Chuck, in fact with a good breakfast under my belt I'll be as good as new."

"That's great! We were worried about you."

Just then the whistle blew and as we scrambled out of our tents and quickly aligned ourselves in columns of three, ready for roll call.

After roll call we had fifteen minutes to wash, shave, and fall out for chow. As soon as we were dismissed, we double timed it to our tents, picked up our soap, shaving kit, and towel, and hurried to the bathroom. In the Armed Forces the bathroom is called the Head. Why they call it the head, I have no idea. Nevertheless the head was a one story wooden structure about one hundred feet long and about thirty feet wide. A bulkhead or wall divided it into two rooms. In each room there was a row of washbowls that lined each wall and directly behind them, out in the open, a row of white glistening stools or commodes were present.

In order to save time it usually was a good idea to wash and shave first and then take care of your bodily functions. On the other hand, if you were slow in getting to the head, you took care of your bodily functions first and then put in your bid for the next vacant washbowl. Every morning the same poignant remarks were expressed;

"Who died?"

"Man will you flush that bowl!"

"Hey Bergoni, your insides must be rotting out!"

"Any one have a roll of toilet paper?"

"I hear they're going to hold our lectures on gas warfare in this head, quipped Chuck.

"Yeah man," replied Tiny as he held his nose.

It wasn't long before we mustered and marched to the Mess hall. After chow, we marched back to our tent area and were instructed to police the area. (clean up) We spent about fifteen minutes picking up any debris we could find, which we placed in large drums and made sure the lid was on good and tight. The whistle blew and we quickly fell in line and stood at attention. All three of our Drill Instructors were present.

"This morning, as every morning from now on, we will inspect you people for cleanliness. Corporal Olson and Pfc Kotowski will assist me in looking you over to see whether you've shaved, washed behind your ears, brushed your teeth, and cleaned the dung from under your nails.

In the Marine Corps, we expect you people to clip your fingernails as close as possible. We don't want to see Victory gardens growing under your nails. We also want you to be clean shave at all times. If perchance you should forget to shave or miss a few whiskers, you will have to dry shave the next day.

"Yes Sir!" we shouted.

"While were inspecting you, we want you to show us both sides of your hands, and also smile so we can see whether you've brushed your pearly white teeth. Is that clear? "

"Yes Sir!" we shouted.

Bulldog started with Tiny and immediately spotted a whisker under his chin.

"Bartells you must be a radio and this antenna protruding from under your chin must be your way of getting better reception! Are you a radio Bartells?"

"No Sir! Tiny responded.

"See me tomorrow morning with your razor."

"Yes Sir! " Tiny unhappily shouted.

Briles was inspecting our line and as he approached me, I knew I was in trouble.

"Pvt. Walewander it looks as if you're clean shaven but yet when I look at you from a certain angle, I see what looks like peach fuzz. Are you a peach Walewander?"

"No Sir!" I shouted.

"Well I think you are! See me tomorrow morning with your razor."

"Yes Sir!"

"Private Bergoni you're a slob. Don't you ever was your hands? Look at your fingernails; it looks like you've been brought up in a pigsty. Report to me tomorrow morning with your scrub brush and soap. "

"Yes Sir!" Sammy groaned.

A few more of us were given penalties and then we proceeded to be marched over to the parade grounds for what would become a daily dose of mass calisthenics.

The parade ground was also called the "black top" because it was covered with asphalt.

In the center of this huge field stood a wooden platform upon which were located two loud speakers and a microphone. Directly in front of the microphone stood a well-tanned muscular individual attired in a white T-shirt, khaki pants, gym shoes and sweat socks. Alongside of him stood his two assistants also quite tan and muscular and dressed accordingly.

"My name is Sgt. Langford and my job is to whip you into shape before you go to the rifle range in two weeks. Every morning at 0900 you people will participate in-group calisthenics and to see that you're not "gold bricking" (not performing the exercises) your D I's will watch you and lend a helping hand when needed.

My two assistants will perform the exercises up here, and you do the same down there.

Now take off your dungaree jackets, and let's get started. For your first exercise - - -

Place your hands on your hips and twist your torsos to the left and then to the right. Now let's go!

Turn to your left, turn to your right, your left, your right, etc. Come on stretch those lazy muscles, left, right, left, right, etc.

While the physical educational instructor was calling the shots his two assistants were performing the exercises on the aforementioned stage. After this exercise we were subjected to a few more, such as; touching our right toe with our left hand, left toe with our right hand, doing pushups, knee bends and topped off by what is called " Fireman's carry."

In Fireman's carry you pick up an individual and balance him across your shoulders, distributing his weight accordingly, thereby making it a very simple task to carry or even run with a much heavier person than yourself. This is a very important technique to know especially in combat.

Chuck and I carried each other and we were bushed when we were done. I thank God I didn't have Tiny to carry.

When we were finished with Fireman's carry we were told to pick up our dungaree jackets and fall in line.

"At ease!" Briles announced. "The rest of this morning we will spend in Close Order Drill. This afternoon, after chow, you will be issued an M1 rifle. These rifles have a good coating of cosmoline (grease), which you will remove with gasoline. You will then take your rifle apart, learn the name of every part, and then dry, oil and put it back together again. The manual that you were issued yesterday will show you how to take this rifle apart. Your rifle is your best friend, treat it with respect and it will never let you down. You will keep it oiled and clean at all times and be able to identify every part if asked to do so. Is that clear? "

"Yes Sir!" we acknowledged.

"I may call on you to dismantle and reassemble your rifle in the dark and God have mercy on your wretched souls if you can't do it. And one more thing, don't ever let me hear you call your rifle a gun.

If you don't know the difference, look it up in your bible (Marine Corps Hand book.) Is that clear? "

"Yes Sir!" we replied.

"And by the way, I want each and every one of you to memorize the eleven General Orders of a sentry on Guard Duty by tomorrow evening. Is that clear?

"Yes Sir!" we shouted.

"Corporal Olson and Pfc. Kotowski will take over this morning and I told them to work your butts off. All right Corporal , take over, and see if you can teach these sad sacks how to march properly."

Corporal Olson and Pfc. Kotowski acknowledged Sergeant Briles by a salute and when Briles departed, Olson did an about face, addressed our platoon and began marching us back and forth across the parade grounds. When he got tired, Bulldog took over. He marched us until he got tired. This continued for the rest of the morning. When we got back to our tent, I immediately removed one of my boon-dockers to see what my new blister looked like.

"Man another blister?" Chuck remarked. "How in the world were you able to walk with another blister on your foot?"

"It's on the other foot, so it wasn't so bad," I winced.

Just then somebody shouted, "Mail Call"

"I'll pick up your mail Lee, you finish dressing that blister," Chuck remarked as he followed the others out of the tent. I meanwhile pricked the blister with a needle, drained the fluid and then rubbed a little Vaseline over it and put on a clean pair of socks. It felt a lot better.

"Any mail Chuck?" I asked when he returned.

"Very little, none for us though."

"I guess it's too soon to expect mail, after all this is only the second day at boot camp," I replied.

"Yeah, you're probably right."

Once more the whistle blew and we fell out for chow.

We were told to report back to our tent on our own and write a letter home so our parents wouldn't worry about us.

As Chuck and I left the mess hall we were deep in thought, and forgot to salute an officer when he approached us.

"As you were!" shouted the Captain.

We quickly saluted but the damage was already done.

"What are your names?"

"Private Walewander," I stammered.

"Private O'Leary," Chuck gulped.

"What is your Platoon number?"

"676! Sir!" we replied."

"Haven't your D.I's instructed you in the art of saluting and showing respect to your officers?"

"Yes sir, they have sir."

The Captain smiled and said, "Since it's your second day in boot camp, we don't want to make it too rough on you boots, so I'll forget it this time, but don't let it happen again.

"Yes Sir! We won't!"

We saluted the Captain, he acknowledged, and he was on his way.

"Wow, that was a close call Chuck, just think what Briles and Bulldog would have done to us if the Captain reported us."

"I don't want to even think about it."

Just then we heard Sammy yell, "Hey guys wait up for me."

As he double-timed it towards us, I couldn't help but wonder how one's opinion of someone changes so drastically.

When I first met Sam Bergoni I thought he was obnoxious and didn't want any part of him and here we are a few days later and he's growing on me.

It wasn't very long before the whistle blew again and we were off to the Ordinance Depot to receive our rifles. They were packed in cosmoline as they said they would be.

When we got back to our camp area, we spread our ponchos on the deck and began cleaning our rifles with the gasoline that the D I's brought us. We also had an abundance of rags at our disposal.

It took a lot of scrubbing with gasoline and hot soapy water to get them clean. Once the grease was removed, I pushed the cleaning rod with a flannel patch attached, through the bore a few more times until I was convinced that the bore was good and clean. I rinsed the parts in a bucket of clean water and dried every part immaculately. I also soaked a piece of cloth in machine oil and began to spread a thin film of oil on all parts, prior to assembling the rifle.

As I began to put my rifle together, I had an idea that should make the memorizing of these parts a little easier.

"Hey guys, since we have to learn the names of these parts, why don't we make a game of it. I'll hold up a part and you guys tell me its name. Okay? "

"Sounds like a good idea," Chuck and Sammy remarked.

So with our bible in our laps we each took a turn of holding up a part and asking each other what's it called.

I started out by asking what the name of this part of the rifle is called.

"That's the plate butt," Chuck replied as he pointed to a picture of it in his bible.

"What's this part called? Sammy asked.

As we browsed through our book we almost simultaneously shouted out "stacking swivel."

"Right!"

"What about this part?" Chuck asked.

"Bolt assembly!" we replied.

We continued playing our little game when all of a sudden Bulldog appeared on the scene. "How are you guys doing? Any trouble?"

"Yeah," Sammy replied. "I have an extra part and I don't know where to put it?"

"I'll tell you where to put it!" barked Bulldog, and what's this yeah business you're giving me.

Don't you know you're supposed to address me as Sir?"

"Yes Sir!" Sammy shouted.

"Because of your forgetfulness I want you to pick up all the oily rags in our platoon and deposit them into that G I can. Is that clear?"

"Yes Sir! " Sammy once more shouted.

"All right now hurry up and assemble those pieces, we're going to have rifle inspection in fifteen minutes. Bulldog left shaking his head and once gone all eyes turned to Sammy.

"Man what a "chicken shit" outfit. It seems that every move I make gets me in trouble. If this keeps up I'll go over the hill tonight. "

"You better get your rifle assembled Sam, or you'll be getting more shit details," I added.

"Yeah, I guess you're right," he surmised. He then determined the part he had in his hand was a part of the bolt assembly. It wasn't a minute too soon. The whistle blew and like dogs on command, we mustered, and fell in line.

"Ten Shun!" commanded Sergeant Briles. "You people have been issued a .30 caliber, M1, United States rifle. It is gas operated, clip loaded, air-cooled, semiautomatic, self-feeding, shoulder weapon.

It weighs 9.5 pounds without the bayonet. The bayonet weighs an additional pound. The ammunition is loaded in clips of eight rounds.

This M1 rifle has taken the place of the 1903 Springfield rifle because of its ability to deliver a large volume of accurate fire in a very short time. It is your baby or sweetheart for as long as you stay in the Corps. It will be at your side constantly and you will have to know how to fire, clean, march, and drill with it. Pfc. Kotowski will demonstrate the proper procedure employed in carrying the rifle, the position taken at attention, and the proper procedure used in executing rifle commands.

Bulldog stepped forward, rifle in hand, and began to deliver his well-memorized speech.

"Boots, I want you to pay strict attention because I don't intend to go over this part of the manual of arms again. I'm going to start with the position taken at order arms, and continue through inspection arms and wind up with the dismissal of the platoon.

At Port Arms, the butt of the rifle rests on the ground in line with the toe of and touching the right shoe, thusly. The barrel is pointed to the rear and the rifle is grasped between the thumb and fingers of the right hand. The left hand is carried the same as at attention without arms."

Bulldog continued at some length and when it appeared as if we knew what he was talking about we were told that now our rifles would be inspected.

"Tetch hut! Order--Arms, Port----Arms, Inspection ----Arms."

Upon the command of Inspection Arms we were to place our left thumb on the operating rod handle and push it smartly to the rear until it was caught by the operating rod catch; lower the head and eyes sufficiently to glance into the receiver to see that it was empty, raise the head and eyes to the front and at the same time regrasp the piece with the left hand at the balance.

Being in this position, Briles and Bulldog began inspecting our rifles.

"Too oily!"

"Dirty bore!"

"Front sight dirty!"

"Sling is too loose!"

Not one of us passed rifle inspection but I guess that was to be expected.

"You people go back and clean those rifles, and in fifteen minutes we're going to have another inspection. Now fall out."

We double timed it back to our tents, spread our poncho on the deck and proceeded to dismantle and clean our rifles.

"I have to find that speck of dirt," quipped Chuck as he looked into his receiving chamber.

"You want to use my magnifying glass?"

"How about a telescope" Sammy jested.

We had a hearty laugh but continued to clean our rifles even though we knew they were spotless. No sooner were we finished, than the whistle sounded and we mustered once more for rifle inspection. Corporal Olson joined Briles and Bulldog during this inspection and after it was over with Briles bellowed out.

"Bergoni you will start stringing up those 100 cigarette butts immediately after you do your wash. Walewander you will stand guard duty in the head. Your duties are to make sure all toilets are flushed; no paper on the deck and the place is spotless. Is that clear? "

"Yes Sir!" we replied and with that we were dismissed to do our afternoon wash.

"I guess Briles didn't forget about us after all, did he Sam?"

"No he's like an elephant."

"Sam where in the world, are you going to find 100 cigarette butts?"

"You know Lee I think I know where I can find them."

"Where?"

"As soon as I'm finished with my wash, I'm going to double time it behind the Beer Hall and check those garbage cans. I think I'll find what I'm looking for, don't you think?"

"Yes! I think it's a great idea, what made you think of it.?"

"Elementary Lee, purely elementary," he smiled as he inspected the crotch of the skivvies he just washed. Almost everyone passed our afternoon clothing inspection.

We hung up our wash to dry and proceeded to do our penalties. Sammy headed for the Beer Hall, while I picked up my cartridge belt and "Billy club" and departed for the head. The rest of our platoon went back to their tent to either write letters, shine their boondockers, or memorize the General Orders of a Sentry.

When I got off guard duty, I returned to my tent to find Sammy sitting on the deck, stringing up cigarette butts, which he was taking out of a brown paper bag. Whenever he came across one that was over an inch long, he cut it in half'

"I see you hit the jackpot Sam, how many butts did you find?"

"Enough to string up 100, that's for sure."

"Oh by the way, how was guard duty in the head?" Sammy asked.

"It stunk!" I replied.

Our little chitchat was interrupted by chow call. We stood at attention and waited for Sergeant Briles to tell us what's on the agenda for this evening.

"This evening, at 1900 we will attend a lecture dealing with fires. As Marines you may be called upon to help put out forest fires or even fires that may be caused by an exploding bomb or a Molotov cocktail.

Pay attention because I may ask you questions about the nature of some of these fires. Is that clear?"

"Yes Sir!"we shouted.

"Okay, let's get some grub. Rite face, fohward march, yo lept, yo lept, yo lept, rite lept,etc.

Immediately after chow, we departed for the amphitheatre where the lecture on fires was to take place. After we were seated and quiet, a robust Master Sergeant walked across the stage and introduced our lecturer Lt. Marson.

"Good evening, Marines. Tonight our lecture and demonstration is on fires. You never know when a fire will occur and once burning how do you extinguish it?

Fires are classified as either an A , B, or C . First of all for any fire to take place three conditions have to be met;

1. You must have a fuel or something to burn.
2. Secondly you must have air or the oxygen that's present in air.
3. The kindling temperature of the fuel has to be reached.
   If any one of these conditions are removed, a fire cannot take place."

Just then the Master Sergeant hauled out three large drums onto the stage, which had an A, B, and C painted on them.

"The first type of fire and the most common is the A fire. The fuel in the A fire can be paper, wood, straw, coal, etc. A couple of Marines came on stage and placed some paper and wood in the A drum and lit it. As the fire burned, Lt. Marson told us that this type of fire could be put out with water, or with a Carbon Dioxide extinguisher, which suffocates or removes the air from around the burning fuel.

No sooner had he said this, one of the Marines poured a bucket of water onto the fire and the other one used the carbon dioxide extinguisher.

The fire was extinguished but a lot of smoke was produced.

The B fires consist of paints, gases, oils, greases, etc. The best way to put out this type of fire is to smother it with sand. If you use water, it will only spread.

Once more the two Marines that were assisting Lt. Marson placed some paint, gasoline, grease and oil into the B drum and lit it. This type of fire produces a lot of smoke and heat. The assistants then poured a couple of buckets of sand into the B drum and the flame was extinguished.

The last type of fire that I'm going to talk about is electrical in nature. It usually starts with some electrical device shorting out, sparking and igniting some type of combustible material.

Usually the coating on the wire itself may start to burn and it in turn ignites nearby material.

To show how electrical fires start the Lieutenant placed an electrical motor with wires attached on top of the inverted C labeled drum. He then plugged in the motor and lo and behold sparks were flying everywhere, igniting a nearby curtain.

"The best way to put out electrical fires is by using a Carbon tetrachloride fire extinguisher, like this one here," he replied, as he held it upright for all to see.

He then proceeded to spray the fire, which extinguished it immediately.

The lecture was finally over. We left for Tent City and sack time.

****

Chapter 4

Gabriel blew his horn and another hectic day of boot camp was about to begin. We made up our sacks, fell out for roll call, and hurried to the head.

"Hey Lee, you're going in the wrong direction" shouted Tiny.

I stopped suddenly, and remembered that Bulldog wanted me to dry shave this morning. I did an about face, picked up my pocket mirror and double-timed it to our D I's tent. When I entered, some of my friends were already busily engaged in scratching off their beards.

"Hubba, Hubba," (Hurry up!) Walewander, get in here, or I'll have you come back every morning for the rest of the week," growled an angry Bulldog.

"Yes Sir!" I hurriedly replied.

Holding a mirror in one hand and a razor in the other, I began to dry shave. My first stroke was a little deep and I could see and feel the warm blood trickle down my cheek. Fortunately Bulldog had many styptic pencils handy because we sure needed them.

In the meantime, Sammy along with a few more of our platoon members we're crouched over their buckets scrubbing their hands. I couldn't help but notice how red their hands were when they showed them to our DI's. We were finally dismissed and given a few more minutes to take care of our needs.

Immediately after chow and before our morning calisthenics, our DI's told us about a little drill they made up to see how fast we could carry out an order.

"I want you to go back to your tents and put on your U. S. Marine overcoat and get your butts out here as fast as you can. The last one out get's a detail. Is that clear?"

"Yes Sir!" we shouted.

"All right- dismissed!"

We took off like "bats out of hell" and began to empty or seabags onto our cots. Since all our belongings are neatly rolled up in our seabags, our overcoat which we haven't used as yet, was down at the bottom of our bags. Skivvies, T-shirts, shaving kits, bars of soap, shoe polish and other articles were flying about as everyone was digging out their overcoat. I finally pulled out my crumpled overcoat from within, and proceeded to put it on as I double-timed it out of the tent. Everyone was accounted for except poor Sammy and an enlistee who was nicknamed "Porky". It now became a contest between these two and words of encouragement were being voiced.

"Hurry up Sam," Chuck and I screamed.

Just then two disheveled figures emerged almost simultaneously from their tents and began to double-time towards us.

"Hurry Sam," Chuck and I continued screaming.

"Come on Porky," others shouted.

It was a close race but Sammy won.

"That was pretty damn slow, so we'll try again, only this time I want you to go back to your tents and pack away everything that is yours, including your cot, bedding and rifle. The last one out gets a detail, and don't leave anything behind.

"Dismissed!"

A cloud of dust emerged as we stampeded to our tents. As I ran, I tried to remove my overcoat but almost stumbled in the process so I quickly gave up on the idea. When I entered the tent, I immediately grabbed my empty seabag and began stuffing it with anything that was on my cot or nearby. Once I got my seabag filled and secured, I pulled out the supports on each side of my cot, caved in the legs and wrapped my mattress around it. I placed my pillow and sheets inside my bedroll and then covered them with my camouflaged poncho.

I then placed my sea bag over my right shoulder, slung my rifle over my left shoulder, picked up my bedroll with my left hand and hobbled out of the tent.

In the process I tripped over some one's pillow and my pit helmet kept falling over my eyes. My bedroll finally fell apart but luckily a few feet from our platoon. I wasn't worried, I knew when I left my tent there were a lot of guys still packing their seabag so I knew I wouldn't be the last one. As I stood there panting, I noticed that Chuck was present but Sammy wasn't. I looked for Porky and he too was having trouble. Sammy struggled but still managed to beat out Porky and Tiny. So it looked like it was going to be Porky and Tiny once more.

While all this was going on our D I's stood there with shit eating grins on their faces. They were enjoying this torture they were putting us through and it wasn't over yet. When we were all present and accounted for, Porky and Tiny were called forth by Briles.

"You two snails will pick up your seabags and run down this road up to that fourth row of tents and back again. If you don't make it in 40 seconds you'll have to do it over again. Is that clear! "

"Yes Sir!" they shouted as they tried to catch their breath.

"Now get going," he ordered.

Porky and Tiny took off down the road and Tiny being the stronger and in much better shape had no trouble getting in under 40 seconds. Porky as his nickname suggested had one hell of a time. He was overweight and out of shape but had guts. We all shouted words of encouragement and for a split second it looked like he wouldn't make it but he put on a burst of speed and got in just under the wire.

"I'll give you people ten minutes to get your gear squared away, after that we fall out for out for calisthenics. Tetch hut ! Dismissed!"

-44-

We dragged our tired bodies into our tents, and began the unhappy task of setting up our cots, making up our sacks and rolling up our clothes and packing them back into our seabags.

"Man, am I bushed," complained Sammy

"If you're bushed how do you think I feel? Tiny moaned, "I had to double-time it with that seabag on my shoulders,"

"Yeah! What a bummer."

The whistle blew and we were on our way to the black top and calisthenics. We performed pretty much the same exercises we did yesterday, which included and ended with the dreaded Fireman's carry. We spent the rest of the morning marching with our rifles.

That afternoon Briles informed us that we were going to the indoor swimming pool to see how many non-swimmers we have in our platoon. A non-swimmer is anyone who can't swim 50 yards. If you don't qualify, you will be taught how to swim, in the evenings, when the rest of the platoon has some free time.

As we entered the pool area, we were instructed to put our clothes into a wire basket, shower, put on a pair of swim trunks and report back to the pool area. We complied and as we stood there looking at the cool, limpid water we were interrupted by a tall sinewy instructor who emerged from the pool.

"All right gentlemen, in order to qualify you have to swim the length of this pool twice which is 25 yards long. It doesn't matter how you do it, floating, dog paddling, breaststroke etc. just so you do it.

If you think you can swim 50 yards stay here, the rest of you report to the other side of the pool."

"I can swim this pool ten times," Chuck bragged. "How about you Lee?"

"I doubt it!" I replied. "I spent my free time on the ball diamond not on the beach. I can swim a little but I don't think I can swim 50 yards. I'm going to try it anyhow. What have I got to lose?"

The pool was about 25 yards wide, which meant that at least five of us could try to qualify at the same time. Around the pool were the instructor's assistants whose job it was to pull out anyone who was having trouble. They had long bamboo poles with a hoop at the end.

Since I knew I would have a hard time qualifying, I wasn't too eager to get into the pool. When I finally got enough courage, I dove into the pool and swam under water as long as I could. When I came up for air, I couldn't synchronize my air intake with my arm movements and consequently swallowed a couple of mouthfuls of water. I then began to dog paddle but it seemed like I wasn't moving. I began to panic, which is the worst thing you can do when you're swimming. I furiously beat the water with my arms but to no avail. I swallowed another mouthful of water and sank. I grabbed the hoop and was hauled out of the pool. I was a non-swimmer.

"Too bad Lee," Sammy commented. "I thought you were going to make it, but when you got panicky I knew you've had it. Oh well you might as well learn to swim; you never know when it might come in handy and besides you can keep me company."

"Yeah right!"

"Hey boot, get your butt over here and sign up for the non-swimmers club," shouted one of the assistants. I reluctantly did.

Out of our platoon of sixty, there were fifteen non-swimmers, which of course included Sammy and myself.

When everyone had a go at it, we showered, dressed and assembled in front of an unhappy Sergeant.

He didn't say much to us, but disgust was written all over his face. Who ever heard of a Marine who couldn't swim, he probably thought, as he double-timed us to our camp area.

We were dismissed, washed our clothes and began to memorize the General Orders of a Sentry. We were scheduled to report to our D I's tent tonight.

Sammy meanwhile was stitching together the last of his cigarette butts while Chuck was trying to get a shine on his boondockers.

"Hey guys, guess what? I figured out a way we can get a shine on our boondockers? "

"How?" we asked.

"You lather them with shaving cream and then shave them like you do your beard."

"Does it take a shine? I asked.

"Does it ever? Look at this shoe" Chuck replied.

"Man it looks great!

Immediately everyone began lathering their boondockers except for Sammy who was busy counting the cigarette butts he had strung up.

"I'm done," he gleefully shouted, as he double-timed it out of our tent. When he came to our D I's tent he asked permission to enter.

"What is it Pvt. Bergoni?"

"Private Bergoni reporting Sir, with one hundred cigarette butts as ordered, Sir."

"Come in, and count them aloud for me."

"Yes Sir," Sammy replied as he began to count his booty.

"Where'd you find all these butts?"

"Around Sir"

"Around? Where?"

"Ugh, aw, around the areas of other platoons Sir. They're not as clean and spotless as our area."

"Yeah right," he sarcastically responded, as he looked at his tent cronies.

"Bergoni if I ever catch you crapped out in that sack again, I'm going to give you a permanent butt detail. Is that clear? "

"Yes Sir!"

"Now get your ass out of here and get your Chicago hoodlums ready to fall out for chow."

"Yes Sir!" Sam shouted.

As soon as Sammy got to our tent, the whistle blew and we fell out for chow.

The meals we're pretty much the same. They were nutritious but nothing out of the ordinary. We always had some kind of meat product, and always a variety of vegetables to choose from. The beverage was water, milk or iced tea.

After chowing down, Chuck, Sammy and I were walking back to our camp area when I inadvertently asked my buddies what our lecture is going to be tonight.

"I hear they may show us movies on the prevention of venereal disease," Sammy replied.

"No I think they save that movie after we're through with boot camp and ready to go on furlough," Chuck surmised.

"In a way I hate to see these films because I feel like putting it in storage and keeping it there," Sammy laughed.

"Yeah man," we replied.

The whistle blew; we stood at attention with Corporal Olson in charge.

"Tonight we're going to hear a lecture on gas warfare," Cpl. Olson informed us. "Our lecturer is a top notch research chemist who is in charge of chemical warfare at this base. In a few days you people will be issued gas masks and be required to enter a room filled with tear gas. If you don't have your masks adjusted properly, you'll start to choke, cough and your eyes will water.

This is mild compared to how you'd react if it were mustard gas. So tonight, don't let your minds wander. Pay attention, your life may depend upon it."

When we were all seated in the Amphitheatre, a Major appeared on the stage.

"Good evening, my name is Major Bolston and I'm here to teach you a little about Gas Warfare. The world war we find ourselves in is one where no holds are barred. Poisonous gas was used in World War I by the Germans and we lost a lot of men because we weren't prepared for it.

Well we're prepared for it now and intend to stay that way. The scuttlebutt is that the Japanese have a gas that not only puts you to sleep it also tears your guts out at the same time. When you men go into combat, a gas mask will be a part of your ensemble.

It won't do you any good if you don't know how to use it; so after this evening's discussion, I hope you have a better understanding of poisonous gases.

The first gas that I shall discuss is the one most of you are familiar with, namely Mustard gas. The reason it's called Mustard gas is because its odor strongly resembles mustard, garlic or horseradish. Its chemical name is Dichlorodiethyl sulfide. It occurs as either a liquid or gas. It has a delayed effect on the subject.

It burns the skin or membrane and leads to an inflammation of the respiratory tract and finally to pneumonia.

How does one protect himself from this gas? Well he wears his gas mask and protective clothing, and when no longer exposed to this gas, he rubs his skin with a bleach paste or kerosene.

The next gas I want to talk about is Phosgene. Its chemical name is Carbonyl chloride. It has an odor of musty hay or green corn and is much deadlier than Mustard gas."

As the Major continued his dissertation on these gases it was getting quite late, maybe late enough for us to recite the General Orders of a Sentry. And late it was! The bugler was beginning to blow taps and a weary, brow beaten, tired platoon was on its way to Tent City and some shuteye.

Chapter 5

Reveille sounded, roll call was held, and another day was upon us. We shaved, washed, brushed our teeth and marched to chow.

"I wonder what we're having for chow this morning," Chuck asked.

"I hope its "S O S" (Shit on a Shingle) Sammy remarked.

SOS was toast covered with s kind of gravy that had bits of ham or beef cut into it and was a steady diet for all service men. When we approached the entrance an aroma of grease was evident and we knew French toast was on the menu, not SOS. Perhaps Sammy will get his SOS tomorrow.

"Are you going to take your ten day furlough?" Chuck asked, as I dipped my tray into hot soapy water and swirled the swab across its compartments.

"What do you mean, am I going to take my ten day furlough? Of course I am! Why shouldn't I?"

"Well the scuttlebutt is that if you defer your furlough until your next assignment, you'll get fifteen days instead of ten."

"Sounds good, but I'll have to think about it," I replied.

When we got back to our tent, the whistle blew; we mustered and marched over to the black top for our morning calisthenics. Afterwards, Sgt. Briles marched us over to the boon docks, which was a vast open field with a multitude of sand and a few trees. We were issued a bayonet and a scabbard (Cover for the bayonet) and told to snap on our bayonets onto our rifles.

"This morning, you people will learn how to use the bayonets that were just issued to you. The first thing I want you to do is to place your scabbard over your bayonet and listen up.

As you know, we're engaged in a war that most of us want no part of. Some of us are professional fighters whose job it is to protect our country at any cost. Killing is a part of our training and we have to teach you how to kill or you won't be coming back to see your loved ones after the war is over. Since most of you will be engaging the enemy in the South Pacific, and in jungles, and in close quarters, bayonet fighting is a must. Cpl. Olson and Pfc. Kotowski will demonstrate how the Japanese use their bayonets as compared to our methods.

To be perfectly blunt, you never engage the enemy in bayonet combat unless you have to. Don't let the yellow bastards come close to you. Blow their brains out before they can lob a grenade your way, is that clear?"

"Yes Sir!" we shouted.

"But if you do encounter the enemy, we want you to be able to tear his guts apart before he gets at yours. So that's why you're here this morning. My two assistants will demonstrate how to use the bayonet properly.

In bayonet fighting you place your left foot forward and plant yourself in such a position that you have your balance at all times. The stock of your rifle butt is placed under your right arm and your left hand holds the front hand guard just below the bayonet. If a Jap charges you with his bayonet pointing towards your chest, you parry (turn aside) his thrust and aim your bayonet right for the base of the bastard's neck. If your bayonet doesn't come out, squeeze off a round and pull, I'll guarantee that it does, a little bloody perhaps, but out!"

Cpl. Olson and Bulldog were going at it, parrying and thrusting. They had their scabbards on so no blood was shed.

"Ok men, spread out at arm's length.

Set yourself so you can't be shoved off balance by your D I's is that clear? "

"Yes Sir," we shouted.

As we squared away, Bulldog approached Sammy with his rifle, faked a parry and slammed Sammy's rifle to the ground.

"Bergoni you'd be dead right now if I were the enemy. Now pick up that rifle and hold it firmly at your side. Let's try it again!"

Sammy picked up his rifle, gritted his teeth and faced Bulldog once more. Sammy parried and when he thrust his bayonet forward, Bulldog locked Sammy's rifle with his own and at the same time placed his foot behind Sammy's and lo and behold Sammy was flat on his back, with Bulldog's bayonet resting on his throat.

"Not good Bergoni ! Not good! "

We all had to laugh, but very shortly afterwards found ourselves biting and hitting the sand just as Sammy did. Briles gave me a good going over, and when it was Bulldog's turn I was really pissed off, and prepared. He proceeded to rush me but instead of standing still, I jumped aside, stuck out my leg, and lo and behold there was Bulldog face down in the sand.

"Nice going Walewander, you're learning fast. Who knows, we may make a Marine out of you yet." Bulldog replied, as he spit out some sand from his mouth.

"Let's try it again," he suggested.

"Take your position and pretend I'm your enemy. I did, but I didn't have to pretend he was my enemy. He was an asshole.

As we parried and thrust our bayonets at each other, I thought I had an opening, so I quickly thrust my bayonet forward only to have Bulldog parry it and slam me to the ground.

As I got up I noticed our D I's were having a field day. They were spilling us into the sand and loving every minute of it.

After a couple of hours of this torture, we marched back to Tent City to clean our rifles of all the sand and be ready for rifle inspection, immediately after noon chow.

We spread out some ponchos on our wooden decks, and proceeded to dismantle and clean our rifles. We knew we had about a half an hour to complete our task before chow and no time afterwards.

That afternoon, after chow, we fell out for rifle inspection. Bulldog was at the helm.

"Ten Shun! N'spection Arms!" he commanded.

He moved militarily from man to man finding dirt or sand on every rifle.

"When did you clean your rifle, Pvt. Walewander?"

"This morning before noon chow," I shouted.

"Just before noon chow, what?"

"I cleaned my gun sir!"I shouted, emphatingly.

"Cleaned your gun! Did you crapheads hear what he called his rifle? He called his rifle a gun. Everybody knows the difference between a rifle and a gun, don't we?"

"Yes Sir!" the platoon shouted.

"A rifle is what you have in your hands right now, a gun is what you have between your legs. One is for fighting and the other one is for fun. Do I make myself clear? "

"Yes Sir!" we shouted.

" Private Walewander, just so you never forget the difference, this afternoon, after clothing inspection, you will march up and down the camp area, reciting these words;

"This is my rifle, this is my gun.

This is for fighting and this is for fun!"
As you chant this ditty you will point to your rifle when it's for fighting and point to your genitals when it's for fun. Am I making myself clear?"

"Yes Sir! Very clear Sir!" I shouted, as I stood rigidly at attention.

Bulldog sneered and continued his inspection, constantly beating his gums, (complaining) in the process.

We performed Close Order Drill with our rifles for about an hour and then were told that the smoking lamp was lit. (Could smoke) Those of us that didn't smoke just sat down, and relaxed, as best we could.

After about five minutes, Bulldog blew his whistle and we fell back in ranks.

"Do you people like to play games?" he asked our platoon.

"Yes Sir!" we loudly replied.

"Good, because you're going to play this game whether you like it or not. As you very well know, a Marine has to be alert and attentive at all times. If an order is given he has to carry it out to the best of his abilities. No questions asked. To see how attentive and alert you are, you will carry out an order only if it's proceeded by Maggie says. Is that Clear? "

"Yes Sir!" we acknowledged.

"All right now, Ten shun!" He ordered.

As we came to attention, Bulldog started to yelp. "You stupid idiots, did I say Maggie wanted you to come to attention?"

"No Sir!" we responded.

"Then why in the world did you come to attention? Can't you follow instructions? Now let's try again and remember don't flinch an eyelash unless my orders are proceeded by Maggie says. If you move you will step out of the platoon until only one man is left. Okay now, Attention," he commanded. No one moved!

"Maggie says, Attention!"

We all responded.

"At ease!" About five from our platoon moved, and were called out of ranks by Bulldog.

"Inspection Arms!"

Two more flinched.

"Maggie says, Inspection Arms"

We responded.

This little game continued until only two men were left. Chuck was one of them and eventually the winner.

We spent the rest of the afternoon drilling until it was time to hit the wash racks and do our laundry. After our wash was inspected, I began my tour of humility.

"This is my rifle, and this is my gun,

This is for fighting and this is for fun," I shouted, and motioned, as I made the rounds of the camp area. I felt so embarrassed; yet there was nothing I could do about it.

"Hey Gyrene, someone shouted you've got the wrong words to your ditty. It should be,

"This is my rifle and this is my gun.
They feed us Salt peter so we don't have fun!"

As the uproarious laughter continued, I felt like Sammy at this time, wondering why in the hell I chose this branch of the service. I must have recited this ditty five hundred times before Bulldog told me to knock it off.

"Hey Walewander," he barked, "I can't stand your voice anymore, so knock it off and get ready to fall out for chow."

As much as I detested Bulldog for the ridicule he put me through, I was elated to get off this horse shit assignment. I returned to my tent, stacked my rifle, washed and was ready for chow.

"This evening we're going to the fights, that is everyone but the non-swimmers," rejoiced Briles.

"Corporal Olson will escort the non-swimmers to the pool, for their swimming lessons.

After the fights, you people will report to my tent to recite the eleven General Orders of a Sentry which I assume, you have memorized by this time.

"Is that clear?"

"Yes Sir!" we shouted.

"All right now, the non-swimmers will fall out, pick up their trunks and report to Cpl. Olson's tent on the double. The rest of you will fall out in about fifteen minutes. Dismissed!"

Sammy and I double-timed it to our tent to pick up our swim trunks.

"Man would I love to see these fights," Sammy sighed. "I used to attend the fights every Wednesday night at the Rainbo Arena back in Chicago."

"Sam I'm sure there will be a lot of fights you'll attend while you're in the service. Don't the Armed forces have boxing exhibitions against each other all the time?"

"Yeah, I guess you're right," Sammy replied.

We picked up our trunks and trotted over to Cpl. Olson's tent where most everyone was already there and waiting for us.

"Men, I'm going to march you to the pool where you'll be given your first swimming lesson. While you're at the pool, I'll be at the fights. When you're through with your lesson, I'll be out front waiting for you. Is that clear?"

"Yes Sir," we replied.

We marched to the pool, undressed, showered and assembled at the pool's edge.

"Now hear this," bellowed the instructor.

"You people are probably wondering why it's so important to be able to swim 50 yards? Well I'll tell you. As Marines, you will probably spend more time aboard ship than a great many Swabbys do.

As you island hop, you will be transported by various types of ships which will include troop ships, destroyers, air craft carriers and of course landing crafts.

At times the Swabbys won't be able to get their landing barges up on the beaches so you'll be in water over your head so we don't want you to drown during the invasion.

Some of these ships may be torpedoed and bombed, so it is imperative that you be able to swim at least 50 yards or be sucked in by the sinking ship.

We believe that 50 yards is minimum for the course, so before you get out of boot camp we see to it that you swim this distance.

Before you can learn to swim properly, you have to feel at home in the water. Your body will float if given half the chance, but if you get excited and tense you'll sink like a lead weight. Now watch how easy it is to float when you're relaxed.

He dove into the water, came up; turned over on his back and began to float leisurely.

"I can probably fall asleep in this position," he said, as he maneuvered himself towards us.

"This evening we shall start at the shallow end of the pool and practice floating. Pick a partner so you can hold each other afloat until you can do it on your own. My assistants and I will be amongst you, so relax and enjoy yourselves."

Sammy and I quickly jumped into the pool as we were determined to learn how to swim. I always loved the water but as youngster, if I had a chance of going to the beach or play baseball, I always chose the latter. I don't know what Sammy did as a youngster, but I'm sure he didn't spend much time on the beach. Sammy also wanted to qualify in swimming so he could see a few fights before Boot camp was over with. I just wanted to learn how to swim because I love the water very much.

Before we knew it, the whistle blew, and our first session was over. We showered, dressed, and assembled outside the pool where Cpl. Olson was waiting for us. We marched back to our camp area while our platoon was still at the fights.

Usually when the Navy, Army, or Air Force visited our base with their pugilists, you can bet your bottom dollar that a lot of betting will be taking place. Today was no exception.

Sammy and I sat down on the deck and began reviewing the General Orders of a Sentry on Guard Duty. "How are you doing Sam," I inquired.

"Not so good Lee, I was never one for memorizing anything except how many Aces or Kings were still in the deck. How about you?"

"Not bad, except I'm having trouble with the last two."

Just then Chuck barged into our tent, shadow boxing all the way.

"Boy, did you guys miss some good bouts," he gleamed.

"The Marines whipped the Swabbys but good, and by the fist full of greenbacks Briles and Bulldog had in their hands they must have made a killing. We should try checking out on the General Orders tonight while they're in such a good mood."

"Good idea," I replied but let's go now before the line gets too long."

We left our tent and walked over to where our D I's were busily engaged in counting their winnings.

There were three lines, one for Briles, one for Olson and the other for Bulldog. Bulldog's line was the shortest, I wonder why? Since I knew my General Orders pretty well, I chose Bulldog's line.

When it was my turn, I knocked on the signpost and called out; "Private Walewander requests permission to enter and recite the General Orders of a Sentry on Guard Duty, Sir?"

"Permission granted," he slurred.

I entered, saluted, and began my recitation.

1. "The General Orders of a Sentry on Guard Duty is to take charge of my post and all government property in view.

2. To walk my post in a military manner, always keeping on the alert and observing everything   that takes place within sight and hearing. To report, etc.

As I stood at attention, rattling off the General Orders, Bulldog with a cigarette dangling from his lips, was busily engaged in counting his winnings and seemed oblivious to what I was saying.

"Okay Walewander, you passed."

"Yes Sir!" I saluted, did an about face, and left. I went back to our tent, crapped out on my sack and waited. Chuck was the first to enter and by the smile on his face, I didn't have to ask how he fared. I was a little worried about Sam, but when he entered with a shit-eating grin on his face, I knew he also passed.

"I made it!" he laughed.

"When I saw Bulldog so uninterested in what you guys were reciting, I chose his line and it paid off. While he was counting his greenbacks, and looking through his little black book, I kept repeating the same General Orders over and over again. I knew once I stopped I was a dead duck so I kept talking until Bulldog dismissed me. We joined Sammy in his uproarious laughter.

That night before we fell asleep, Sammy asked us if we thought the Marine Corps was slipping in some Salt Peter into our meals, to curb our sexual desires.

"Why do you think they do?" I asked.

"Well every morning, I would wake up with an erection, but since I've been in the Marine Corps, no erection!"

"Well I've heard that rumor too, but you know what Sam, we're so exhausted at the end of the day that I don't think Lana Turner would be able to turn us on," Chuck laughed. We agreed and another day came to an end.

Chapter 6

"Up and at Em," shouted Chuck as the bugler tooted his shrill notes. We dressed, fell out for roll call, washed, shaved, and went to chow. After chow we policed the area, and fell out with our rifles for Close Order Drill. Cpl. Olson had the detail of calling cadence this morning. Briles and Bulldog were hung over and sleeping off a rough night.

We practiced marching and drilling with our rifles for about an hour and then proceeded to march to the black top where Sgt. Langford was waiting for the various platoons to assemble. At a specific time every morning, the D I's marched their platoons to the black top where the physical educational instructors took over. As we performed calisthenics with our rifles, the D I's of the various platoons would gather in small groups and "chew the fat." (talk)

When Briles and Bulldog finally arrived, they looked very haggard, which made us very happy because regardless of how they felt an exacting schedule had to be met. After all, we were being trained in half the time and time was a top priority. We were slowly becoming fit machines, molding our baby fat into rippling muscles. We stacked our rifles, and ended our exercises with the dreaded Fireman's carry. The rest of the morning we spent in close order drill and then went to chow.

"This afternoon we're going out to the black top and participate in mass boxing," Sgt. Briles informed us. "You will wear 16 ounce gloves so don't worry about getting hurt. Move quickly and strike with force but don't hit anyone from behind, is that clear?"

"Yes Sir! We promised."

"Maybe a good belt in the kisser will snap some of you out of your senses," he sneered.

We disagreed, but maybe we weren't tough enough by Marine Corps standards.

Nevertheless, we marched to the blacktop, stripped to our waists and began helping each other put on our gloves. About five other platoons were already awaiting the gong and it looked as if would be a fight between platoons rather than fighting amongst ourselves.

The whistle blew and before I knew what had happened, somebody hit me from behind and sent me reeling. As soon as I got up I was hit again from the side and was getting nowhere fast when Sammy shouted at me.

"Hey Lee, get your ass over here or you'll get your brains beat out. These guys are hitting from behind, so stand back to back with me and we'll protect each other's backs."

"Sounds good to me," I replied, as I ducked a punch and countered with an uppercut.

"Much better Lee!" Sammy grunted as he sat another boot on his can. We fought back to back for about a half an hour when finally the whistle blew and we were told to stop fighting.

"Men we played a dirty trick on you in allowing you to fight without giving you boxing instructions first. We wanted you to get the shit beat out of you so you'd be better pupils. You will now get some pointers on how to box from Sgt. Dakins, a former middleweight contender.

Sgt. Dakins jumped up on the platform and looked us over.

"Some of you couldn't punch your way out of a wet paper bag," he laughed.

"As I watched you boxing out there, I couldn't help but wonder what a pleasure it would have been to have some of you as my opponents in the ring. If that was boxing, I'm Grandma Moses," he laughed once more. "You men are going to become Marines and as Marines you should be able to defend yourselves not only against the Japs, but the Swabbies and Doggies as well."

A good boxer is one that protects himself from being hit and at the same time "clobbers" the hell out of his opponent.

Some of these defensive tactics include, blocking, ducking weaving, parrying, side stepping, and slipping. The offensive tactics include the straight right or left to the head or body. The right cross, and left cross are very important as they're powerful enough to knock out your opponent. The short jab and hook are important because they keep your opponent off balance and if you put your shoulder behind these blows you won't have any trouble knocking him out. Last but not least is the uppercut. It is very useful in infighting or night club brawls.

Remember the most important phase of boxing is to block your opponent's blows, and the best way of doing this is to keep your "dukes" high and watch his eyes. Now let's get started, and remember one of you is on defense the other on offensive.

Sammy and I paired off. I was on defense. By watching Sam's eyes I was able to ward off or block most of the punches he was throwing. It was quite exasperating to have most of your punches blocked but then again we were using boxing gloves as big as pillows. After about a half hour of these pugilistic endeavors our arms were so tired that we wound up clinging to each other just so we wouldn't fall down.

When Briles saw how tired all of us were, he told us to knock it off and then he marched us back to our camp area so that we could do our daily wash.

After clothing inspection, we showered, and spent the remaining time cleaning our rifles, shining our shoes, and getting ready for chow.

A hearty dinner and off to the Amphitheater, for still another lecture and demonstration. We sat down on the hard benches as three Marines attired in their fatigues walked up onto the stage. One of them stepped forward and introduced himself and his two cronies.

"Tonight's lecture is on "Judo and Jujitsu." Jujitsu is a popular sport in Japan. The difference between the two is very slight. Judo is often thought of as the dirty form of Jujitsu. The Japanese use Judo in hand-to-hand combat and our job is to teach you how you can defend yourself against them. The theory behind Judo is to become familiar with the weak parts of the human body. The vital areas are just below the ribs, the Adam's apple, the area behind the ear, and the upper lip. A sharp blow with the side of the hand at any of these regions will stun the individual and leave him open for a direct attack. Death will result if the attack is vicious enough, because the nervous system and brain have been damaged. Before you can strike these deathly blows you must have your enemy off balance. My two assistants will demonstrate how easy it is to throw a person off balance. Corporals Snider and Jaskovich will show us a few holds. Okay fellows, let's go."

We watched Cpl. Jaskovich approach Cpl. Slider, and as he did, he quickly grasped his hand, turned his body very quickly so that his back was towards him and flipped him over his shoulder. We were amazed because Cpl. Snider was twice the size of Cpl. Jaskovich. As Cpl. Snider got up he pulled out a knife and was quickly disarmed by Cpl. Jaskovich and thrown flat on his back. Cpl. Jaskovich made a motion with his hands where he would have struck Cpl. Snider if he were the enemy. The Sergeant interrupted the proceedings by saying-
"As you can see, size isn't important in Judo, in fact it may work against you. You've heard the saying—

"The bigger they are, the harder they fall," well it's true in Judo. Judo requires quick thinking and fast footwork. Tomorrow, you people will be given Judo lessons by your D I's who in most cases are combat veterans well trained in Judo tactics. Before we adjourn, Cpl. Jaskovich and Cpl. Snider will demonstrate a few more holds.

"Okay guys, let's finish up."

As Cpl's Jaskovich and Snider were flipping each other all over the mats, I couldn't help but wonder what it would be like tomorrow when Briles and Bulldog take over. If I know our D I's they'll give us a good going over.

The lecture and demonstration was over and another day was coming to an end. We filed out of the Amphitheater, and marched back to our tent area. After being dismissed we headed for the head where we brushed our teeth and took care of our bodily functions.

Every night, we would climb into our sacks and before taps were blown, we would chew the fat. It seems like our discussions always wound up, where we talked about girls. Sammy and Chuck had a lot more experiences with girls than I had, so, I was getting an education just listening to them.

"When I go home on my ten day furlough, I'm going to buy me some dress blues," Sammy remarked.

"Dress blues! Do you know how expensive they are?" Chuck asked.

"Yeah, about $80 dollars," Sam replied, "but it's worth it. When these broads see me in my Dress blues they'll chase me around with a mattress on their backs," Sammy laughed.

"Yeah right!" we laughingly replied.

Traditionally, Dress Blues are only issued to the guards at the White House, at our Embassies, or aboard ship. Most everybody else is issued the traditional dark green uniform.

"Not to change the subject," Chuck cut in, "why don't the three of us get together after we graduate from Boot Camp and get good and drunk."

"I'm all for it, how about you Sam?"

"I am too," Sammy replied. "Who knows, we may never see each other again."

"Don't say that Sam!" I replied, "I'm getting used to you guys."

Gabriel blew his horn and we went to sleep. Gabriel blew his horn and we woke up. This is how every one of our days started and ended.

This morning was pretty similar to all the others, except for the Judo lessons that we were to receive. Cpl. Olson marched us to the boon docks where Briles and Bulldog were already practicing Judo holds.

"Men," Briles uttered.

"Last night you saw a demonstration on Judo by two men who are well trained in the art of self defense. You people won't be half as good as they are, but you'll be twice as dirty. Once you're familiar with the weak points of the human body you can kill your enemy if you get the drop on him. Remember your life is at stake, so don't be afraid to kick him in the balls if you get a chance to do so.

A quick blow to this area will buckle any man, and when he's buckled over, bash his brains out with the butt of your rifle. Sure it's dirty! But would you rather be a clean dead Marine, or a dirty, no good S.O. Bitchen live Marine?"

"A dirty no good S.O. Bitchen live Marine," we shouted.

"Good! Now let's get this show on the road," Briles replied as he looked us over.

At that moment Sammy whispered something about Briles that brought a smile to my face. I may have had a shit 'eatin' grin on my face and once Briles noticed it, he called me out of ranks.

"Pvt. Walewander step forward so I can demonstrate a few Judo holds.

As I came forward, Briles put both of his hands on my fatigue lapels, fell backward, and in so doing, pulled me forward, whereby I was falling on top of him. But just before I fell on top of him, his feet caught me in the pit of my stomach and projected me about ten feet into the air. I landed flat on my back into the warm soft sand.

As I looked up, Briles extended his right hand and as I grasped it to get up he flipped me over his shoulder and I was flat on my back again.

"So you don't hurt your back, you have to learn how to cushion your fall. The best way is to strike the sand with the palms of your hands and arms just before you land on your back. Pfc. Kotowski and Cpl. Olson will now demonstrate how to cushion your fall.

As we watched with delight, Cpl. Olson grabbed Bulldog by his lapels and suddenly Bulldog was airborne. We hoped he'd stay airborne but no such luck. Just before his back hit the sand he cushioned his fall by striking the sand with the palms of his hands and arms.

"Now that's the way it's done, any questions?"

"If not, let's get going and remember, never let your enemy up! Bash his brains out while he's still on the ground, is that clear?"

"Yes Sir!"our platoon shouted.

"Now let's get started and practice the first of the Judo holds I just demonstrated."

Chuck and I paired off and since I was Brile's guinea pig, I knew exactly what to do. In slow motion I showed Chuck what Briles did to me, which made it a lot easier for us to practice this tactic. We got pretty good at it.

"Pvt. Oleary, you look like you're getting pretty good, why don't you come forward and throw me," Bulldog suggested.

"Yes Sir," Chuck replied.

Chuck came forward, quickly grabbed Bulldog's lapels but before Chuck could pull him backwards, Bulldog shot both of his hands upward breaking Chuck's grip on his lapels, sending both of Chuck's arms down to his side. Bulldog's arms came down; they were open and rigid and aimed right at Chuck's neck.

"You'd be a gonner,' Oleary. Now that's how you break that hold!

Got it? "

"Yes Sir!" Chuck replied.

We spent the rest of the morning practicing different holds and techniques and finally had to call it quits when it was time for noon chow.

That afternoon, we marched over to the Quartermaster Depot where we were issued gas masks. When we assembled outside the depot, Briles bellowed out; this afternoon we will take a little trip to the gas chambers and check out your gas masks. If you have a faulty gas mask we want to find out now. It's much better, to inhale a little tear gas now than, Mustard or Phosgene gas later on, don't you agree? "

"Yes Sir" we replied.

We left the Quartermaster Depot and marched over to a Quonset hut that was converted into a gas testing chamber. At one end of the chamber was the entrance at the back end was the exit. Just before we went in Sgt. Briles briefed us on our masks and showed us how to check for leaks. The gas masks were quite cumbersome and when placed over the face a corrugated rubber hose extended downward to a canister that was attached to the case.

When we were certain that our gas masks were functioning properly we entered the gas chamber. We formed a circle around a large G.I. can (garbage can), from whence a white gas was bellowing forth. I wasn't affected by the tear gas, which indicated that my gas mask was working properly.

A few of them weren't and consequently choking, gasping and running toward the exit were experienced by a few. To make sure that we would appreciate our gas masks, we had to remove them before we left the chambers. I tried to hold my breath so I wouldn't inhale this tear gas but to no avail. I inhaled this gas, which made my lungs and eyes burn. I was gasping for air and as I staggered out the door.

I started to cough and wheeze while tears were streaming down my face. I glanced up and noticed that everyone else was either coughing, wheezing or had tears streaming down their cheeks. After we coughed out enough of this gas, and inhaled mother nature's content, we put our gas masks back into their containers and marched back to our tent area. Just before we were dismissed, Sgt. Briles made an announcement.

"These gas masks are to be taken care of, in the same manner as your rifles. Don't ever let me catch you putting any of your gear inside the mask or container. If you do, It'll be your ass! So put away your gas masks and fall out with your rifles for a little close order drill.

Dismissed!"

We scrambled back to our tents, put our masks away, and fell out in the matter of seconds.

"Ten Shun !"

"Right Shohlder Harms!" Briles bellowed

"Make those pieces ring out! Hit 'em' hard! Right sholder harms! Left sholder arms! "
We hit our pieces as sharply and as loudly as possible with very little effect on our calloused hands.

"That's better," Briles shouted.

We marched and drilled till 1500 at which time we called it quits to do our daily wash and get ready for our evening chow. After I showered, I had about a half hour of free time, before chow, so I wrote a letter to my parents and to my pretty cheerleader in Kingsport Tennessee.

Since all our mail was censored I was limited as to what I could write. If I wrote something bad about the Marine Corps they would cut it out.

We ate chow, reported back to the camp area and awaited another lecture, demonstration, movie, etc. Well tonight we had a treat; we were going to listen to the United States Marine Corps band, except the non-swimmers who reported to the pool for our second lesson.

We practiced kicking and dog paddling. Sam and I were becoming quite at home in the water and weren't too eager to qualify. The whistle blew; we were dismissed for the evening.

Bulldog had the detail of escorting us to the pool this evening and since it was still quite early, he marched us to the auditorium to hear a few closing numbers by the Marine Corps band.

The next few days of boot camp were going to be devoted to running the obstacle course. The course consisted of a row of tires laid side by side, a long wooden rail to traverse, a series of cut out drums that you had to crawl through, a twelve foot wall that you had to pull yourself over, and finally run about fifteen yards, leap, grab a rope and swing over a muddy stream, crawl under barbed wire and double time it about twenty five yards where our D I's were checking our time with a stop watch.

When all of us finished running the obstacle course, the smoking lamp was lit, and we took a fifteen minute break. Afterwards we were informed that we would run this course again only this time we have to beat our previous time.

Chuck and I had no trouble beating our previous time but Sammy and Porky who already fell into the muddy stream on their first run were really bitching.

"I'll never beat my previous time," Porky lamented.

"I made about five passes on that God damn wall, before I realized I couldn't make it."

"How'd you get over it, I asked?"

"I didn't! I ran around it! "

"Didn't Olson say anything?"

"Nope! He turned his back so he couldn't see what I was doing."

Most of us beat our previous times and those that didn't were to come back during their free time to try it again.

We were also told that after we get back from the Rifle range we will run this course with a full pack and rifle.

Porky, who Briles called "Lard Ass" was told that he was going to be put on a special diet which would cut out the mashed potatoes, gravy, sweets and other carbohydrates that he loved so much or he'd never make it as a Marine.

"This afternoon you people are going to have a group picture taken of your platoon, so I want you to wear your dress green pants, khaki shirt, field scarf, piss cutter and polished boondockers for this picture.

After your picture is taken we are going to march over to Sick Bay and have you donate a pint of your blood. As you know there is no substitute for whole blood. With all the Marines that are being wounded and lose blood it is imperative that we have it on hand when needed. To let you recuperate your loss, you will have the rest of the afternoon off and this evening you will be treated to a movie."

"Hooray!" we shouted.

We were dismissed, went back to our tents and began to dress for our group picture. Bulldog marched us over to the photographers and our picture of platoon 676 was taken against the background of a white building. We were told that each picture that we ordered would cost us fifty cents which would be taken out of our monthly salary. Since cameras were prohibited in boot camp, we all ordered more than one picture.

"Hey Lee, do you think they have some good looking nurses at the base hospital?" Sammy asked.

"I don't see why they shouldn't," I replied.

"Oh to be next to a skirt again," sighed Sammy.

"Sam you act as if you've been imprisoned for years, and in reality it's less than a week," I replied.

"I know, but it seems like a year."

676th PLATOON U.S. MARINE CORPS
SAN DIEGO
1943
U.S. MARINES — FIRST TO FIGHT

We entered the base hospital and began to fill out a few forms.

"What's your Rh factor, Lee?" a pretty nurse with red hair, and dimples asked me.

"My what?" I asked her.

"Your Rh factor, it's right there on your dog tag," she pointed.

She flipped over my dog tag and read aloud. "Type O, Rh positive."

"You know Lee you're what we call a universal donor. Your blood can be used by anyone."

"That's good to hear," I facetiously replied.

I was told to roll up my sleeves and lie down on the bed.

"Not frightened are you Lee?"

"No, but how come you know my name?"

"It's on the form you filled out, silly."

"Since you know my name what's yours?" I smilingly asked. "Rita Shaw" she replied.

"Rita, I never knew any girls named Rita.

"Well you do now, she smiled."

She proceeded to wrap a rubber diaphragm around my biceps, inflated it with air, which made my veins pop out. She then cleaned an area with alcohol and inserted a needle into a large vein and taped it down. I watched the blood trickle into the bottle as I squeezed the rubber ball.

"All finished Lee," she smiled, as she pulled out the needle and placed a piece of moist cotton over the punctured area.

"That wasn't so bad was it"

"No, not at all, but I think you had a lot to do with it," I winked.

"Oh I'll bet you say that to all of the nurses."

"No, only the pretty ones like you."

I could sense that Rita was attracted to me as much as I was to her but since I was in boot camp I wouldn't be able to ask her out for another six weeks.

Oh well, at least I know her name and where she works so maybe I'll give her a call when I'm out of boot camp.

After we donated our blood, Bulldog marched us back to our camp area and told us that we had the rest of the afternoon off and that we could crap out on our sacks, if we wanted to. I was pretty tired so I dozed off for what seemed like only a few minutes before the whistle blew for us to fall out for chow.

That evening, Cpl. Olson escorted us to the base theatre where we were to see a U. S. O. show followed by a movie. The U.S.O. troupe was very good, especially the all girl orchestra that played and put on a few skits for us.

After the vaudeville portion of the show was completed, we saw a movie entitled, "Seven Days Leave" which starred Victor Mature and Lucille Ball. The picture was a little silly, but everyone seemed to enjoy it.

We left the theatre and were marched back to our camp area by Cpl. Olson and got ready for sack time.

When the bugler got us up we were informed that it was Sunday morning and everyone has to attend church whether they like it or not.

"I don't care if you're an Atheist or an Agnostic you better convert immediately or you'll be cleaning out the heads for the rest of the day, is that clear?

"Yes Sir." We shouted.

We went to chow, and then fell out to go to church. Since Sammy, Chuck and I were all Catholics so we all attended the Catholic Church. We returned to our camp area only to find out that the non-swimmers were to fall out in ten minutes for another lesson. The rest of our platoon either played Volley ball or wrote letters to their loved ones.

At the swimming pool we were introduced to the Australian crawl and practiced how to breathe while swimming.

Sammy and I were getting pretty good, and if we had to, I'm pretty sure we could swim the prescribed 50 yards.

The afternoon session consisted of extended close order drill, some Judo drills, and of course rifle inspection. We also had to dismantle our rifles and name the parts as our instructors pointed to them. We did pretty well!

We had just finished one week of boot camp and had to spend another week in Tent city before we would pack our gear and spend the next three weeks at Camp Mathews and the rifle range.

Our last week in Tent city went by very quickly and before we knew it we were told that tomorrow we were leaving our beloved Tent City and spend the next three weeks at Camp Mathews. Unfortunately our D I's would accompany us and still be in charge.

Chapter 7

Today, was the day, we've been looking forward to. The day we left the Recruit Depot and headed for Camp Mathews and the rifle range. We fell out for roll call, washed, shaved, and fell out for chow.

"This morning right after chow, I want you people to pack all of your gear and be ready to board the trucks for our trip to Camp Mathews," ordered Briles."We will spend three weeks at the range and then return to Tent City for the remaining two weeks. Is that clear?"

"Yes Sir!" we replied.

"Ten Shun! Rite Face, Fohward Hartch," he bellowed.

Immediately after chow, we packed our seabags, rolled our bedrolls around our collapsed cots and policed the area. We then carried out our gear to the convoy of trucks that were parked nearby.

Ours wasn't the only platoon leaving; in fact there must have been at least fifteen leaving this morning. A platoon consisted of sixty men, and twenty were instructed to board each truck. Briles stood in front of one of the trucks, clipboard in hand, pencil poised and began to call roll.

"Abrams? "

" Here Sir!"

" Albert? "

" Here Sir! "etc.

As his name was called, each recruit boarded the truck and sat down on the benches provided. When twenty of us were in the first truck, Bulldog secured the tail gate and hopped into the truck to make sure that no one decides to go AWOL. I guess over the years too many unhappy recruits disappeared during this trip, so now a D I has to be present in every truck.

As the caravan of trucks began to pull out of the area, we were greeted by the usual, "You'll be sorry!" from Marines that were marching nearby.

The trucks picked up speed and as we rumbled along someone began to sing the Marine Hymn. We all joined in –

" From the Halls of Montezuma
To the shores of Tripoli.
We will fight our country's battles
On the land, the sea and air.
First to fight for right and freedom,
And to keep our honors clean;
We are proud to bear the title of
The United States Marines.

I personally believe that everyone here in our platoon was very proud to be a United States Marine, even though their constant bitching didn't show it.

We arrived at Camp Mathews and began to move into our new quarters. We were assigned huts that already had bunk beds and closets. These huts resembled miniature barracks neatly aligned in rows of ten, and heated by a pot-bellied stove. Chuck, Sammy, Porky, Hillbilly and myself all moved into one of these huts.

We drew straws for upper and lower berths and I was one of those that lost. I soon realized that an upper berth has certain advantages. First of all it was easier to keep clean and when visitors came to visit, especially to play cards, they used the lower bunk as their table.

We squared away our gear and fell out when Briles blew his whistle.

"Men, this is going to be your home for the next three weeks. The first week is going to be devoted primarily to what we call the "Snapping In" period.

During this period of time you will be taught the different firing positions, become familiar with the 22 Caliber rifle, the 45 automatic pistol, the Carbine, the Browning automatic rifle and of course you're M1.You will also learn to simulate the exact procedures used on the firing lines.

The Sergeant who is going to instruct you is an expert marksman, in fact every one of these men had to shoot expert or they wouldn't be out here. But, so much for that, right now, I want you to pick up two of these leather patches and sew them on your sleeves, just behind the elbow. When you bend your arm that leather patch better be right over the elbow or you'll be battered and bruised before you know it. Am I making myself clear? "

"Yes Sir!" we acknowledged.

We picked up our leather patches, went back to our huts and began to sew them onto our sleeves.

"Ouch!" bitched Sammy. "Who ever thought I'd be doing my own wash and sewing? Not me, in fact if my friends back home could only see me now they'd demote me to stripping cars."

I looked at Sam and had to laugh. He looked so ridiculous. Can you picture a big burly character, scar and all, sitting on the edge of his bunk, puffing on a big smelly cigar, trying to thread a needle? Well if you can that is exactly how he looked.

We completed our chores, and fell out for chow. The chow in the Marine Corps was the same no matter where you were, except of course, if you're stationed overseas and then it varied.

We returned from chow and fell out with our rifles. It took us about fifteen minutes to march to the dummy range. The reason they called it the dummy range was because no firing was done here, only practice, practice and more practice. Sgt. Briles introduced us to our new instructor.

"Men, I want you to meet Sgt. Catlon, an expert marksman and a man who is going to teach you all there is to know about firing different weapons.

If you don't qualify, it won't be because of Tex's, ugh, I mean Sgt. Catlon's doing. He has more patience than any one man I know."

Sgt. Catlon seemed like a very easygoing, relaxed sort of person. While Briles was introducing him, he was starring at the ground or out at the mountains, not once looking directly at us. He was about six feet two, big boned, broad shouldered, and a little on the lean side. He had pitch-black hair, steel gray eyes and chiseled features. He wore a shooting jacket and the old Marine Corps campaign hat. We soon found out that only the expert marksman was permitted to wear this hat, so whenever we saw a cocky Sergeant wearing one of these hats, he had every reason to be proud of himself.

Sgt. Catlon stepped forward and said --

"Men my job is to teach you how to fire your rifles expertly. But in order to do so, you'll have to be taught the various firing positions, the proper procedure used on the firing line and last but not least how to use your weapons expertly. You will be out here from early morning, till dusk, and only leave this dummy range to go to chow and sack time. This afternoon I shall demonstrate the different positions that you have to learn before you go out to the actual firing range.

There are four basic positions: the prone, sitting, kneeling and standing. We shall start with the prone position and practice it for the rest of the day. Any questions? If not, I shall begin with the Prone position. Now in the Prone position you lie flat on your stomach, your legs and feet are far apart and the heels are in and down," he said, as he knelt down and sprawled out on the ground.

"The position must feel comfortable and you should lie at an angle of 45 degrees to the line of fire with the spine good and straight. Your left hand is in the rear of and against the lower band. The rifle rests in the palm of the left hand, and the fingers of the left hand should exert no pressure. The left elbow is directly under the rifle and the loop of the sling is tight and well up on the left arm.

If you don't have your leather patches positioned properly, you'll get bruises on your elbows because of the pressure exerted upon them. After the rifle is grasped properly, your right eye should be close to the cocking piece and the right cheek is placed hard against the stock. You never jerk a trigger, you squeeze it gently, just like you would, a little "ole tit" he quipped.

The right hand, as you can notice, grasps the rifle at the small of the stock with the right thumb alongside the stock. The butt of your rifle is high in the shoulder and the right elbow is well out bringing your chest close to the ground."

The sight of Sgt. Catlon in this unorthodox position brought on our aches and pains suggestively.

"Okay men," Now it's your turn. Take a position at one of the markers and fall into the Prone position. Remember you have to be as close to the ground as possible or you'll get your ass shot off by the Japs"

We moved out, loosened our slings, fell to our knees by cushioning our fall with the butt of our rifles and then dropped down onto our stomachs and assumed the Prone position. To see that we were low enough to the ground, Sgt. Catlon and our D I's would walk around checking our positions, stepping or sitting on our backs if necessary.

As we laid down on the ground in this very uncomfortable position, Sgt. Catlon and our D I's would walk around and you can hear comments such as, "Tighten your sling a bit!

Prone position

Bring your left elbow over to the right! Spread your legs! Turn in your heels! Get lower to the ground! etc."

I thought I was as close to the ground as I could be, but evidently I wasn't.

"Get closer to the ground, Walewander," Bulldog shouted at me. I tried, but I was locked in this position and couldn't move.

Bulldog waited a few minutes and when he saw no improvement, he sat on my back. All of a sudden the bones in my back began to crack and I finally felt the ground beneath me. I thought I was going to die!

"Now you're perfect!" he sarcastically remarked.

As every bone in my body throbbed, I wondered how Sam and Chuck were doing. I didn't have long to wait.

"Oh my aching back! I think he broke every bone in my body," Sammy groaned.

"My shoulder joints must be dislocated! Chuck moaned.

"My balls itch! Porky cried.

All these comments were being strewn about while we laid in this ideal position. I never heard so much bitching in my life, but then again we had every reason to be pissed off.

"Everybody up on the firing line," Catlon ordered.

As we got up, we were instructed to keep our rifles pointing in the direction of the targets and our bodies turned at about a 45-degree angle to the targets.

Let's try it again!" Catlon shouted.

And try we did, over and over again. I began to appreciate our aching bodies before we had to fall out for chow. The leather patches that we sewn onto our dungaree jackets helped a lot but even with these patches my elbows were taking a beating.

Our afternoon session came to a halt. We assembled, marched back to our camp area where we spent the rest of the afternoon cleaning our rifles, washing our clothes, and resting

After chow, we marched back to the dummy range and became familiar with the sitting position when firing a rifle. This position was much easier to assume than the prone position, but it too had its drawbacks.

There were three authorized sitting positions but the one we employed was the most comfortable. In this position you sit down and bend your legs. The right elbow is inside the right knee and the left elbow extends over the left knee.

The rifle is cradled in the normal manner except that it steadied by resting the arms on the knees.

We practiced "Snapping In," until dusk fell upon us, at which time we picked up our aching torsos and headed back to our camp area and some serious sack time.

It was 0530 when the bugler began to toot his horn. We hated that sound especially when we're so tired. Nevertheless, we made up our sacks, and fell out for roll call. After roll was taken, Sgt. Briles addressed us;

"Because we're at the rifle range that doesn't mean we forget about our morning calisthenics. Every morning right after roll call we will have our limbering up exercises. Today is no exception, so let's get started."

We moved out at arm's length from each other and began bending and twisting to Briles monotonous chants. We concluded our exercises with Fireman's carry around the huts. We went to the head to wash, shave, and get ready for chow.

Immediately after chow, Bulldog double-timed us back to the rifle range so that we could practice the kneeling position.

"Good morning, mates," he uttered. "This morning we will cover the kneeling and standing positions. In the kneeling position, you kneel on your right knee and sit on the right heel. Your left foreleg should be nearly vertical, and your left foot should be flat on the ground and on a vertical line between the right foot and the right knee.

"Any Questions?"

"If not, then move out and take up the kneeling position."

We selected a marker, adjusted our slings and began to assume a kneeling position. I tried sitting on my right heel but found it so unsteady that I changed to sitting on the side of my right foot.

"Hey Sam, try sitting on the side of your right foot and you'll get rid of your shakes," I laughingly remarked.

"Shakes! What Shakes? I'm as steady as an alcoholic trying to walk a straight line," Sammy replied as he fell over backwards. We began to "goof" around when Bulldog spotted us.

Kneeling position

"Bergoni !, Walewander! What the hell are you two crapheads laughing about? This isn't a laughing matter, there's a war going on out there and you fartheads are wasting the taxpayer's hard earned money. Just so you two idiots don't forget, I want you to step off the line and raise your rifle 100 times over your head Is that clear?"

"Yes Sir!" we shouted.

We stepped off the line and began lifting our rifles over our heads, counting off each lift vocally. The first 50 lifts were pretty easy, but from that point on, everyone was getting a little heavier. My arms were so fatigued I began to cheat a little by dropping my head under the rifle rather than lifting it over my head.

While Sam and I were doing our lifting, the rest of our platoon was busily engaged in snapping in. When we were finished we went back to snapping in and kept our mouths shut.

"You men are doing just fine," Sgt. Catlon added.

"I'll demonstrate the standing position and then we'll knock off for chow. How does that grab you?"

"Just fine! We shouted."

"Now the standing position is probably the easiest of the four to assume. In this position the body is naturally erect and the weight of the body rests equally on both feet.

The feet should be about twelve inches apart. The left elbow, as you can see is under the rifle and free from the body, while the right elbow is above the height of the shoulder. The left hand is slightly forward of the rear sight leaf and the fingers of the left hand should exert no tension.

The butt of the rifle rests in the hollow of your shoulder and when you squeeze the trigger you'll hit pay dirt every time," he grinned.

"Yeah right!" I mumbled under my breath.

We assumed our standing positions and obviously we're doing very well because very shortly thereafter we were dismissed to go to chow.

"I don't know if the meals are getting better or if I'm getting hungrier," savored Porky, as he reached over for a slice of bread. Just then Sammy tapped Porky with his spoon.

"Naughty, Naughty, you promised, remember?"

"Must you remind me, big mouth!" He sadly remarked, dropping the bread back onto the plate.

"Who wants my dessert?"

"I'll take it Porky old pal," Sammy beamed.

"No you won't buddy, you're almost as fat as I am! How about you Lee, you want my ice cream? "

"Nah! Give it to Billy. He looks under-nourished."

Hillbilly gladly accepted and to show his appreciation he grinned with every savory mouthful.

We continued "Snapping In" for a few more days, at which time Briles informed us about our qualifying.

"If you shoot Expert the government will give you five dollars more per month.

If you're a Sharpshooter the government will give you three dollars more per month. If you qualify, which is a Marksman, the government will give you a pat on the back, no money. We expect each and every one of you to qualify and if you do better you'll be compensated accordingly.The word got around that the D I's bet heavily on their platoon scoring better than the other platoons.The platoon qualifying the most number of men would be the winner.

Our D I's assisted Sgt. Catlon as best they could, trying to whip us into shape in the allotted time. We were working in pairs now, one of us slamming the operating bolt handle every time the trigger was squeezed.

Normally when a round is fired' it passes the gas port wherein some of the gas enters through the port into the cylinder; striking the piston end of the operating rod with sufficient force to drive the operating rod backwards, ejecting the shell and putting another round into position.

But we weren't firing live ammunition, so the operating rod handle had to be operated manually. We wrapped our handkerchief (snot rag) around our hand to prevent it from becoming too bruised.

"Slam that operating rod handle sharply," Catlon drawled. "Let 'em' get the feel of the kick.

"Don't jerk that trigger Bergoni, squeeze it like a lemon. Get those elbows in O'Leary! Walewander you want your heels shot off? Turn them in!"

We snapped in unhesitatingly for the rest of the day.The next day was upon us, and after the usual, we marched over to the 22 Caliber range to fire some live ammunition. The 22 rifle was like a toy in our hands, it was a lot lighter. We enjoyed firing it! We practiced breath control and worked on how to squeeze the trigger, not jerk it.

"The trigger should be squeezed so steadily that the rifleman doesn't know the instant the rifle will fire. If he does, he will flinch and the shot will go astray," Sgt. Catlon informed us.

We were shooting at targets similar to the one's you'd see at a County fair.

"Hey Lee I'll bet you a beer on who gets the most bulls eyes"

"You've got a bet Chuck , but where are you going to get a beer"

"When we graduate from Boot Camp we'll meet at the Beer hall."

"Hey what about me? I want a little of this action too," Sammy asked.

"Sure! The more the merrier," Chuck replied.

We fired away and when it was over, my two buddies owed me a couple of beers.

"Pick up those empty shells, deposit them into that large container, and police the area, before you leave. Is that clear?

"Yes Sir!" we replied.

We were then escorted to what looked like a classroom with a huge chalkboard hanging on the wall.

"Today, I'm going to talk about making your rifles more efficient. Every rifle is different, and in order for it to hit the target you're aiming at, it has to be adjusted for elevation and wind age. This is called the Zero point of your rifle.

If there's a strong wind blowing, you have to correct for it. The windage knob on your rifle will move your strike zone to the left or right. One click on the wind age knob will move the hit of the bullet one inch for every one hundred yards.

At two hundred yards, two inches, etc. If you're hitting high or low, you turn the elevation knob and again one click of the knob moves the hit, one inch for every one hundred yards. Any questions?

How do you know how fast the wind is blowing, Sir," I politely asked.

"The velocity of the wind will be told to you on the firing range, but in a pinch here's what you do.

Pick up some grass or leaves and drop them from shoulder height and when they settle, point to them.

The angle formed between the body and outstretched arm, if divided by four will give you an approximate wind velocity. If your answer is 3.2 you turn your wind age knob three clicks," is that clear?"

"Yes Sir," I replied.

"Anymore questions? If not let's work out a few hypothetical situations. Supposing a Jap sniper is perched in a tree top about 200 yards away and the wind is blowing about twelve miles per hour.

Your wind age knob is set at 0600 what corrections would you make? "

Chuck quickly raised his hand.

"None Sir, because winds at 0600 and 1200 will not affect the path of the projectile and therefore require no windage adjustment. A strong wind coming in at 1200 hours may retard it somewhat, and the winds at 0600 hours may accelerate it a bit, but will not require a correction in elevation up to 500 yards, Sir"

"Very good O'Leary," Catlon replied. "I'm impressed!"

So were we!

We continued talking about hypothetical situations that we may encounter in jungle warfare when Briles informed Catlon that it was time for afternoon chow.

That afternoon, we went to the Rifle range to work in the Pits of E Range.

The Pits is the area behind a concrete wall where the targets that the recruits are firing at, are spotted and marked. After the recruit fires at the target, the men working in the pits lower the target and check to see what he hit.

-87

If he hit the bulls-eye the target is raised and a large white disc is raised by one of us to indicate to the recruit what part of the target he hit. Then he can zero in his rifle accordingly.

So if you hit the bull's eye, a white disc is raised and you get five points. If you're right next to the bull's eye, a red disc is raised and you get four points.

If you're two rings away from the bull's eye you get three points and a black and white disc is raised. If you're in the last ring you get two points and a black disc is raised.

If you miss the target completely, a red flag, or Maggie's drawers is waved across the target.

We were then instructed to break up into groups of three and instructed as to what they wanted us to do.

"Remember when you're in the Pits, I want you to raise and lower the targets when ordered to do so. After a round is fired, the target is lowered and a spotter is placed in the shot hole.

The target is then raised and the appropriate place and value of the shot indicated. Once the target is lowered, you remove the spotters and paste up the holes with the appropriate colored paper. Is that clear? " Sgt. Catlon asked.

"Yes Sir!" we replied.

We took turns spotting, pasting and raising and lowering the target. Sammy got a big kick out of waving "Maggie's Drawers."

"One of my girl friends has a pair exactly this shade," Sammy replied as he waved the flag in front of us. "Summer or winter issue?" Chuck smilingly snickered.

"Winter!" Sammy quickly responded. "She never wears panties in the summer time!"

"Yeah, right!" we laughingly replied.

We laughed, worked and before we knew it, another crew relieved us.

The next few days, were devoted to the same old grind. Besides firing the 22, we also became familiar with and fired the 45 automatic pistol. We were also taken out to the bayonet course and as we were prepared to run it, Sergeant Briles bellowed out

"Men there are a lot of stuffed dummies out there that resemble the Japanese soldier. When you run this course I want to hear a lot of blood curdling screams. Some of these dummies are set up in such a way that if you don't parry and thrust, you cannot stick a bayonet into them. Don't slow down! Do what we taught you! Bash their brains in, rip their guts out, and bury your bayonet into their bellies and Yell!

As I waited my turn, the blood curdling screams tied my stomach into knots.

"Go Walewander!" was the command.

With my rifle at waist level, I double- timed it to the first dummy, screaming like a mad man. My bayonet ripped through one dummy, knocked the head off another, caved in the shoulders of a third as I continued to scream and take out my aggression on a few more. When I was done, I was breathless.

The first week on the Rifle range was coming to a close. We were letter perfect as far as procedures and positions were concerned. What Sgt. Catlon drilled into us all week long would be put into use during the next two weeks.

We attended our respective church Sunday morning; attended a lecture in the afternoon, and were treated to a movie that evening. We went to bed wondering what it will be like to fire our babies

Chapter 8

We marched to E Range and took up our positions behind the designated markers that were assigned to us. Each of us was assigned an instructor to help us Zero in our rifles.

"My name is Sgt. Drexler," a booming voice informed me.

"Pleased to meet you Sir, I'm Private Lee Walewander."

Sgt. Drexler was of medium height, well built and on the elderly side. He had blue eyes, a balding head and an infectious smile.

"Well Lee, are you ready to Zero in your rifle?"

"You bet I am sir, I've been waiting all week to fire my baby."

"Okay Lee, but before we start, go over to the smudge pot and blacken your front and rear sight."

"Yes Sir!"

After putting a good coat of lampblack on the sights, I returned to the firing line and assumed the prone position. The Prone position is the position used to Zero in rifles because it's the most reliable.

"Okay Lee, your prone position looks perfect so now I want you to aim at the bull's eye and squeeze off a round. I did as instructed and when Sgt. Drexler was convinced that my breathing and squeezing were passable, he handed me a clip of ammo which contained eight rounds of .30 caliber bullets. I inserted it and lined up the peep sight at 6 o'clock. I began to apply a gentle squeeze but at the last second jerked the trigger; got a good solid kick in the shoulder and the familiar wave of Maggies drawers flashed before me. I felt like shit, but Sgt. Drexler calmed me down.

"Don't worry about it Lee, most everyone gets Maggie's drawers when they fire their first shot. Just relax and remember to take in a deep breath, hold it, and squeeze the trigger as you would a little "ole" tit," he quipped.

I had to smile when I thought of the number of times this little "ole" tit has been squeezed since I've been out here. Nevertheless, I relaxed, took a deep breath, lined up my sight at the center of the bulls eye and started a gentle squeeze on the trigger. When I least expected it, the rifle discharged and as I looked up a black and white disk was starring me in the face, at about 8 o'clock.

"Try it again Lee. If you hit the same spot, we'll have to give it a little right wind age and elevation."

"Yes sir!" I replied.

I squeezed off another round, and lo and behold I hit the same spot.

"Okay give her one click of right windage and elevation," Sgt. Drexler instructed. I did, and as I squeezed off a round, I waited to see what I hit. I didn't have to wait long! A red disk at 9 o'clock appeared on the target.

"Elevation should remain the same so all I need to do is give it one click of right windage" I thought aloud.

Sgt. Drexler didn't say a word just watched. I turned the wind age knob one click and proceeded to fire another round. All of a sudden a white disk appeared over the bull's eye.

"My first bull's eye! I shouted with glee.

"Nice going Lee that looks like your Zero point of your rifle this morning."

I squeezed off another round and once more I hit the bulls- eye.

Sgt. Drexler then told me to line up on the bull's eye only this time he would squeeze the trigger. I held my breath, the rifle recoiled and a bulls eye was recorded.

"That's it Lee, so now I want you to fire a clip of ammo in the Prone, Sitting, Kneeling and Standing positions."

"Yes Sir," I happily replied.

I was really enjoying this part of boot camp. I was getting pretty cocky with my scoring because if I didn't hit the bull's eye I was close to it. I soon discovered that the standing position was the hardest to master.

In addition to firing our rifles we practiced the protocol used on the firing line. The familiar, Ready on the right? Ready on the left? Ready on the firing line? was becoming a part of our dreams.

For the rest of the week we were firing our rifles or working in the pits and running the bayonet course.

The last week began with us learning how to fire the baby M1 or Carbine at a very unique range. This particular range had Japanese dummy's rigged up in a jungle setting, that when you approached they would spring out of their hiding place and disappear just as quickly. You were to shoot at them very quickly but sometimes a U.S. Marine would appear and if per chance you shot him you'd never hear the end of it. To make sure we wouldn't kill each other, the D I's made sure that only one of us was on the course at one time. This type of practice was very important because it taught us to react quickly and efficiently.

"In jungle warfare you don't have time to aim," barked Bulldog. "You have to get that round off very quickly or the show will be over."

We agreed wholeheartedly and realized the significance of this training.

Since we've been out here, we fired all the prescribed weapons and now all that was left for us is to do, was to qualify with our M'1s. Our platoon wasn't doing very well in the preliminaries and this made our D I's very nervous.

"What's wrong with you Chicago hoods? Would you do better with a sub-machine gun? " Briles angrily asked.

"In a couple of days you're supposed to qualify with your rifles, and I for one don't know how some of you are going do it.

How do you expect to shoot a Jap if you can't hit a huge target 500 yards away? You can't hit a target if you jerk the trigger or breathe as you're squeezing off a round. It can't be done! This evening, I want the following men to fall out for extra practice on the firing range. The rest of you can catch up on your letter writing. Is that clear?"

"Yes Sir!" we replied.

Sgt. Briles began to read of the names of people that at the present time were not qualifying. About 20 names were called; Chuck, Hillbilly and I were not among them. After they had departed, Chuck said,

"Lee what about sneaking off to a movie tonight?"

"Are you kidding? What if Briles calls roll? "

"Oh he won't! He hasn't for the last two nights and besides we may be back before they come back from the range."

"What's playing?"

"A western, starring Gary Cooper."

"Let's go!" I excitedly replied.

We went back to our tents, changed out of our dungarees and departed. The movie was very good but lasted a little longer than we anticipated. As we walked back to our camp area, we were very quiet so as not to disturb anyone.

"Do you think they're all asleep?" I asked.

"Yeah they must be its way past taps."

Just before we reached our camp area, we heard a lot of noise emanating from the general vicinity of our huts. We approached very quietly and peeked out from behind our hut.

"There they are!" someone shouted.

"I'm afraid we've had it," I blurted out.

"Yeah, I can't imagine what's going to happen to us as we walked towards our platoon, like two beaten dogs dragging their tails; our platoon seemed to have turned against us.

They were hissing and jeering like a lynch mob, while Briles, Olson and Bulldog were sitting nearby. Meanwhile our platoon was supposed to be at attention, but now they weren't.

"Good evening, gentlemen. Did you have a good time? " Briles sarcastically asked.

"Yes Sir!" we sadly replied.

"Did you attend the Opera per chance?" Briles continued with his sarcasm.

"No sir!" we replied, "We went to the movies?"

"Oh! A couple of movie fans, isn't that nice," Briles calmly remarked.

Suddenly he jumped to his feet, grabbed me by the lapels and spun me around in my tracks.

"Do you crapheads know how long your buddies have been standing at attention?" he shouted.

"No sir!" we replied.

"About an hour! Would you like to stand at attention for one hour?"

"No sir," we shouted.

"I just had a sneaking suspicion that some of you fartheads would pull off something like this, so I purposely called roll in order to catch you. So that I wouldn't have to wait for you two idiots alone, I had your buddies wait for you too, only at attention. Tomorrow morning I want you two yard- birds to report to my hut before the bugler finishes blowing reveille. I have something in store for you."

"Yes Sir!" We shouted.

"Okay. Now Fall out!"

A grumbling, bitching platoon headed back to their huts and sack time.

As soon as reveille beckoned, Chuck and I quickly dressed and reported to our D I's hut.

"Private Walewander and Private Oleary reporting, Sir."

"Oh yes, the movie fans," Briles grumbled.

"Make up our sacks, and clean out this hut," Briles demanded.

"Yes Sir!" We replied.

Our D.I.'s picked up their towels, shaving kit and departed for their own head. We snapped to and had the place spotless upon their return.

"You two movie fans go get your rifles and when you return I want you to lift them over your heads two hundred times. Is that clear?"

"Yes Sir! We replied.

We double timed it to our huts, picked up our rifles and very shortly thereafter began the arduous task of lifting our 9.5 pound rifle, over our heads. While we were struggling with our punishment, our D I s were brewing some coffee and talking about liberty in Los Angeles.

"We're   through   Sir!   Chuck   gaspingly announced.

"That's what you think, "Movie fans." Put your rifles away and get back here on the double. "

With our platoon standing at attention, Briles called Chuck and me out of ranks.

"Walewander get down on your knees and with arms out stretched, bend down and say, Allah, I'm a movie fan. O'Leary you kick him in the ass every time he bends down? "

"Yes Sir," Chuck replied.

"Walewander, every time somebody walks by I want you to tell them, loud and clear, that you're a movie fan."

"Is that clear ? "

"Yes Sir ! " I replied.

He blew his whistle and our platoon of 58 pissed off Marines walked by me one by one whereby I shouted "Allah, I'm a movie fan! Chuck meanwhile kicked me very gently in the buttocks with the side of his foot, which infuriated our D I's.

"O'Leary kick him harder or I'll kick your ass in myself," Briles angrily shouted.

"Allah! I'm a movie fan!" I shouted as Chuck kicked me pretty hard.

"Take it easy, I winced, remember yours is still to come."

After the entire platoon filed by, it was Chuck's turn. He got down on his knees and I did the kicking.

"Allah! I'm a movie fan," Chuck shouted and with that the side of my boondocker found its mark. After the entire platoon filed by, we went to chow and later to the rifle range. Our asses ached for a couple of days. I hate movies !

We spent the entire day on the range, practicing zeroing in our rifles. Since weather conditions vary from day to day, we have to know how to zero in our rifles or we won't be able to qualify. During our practice rounds we can ask for help, but not on qualifying day. Tomorrow was the big day, so we were given last minute instructions, and told to clean and oil our rifles after leaving the range.

"Do you think you'll qualify?" Chuck asked me.

"Yes I do," I replied, "If I zero in my rifle correctly."

"How about yourself,"

"I'd like to shoot Expert but if I have trouble zeroing in my rifle, who knows what I'll shoot."

"Oh come on, you've been shooting Expert all week, why wouldn't you do the same tomorrow?"

"I may choke!"

"Yeah right!" I laughingly replied.

Sammy and Porky were listening to our' chit chat' and so not to ignore them I directed a question to both of them.

"How about you guys? Expert or Sharpshooter," I kiddingly asked.

"I haven't qualified all week so unless a miracle happens tomorrow I don't think I will," Sammy replied.

"Porky, how about you?"

"It doesn't look good."

As for myself, I was pretty sure I would qualify. After all I've been shooting Sharpshooter all week so I hope nothing changes tomorrow. We hit the sack and awaited the big day in the life of a Marine- "Qualifying Day!"

Qualifying Day was exceptionally beautiful! The sun was peering from over the horizon; sending its golden rays through the earth's atmosphere.

"Looks like we're going to have a good day," Chuck happily remarked, as we left the mess hall.

"You know what Chuck, the way our platoon has been doing, we need every break we can get."

"You're not kidding. Only a miracle can save our D.I's from losing that pool money," Chuck laughed.

We agreed, left the mess hall, cleaned and oiled our rifles and fell out for our last trip to E Range. Upon arriving at the range, Sgt. Drexler was there to meet me.

"How do you feel this morning Lee? Butterflies in your stomach?" he asked.

"A little nervous I replied, as I coated my sights with lamp black.

"Don't be, just zero in your rifle as you have all week, and you won't have any trouble qualifying," he calmly replied.

I zeroed in my rifle and nervously awaited my turn on the firing line.

"Good luck Lee," Drexler said, as I took my position on the firing line. I faced the target and on the command of load, placed a clip in my chamber.

You only have a certain amount of time to get off your rounds, so everyone starts and finishes firing at the same time.

"All Ready on the Right! All Ready on the Left! All Ready on the Firing Line ! Fire ! " Was the order.

I dropped down into the Prone position and began to fire at a target 500 yards away. It was now or never! Sgt. Drexler was at my side and kept a running account as to how I was doing and encouraged me constantly.

I was shooting at the Sharpshooter level until I started the Standing position. I don't know what happened to me but I couldn't keep my rifle steady and I knew I blew my chance to be a Sharpshooter in the United States Marine Corps.

Since the starting times were so different, each Platoon Sergeant stood by with his roster, and when you finished firing, you turned in a score card to your Platoon leader. My score card was signed by Sgt. Drexler and the Captain in charge.

"Sorry Lee, you missed being a Sharpshooter by two points. That standing position did you in. You qualified but only as a Marksman," Sgt. Drexler sadly informed me.

Meanwhile Chuck and Hillbilly shot Expert, as everyone expected them to do. Sammy and Porky didn't qualify and as it turned out almost one third of our platoon didn't qualify.

Sgt. Briles, Cpl. Olson and Pfc. Kotowski were really pissed off at us because they lost their bets. They decided to punish us in one way or another.

"You people should feel pretty damn proud of yourselves," Briles raved.

"No platoon in the history of the United States Marine Corps has failed to qualify as few men as we did today. We went out of our way to help you people qualify, but no, some of you jerks didn't take advantage of it and now you're on the Marine Corps shit list.

Who ever heard of a Marine that couldn't qualify with a rifle?

We're supposed to be the best, you "Shit birds," and I'm so God Damn disgusted with you "yard birds" that I'm going to march you sad bastards until you beg for mercy," he ranted.

That afternoon, Briles, Olson and Bulldog marched us over to the black top and began our marching marathon.

"Right flank, hartch ! Left flank, hartch ! To the rear, hartch ! Left oblique, hartch ! To the rear, hartch! Column right! To the rear, hartch! First squad to the rear, hartch! Second squad to the rear, harch! Third squad to the rear, hartch! Etc.

When Briles got hoarse, Bulldog and Olson would take over and drilled us unmercifully. When one of our D I's was drilling us the other two would sip cokes knowing full well that we were dying of thirst.

"I can't go on !" cried Porky.

"Don't be a chicken! Stick it out ! Don't give in to those bastards," Sammy rasped, "that's what they want us to do."

"I'll try, but I'm getting awfully weak," Porky shakingly replied.

We marched continuously for about three hours and the drill or should I say punishment was taking its toll. Porky fainted about a half hour ago and was taken to sick bay. We kept reassuring ourselves in ranks, but even this didn't help. Two more recruits passed out almost simultaneously and were dragged off to the side and then to sick- bay. We just about had it when out of nowhere a Colonel appeared.

"Who's in charge of this platoon?" He shouted.

"I am sir, "Briles answered, saluting the Colonel as he did so.

"Sergeant I've been watching your antics for the last hour, and don't like what I've seen. I don't know what these men are guilty of doing but if you don't knock it off this instant, I shall put you on report, and have your stripes, is that clear?"

"Yes Sir, Loud and clear."

"Good ! And furthermore, I want these people to attend a movie tonight, and you three are to accompany them. Is that also good and clear?"

"Yes Sir! they replied, in unison.

The disgusted Colonel left, not even waiting for a salute from Briles.

We never saw our D.I's become so passive. They told us that we had the afternoon off and we could crap out on our sacks if we wanted to.

"Man did you hear that Colonel eat Briles out?" Sammy chuckled.

"Yeah I hope they bust his ass down to a Pfc." Chuck replied as he checked his feet for blisters.

"Why not a Private," I remarked as I dropped onto my sack.

We agreed, and without compunction sacked out for about an hour; showered and awaited chow call.

After the movie we were instructed that tomorrow morning we are heading back to the Recruit Depot, and two more weeks of Boot Camp.

Chapter 9

We piled into the trucks and headed back to San Diego and the Recruit Depot for our last two weeks of Boot camp.

Two more weeks and then what? I thought to myself as I disembarked from the truck and awaited further orders. Briles and his cronies were laughing about something perhaps a joke, and then he turned around very disgustedly and said.

"You people have two more weeks of boot camp and then you'll be assigned to different outfits in the United States Marine Corps. At the present time the Marine Air Corps is in desperate need of pilots, gunners, and mechanics. Some of you will qualify for Officer Candidate School (OCS), pilot training, gunnery school and the Line Company. Those of you that are fortunate enough to get into a Line Company, will get more infantry training and probably be in on the next push in the south Pacific. But before you leave Boot camp, we have a very busy schedule ahead of us, so fall out and get squared away; we fall out in fifteen minutes.

We no longer had to live in tents. We graduated to huts; similar to the ones we lived in at the Rifle range. The five of us picked out a hut, made up our sacks, got our gear squared away and fell out for a jaunt to sick-bay. We were given two more booster shots and then marched to the base barber shop where three weeks of hair were quickly removed..

Our next trip was to the Quartermaster Depot where we got the blouse to our dress uniform and also a pair of dress shoes. We marched back to our camp area and were dismissed to do our daily wash.

"How do I look in my uniform?" Sammy asked us as he strutted about.

"Like a million bucks," Chuck winked.

"Of course the blouse has to be pressed, but otherwise it fits like a glove," Sammy responded as he paraded back and forth.

"Sam don't forget to use a little spit and polish on those new shoes," I said, as I applied another coat of polish to mine.

"Don't worry Lee, mine will look like mirrors when I'm through," Sammy boasted. We spent our free time writing letters, shining shoes, buckles and ironing our blouses and trousers. After all, a Marine's appearance is supposed to be immaculate, and we had no intention of changing it.

The next few days were quite hectic; we fell back into the same routine of marching, calisthenics, judo and more lectures.

This morning we went to the boon docks to learn about different types of grenades and what makes them tick.

"This morning, you people will become familiar with the Fragmentation Hand Grenade, MKII. This is the baby, right here," he said pulling out a yellow painted grenade out of his pocket.

"As you can see, it resembles a large lemon, and is deeply serrated, horizontally and vertically. It is made of cast iron and weighs about 20 ounces. The grenade is serrated, so when it explodes it forms fragments of uniform and effective size. There are three principal parts of a grenade; the body, bursting charge and the fuse. I shall take this demonstration grenade apart and show you what makes it tick." He did just that, and then said; "This lever will not disengage unless this cotter pin is removed. When you pull out the ring, you automatically remove the cotter pin and the lever is released.

The pressure created by a spring, which rotates a striker, which in turn ignites a primer charge. The primer charge in turn ignites a 2 inch fuse which in turn will ignite the main charge and "Whoom" you've had it!"

Chuck raised his hand and wanted to know how much time we had before it would explode in our hand when the cotter pin is pulled?

"From the time the lever is released, you have approximately 5 seconds to get rid of it," he said.

"Wow! That's not very long," Chuck surmised.

"No it isn't!" Briles responded.

"I have a few more dummy grenades that I shall pass around for your inspection. Cpl. Olson and Pfc. Kotowski will be here very shortly with some live grenades which each and every one of you will throw over this brick wall." It wasn't very long before Olson and Bulldog drove up in a Jeep with a few crates of live grenades.

"All right, let's knock it off, Pfc. Kotowski is going to demonstrate the proper way to throw a grenade. Pay attention, or you'll throw your arms out," Briles snapped. Bulldog picked up a dummy grenade and said; The grenade is held with the throwing hand with the thumb and forefinger encircling the upper horizontal serration. The left arm is outstretched so as to give you balance and the throw is more like a heave. You never line up directly with the target but at a 45-degree angle to it. This 45 degree angle seems to give the thrower the maximum distance when he heaves the grenade. The straight left arm not only gives you balance it also points to your target. Any questions?"

"What's the record throw?" I asked.

"I'm not sure but I think it's about 70 yards, and you people should be able to heave it about 35 yards after a little practice. Now enough of this "bull crap" and let me show you how to fling these babies.

First of all there's no set position for throwing grenades. You can throw, fling or heave "em" from a standing, kneeling or prone position. Pick your target; Pull the pin; prepare to throw; throw and hit the deck so the shrapnel from your grenade doesn't hurt you, if it goes off before the 5-second interval. Got it? "

He then pulled the pin on a dummy grenade and heaved a perfect spiral about 50 yards. He then threw from a kneeling and prone position just as accurately.

"Okay let's go at it. Pretend like the Japs have a machine gun nest where that GI can is situated. See if you can hit it!"

We moved out, spread out and began practicing throwing these dummy grenades. Since I was a ball player I knew how important it was to warm up before I threw a fast ball, so I took it easy throwing these dummy grenades. After awhile I was beginning to hit this garbage can, which impressed Bulldog to no end.

"Hey Walewander where'd you learn to throw so accurately," he asked.

"I'm a natural!" I kiddingly replied.

"Yeah Right!" he snickered.

We practiced throwing grenades for about a half hour at which time Briles told us to knock it off.

"Each of you are now going to throw a live grenade over this 6 foot wall. Now here's the procedure. I will hand you a grenade, you pull the cotter pin and heave the grenade over the wall. Don't freeze up on us or we'll have to belt you in the kisser and get rid of it for you. Is that clear?"

"Yes Sir!"we acknowledged.

"You men will come up one at a time. The rest of you will be behind the other wall. If a grenade should explode before you have a chance to get rid of it, we want the rest of you to be out of Harms way. Is that clear? " "Yes Sir," we gulped.

The wall in question was about 100 yards long and had side- walls jutting out every 10 yards or so. Great precaution had to be taken as one mistake could mean the death or injury to the recruit and our D I s.

Everything was working smoothly until one of the grenades slipped out of a boot's hand whereby a pouncing Bulldog retrieved it and quickly threw it over the wall. The grenade exploded in the air.

Briles looked at Bulldog, sighed and meekly said, "The smoking lamp is lit!"

Shaky hands fumbled with their cigarette packs; crumbled cigarettes were being lit! and those of us that didn't smoke, wanted to !

Fortunately we completed our grenade drill without losing anybody and marched back to camp. Sammy was caught talking in ranks and for his punishment he had to walk around the camp area with a bucket on his head, shouting;

"I'm a talking yard bird! I'm a talking yard bird!" he shouted as he stumbled along peering from under his bucket. Sammy was greeted by the usual wise cracks, and pebble after pebble bouncing off his bucket. I sympathized with Sammy, knowing first hand, the humiliation involved. When he got off this detail, we left him alone; he was just itching to square off and clobber somebody.

Sammy and I spent our evenings in the pool practicing the various strokes that were taught us. We were enjoying ourselves and weren't too eager to qualify.

"You know Sam the scuttlebutt is that non-swimmers will not get their ten day furloughs if they don't qualify."

"You're kidding aren't you?"

"No I'm not! You want to try it tonight?"

"Why not! I think we can swim fifty yards easily, you agree?"

"Yeah, I do!" I replied.

"Let's do it!"

We called our instructors over and told them we were ready to qualify. That night we were two determined swimmers. We had no trouble qualifying in fact we swam 75 yards instead of the minimum of 50. We were very pleased with ourselves and so were our Drill Instructors.

One afternoon, during our pause in our busy schedule, Bulldog held a bull session. "Men in four days you'll graduate from Boot Camp and become full fledged Marines. As Marines you have the tradition of the Corps to uphold. Every one of you will have to pass a rigid inspection before you're permitted to leave the base. Your appearance has to be immaculate. It should make people marvel at the crease to your uniforms and the sparkle of your shoes. Some of you will get into brawls whether you like it or not. Don't ever stand by and let a Gyrene get his brains beat out by some Doggie or Swabby. Help each other out! Is that clear?"

"Yes Sir!" we smiled.

" If it's a choice between the Swabbys and Doggies go along with the Swabbys, after all, they furnish us with the transportation to our battlefields, and besides we technically are a part of the Navy, as much as I hate to admit it.

Furthermore, if some big bastard is giving you a hard time, remove your belt, wrap it around your fist and with the large brass buckle dangling freely, wrap it around his skull. Always have an "equalizer" in your possession. Remember you wouldn't expect a heavyweight, fighting a lightweight, and so it's no different in bar room brawls. If you can't use your belt, a broken beer bottle if handled properly will do just fine, he winked. One more thing, the Marines are always courteous to little old ladies and are Don Juans as far as the broads are concerned, so don't ruin our reputation," he quipped.

That evening we were told we were going to see a couple of films on sex.

"Hey Sam do you think these movies are like stag movies" Chuck asked.

"Not only are they stag, but they're imports from France!"

"Yeah, right!" Chuck replied.

"No I'm not kidding! I got my information from a good source."

Well Sammy's source was way off base. The film we saw was strictly biological in nature. It explained the functions of the sex organs and the diseases that are associated with them. The possibility of a promiscuous girl having syphilis or gonorrhea was impressed upon our fertile minds.

"A girl may look beautiful and wholesome on the outside but a vicious killer and crippler on the inside," commented the Doctor in the film. "She may be the carrier of this spirochete bacteria and not know it. Syphilis may exist in the sex organs and in the blood streams for many years before striking its blow. Your wife or child may be the victims of your sex escapades. If you can't control your sex drive than you better know how to protect yourself. Wear a rubber or condom every time you have sex or this is what can happen to you.

The film then showed us in graphic detail, how these diseases affect various organs of the human body. I was getting nauseous and felt like vomiting. When we left the theatre we were also given a Prophylactic Kit, which was to be used if we had un-protective sex. It consisted of a tube of ointment, some Isopropyl alcohol and some cotton swatches. The ointment was to be squeezed into our penis before and after we had sex. Good Luck !

The next few days flitted by very quickly. We arose one morning and Graduation Day was upon us. We showered, shaved and put on our pressed dress uniforms. Our shoes sparkled as brightly as our brass buckles. After a preliminary inspection by our D I's we proceeded to march to the parade grounds and fell in line with the other graduating platoons.

As we stood at attention, we listened to various dignitaries and Officers speak and then were inspected by one of the visiting Colonels.

We passed inspection and awaited the finale to Boot Camp, the "Grand March."

Just then the United States Marine Corps band began to play the Marine Corps hymn, and each platoon began to march towards the Review stands.

Meanwhile my heart was pounding rhythmically with every step I took and as I marched a strange, pleasant feeling came over me that was unforgiving. I survived Boot Camp, I did what was required of me and now I was a United States Marine. No one can ever take that away from me. I was proud to be a Marine!

"Eyes Right!" Briles commanded, as we approached the review stands. As we passed the stands we saluted Old Glory a flag that we were willing to fight for and perhaps die for. We were Marines!

Before we were dismissed, Sgt. Briles, Cpl. Olson and Pf Kotowski stood before us. Briles was the first to address us.

"First of all, I want to congratulate you people on the way you performed this morning. You were just great !

You are now Marines and as Marines you have certain privileges. One of these privileges is to be able to guzzle beer at the base Post Exchange or better known to all of us as the "Slop shoot. It is also traditional for you people to get drunk with your D I's and let bygones be bygones so we'll see you at the slop shoot tonight. That's an order!"

"Yes Sir! we shouted very loudly.

Tomorrow morning, you people are going to ship out to your new assignments and from there you will get your ten day furloughs.

As I told you people before, most of you are being assigned to the Marine Air Corps, while some of you will be assigned to Camp Ellington and Camp Pendleton.

Chuck looked at me and said, "I hope I get assigned to Camp Pendleton or Camp Ellington. I want to see some action," he hopefully stated.

I wasn't sure what I wanted, but if I had a choice I'd rather be playing baseball for the United States Marine Corps instead of fighting for them. Oh well, what is to be, will be.

"When I call your name I'll address you as either Pvt. or Pfc. and tell you where you've been assigned. Usually you're promoted to Pfc. if you qualified with your rifle, swam 50 yards, ran the obstacle course in a certain amount of time etc., but most importantly, the three of us decide if you're promoted or not.

> Private Abrams - Camp Miramar (Air Corps)
> Private Albert   -   Camp Miramar(Air Corps)
> Pfc. Artford   -   Camp Pendleton (Infantry)
> Privae Bartels -   Camp Miramar(Air Corps)
> Private Bergoni   Camp Miramar(Air Corps)
> Etc. ------------

When the names were read some of us were very unhappy to be assigned to the Marine Air Corps and not to the Line Company.

We were very happy in a sense because all five of us were assigned to Camp Miramar. Chuck and Hillbilly were really disappointed because they joined the Marine Corps to fight not to be machinists, cooks, aerial gunners, pilots, etc.

We were given the rest of the day off, so we went back to our tent area and on the way there we saw a platoon of recruits that were just starting out.

"You'll be sorry! You'll be sorry"! We shouted, getting even with the times we had to hear those words.

Our last night in boot camp was pretty memorable. We put on our dress greens and moseyed over to the "Slop shoot."

"Let's sit at that large round table in the corner," Chuck suggested, as he led the way.

"I'm going to get' pissy eyed drunk before this night is over," Sammy boasted.

"Me too!" Hillbilly yelled.

"You guys haven't seen beer guzzling until you've seen me put it away," Porky chided as he patted his stomach.

"Yeah right! I'll drink you all under the table," I kiddingly, replied.

"We'll see who drops out first," Sammy replied as he brought a couple of pitchers of beer to our table.

"Seeing it's our first drink together, let's make a toast." I suggested.

"Let me do it!" Porky begged.

"Go ahead," we replied.

"Here's to our friendship and here's hoping that we can all return to our loved ones in one piece."?

"Here ! Here!" we shouted.

"Down the hatch!" Sammy ordered.

I wasn't much of a beer drinker; in fact if you gave me a choice of a black cow or a beer, I would always pick the black cow.

"Come on Lee, down the hatch!" Sammy said, as waited for me to take the first swig. I complied, and almost choked to death! I began to cough and wheeze.

After the laughter subsided, I forced the drink down my esophagus without stopping.

"Another round," I shouted, trying desperately to save face. There weren't any waitresses in the Slop shoot, so we had to fetch the beer ourselves. We kept drinking and toasting. I felt bloated, but as yet the beer had no effect on me, so I thought. Another round was ordered and the familiar, Down the Hatch, bounced off my ear drums. I began to feel the warmth in the pit of my stomach. I belched and drank some more."Where the hell are our D I's?" Hillbilly slurred.

"It's early yet," Chuck replied.

"Whose going to buy those ass holes a beer? I'm not! Sammy belched.

"They really gave me a hard time. If I didn't have this physiological defect, I'd have gone over the hill as I promised."

"What phys—physiolo --- what defect ?" Porky blurted out." No guts !" Sammy screamed.

" Hey, das a goo one, No guts," Porky roared.

We sat there drinking, telling jokes and visiting the head. Finally someone shouted, "Ten Shun!" as our D I's approached.

Forgetting that we were no longer recruits, we staggered to attention knocking over a pitcher of beer in the process.

"At ease men, you guys are no longer in Boot camp," Briles remarked.

"Is it alright if we join you for a drink," Cpl. Olson asked.

"Sure why not! Pull up a chair and help yourselves," Chuck suggested.

As Bulldog poured himself a beer he looked at me and said.

"Movies better than ever Lee?"

"Can't stand them Bill, but I did clean my gun today," I laughed.

The laughter was uproarious and when it subsided we ordered a few more pitchers of beer to take care of our visitors. I don't know how many beers I drank but at this stage of the game, I didn't care. My companions were becoming twins and my tongue didn't want to move.

I looked at Bulldog and asked, "Hey Bill were "wou" picking az me?" I slovenly asked.

"You bet I was Lee. I knew I could make a man out of you if I gave you a rough enough time," Bulldog replied.

"You didn't suk seed did you?"

"I think I did!"

"Well you soor pizzed me off az times."

"Yeah,"Sammy cut in, "and was it ever hot with that bucket on my head."

"I can imagine."

Just then Briles interrupted our conversation and asked, Sammy how he was able to find 200 cigarette butts in a spotless area.

"Well Danny old boy, I raided the G I cans behind the slop shoot when you weren't looking." Sammy laughed.

"I figured you did something like that," he smirked.

Our D I's had a couple of beers with us and then joined another group of men from our platoon at another table and then another table and –

I don't know how many beers I drank but I would bet more than I ever had in my entire life. The slop shoot finally closed and we were kicked out into the cold night air. As we staggered back to our hut, I can't imagine what five pissy eyed, drunken Marines must have looked like with their arms around each other staggering back to the camp area.

Chapter 10

Camp Miramar is located about sixty miles from San Diego. It is the stopping off place for Marine Air Corps personnel to and from the islands. It is also the transient area for Marines going to Aviation school.

We arrived at Camp Miramar early Saturday morning and were assigned to ATS, 131 MCAD. This stands for Aviation Training School, Marine Corps Air Depot. Forty of us were assigned to the Marine Air Corps but as yet we had no idea in what capacity. As we were getting our gear squared away in one of the wooden barracks, Chuck broke the silence.

"Lee, I don't know if I'm going to like the Air Corps very much. I wanted to get into the thick of things not get stuck behind a desk for the rest of the war."

"Why don't you try to become an Aerial gunner like me?" I replied. "You get all the fighting you want, with very little walking."

"Maybe you're right Lee, maybe I'll give it a shot." One of the prerequisites of trying out for gunnery school is that you had to have qualified with your rifle. They probably figured that if you can't hit a stationary target how in the world can you hit a Jap zero. It makes sense, I thought.

Just then the whistle blew; we fell out and were told that a battery of tests awaited us in a nearby building. We spent the rest of this morning taking these tests which were primarily aimed at determining what we're going to do in the Marine Corps.

Camp Miramar was run very strictly. Every Tuesday and Friday was locker inspection. Every article of wearing apparel had to be neatly folded and according to the diagram that was stapled on the inside of every locker door. If you didn't pass inspection, you were restricted to the base along with the D I's who were in charge of your barrack.

There were two D I's assigned to every barrack and they were responsible for at least 60 men. Every barrack had a room at one end where the DI's slept. The DI's loved their liberty and raised Holy Hell if they were restricted to the base. We haven't had liberty yet and we're awaiting it eagerly.

We passed our first inspection and were told that we could go out on Liberty that evening if we chose to do so. They also told us about the buses, curfew and to stay out of trouble. We double timed it to the head, showered, shaved and went to chow. Immediately after chow, buses were waiting for us to take us to San Diego. The bus company had a regular scheduled route with Camp Miramar. It took the Gyrenes to San Diego and then picked them up at certain times. We bought round trip tickets and boarded one of the buses.

"I've got to find me a nice "wench" to shack up with," Sammy gloated.

"Are you forgetting that film we saw on sex," I asked.

"No I haven't, but you heard what the man said, If you can't keep away from it, make sure you protect yourself. Well I've got a pocket full of condoms and if I meet someone who doesn't like for me to use a condom, I also have my little ole Pro Kit to fall back on right here in my pocket," he boastfully replied.

"You're really well prepared, aren't you Sam. I hope you don't strike out."

"Don't worry about me, Lee, what about you guys?"

"I don't know! Since Chuck and I are under age, we can't get into the night clubs. It's a shame they have our pictures on them otherwise we could use somebody else's I. D. card. Oh well, we'll have to play it by ear," I rationalized.

Sammy sat their smiling.

"Listen guys, let me know where you'll be so if I get lucky, I'll see what I can do about getting you two a couple of broads."

"No thanks Sam, I don't think I'd be interested in that kind of girl."

"What do you mean you wouldn't be interested? What about that red head in the hospital? You seemed to be interested in her?"

"Well, she seemed different."

"Lee, don't be so naïve. You've got a lot to learn. I'll bet your little red head is no angel and I'll bet she's out on liberty looking to score like we are."

" Forget it Sam, even if she is, I'm not interested."

Chuck wasn't saying much, but he was listening.

"You know what Lee, let's look over the town and as a last resort we can go to the USO (United Service Organization) Canteen center here in town. They say the hostesses are quite pretty. Who knows we may even bump into some movie stars."

"Sounds great!" I happily replied.

We settled back in our seats and enjoyed the beautiful California Mountains that looked like a post card. It wasn't very long before we pulled into the station, got off the bus, and walked out into the sunlight.

"Man I didn't know San Diego was so beautiful? Chuck noted.

"Yeah and these broads are pretty cute too," Sammy added as he proceeded to give a couple of girls a wolf call. The girls seemed to be flattered and looked back at us when they were some distance away.

"Why don't you guys pick em up?" Sammy asked. "They look ripe for plucking and just look how they're cramming their necks," he laughed.

I looked back and sure enough the girls stopped at a store window and kept looking at us.

"What do you say Lee, you want to pick them up?" Chuck excitedly asked.

"Nah, let's look over the town for awhile and see what happens."

"Okay, but Sammy's right. They look pretty eager,"

Sammy must have known that we were going to curb his style so he doffed his barracks cap and said, "I'll see you two squares later," as he walked toward the night club district.

"Where's Sam going?" I asked.

"Oh he'll hit the night clubs and wind up in the sack with some broad."

"Yeah right!"

We proceeded to look over the town, noting especially the theatres, night clubs, dance halls, roller rinks, and the USO canteen.

"Hey Chuck there's a Burlesque show up ahead, what do you say we drop in for awhile.

"You think they'll let us in?"

"They better!"

I looked at the posters of the girls scantily dressed and wondered what they looked like without the heavy makeup. I never attended a Burlesque show and was very curious. My curiosity got the better of me and after we bought our tickets we were lucky to find a couple of seats in the back of the theatre. The Hollywood Burlesque Theatre was filled to capacity with service men of the Marine Corps, Navy, Army, and Air Force. All ranks and all ages were represented.

"Take it off!" they yelled. The girls did just that! When a stripper got finished with her number, a couple of comedians filled in until the next girl got ready. I soon realized that many people frequented the burlesque theatre because of these comedians. There jokes were off color, and very funny.

"Now ladies and gentlemen, for our feature attraction of this evening, the one, the only, the beautiful and talented, "Juanita" the body beautiful," the Master of Ceremonies announced.

The drums began to roll, the lights were dimmed and a beautiful dark haired goddess appeared on the stage. The colored spotlight presented her in all her loveliness and as the band struck up, "A Pretty Girl is Like a Melody,"

Juanita began her slow, tantalizing movements. She was getting to me! I swallowed hard as I took in every movement. She slowly took off all her clothes until only a transparent brassiere and panties remained. Bedlam broke loose and shouts of, "Take it off Juanita ! Go all the way doll!" Were the cries.

Juanita responded by taking off her bra and twirling it around her head as she bounced around on the stage. Her busts were perfectly molded and responded to her every whim. When she completed her number the audience clapped, whistled and shouted.

"Take it off baby, go all the way!" they shouted, but Juanita couldn't because the city ordinance prohibited it. I'm sure she wanted to oblige, but if she did, the place would be shut down. The most she could do was to pull her G string slightly forward, and then left the stage. The applause was deafening and once more the comedians came out with their slap stick humor.

I don't remember how many girls performed, but we sat there for over an hour and a half and the show was still going strong. The high point of the show was when the chorus girls came down to the audience and sat in the service men's laps. The girls would kiss and hug the servicemen and give them autographed pictures of themselves. The front row was therefore very popular and we soon found out that some of the servicemen would wait in line for hours just to make sure that they got one of these choice seats.

"Wait till Sammy hears about this place. I'll bet he'll want to come here every night." I laughed.

"You know what, I may want to join him," Chuck laughingly replied.

We left the Burlesque theatre, and headed out for the USO (United Service Organization) canteen. The Canteen was crowded to the hilt with servicemen, and as we entered we were greeted by one of the hostesses.

"The food is to the left, and the entertainment to your right."

We doffed our piss cutters and headed for the food. "Look at all the food they have laid out here, I'll bet there's enough here to feed our platoon," I remarked.

"At least," Chuck replied.

I picked up a ham sandwich, bag of potato chips and a glass of milk and sat down at one of the tables. Chuck joined me and as we munched on our sandwiches, and looked over at the various hostesses. Some of them were dancing, some serving drinks and food, but the majority of them just sat around and talked with the servicemen. As I glanced around the room I thought I recognized a girl I met at the hospital when I donated blood.

"Well, I'll be, it's the red head I met at the hospital. Now I wish I could remember what her name was?" I thought. All of a sudden it came to me, Rita Shaw!

"Well what are you going to do about it?" Chuck inquired

"I figure I'll go over and make a fool of myself, that's what I'm going to do."

"Well you better hurry, I see a couple of Swabbys looking her over.

I strutted over to the sandwich counter and walked up behind her.

"Hi Rita!" I stammered.

She abruptly turned her head and when she looked at me a big smiled crossed her face.

"Hi Lee, what a welcome surprise. I thought you were still in Boot Camp?

"You're not AWOL are you?"

" No, silly, we graduated a few days ago and right now I'm stationed at Camp Miramar waiting to qualify to go to Aerial Gunnery school."

"When would you start?"

"First I have to qualify, and then they'll send me to their gunnery schools in Florida or Texas."

"How long does it take to become an aerial gunner and isn't it a little dangerous? From what I hear a gunner's life is a very short one." She remarked.

"I don't know how long it takes but when they asked me if I would be interested in becoming a gunner, at the time it sounded exciting."

"How long will you be at Camp Miramar?"

"I don't know, it could be a week even a month, it all depends on how crowded the schools happen to be. But you know what? We have Liberty every night just as long as we pass barracks inspection."

"That's great! Maybe we can see a movie together," she asked"

"I'd like that!" I happily replied. "Oh by the way would you like to meet my buddy Chuck?"

"I'd love to!"

We walked over to where Chuck was sitting. I introduced her to him and after the usual small talk she asked me if I'd like to dance.

"I'd love to," I replied. The band played, "You'll Never Know" which was a nice slow number for me to hold her close to me.

"You dance very well Lee, who gave you lessons"

"When you grow up with three older sisters you don't need lessons," I laughed.

"Yeah right!" she smiled.

Just then the band started to play, "One O'Clock Jump", a fast jitterbug number. "Do you know how to Jitterbug? Rita asked.

"Do I ever! I love it!

We started to jitterbug and to my pleasant surprise we danced very well together. Rita loved to dance and so did I which made our meeting something special. We danced for awhile and then sat down at a nearby table, had a light snack before heading back to our respective bases.

Chuck, meanwhile, was occupied with a pretty hostess and told me he'd meet me at the bus station later on.

"Okay," I waved to him, as Rita and I moved towards the door.

The cold night air was invigorating and as we walked, hand in hand, to the bus stop, Rita asked me,

"Lee do you have a girlfriend waiting for you back home in Chicago?"

"No I don't, but I did meet a girl I liked very much when I was playing professional baseball in Kingsport Tennessee. I haven't heard from her in awhile so I figure she must have met someone else in College and dumped me."

"How about you, any boyfriends?"

Well believe it or not, I was engaged until I caught my fiancée cheating on me with my best friend, so I dumped both of them. To get away from them, I joined the Waves and I'm now in the process of becoming a naval nurse."

I didn't know what to say, so I just kept quiet, but I did squeeze her hand a bit, to how that I cared.

"Rita," I stammered, "Would you like to go out tomorrow night? I could meet you here at the canteen and then we can take in a movie."

"I would love to!" she smilingly replied, "and after the movie we can come back to the canteen and pretend were Ginger Rogers and Fred Astaire," she giggled. She then scribbled her phone number, on a piece of paper that she took out of her pocket. We gave each other a hug, no kiss, and boarded the buses that would take us back to our respective bases. It was 0100 in the morning.

As I sat there in the bus waiting for Chuck to appear, I must have fallen asleep because the next thing I knew I heard the bus driver announcing that we were in Camp Miramar and he wanted everyone off his bus. So my first night of Liberty was one that I shall never forget!

Sunday was a day of rest and boy did we need it! After roll call, I hit the sack once more as did most of the others. I missed Church services for the first time since I've been in the Corps. I got up late that morning, showered, shaved and went to the afternoon chow. Chuck and Sam did the same.

During lunch, we talked about our first night of liberty.

"Man what a night I had," Sammy said, in between mouthfuls.

"Did you make out Sam?"Chuck asked.

"Sammy always makes out," he bragged. "How did you guys do?"

We told Sammy about the Burlesque show and how the strippers came down and sat on the laps of the servicemen.

"No shit! You guys are pulling my chain, aren't you?"

"No we're not, and if you don't believe us ask around and you'll see that we're telling the truth."

"Well if that's the case, we better get there early this evening."

We didn't pass barrack inspection and so no liberty for us tonight. I called Rita and told her what had happened and of course she understood.

I told her that I'll call her when we do get liberty and we'll go to the movies and canteen as we planned. I also told her how much I enjoyed her company and what a wonderful time I had last night. She said she did too and can't wait to see me again.

Since we were restricted to the base, we caught up on our letter writing, and had a good opportunity to wash our clothes. While we were waiting for our clothes to dry, we checked out a basketball, chose up sides, and played about as rough and tough basketball game as would be expected without a referee. It felt like Judo all over again.

That evening we attended the base theatre, slop shoot and retired early.

A typical day at Camp Miramar is as follows:

The bugler wakes us up at 0600 for roll call. After roll is taken, we wash, shave and go to chow. Immediately afterwards, we clean our barracks, police the area and fall out for school announcements. Every day a list of names are read off telling you where you're being sent. If your name is not called you stay where you're at until your name is called.

Meanwhile, those whose names were not called had to be kept busy for the rest of the day. The Sergeant in Charge was an old campaigner with at least twenty years of service life under his belt.

He was in his early forties, stood about six feet tall, and was the proud possessor of a huge stomach that protruded over his belt. His face was pocked, he had small beady eyes and a network of veins on his big red nose. He was always smoking a cigar and went under the name of Daniel O'Shannon. His job was to keep us busy until we were assigned elsewhere. He was appropriately called "Beer Belly" O'Shannon by those who disliked him.

At the present time he was in charge of six barracks which held a compliment of sixty men each, not counting his stooges.

If the schools weren't crowded, O'Shannon had very few Marines to keep busy, but at this time he had over three hundred men that he was responsible for. These men had to be kept busy so he often took us on all day hikes whenever he was well rested.

If we didn't go on a all day hike, his D I's (Stooges) would give us Close Order Drill or put us to work cleaning out the heads, peeling spuds or unloading trucks for the Quartermaster Depot. We couldn't wait to get out of here.

When Beer Belly O'Shannon went out on liberty, we knew we were in for it. He would stagger into his barracks at 0200 in the morning, and began cranking a siren that he had attached outside his barrack door.

Once we heard this air raid siren we were to dress and double time it outside for roll call. It sounded like an air alert, but we knew it wasn't. His stooges, meanwhile, were running through the barracks with flash-lights dragging out any one who hid under his bunk or in his clothes closet. The last one out in each barrack would have to do push-ups with a couple of loaded seabags on their back.

After the barracks were turned inside out and the last one from each of the barracks punished, he began his drunken dissertation about the old Corps, while we shivered in the cold night air.

"If we had an air raid tonight, you sad bastards would be dead," he bellowed, as he weaved forwards and backwards.

At times he talked for an hour before we were dismissed.

Whenever O'Shannon went out on liberty, we knew what to expect, so we slept with our clothes on. We didn't like the idea of doing push-ups at two in the morning.

On many occasions, you can see a lot of the men in their stocking feet just so they wouldn't be the last one's out of their barrack. It was getting so unbearable that men would bypass their school and sign up for oversea duty.

There was a sign posted in the Mess Hall which stated that if you don't want to wait to go to school you can sign up for oversea duty and hopefully get your training overseas. This would mean a transfer to the Aviation Replacement Squadron, which was on four-hour notice and ready to ship out. While they were waiting, they were given infantry training.

When Chuck read this notice he was beside himself. He could sign up and get the fighting he was looking for, and not put up with all this bull shit.

I on the other hand, wasn't in much of a hurry. I enjoyed being with Rita and dancing at the USO. Sammy and Porky were going to the Burlesque show every time we got liberty so they weren't eager to sign up either. The only ones ready to sign up were Chuck and Hillbilly.

Since Chuck wanted the three of us to stick together, we made somewhat of a pact. We wouldn't sign up for oversea duty until that time when all three of us are ready to do so. Chuck was ready, but Sammy and I weren't

Chapter 11

One day, when I had the detail of raking the baseball infield, I stuck around to watch the team work out. Being a professional ballplayer, I was eating my heart out. I just had to play once more. I wanted to find out who was in charge but couldn't leave the detail because one of O'Shannon's stooges was watching me.

Camp Miramar had a very good baseball team. All of its players were professionals and consequently a good brand of baseball was being played. If you were a baseball player, you had certain privileges. Most of the players were catered to and spent their time on the ball diamond. If they played away from home, they had their own bus to travel in and were given liberty after each game.

On many long road trips the team would be away for three days or more. I figured I could be an utility infielder on this team while I'm waiting to go to school. After all, they're just keeping me busy on these "shit" details. I was determined to get a try out but I knew I had to go through the proper channels. The first obstacle was to get permission from Sgt. O'Shannon.

The next morning, I knocked on his door and asked permission to enter.

"Come in," He gruffed.

"Private Lee Walewander asks permission to try out for the Camp Miramar baseball team, Sir"

O'Shannon looked up from his "girly" magazine he was reading.

"You a ball-player Walewander?"

"Yes sir!" I boastfully replied.

"Well I play with my balls, too!" He roared with laughter.

"Walewander, get your ass out of here and get back on that God Damn detail where you belong," he shouted.

As I left the barracks, I cursed him under my breath. When I met Chuck and Sammy I told them what had happened.

"If that drunken slob thinks he's going to keep me from trying out for the team, he's nuttier than I think he is," I angrily replied.

"Don't go over his head Lee or he'll really make life miserable for you," Chuck reasoned.

"I know I can make the team Chuck, I just know it! And he isn't going to stop me. I'm going to sneak away this afternoon and see if they give me a try out."

"Lee if you want to see your red head again you better not cross Beer belly," Sammy cut in, "he'll give you the worst shit details he can muster."

"I don't give a shit!"

That afternoon, we were detailed to unload a truck full of ammo at the Quartermaster Depot. As soon as the opportunity presented itself, I left the detail unnoticed. I double-timed it to the ball diamond where the team was having practice. I walked over to one of the pitchers who was in the process of warming up and asked who was in charge.

"Lt. Gross, he's also our first baseman."

I walked over to the first base side and watched the Lieutenant maneuver around first base.

"Lt. Gross may I bother you for a minute."

"Sure Private, what is it?" he asked, as he picked up a towel and began wiping his face.

"Sir, I'd like to try out for the team"

"I'd like to oblige you Private, but I don't think you'd stand a chance. Every man on this team played Professional baseball and we don't have the time to give try outs to every Tom, Dick and Harry.

"But I'm also a Professional Ballplayer," I stated.

"You are?" he smiled.

I knew he didn't believe me, so I pulled out my wallet and took out my release and a clipping I carried with me.

"Here sir, take a look at my release and also this clipping"

The lieutenant took the release and clipping and began to read them.

"Lee Walewander rookie shortstop from Chicago has made the team and along with Vince Fauci should give us the best keystone combination in the Appalachian League." The clipping and release were passed around for the players to verify.

"Okay, Lee, you've got your tryout. Go to the gym, pick up a uniform and glove and we'll see what you can do."

I went over to the gym and told the equipment manager that I was trying out for the team and needed a glove, a pair of spike shoes, a cap and a comfortable pair of baseball pants. I wore my own green T shirt.

When I returned to the field, I warmed up for about ten minutes and when my arm felt loose I took my position at shortstop.

"Okay Lee, let's see what you can do," he shouted.

He proceeded to hit a sharp ground ball to me which I cleanly picked up and rifled a perfect strike to first base. The next few were right at me again and then he began hitting them to my right and then to my left. I didn't make an error which impressed the Lieutenant very much.

"Okay Lee, right through the box," he shouted, as he hit a sharp grounder over the pitcher's mound heading for center field.

I instinctively broke for second base, speared the ball behind the sack, and pivoted somewhat throwing a perfect strike to first base.

Kingsport's Wonder Boys – Vincent Fauci and Lee Walewander, rookie keystone combination are ready to give any other combine in the league a run for its money. These two youngsters who have shown remarkable speed and accuracy during the entire training period, have been highly praised by Manager Neil Millard and should prove the strongest department of the entire club.

The next ground ball was either going to make me or brake me. Since the Lieutenant hadn't hit one in the hole as yet I anticipated that he was going to.

He didn't disappoint me. He drove one in the hole and by my breaking immediately I was able to back hand it and spin around in the air, throwing a strike to first base.

"Atta baby Lee," someone shouted.

"Move over to second Lee," the Lieutenant beckoned.

I did and then worked out at third base.

"Bring it in Lee," the Lieutenant once more shouted, as he dropped a bunt down the third base line. I raced in, picked up the ball with my bare hand and while still in the crouched position, snapped the ball to the catcher. During all this time the team stood around and watched me perform.

"If you can hit, you're on the team," the Lieutenant informed me.

I stepped into the batter's box and proceeded to bunt the first two pitches. One down the third base line; the other down the first, both balls stayed fair. The next two pitches were outside so I didn't swing. The next pitch I lined into left center, which split the outfielders.

"That's a two bagger," one of the ballplayers shouted.

I proceeded to hit a few to left and then to center. Meanwhile Lt. Gross was standing behind the batter's cage watching my every move.

"Hit and run!" he shouted.

I shifted my feet and drove the ball between first and second and raced to first base. My speed was better than average. I returned to where Lt. Gross was standing and was congratulated by most members of the team.

The Lieutenant shook my hand and said.

"Lee you're on the team. You came to us at the right time. Our regular second baseman broke his ankle sliding into third base the other day and we can use a good utility infielder.

Are you interested?"

"You bet I am!" I happily remarked.

"By the way Lee, what's your status here at Camp Miramar.?"

I told him I was waiting to go to Gunnery school and was assigned to ATS 131, Sergeant O'Shannon's outfit."

"Oh, you'll probably be around for some time. The schools are very crowded right now," he said.

"By the way Sir, I would appreciate it if you could write a note to Sgt. O'Shannon informing him that I'm on the Camp Miramar baseball team.

"Sure Lee, I'll write it right now and you can show it to Sgt. O'Shannon this afternoon, and furthermore Lee, as a ballplayer you will be away a good part of the time because we do play quite a few road games."

"Yes Sir," I know.

I went back to the gym and put on my dungarees. I went directly to O'Shannon's barrack and knocked on his door.

"Come in," he rasped.

When I entered, O'Shannon was crapped out on his back and didn't make an attempt to get up.

"What the hell do you want now, Walewander?"

"Sir, I have a note from Lt. Gross."

He slowly arose, sat on the edge of his bunk, and took the note. His hands began to tremble as he read it, and I could see that I was in for it.

Walewander, you no good bastard, what do you mean by going over my head and trying out for the team. I told you that I didn't want you to, didn't I?"

"Yes Sir!" I replied.

"Walewander, I'm going to restrict you to the base whenever you're not playing ball. No more Liberty for you Walewander. Do you hear me?"

"Yes Sir! Loud and clear," I replied.

"When you're not playing ball I'm going to give you the worst God Damn shit details, I can think of," he raved.

He got up, tore up the note and threw it in the garbage can, and shouted:

"Corporal Fischer get your ass over here, I have an assignment for you."

"Stooge" Fischer entered very quickly and awaited his orders.

"Corporal, this shit bird has disobeyed my orders. I want you to give him the worst jobs you can find, and I want you to start right now. Keep an eye on him and if he gold bricks just once, I'll have him court martialed and thrown into the brig. Now get his sorry ass out of here!" he screamed.

My first job that afternoon was digging holes for fence posts. In the evening I guarded a pile of coal. I came back to the barracks at midnight and woke up Sammy.

"Hey Sam," I whispered. "Did Beer Belly go out on liberty tonight?"

"Naw, I always sleep with my clothes on," he mumbled, as he rolled over and went back to sleep.

I went to my bunk, and didn't even bother to get under the sheets. I threw an extra blanket over myself and awaited the blast of the siren.

"There it is!" somebody cursed.

The siren screamed as if it were in pain. I threw off my blanket and was jostled out of the barrack with the rest of the sleepy unhappy men. Beer Belly stood there rocking and reeling as his stooges stormed through the barracks.

"What the hell is that drunken slob going to talk about tonight?" Sammy yawned.

"What else, the Old Corps," I replied.

Sure enough, "Now in the Old Corps, etc.

He ranted for about an hour, and then retired to his room. We undressed, and hit the sack for the few remaining hours that were left.

The only consolation with Beer Belly going out on Liberty was that we wouldn't go on an all day hike. He had to sleep off his drunken stupor and hang over.

"Get those pots and pans cleaned" ordered the Mess Sergeant, as he escorted me into the galley. I took off my dungaree jacket, picked up a scouring pad and began the arduous task of rubbing off the baked food that was stuck to the skillet. The hot greasy water was beginning to stain and scald my hands.

"I hate that fat drunken bastard," I said under my breath.

Just then the door opened up and more pots and pans were put into my sink. I don't know how many I cleaned but my hands looked like beets when I finally finished.

I looked forward to the afternoons because we either practiced or had a ball game.

I was now our team's lead-off man and filled in at short, second or third base. I also pinch ran for some of the slower players. I was the youngest player on the team and the only player to have played Class D ball.

Whenever we played on the road, our opponents would set us up at their base. We had our own sleeping quarters and ate our meals at their mess hall. We did the same for them when they visited us.

After the game, we showered, shaved and went to their mess hall to partake of their chow. We then piled into our bus and liberty. The bus driver would park our bus in town and we migrated from there. We were told when the bus would leave and to make sure we were there, otherwise, we take a cab back to the base.

Sometimes I would return to the bus a little early only to hear a girl's giggling voice somewhere in the darkened surroundings. Since I was too young to get into the dives they frequented, my teammates never asked me to join them. I always told them that I had relatives in town and that I would go to visit them. I wound up watching a movie!

One day, as we were planning to leave Camp Miramar to play the San Bernadino Air Force team, Bill Campell our shortstop called me over.

"Lee, I want to do you a little favor, if you let me."

"Sure Bill, what do you want to do for me?"

"Well Lee, we all like you, and would love to take you along on liberty with us, but because of your age, we can't. So if you give me your I. D. card, I can make you 21 in about an hour and you'll have a ball with us in San Bernadino."

"Isn't that illegal," I asked.

"Only if you get caught. You'll have two I D cards, one for the Corps and one for the nightclubs.

I thought of the miserable nights I spent, seeing double feature movies, so I wouldn't have to report to the bus too early. I was torn between honesty and despair and the latter won out.

I called Rita, or Rita called me almost every day. She hated O'Shannon for not giving me liberty, but she was happy I was playing baseball again. Just before we left for San Bernadino, I put in a hurried call to San Diego.

"Hi Rita, it's me. We're playing the San Bernadino Air Force today and I'm just wondering if you could meet me there."

"I'd love to Lee, but I have duty this weekend. If you let me know a few days ahead of time I may be able to work it out so I can see you play."

"That's right, you haven't seen me play ball, have you?"

"No I haven't!"

Some of the players were absent when this picture was taken.

Camp Miramar baseball team, (1942)

"Well when you come out I'll get you a seat right behind our dugout. Would you like that?"

"I'd love it, and if you promise to give me your autograph, I'll take you out for a steak dinner."

"You sound like a "groupie" I laughed. "But I accept!"

I had to cut the conversation short as the team was boarding the bus.

"Bye Rita, they're boarding the bus. I'll talk to you later."

I was the last one aboard and as I sat down next to Bill, he presented me with two I D cards. I looked at the cards and they were identical except for the age difference.

"How did you get my picture on this card?" I asked.

"Pretty good, huh?" Bill winked.

"Lee if you know the right people, anything is possible."

I took the forged I D card and placed it in my shirt pocket and the original in my wallet.

"Thanks Bill."

"You're welcome!"

We were scheduled to play a double header Saturday so no liberty for us tonight. Lt. Gross knew that if the players went out on liberty tonight, they'd be hung over tomorrow for our double header. We arrived at the Air base in time for chow and a little practice. We attended the base theatre and retired early.

The next day we arose at 0800, had a late breakfast and reported to the field. We had some batting practice, ate a light lunch and prepared for the conflict ahead. The stands were filling up and it looked like a sell-out. The San Bernardino Air Force team was loaded with professionals and we knew we had a battle on our hands. They were testing the Public Address system while we were taking our infield practice.

We looked exceptionally sharp today perhaps because of the amount of sleep we received. We brought the ball in, and headed for the dugout.

"Nice crowd!" Lt. Gross said, as he looked up from the dugout. We nodded affirmatively; wiped the sweat from our faces and necks and watched our opposition take infield practice.

After the Air Force brought the ball in, the ground crew raked and lightly sprayed the infield. The game was about to start.'

"Ladies and Gentlemen our National Anthem. We lined up outside the dugout, took off our caps and placed them over our hearts. We faced the center field scoreboard where Old Glory furled in all her majestic beauty. As I looked at our flag, I was so proud to be an American and happier still that I was willing to give up my life for her.

The Air Force being the home team took the field and the ball game was under way.

"The first batter up for the Camp Miramar Marines is Pvt. Lee Walewander playing second base," was the announcement over the P A system. The reason I was playing second base and leading off was because our regular second baseman was still injured.

I worked the count to two and two and then drove the ball pass third base for a single. Our next batter sacrificed me to second. My Keystone partner Bill was up next and the pitcher really had his number. The first pitch was thrown right at Bill's head and as he hit the deck the ball broke inward for a strike. The next pitch went right for his head again and once more Bill hit the deck only to have strike two called on him.

"Wow this guy really has a good curve ball," Bill surmised as he stepped up to the plate again.

The pitchers name was Steve Kowalics and his nickname was sling shot because of the way he delivered his pitch.

He would reel back on his right foot and snap the ball towards the plate in the same manner a child would use a sling shot.

He was very erratic which didn't help matters very much. He lost all of his games because of his wildness, so we just had to wait him out. If his game was on, he was impossible to beat.

As I stood there at second base, I could see what kind of a pitch Sling shot was ready to throw to Bill so I held my hand in the air and flipped my wrist as you do when you throw a curve ball. Bill caught my signal and when Sling shot sent one towards his head, he stood his ground and when the ball broke he stepped into it and drove the ball into left center enabling me to score from second base. We didn't score any more runs but fortunately for us the Air Force didn't either. We won the first game by a 1 to 0 score.

Whenever we played a double header, we always used our best pitcher in the first game so that we could be up on our opposition.

Our best pitcher was a tall left hander by the name of Brown whom we affectionately nicknamed him "Farmer." He pitched a three hitter while Sling shot walked 10 batters and struck out 14. I went one for three, with one hit, a walk, two strike outs and I scored the only run of the ball game. I played errorless ball in the field.

The second game was a slugfest. We started the game by scoring four runs in the first inning.

"Looks like we have a yawner," Bill said, as he awaited the peg to second base. "Don't count your chickens before they're hatched or should I say a ball game is never over until the last man is out!"

"Yeah right!" Bill laughed.

I don't know if I jinxed us by reciting these proverbs but our pitcher walked the first two batters, followed by a base hit, a hit batsman and a home run and we were one run behind with nobody out.

The fans screamed as Lt. Gross pulled Durks and put in Kieber, a lefty. Before Kieber could get the side out another run scored and when we came to bat in the second inning we were two runs behind.

We scored a run in the second inning only to have the Air Force score two more in their half. Hits were being sprayed all over the outfield and it looked like anybody's ball game. When we came to bat in the first half of the seventh, we were still three runs behind. The score at this time was 12 to 9. The first man up walked. The next man blooped a Texas Leaguer over third, holding the runner at second. I came up to the plate and the coach flashed us the Hit and Run sign. As the runners broke for third and second, I drove the ball right in the hole between first and second and two more runs crossed the plate. That made the score 12 to 11 with nobody out. After a few more pitches, I got the steal sign. I took a normal lead off, broke for second, and the race between man, catcher and ball was under way.

The peg was a little high and towards the first base side. I hook slid on the inside, evading the futile stab by the second baseman.

"Safe!" was the call.

My stealing second went for naught, as Bill came up and hit the next pitch over the left field fence. As I crossed home plate, I waited to congratulate Bill who was leisurely jogging around the bases. We scored two more runs in the ninth inning and won the game 14 to 12. Wow! A double victory

"Perhaps they won't feed us," Lt. Gross quipped. They did! In fact they complimented our sportsmanship and good play.

A victorious, joyous group of Marines boarded our bus, on our way to San Bernandino and liberty. Bill Campbell and Joe Vendetta one of our pitchers asked me to go out on liberty with them. Since I had a new I D card, I consented.

The city of San Bernandino was overrun with "Doggies" which in a way was good because it made us stick out like a sore thumb. Bill and Joe were a couple of smooth operators and were very proud of their achievements. They had the uncanny ability to size up a woman and tell you whether it was worthwhile to spend your time with her or not.

"Lee when you go out on liberty with us, you can't be shy," Bill instructed.

"The women that we're interested in aren't the young chicks that roam the streets. Keep your hands off these critters! They are jail bait! And besides they don't know the score. The women in their late twenties or early thirties are the morsels we're after. They're glamorous, have poise and know their A,B,C's In most cases these gals are married, with husbands stationed elsewhere. They believe that their husbands are having a good time so why shouldn't they. As Marines, we comply. After last minute instructions from Lt. Gross we bid adieu to the rest of the team and went our merry way.

"Let's try out your I D card in this joint," Bill said, "and remember Lee act like you're 21."

"Okay, I'll try."

"As we approached the door, a bouncer was there to greet us. We took out our ID cards presented them to the bouncer. He checked the age and made sure the picture was the same as the individual presenting it. We had no trouble.

The nightclub was called "Jo's Ringside" owned and operated by an old fight promoter. Jo's Ringside had a small dance floor in the center of the room with tables surrounding it.

A combo of musicians were belting out "Caledonia" and a poor man's Louis Armstrong was rasping Caledonia! Caledonia! What makes your big heart so hard , etc.

We sat down at the bar, ordered beers, and looked around to see if there were any girls they would be interested in picking up.

"Hey Bill look at that blond sitting at the table, doesn't she remind you of Ava Gardner, a little?" Joe asked.

"Wow! I'll say she does, is she with anyone?" Bill remarked.

"Doesn't look like it. There's only one drink at the table and she's been nursing it for some time," Joe mused.

I took a quick glance at the girl in question and all I saw was an attractive young lady sitting at a table drinking a coke. Bill looked at me and smiled.

"Lee do you know why we know she's been sitting there nursing her drink.

"No I don't!"

"Well if you look carefully you'll notice that her ash tray is filled with cigarette butts which means that she's been here for some time."

"Yeah, I see what you mean," I replied.

"Lee the best way to pick up someone like this is to work through the bartender. I'll show you how it works."

Bill then proceeded to call the bartender and told him to ask the lady what's she's drinking. The bartender then went over to the lady and when he spoke to her she looked our way and smiled.

"The lady is drinking Scotch and water," the bartender reported.

"Well don't disappoint the lady," Bill replied, as he removed a folded bill from his pocket.

When the bartender placed the Scotch and water in front of her, she gulped down her warm drink and gave us another big smile.

"You see Lee, if you're ever in a bar alone, and want to pick up some babe, the best way to do it is through the bartender.

Just the way I just did. Now go over and introduce yourself and get your feet wet. We'll give you about fifteen minutes and then we'll come to your rescue. Okay?'

"All right, but remember, about 15 minutes."

I picked up my beer and walked over to where she was sitting. "Mind if I sit down gorgeous," I smiled, trying my darndest to act cool.

"No not at all, in fact I'd like some company." She smilingly replied.

"What are all of you Gyrenes doing in San Bernadino?" she asked. "This is Army territory."

"Oh we're a bunch of ballplayers that played the Air Force team this afternoon and now we're just relaxing and having a good time."

"I know where you and I can have a better time. Why don't you ditch your buddies and we can go to my place. We can pick up some Chop Suey on the way and have a nice quiet evening together. What do you say Lee?"

Before I could answer her inviting proposal, Bill and Joe came up to our table and said, "Let's go Gyrene, we have to get back to our base."

Betty looked at me, and her eyes seemed to say, "Don't go! Please, don't go!"

I looked at her and said, "I'm sorry I have to go!" We left Jo's Ringside.

"How did it go Lee,?" they asked.

"Very well! I didn't know girls could be so forward."

"You'd be surprised at how forward some of these girls are," Joe added.

I didn't say anything, but how much more forward can they be.

"Hey Joe, let's take Lee to the Bamboo Inn,"

"Good idea!"

Lee and Bill at Jo's Ringside

The Bamboo Inn was about a block away and was on the same order as Jo's Ringside but a little larger. The walls, tables, and chairs were either lined with bamboo or constructed of it. Chinese lanterns hung from the ceiling whirling lazily with the air currents. As we entered, a bouncer whose job it was to check I D cards once more greeted us. Every one of these nightclubs was required by law to prohibit entrance to minors. The irony of it was that we weren't too young to die but yet too young to drink.

We entered, showed our I D cards, and sat down at a nearby table.

"Lee, this place is loaded with "bar flies," Joe remarked.

"What's a "bar fly?" I asked.

"Well these are girls that work for the club and their job is to solicit drinks from their customers. If you buy them a drink, they usually drink tea or coke and charge you for scotch. They'll sit with you, gulping down these fake shots until you run out of money.

They get a percentage of what they drink, so if you're willing to buy, they'll sit and talk to you all night long.

"Oh here they come," Bill warned us.

I looked around and sure enough, three buxom platinum blonds were approaching us.

"Let me talk to them," Bill said.

The blonds looked like triplets, but close up they were different. Heavy makeup covered their ages and in darkened surroundings they looked very appealing. They reeked with cheap perfume and cologne. Almost on cue, they put their arms around us, and one of them said:

"What are you handsome Marines drinking?"

"Beer," Bill replied.

"How about buying us a drink?" they said.

"Sure but you'll have to drink what we're drinking," Bill remarked'

"Oh we hate beer," one of the blonds frowned.

"How about buying us a shot?"

"Will it be worth our while?" Bill asked.

One of the bar flies who was draped all over Bill and whose bosom was resting on his shoulder, reeled back and said:

"Is that all you guys think about? If that's the case we're leaving."

"Bye girls," Joe laughed, as the girls left us, for a table full of Swabbys.

"Lee, you have to be careful with these bar flies. If they know you have a bankroll, they'll spike your drink with knock out drops just to get at it. If you're interested in shacking up with one of them, make sure you don't drink or eat anything she offers you. If you want to drink, pick up a six- pack. It's the safest way to go," Bill lectured.

As I sat there listening to Bill and Joe it reminded me of all the lectures that we had to listen to, during Boot camp. Only these were a lot more interesting. I learned more about women in one night than most men would learn in a lifetime. They were giving me an education that was priceless.

What probably took years of research in Night Club Universities, I was being taught all of this in one evening. I was always a pretty good student and this phase of the American Culture fascinated me.

Just then a sleek looking brunette with a boyish cut, walked up to the bar.

"Joe, look who just walked in," Bill nudged Joey.

I turned around to look at her, and said, "Let me size her up and you guys tell me afterwards how I did?"

"Okay, she's all yours,"

I began to scrutinize the young lady and this is what I observed. The girl sat down at the bar and immediately struck up a conversation with the bartender. Evidently she knew him, I thought.

She proceeded to light a cigarette and at the same time looked at her watch as if she were expecting to meet someone here. The bartender brought her a drink, which she wasn't too eager to drink. She kept looking at her watch. She looked to me like she could be in show business. I don't think she wants to be picked up; she's waiting for someone.

"Okay, here's my take on this cute broad, I remarked as I began to tell them what I thought she was doing in the bar. When I got finished, Bill and Joey began to laugh hysterically.

"What's so funny?" I asked.

"Well first of all she doesn't want to be picked up, that's for sure Secondly she is waiting for someone but that someone is her girl friend. She's a Lesbian Lee!" Joey laughed.

"How do you know!"

Well the butch haircut gives her away, but the reason we know, we tried to pick her up last week, and she told us that we shouldn't waste our money on her and that she was a Lesbian.

We drank a couple of beers and left. I was relieved to get outside and breathe some fresh cool California air.

"Would you like to visit Suzie's" Bill and Joey asked me?

"It doesn't make any difference to me. Remember I'm your guest."

"Okay, Suzies it is," they replied.

We piled into a cab, and rode out to the outskirts of town where we finally stopped at a well kept wooden bungalow. This doesn't look like a Night Club to me, I thought, as Bill rang the door bell. A matronly lady opened the door and said,

"Yes?"

"Hi beautiful!" Bill whispered in his best pick up voice.

"Billy! I didn't recognize you in the dark, come on in! Who's with you?"

"Only me gorgeous, and a couple of my buddies," Joey replied, as he grabbed her by the waist.

"Joey, you rascal you, I was wondering when you'd come and see me and the girls again."

As all this was going on I was wondering what relationship existed between Bill, Joey and Suzy. I soon found out. Suzy ran a brothel or more commonly known as a "Cat House" by the servicemen.

"Fellows, I've got a couple of young girls that are just beautiful", she bragged.

"All your girls are young and beautiful," Joe said as he pinched her cheek.

Suzy must have been in her early fifties. She was about five feet four, had blue eyes, gray hair, and was quite stout. She walked with a limp and had a very pleasing personality. She looked like she would be the last person in the world you'd suspect of being in this profession. I was introduced to her whereby she said that any friend of Joeys is a friend of mine.

We were escorted into the front room where five girls, including the two new ones, were sitting reading magazines while listening to the radio.

The girls were quite pretty, and they all looked like they were in their late teens or early twenties. They wore robes and slippers.

"Which one do you want Lee?" Bill asked.

"We're giving you first choice, after all you're our guest.

I was on the spot! If I refused, they would think I'm a fag, and I'd never hear the end of it. I had to go through with it, even though I've never been with a girl before and needless to say, I was scared to death.

What will I do? How should I act?

"I'll take that blond sitting next to the radio," I said, as my voice cracked and my body trembled.

"She's yours," Bill said. "Good choice!"

I waited to see what Bill and Joe would do and follow suit. They walked over to the girl of their choice, gave them their hand, and as the girls got up, they followed the girls into their bedrooms.

I can do that, I thought aloud. I then walked over to Blondie, and gave her my hand. She smiled, got up, and I followed her out of the room. We walked down a corridor which resembled a hall in a hotel. All the doors were shut, she opened one of them and walked in; I followed her.

"Shut the door, will you honey; I like to have a little privacy when I work."

I reluctantly did, and as I sat down on the edge of the bed, I took in its surroundings. The room was about 9 by 12, and had a large double bed that I was sitting on. Near the window stood a bureau on which Blondie placed a wash -bowl, soap, water and a towel.

She picked up the washbowl and headed for the door.

"I'll be right back. I want to get some fresh water, and while I'm gone why don't you undress."

I took off my blouse, draped it over the back of a chair and slowly began to take my shirt out of my trousers, when Blondie walked in.

"Come on slow poke, what are you waiting for."

I really didn't know, so I slowly began to remove my field scarf and khaki shirt. I didn't have the nerve to remove my T shirt and skivvies, so I just stood there. She placed the washbowl on the bureau and gently pulled on the cord attached to her robe. The robe sprang open, it slipped lazily to the floor and there she stood, stark naked and business like. I felt the blood rush to my head, and elsewhere, changing my pallor from pale white to a crimson red.

"How do you want it? She asked. Regular, Half and Half, Around the World, etc."

All of a sudden those sex movies we saw in Boot camp ran through my brain.

"She may look beautiful and wholesome on the outside, but on the inside she may be a carrier of a crippling or deadly disease."

"What's wrong Marine? Don't I arouse you? She inquired as she took me by the waist and escorted me to the bureau where she began to inspect and wash my penis.

"Why are you doing all this?" I asked.

"It's just a formality, honey. We know you Marines are in tip top shape but sometimes you may have the "Clap" and not know it."

All of a sudden I wanted out in the worst way. If I were going to have sex for the first time I want it to be with someone I love, not a prostitute.

"I can't go on I stammered," as I began to put on my skivvies.

"What do you mean you can't go on? I may not be Lana Turner but when it comes to giving man pleasure, I'm at the top of the list."

"Look Miss it has nothing to do with you. My erection proves that. I'm still a virgin and when I lose my virginity it's going to be someone I'm in love with, and so I would like for you to pretend like we had sex."

"What's in it for me?"

"I'll pay you, just as if we had sex. Okay?"

"Suit yourself," she said, as she picked up her robe. I started to dress and noticed she had a large scar on her stomach.

"What's with the scar?" I inquired.

"Oh I had an operation performed to tie off my fallopian tubes. This prevents me from getting pregnant and the doctor told me that when I'm ready to quit this business, he'd perform another operation to untie them."

"Sounds like a good idea, if it works."

"It works Honey! Believe me it works!"

I gave her twenty dollars and told her not to say anything to Suzy or my buddies.

"I won't!" she replied, "and I envy the girl who hooks you."

We walked out of the room and entered the parlor. Bill and Joe were waiting for me. The girls were gone evidently more customers came in.

"Man we thought you'd never come out," they quipped.

They looked so happy that I had to smile even though I felt like I let them down. We left Suzies, hailed a cab and returned to the bus. We returned to the Air Force barracks, tired and happy. Tomorrow we head back to Camp Miramar and I for one knew that Beer Belly O'Shannon would be waiting for me when I got off the bus.

Chapter 12

The trip to Camp Miramar was a joyous one. The ball players sang and kidded around all the way back. When we arrived at Camp Miramar I was informed by one of O'Shannon's boys that I had guard duty that night. I entered the barracks, put my gear away and proceeded to go to chow with Chuck and Sammy.

"I see that drunken slob has me scheduled for guard duty tonight," I said.

"I told you that would happen if you went over his head, didn't I" Chuck replied.

"Yeah, but I didn't think he'd be so vindictive,"

"By the way where do you guys go when you're on liberty?" I asked.

Sammy looked at Chuck and began to smile.

"Jim you wouldn't believe it but we're having a ball at the Hollywood Burlesque theatre." Sammy replied.

"I don't get it? Don't you just sit there and fantasize?"

"Should we tell him Chucky?" Sammy beamed.

"We might as well or he'll pester us until we do," Chuck replied.

"Ready Chuck!"

"Ready Sam!"

I didn't know what they were up to and when they proceeded to pull out a couple of water pistols, I was really confused.

"What the hell are you guys doing with water pistols?" I asked.

"This" they replied as they began to squirt me. "Cut it out!" I shouted, as I ran out of their range.

"We squirt the strippers and chorus girls when they least expect it. You should hear them squeal when the cold water hits their fannies."

"Doesn't the management object?"

"I don't know but the audience sure loves it!"

"It's too bad you can't join us," they said.

"Yeah! Right!" I facetiously replied.

My guard duty tonight, was to guard a pile of coal that was piled up behind the Mess Hall. It began to rain so I had to wear my poncho. I don't know how many times I circled this pile of coal in my four hour ordeal? I lost count!

Besides the locker inspections that we have every Tuesday and Fridays, we now have a Colonel's inspection every Saturday. The Colonel was a stickler for neatness. The personnel on his base had to be letter perfect or get restricted to the base. Our uniforms had to be cleaned and neatly pressed and our shoes had to sparkle. We had to be clean -shaven and never in need of a haircut.

Camp Miramar was affectionately called a "Chicken Shit" base because of its orderliness. The sloppy Marines, were never seen by the public; they were restricted to the base. When people complimented the Marines on their appearance it wasn't necessarily of their own doing. If they were out on liberty, they had to be immaculate.

A few days ago we were routed out of our sacks by O'Shannon to go and put out some forest fire. In California these forest fires are pretty common, and how they get started, it's hard to say. Whenever a forest fire does break out, the servicemen of the nearby bases are called upon to help put them out. We quickly loaded the trucks with the necessary firefighting equipment and boarded same. As we approached the area, the skies were illuminated with an orange hue. O'Shannon started to bark out orders as we were climbing down from the trucks.

"You men grab these spades and shovels and start cleaning up this debris so the fire doesn't spread.

The rest of you take one of those "Flappers"and smother the small fires so they don't spread. Now get to it!"

I grabbed a shovel and started digging. Luckily my hands were calloused from the "Shit Eating" details that O'Shannon subjected me to. The fire was spreading rapidly, so we boarded a truck and got out of there. We had to fight fire with fire! We got out in front of the fire and started smaller fires of our own. These small fires burned their way to the main fire and when both fires met, the bigger fire had nothing to burn, so it burned itself out.

On the other side of the fire, we cut down a line of trees and shrubs, well in front of the fire. When the fire burned to that point all the trees in its path were gone and the fire died out. We fought side by side for three days and nights, taking only time off to sleep and eat. We were so relieved when it was over.

The war was at its peak and so the War department froze the furloughs of all Marines that lived east of the Mississippi and we didn't like it! If this wasn't bad enough we've been at Camp Miramar for over a month and still no assignment to a school.

To make matters even worse, Beer Belly O'Shannon was making life miserable for all of us. He was going out on liberty more often and this of course meant more sleepless nights. He even started his own inspection tours, restricting the barracks whenever he so desired. It didn't make any difference to me, because, I was restricted to the base anyway. I went out on liberty, with the ball players, whenever we had a ball game.

Everyday more recruits gave up on their schooling and signed up for oversea duty.

"I don't know about you guys, but I think I'm going to sign up for oversea duty and get out of this Chicken Shit outfit," Chuck vowed.

"I joined the Marine Corps to fight, not to go to school. From what I hear, if we sign up for oversea duty, we get infantry training and fight alongside the Line Company Marines. Just then Hillbilly who was crapped out on his back, jumped up and said:

"No shit!"

"No shit!"

"Well count me in, I didn't shoot Expert to work on airplanes," Hillbilly replied.

" You know what, why don't the five of us sign up for oversea duty, that way we can be together and watch each other's backs," Sammy suggested.

"How about you Lee, are you with us?" Chuck asked.

"Gee I don't know Chuck, I would like to go to school and then again I'm not sure whether I'd qualify for Gunnery school. When I was a young kid I used to get car sick riding the Chicago trolleys, so maybe I wouldn't make it flying in those small planes."

"Does that mean we count you in?"

"Maybe," I replied.

"How about you Porky, you in or out?" Chuck continued his survey.

"I joined the Marine Corps to fight, so count me in."

"I don't want to be a party pooper," I added," but our baseball season ends in a week and Rita hasn't seen me play ball as yet. Could we wait another week, and then we'll all sign up together. What do you say?

The four of them got in a huddle and talked about it.

"Okay Lee, we'll wait for you," they agreed.

"Let's shake on it!'

"We did!"

During that week, we had two games at home and one on the road.

We were scheduled to play the Coronado Air Base at Balboa Field, Saturday afternoon. I called Rita an informed her about the ball game.

"I'll be there!" she said.

This was our last ball game of the season and I wanted Rita to see me play. We boarded our bus and headed for the Naval Air base and perhaps my last ball game for some time to come. Once we arrived at the base, we were directed to our visitor's locker room where we changed into our baseball uniforms. When we started to warm up on the sidelines, the stands were still empty but I'm sure that was going to change by game time.

"How about a little pepper game, Lee," Joey asked.

"You bet Joe! Let her fly!"

Bill joined us in this pepper game and as we crouched side by side, Joey tried to hit ground balls past us. Bill and I were very good glove men, so we seldom muffed a ground ball. This was a perfect warm up drill for infielders. While all this was going on I kept looking for Rita, but as yet she hadn't entered the ball park.

After about fifteen minutes of pepper, we took the field to have our batting practice. The outfielders hit first, so while they were batting I took a position at shortstop to field any ground balls that were hit my way. This was a good way to become acquainted with the infield.

When it was time for the infielders to get their licks, I ran over to the dug out to get a drink of water. As I approached, I heard a melodious voice sing out,

"Number fourteen, may I have your autograph.?"

I looked up, and there stood Rita in her Naval uniform. Her curly red hair was showing from under her navy blue and white "jockey" cap.

She was simply beautiful, I thought, and when she smiled I weakened to a frazzle.

"It would be my pleasure," I smilingly replied, as I autographed her score card.

> "To the most beautiful Wave in the Navy"
> Love and Kisses
> Lee Walewander

"How are you Lee?"

"I'm fine Rita, how about yourself?"

"Well I'd feel a lot better if I can see more of you" Rita pined, "but since O'Shannon won't give you liberty, there isn't much we can do about it."

"Well there's something I'm going to do which will enable me to see you every night, so hang in there."

"Oh really! What is it?"

"I'll tell you about it later on, right now all I'm interested in is beating these Swabbys," I kiddingly replied.

"Don't call them Swabbys, Lee Walewander, after all I'm a Swabby too!" she pouted.

"You look so pretty when you're angry," I laughed, "but you know I'm kidding don't you?"

"Of course I do Lee, but I'm only going to root for you and the Navy. If you do well and the Navy beats you, I'll take you out for dinner. Is it a bet?"

"What if I stink, and we lose?"

"I'll feel sorry for you, so I'll buy you a sympathy dinner."

"How can I refuse an offer like this, you're on!"

Just then Lt. Gross shouted,

"Hey Lee, take your licks, time's a wasting!"

"See you after the game Rita," I waved to her as I picked up a bat and stepped into the batter's box.

After the pre game introductions, the National Anthem was played, and the Swabbys took the field.

We had our best pitcher going for us today. Farmer Brown was carrying a 1.6 Earned Run Average into today's game. The Coronado team had their best lefty going for them. He wasn't very fast but he was very crafty. He had excellent control and a fine assortment of pitches. I was playing second base and leading off. The first ball was a fast ball down the middle.

"Strike one!" the umpire bellowed.

As a lead-off man, my job is to take as many pitches as I possibly can so my team mates can study the pitcher. The next pitch was low and inside for ball one. The next pitch was very much to my liking. It was a slow breaking curve ball, which I reached out for and dropped a perfect bunt down the third base line. As I stood there at first base, I glanced to where Rita was sitting and watched her happily waving her program. Bill our shortstop was up and being one of our better hitters was given the hit sign. I wanted to try and steal second but Lt. Gross thought otherwise. He hit a sharp grounder to short which they turned into a 6-4-3 double play. Lt. Gross flied out and our inning was over.

The next two innings were scoreless but in the bottom of the third inning the Swabbys scored a run on an error, walk and a base hit. I led off the fourth inning and fouled out. Bill tripled down the right field line and it looked as if we would at least tie the score with only one out. Lt. Gross was up and proceeded to hit a hard ground ball to third which the third baseman picked up and nailed Billy trying to score from third. Lt. Gross then tried to steal second but was out on a close play.

Coronado scored one more run it the bottom of the seventh inning and now led 2 to 0. The next few innings were scoreless and when we came to bat in the top of the ninth, we had three hits and no runs. The tail end of our batting was up and we weren't faring too well. Our catcher drew a walk.

The next man up hit a ground ball to short but as he pivoted, he was taken out by our catcher, who then, had no chance of completing the double play. Man on first and one out when our third baseman hit a blooper to center field for a hit. Man on first and second and one out. Brown was replaced by a pinch hitter who worked the count 3 and 2 before being hit by the pitcher. The bases were now loaded and I was coming up to bat. The tension was so thick you could cut it with a knife. There was a delay in the game as they took out their lefty and put in a righty. They were playing the percentages.

After a few warm up pitches I stepped into the batter's box with the bases loaded and one out. The place became a morgue. I thought I heard Rita's voice shouting encouragement. I took a quick glance to where she was sitting and saw her chewing on her program. The hit sign was flashed. A base hit would tie the score, an extra base hit would put us ahead. All I know is not to strike out or hit a ground ball, which they can turn into a double play. Don't over swing! Just meet the ball I said to myself as the first ball almost hit me.

"Ball one!" was the cry.

The pitcher was very fast but a little wild. Should I wait him out, I thought when "strike one," was called.

Can't get behind, I thought, as I fouled off the next pitch. One and two was the count and I was behind and knew it! I proceeded to foul off a few more pitches which must have rattled the pitcher because he came in with a fast ball that was belt high and right down the middle. I met the ball in stride and drove it into right center for a triple. The pitcher was now pissed off so we took advantage of his demeanor by pulling off a suicide squeeze. Bill bunted the ball towards first base.

The first baseman came in to field the ball and seeing that he had no chance of throwing me out at the plate, he tagged Bill out for the second out.

The bases were now empty but the score was now 4 to 2 in favor of Camp Miramar. Lt. Gross ended the inning by flying out to center field.

We took the field for perhaps the last time with a two run lead. Our pal Joey was called in to save the victory for Farmer Brown. The first man up hit a towering long drive which our center fielder caught with his back towards the infield. Their clean-up hitter was up and he drove one into left center for a double. The next man up hit a sharp single to right field scoring the runner from second base. This ball game was far from over, so Lt. Gross called time out, to settle down Joey, and see if Joe had the confidence to get the next man out.

"Joe how do you feel? Do you think you can get this next hitter out ? "

"I think so, I feel pretty good!"

"Joe throw your sinker to this guy! Have him hit it on the ground and maybe we can turn two for you," I suggested.

"What do you think Skipper? Good idea?"

"I think it's worth a try. Okay, let's turn it!"

The next man up was one of their better hitters but not blessed with great foot speed so if he hits it on the ground we can turn two. Joe side armed his sinker which the batter hit on the ground to the right of second base. I streaked for the bag, dove, speared the ball and flipped it back handed to Bill who was in the process of pivoting. As I tumbled to the turf, I saw the first base umpires hand shoot up.

"You're out!"

As I got up, my team mates surrounded me and the fans were giving me a standing ovation. I headed back to the dugout, lowering my head as I ran.

I was too shy to milk this drama for what it was worth.

After showering and shaving, I put on my greens and left the locker room. Bill and Joe knew Rita was waiting for me so they went out on liberty by themselves.

"Oh Lee, I'm so proud of you," Rita beamed, as she took my arm.

"Are you really?"

"Oh yes, it was the most exciting game I have ever seen. You were just great! I think you won that game single handedly"

I didn't say a word. I just listened; loving every syllable of it.

"Lee did you ever think of becoming a Professional baseball player?"

"Yes I have, in fact that's what I was doing before I was drafted into the Marine Corps."

"Oh really! I didn't know! How come you never told me about it"

"I thought I did when we met at the USO" I replied.

"Well I want to hear all about it! She smiled as we walked towards the bus that was going to take us onto a Ferry-boat. While on the Ferry, I told Rita about my love for the game and getting signed by the Kingsport Cherokees. I told her about the little old ladies that bugged me after every game. When I finished, we were docking in San Diego. We got off the Ferry- boat and began to walk to a city bus when Rita asked,

"Do you intend to play ball again, when the war is over?"

"Yes I do, God willing!"

"Where are we going for dinner?" I asked.

"I know a little inn that is just darling and they serve the most delicious food."

"Sounds great! I'm famished!"

After a short drive we entered a quaint little Hungarian Inn where we were seated at one of the tables. In the center of our table, a candle spilled its wax over a heavily encrusted wine bottle. A gypsy violin whined in the background and as I looked at Rita I was happy and contended.

The waitress took our orders and brought us our pre-dinner drinks. Since I had my false I D card handy, I ordered a bottle of Chablis, which the waitress served us without checking our I D's.

"May I propose a toast?"

"Please do Lee!"

We lifted our glasses and as our eyes met, I knew I was falling in love with this beautiful young lady. "Here's to a very beautiful Wave, who's making my life very enjoyable and worthwhile."

"And to one hell of a ballplayer!" she added.

We sipped our wine while waiting for our dinner. I wasn't familiar with Hungarian food so I asked the waitress what she would recommend. She said the beef stroganoff was very good so both of us ordered it. It was very tasty but heavy. We finished our meal, drank our tea and left. Rita insisted on paying for our dinner "A bets a bet," she said.

The evening was just beginning and I felt great. We won our ball game, a delicious meal was under my belt, and a gorgeous Wave at my side. What more can a Gyrene ask for ?

After a short deliberation, we decided to spend our evening at the Mission Beach Amusement Park. I bought a roll of tickets and the fun began. Rita was like a little girl once more. She reminded me so much of my sisters when we attended Riverview Park when we were youngsters growing up in Chicago. She screamed on the Roller coasters, was frightened on the Ferris Wheel and laughed till tears filled her eyes in the House of Mirrors.

Life was fun, with Rita in fact life was beautiful! As we walked down the board-walk, hand in hand, we were oblivious to the terrible conflict that was going on. Germany had over run Europe and was now preparing to strike at England.

In the Pacific, the Japanese were solidly entrenched, and the Marines had just begun to island hop. While all this was going on, Rita and I were deliriously happy.

"Oh Lee, look! "Tunnel of Love, Let's go !

I was a little reluctant, but couldn't refuse my pretty date. I helped Rita into the boat and sat down beside her. The sailor in front of us was all over his girl friend, which made me, somewhat, uneasy. He had his arm about her and was buzzing her ear with butterfly kisses, oblivious to everyone that was watching him. I felt uncomfortable but managed somehow to take Rita's hand. The mere touch of her hand electrified me. The darkness was upon us and as I held her hand, the desire of wanting to kiss her became unbearable. I better not try, I thought, she may get offended and I'll lose her. Better leave well enough alone. I don't know what Rita was thinking about but I felt her get closer to me. I began to tremble, but somehow managed to place my arm around her. She snuggled up close to me and before I knew what was happening my lips were touching hers. Her lips were warm, moist and exciting. I held her tightly and kissed her hard. Every movement of her quivering lips sent tortuous impulses through my activated body.

"Rita, I love you so," I whispered.

"I love you too Lee, very, very much!"

We kissed again and again and from that moment on I knew I was hopelessly and deliriously in love with Rita Shaw.

Our baseball season was over, so the five of us went to the Aviation Replacement Squadron office and told them we're tired of waiting to go to school and want to sign up for oversea duty.

The Captain looked at the five of us and replied- "You guys understand that the minute you leave the Aviation Replacement School you are expendable. Since all you're trained to do is fight you'll probably wind up in the Guard Company guarding our air strips on some God forsaken island in the South Pacific. What you guys will be doing is protecting our airstrips so the Japanese don't put them out of commission. The Japanese will try to knock out these strips, and your job is to see that they don't. At night you will patrol the sleeping quarters of the pilots, gunners and mechanics.
Since our airstrips are close to the ocean the Japanese sneak in at night on rafts and while our pilots and gunners are sleeping they slit their throats.
During the day you will guard our airstrips so that the enemy cannot get to our planes. So you see you will probably see more action than you would if you were in a line company. You still want to sign up," the Captain asked or wait and go to school ?
We looked at each other, and said, "Yeah, what the hell! No school ! Let's go for it!"
That morning a truck came by and all those Marines transferring to ARS were told to put all their gear and themselves into the truck for their short trip to the Aviation Replacement Squadron which was still in Camp Miramar. We did!

Chapter 13

We transferred to the Aviation Replacement Squadron and found life much to our liking. Where O'Shannon made life miserable for us, Master Sergeant Tennell left us strictly alone. The only time we saw him, was in the morning, when roll was called. After roll call, we would go to chow, and then report back for work details. As a rule, the details were poorly supervised so the five of us would usually wind up shooting pool in the recreational hall.

We were on four-hour notice. Our sea bags were packed and ready to go. Where we had locker inspection every Tuesday, Thursday and Saturday in ATS, in ARS we had none. Gambling was forbidden in ATS but in ARS it flourished.

We had liberty every night, unless we were restricted to the base for some reason. We were living the Life of Riley until one sad day a Colonel walked into our barracks unbeknownst to us. Card games and crap games were in full progress.

"Attention!" someone shouted.

It was too late to hide what we were doing.

"As you were!" he barked as he walked through the barracks looking at all the cards and money strewn all over the bunks. He didn't say a word, he just took it all in.

"Who the hell was that? Sammy asked, after the Colonel left the barracks.

"Who knows? Come on deal!" Hillbilly grumbled. I want to win some of my money back."

" How many Lee?"

" I'll take two!"

"Chuck?"

"One!"

"Porky?"

"Three!"

I was becoming quite the poker player. Sammy told me to never change my facial expression when I'm looking at my cards, so I don't. I tried to have a nonchalant attitude whether I'm holding a pair of deuces or four aces.

If I won, Rita and I would frequent the best theatres and night clubs. If I lost, we would either go roller skating, dancing, or take in a movie. I loved Rita very much and I knew we wouldn't be together for very long. We were living on borrowed time and making the most of it.

We soon found out that the Colonel who stalked into our barracks and caught us gambling was our new Commanding Officer, whose name was Colonel Adams. He was injured on Guadalcanal and was made the C.O. of ARS while recuperating from his injuries. He was so shocked by the conditions in his new outfit that he transferred Master Sergeant Tennell out and brought in one of his cohorts, a tyrant by the name of Master Sergeant Donlon.

Sergeant Donlon was a combination of Bull dog and Beer Belly rolled into one. He fought alongside our C.O. on the Canal and previously was with Carlson's raiders. It took a few days to get Sgt. Tennell out, and Sgt. Donlon in, but once that was done, the party was over.

As we stood at attention, our C.O. began his brutal dress down speech.

"As Commanding Officer of the Aviation Replacement Squadron my job is to see that you people get the necessary training before you ship out. As a Replacement Squadron you will be called upon to fight alongside the Fleet Marines if so needed. You are expendable, and I wouldn't be a bit surprised if some of you see more action than if you were in a line company outfit.

Without the proper training, you'd be sitting ducks for the enemy. In my twelve years in the Corp I have never seen a more neglected outfit than this one.

If you were shipped out today, ninety per cent of you would never see the states again.

"Your soft and lazy," he shouted as he smacked Porky across the midriff.

"Oomph!" was Porky's reply.

Sergeant Donlon and I are going to whip you into shape or else. This morning we are going to have an inspection of your barracks and gear. I want the place spotless and every bit of gear you own, laid out on your sacks according to the manual. If you don't have the necessary equipment we will requisition it for you. The barracks have to be spotless at all times and your sacks neatly made up. If I can't bounce a quarter off your sack, you won't get liberty. Is that clear?"

"Yes sir," we grumbled.

"What!"

"Yes Sir!" we shouted.

Boot Camp all over again, I thought, as the Colonel continued his barrage.

"There will be a rifle inspection every day. Close order drills, hikes, judo, bayonet fighting, and combat conditioning is what you have to look forward to while you're still under my command. If you want liberty, shape up and you can go on liberty every night. If you "goof off," No liberty! Is that clear?"

"Yes Sir!," we shouted.

"Now I want you to meet your new Sergeant."

Sergeant Donlon stepped forward, saluted his C. O. and faced us sneeringly.

Our C.O. left!

"My name is Sergeant Donlon. You may have heard some scuttlebutt about me, but don't you believe it. They say I'm a rough tough bastard, but really I'm not!

I'm gentle and kind. I wouldn't hurt a fly, but I'll break every God Damn bone in your body if you don't have your barracks clean in one hour.

And if I ever catch any of you "shit birds" gambling, I'll have you circumcised with a dirty piece of glass and show you stag movies while you're healing." he raved.

"Am I coming through to you "Chowder Heads?" he asked.

"Yes Sir!" we shouted, "Loud and clear!"

"Dismissed!"

We literally flew back to our barracks and began cleaning and sorting our gear.

"I knew it wouldn't last!" Sammy moaned.

"I was thinking of becoming a twenty year man, but the Corps just lost out."

"Yeah right!" We sarcastically replied.

"Hey Sam you better quit bitching and start cleaning up or you won't see that chorus wench of yours tonight," Chuck told him.

I agreed with what Chuck said to Sammy. I looked forward to seeing Rita and so I better shape up, too. Each night could be our last! We scrubbed down the barracks, washed the windows, made up our sacks, laid out our gear, and checked on each other to make sure we would pass inspection. It wasn't a minute too soon.

"Ten Shun!" someone by the door shouted.

We stood at attention as Colonel Adams and Sergeant Donlon inspected our barracks, our gear and us. We passed inspection with flying colors.

The next few days were filled with misery and anguish. We drilled continuously. Ruff Tuff Donlon tried to get us in condition in a couple of days but he wasn't succeeding! But that didn't stop him! Every morning we had calisthenics, followed by judo, bayonet sparring, or going on an all day hike.

Yesterday was a day we shall never forget. It rained continuously for two days and when it let up, we were off on a little jaunt.

The ground was super saturated with water and in no time at all, our boondockers were soaking wet.

We hiked over hill and dale, sinking up to our ankles on many occasions. We double timed it across ravines, waded across streams and stumbled across the brush trying to keep up with Ruff Tuff Donlon. I often wondered where the Marine Corps found these indestructible characters, but they did!

We ate our rations out in the field and headed back to the base. I was so relieved to see Camp Miramar. My feet were sore from my wrinkled socks. I didn't know if the fluid in my boondockers was from my blisters or just plain river water. Ruff Tuff Donlon went berserk! He walked right past Camp Miramar and began to double time us back to the hills.

"That S.O.B. is crazy!" Sammy bitched, as he ran alongside of me with his rifle at Port Arms.

"Don't bitch Sam, if he can do it so can we," I replied, as I puffed along. I forgot that Sammy was a lot older than I was, but with his crew cut and loss of weight, looked very much younger. We finally dragged our asses back to the base, showered, shaved and went to chow. I called Rita that evening to tell her about my day and she understood why I wouldn't see her tonight. I was dead tired!

The next few days were a little better. We were getting back in shape. The hikes didn't bother us, in fact we enjoyed getting off the base. Sgt. Donlon was teaching us Scouting, and Patrolling. We formed scouting parties, rifle and B.A.R squads and simulated jungle fighting. He knew first hand, what it was like fighting in the jungles, after all his last assignment was in Guadalcanal. I felt like we were playing a game, but then again what is war? Isn't it a game, in a way?

We are supposedly the "good guys" and they are the "bad guys." Whoever survives is the winner and they take over the territory.

It was the middle of December, but it didn't feel like it. Back home in Chicago we would have a Christmas tree and our home would be decorated with festive lights.

We would go to the outdoor ice skating ponds and play hockey on a makeshift rink and wind up with a snowball fight afterwards.

We were informed that our contingent of Marines was put on the 1106 detail which was the next group to leave. I was hoping it wouldn't be before Christmas, as I was going to surprise Rita with an engagement ring. I couldn't bear the thought of leaving her and perhaps not coming back, but I had no control over my destiny. She was engaged before and it broke her heart when she found out about her fiancé having an affair with her best friend. Will I break her heart again only this time if I'm killed in action? I'll have to chance it!

I asked Rita to help me buy gifts for my Mom and three sisters. My Dad was no longer in the picture because when I was very young he was killed in a trucking accident. We spent Saturday afternoon buying presents for my family and now all I had to do was buy Rita an engagement ring. Since it was going to be a surprise, I didn't want her around when I bought it. She just loved surprises.

I never realized engagement rings were so expensive! The cheapest one that I could buy was about $200. All I had was about $150 so I had to borrow ten bucks from each of my buddies. I purchased a quarter of a carat for about $200. The ring to me looked beautiful. It had a center diamond and two smaller side diamonds imbedded in a matched heart design. The ring was enclosed in a small blue velvety box.

"I hope she likes it?" I remarked, as I passed the ring amongst my friends.

"Are you kidding Lee?" the girl loves you, she'd be happy if you gave her a "Cracker box" ring, Sammy replied.

"Sammy's right Lee. It's not the ring that counts, it's what comes from the heart, that counts," Chuck added.

"Roger!" they acknowledged.

Time was running out for our group and I was getting antsy. My Christmas presents to my Mom and my sisters three were mailed out a week ago. Rita loved surprises, so I bought a large box of candy, removed a few chocolates from the center and placed the blue velvety box with the engagement ring inside, in their place. I had the candy gift wrapped and awaited eagerly Rita's expression when she opens it.

I made a reservation with Papa Igor, the owner of the Hungarian Inn, for a booth where we could have a little privacy. This was our favorite restaurant. It was here, over candle light, that I fell in love with her. I left Rita's gift with Papa and told him what I was going to do. I think he was as excited about it as I was.

When I arrived at the Naval Hospital, Rita was already waiting for me.

"I'm sorry Rita, but I missed my bus," I lied.

"I thought you might have been restricted to the base," she replied.

"No we've been behaving," I laughed.

"We better get going. I made a reservation at our favorite restaurant so we can celebrate Christmas Eve together."

"That's great! I was hoping we could go there tonight."

We boarded a bus and rode out to Papa Igor's Hungarian Inn. Papa Igor greeted us warmly and escorted us to our booth.

The drapes were drawn, but when he pulled the cord was I ever surprised. In the center of the table stood a miniature Christmas tree.

Presents were on the table and I wondered how they got there. I noticed Rita's gift, but where the others came from I had no idea.

We sat down, the drapes were drawn, and by the light of our little Christmas tree, I leaned over and partook of her warm sweet lips.

"Merry Christmas, darling!" I whispered into her ear.

"How did you know I was going to bring you here for Christmas Eve?" I asked.

"Well I know you like this Inn so I made arrangements with Papa Igor beforehand."

"So did I!" I laughed.

"Shall we open our gifts?" Rita asked, "You first."

I took my sweet time in opening my present, as I wanted this moment to last.

"Rita, you shouldn't have," I said as I examined a beautiful shock- proof wrist- watch.

"It's nothing really!"

I kissed her warmly after each gift. Besides the wrist-watch I received an identification bracelet with the following inscription.

"To Lee Walewander whom I love very much!"

                                                              Rita

In addition to these two gifts, I also received a large photograph of Rita and some wallet sized snapshots of her. I think I valued these more so than the watch and bracelet. She also had a few "booby" gifts, one that scared the hell out of me when it jumped out of the box. She giggled like a little school girl when this occurred.

"Oh Rita, I love you so!" I sighed as I took her in my arms and kissed her tenderly. Her warm sweet lips seemed to ask for more. I obliged.

It was Rita's turn to open her gift, and I could see that she was disappointed when she picked up the package. She knew it was candy but tried desperately to keep her composure. She kept looking around as if there were other gifts to be found.

I watched her every move and when she removed the wrapper and spotted a two pound box of candy, I thought she was going to cry.

"Merry Christmas Dear! I didn't know what to buy, and knowing how you like this brand of chocolate, I thought you'd enjoy it!"

"Thank you Lee," she remarked, her voice cracking in the process.

"May I have one?" I asked

"Of course dear," she replied.

As Rita opened up the box, she immediately spotted the blue velvety box. She clasped her hands in amazement and just starred at it.

"Go ahead and open it! "

She looked at me, with tear filled eyes and I knew that she knew what I was up to. She slowly opened up the box, let out a sigh and began to cry.

"Oh Lee, she cried as she threw her arms about me."

"Don't cry dear, will you be my girl for always?"

"I will forever and ever and ever," she smiled, as she showered me with electrifying kisses. I took the ring out of the box and placed it on her finger. I then took Rita in my arms and lovingly kissed her. I don't know how long we were in each other's arms, but hours went by like seconds when I was with Rita.

Papa Igor tactfully interrupted us with dinner and a bottle of wine, which he told us was his Christmas present to us. We dined, danced and when midnight approached we thanked Papa Igor for his hospitality. We boarded a bus and attended midnight mass. It was a Christmas Eve I shall never forget.

The next day was Christmas and we were treated to a special Christmas Dinner at our base. I hope it isn't my last.

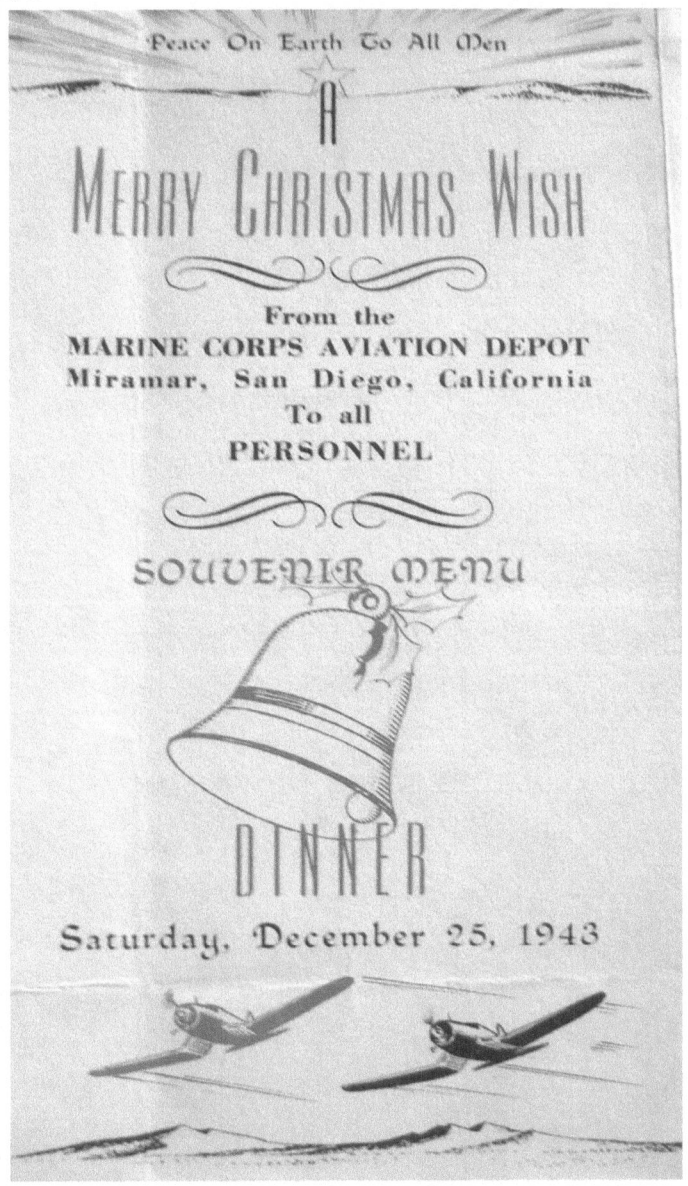

Peace On Earth To All Men

A
MERRY CHRISTMAS WISH

From the
MARINE CORPS AVIATION DEPOT
Miramar, San Diego, California
To all
PERSONNEL

SOUVENIR MENU

DINNER

Saturday, December 25, 1943

* DINNER *

ROAST TURKEY

OYSTER DRESSING

BAKED HAM

GIBLET GRAVY   CRANBERRY SAUCE

SNOWFLAKE POTATOES   CANDIED YAMS

CAULIFLOWER, DRAWN BUTTER

CARROTS AND PEAS

MIXED SWEET PICKLES

RIPE OLIVES   CELERY   STUFFED OLIVES

MINCE PIE   PUMPKIN PIE

FRUIT CAKE

MIXED NUTS   HARD CANDIES   FRESH FRUITS

ICE CREAM   COFFEE

CIGARETTES

CIGARS

Our detail was as hot as a firecracker. Our sea bags were being stenciled in code and any day now we would be sailing out for parts unknown. Our sailing day was kept a secret so that the enemy wouldn't get a "Bee line" on us. One fine morning we would get up early, board ship, and silently sail out of the harbor while its residents still slept. Rita too!

Commanding Officer Adams had us up in the hills every day. Ruff Tuff Donlon and his assistants were giving us advanced training in jungle warfare. We practiced crawling and creeping with full packs and rifle.

"Dig in!" Donlon would shout and we did. We used our mattocks and spades to dig foxholes while still in the prone position. We crawled, ran, hit the deck and crawled some more. We used all the combat signals and used them repeatedly.

"Enemy in sight ! "Donlon signaled as he raised his rifle horizontally over his head.

"Double time, Rush!" was the next signal as Donlon carried his fist to his shoulder and began pumping it up and down several times.

We sprang up and began to run towards the imaginary enemy. We never ran in a straight line but kept weaving and bobbing constantly. Donlon then carried his hand to his shoulder, extended his arm vertically with the palm of his hand toward us. This meant, "Halt!"

We also practiced, "As Skirmishers, Right and Left, Fix bayonets, Change direction, lie down, Take cover, etc. Hand signals were always used in combat because they were simple, direct and efficient. We were apt students.

Chapter 14

Rita made arrangements for me to meet her sister June, who lived in Malibu, California. She was married to a wealthy manufacturer almost twice her age. Rita told me that her sister had everything she wanted but love. They owned a palatial estate in Malibu, a beach house near the ocean, a yacht, sports cars and most everything a girl would want.

She met Van Stewart during a beauty contest that she had entered. He was one of the judges and was smitten by her beauty. His influence enabled June to win hands down. She was given a screen test, by one of the major studios, and while awaiting the outcome, Van wined and dined her. A mink coat, a sports car, a diamond bracelet were just some of the gifts June received. He took her everywhere with him. She met celebrities and was treated like royalty. When Van proposed marriage she was flattered knowing full well that most girls would die to marry him. She thought that even though she didn't love him, in time, she may. So she married Van and has been miserable ever since.

We weres given a 72 hour pass and so Rita was able to finagle one too. I waited for Rita at the Mercy Hospital waiting room while she packed a few things to put in her overnight bag. This was probably going to be our last time together and Rita wanted me to meet her sister before I shipped out.

"Hi sweetheart!" I greeted her with a great big smile.

"Here, let me take your bag."

"Have you been waiting long?" she asked, tilting her pretty face towards me.

"No I haven't," I replied, as I kissed the tip of her nose and then her sweet lips.

We boarded a bus for Malibu which was about 150 miles feom San Diego and made ourselves comfortable.

Rita told me more about her sister and her unhappy marriage.

"Oh you'll like June," Rita said.

"If she's anything like you, how can I not like her," I replied.

As a rule I would hate this long bus ride, but with Rita alongside of me, the trip was short and sweet.

When we arrived in Malibu, we took a cab to June and Val's home.

"Man what a palace!"I awed, as the cab pulled into the driveway. I paid the cabbie as Rita rang the doorbell.

"Rita! I'm glad you could make it! "

"Hi June, I want you to meet Lee Walewander my fiancé."

"Pleased to meet you Mam," I replied.

"The names June," she smiled.

"Pleased to meet you June," I corrected myself.

"So you're the ball playing Marine who swept my kid sister off her feet."

"Is that what she told you?" I remarked.

"Yes and she also told me that you're a pretty good ballplayer."

"Just average," I modestly replied.

"Don't believe him June, he's terrific. He beat the Coronado Air Force team single handed."

"Please Rita, you're embarrassing me."

"Oh a modest Marine! I didn't think any existed.

As we were escorted into a large living room, I noticed that June was a little taller than her sister, but again it was hard to tell because she was wearing high-heeled shoes. She was blond, beautiful and well tanned. Her tan made her blond hair even more striking. She wore a black tight fitting dress that seemed to be molded to her well-proportioned body.

When she smiled, two dimples formed crevices on each cheek. There was a striking resemblance between the two sisters, only Rita, was prettier. Perhaps I'm biased!

"Would you like something to drink? June asked.

"Do you have beer?" I asked.

"Lee, we have a butler who can make you any drink you like?" June replied.

"Good, then I'll have a beer."

"How about my baby sister?"

"I'll have a coke."

"Are you guys hungry? How about a sandwich with your drinks?"

"That would be fine," we replied.

We entered the dining room and sat down at a huge mahogany table. The butler and maid were busily engaged in preparing our sandwiches. As I sat there I couldn't help but notice the huge chandelier that hung directly above us. The crystal clear beads sparkled brilliantly and occasionally tinkled melodiously while we ate.

"June who's at the beach house?" Rita asked her sister.

"Why no one," June replied.

"Since Van is away most of the time, I seldom go up there alone."

"May I show it to Lee?"

"Of course! Why don't you take the M.G. and spend the rest of the day there. You'll find some swim suits in the hall closet if you feel like going for a swim."

"Would you like to join us?" Rita asked.

"I'd love to, but I'm expecting Van at any time. He's been away on a business trip for almost a week and I want to be here when he comes home. We have a New Year's Eve party planned for tonight so have fun this afternoon and remember be back here by ten.

"We will!" Rita replied as we ran to the M.G.

Since I didn't have a driver's license, Rita did the driving. The MG handled beautifully and in no time at all we were there. We soon drove up to a beach house that was situated very close to the beach.

The beach was deserted, as this was all private property. What a shame to waste all this property, I thought, as Rita unlocked the door with the key June gave her.

"Man this place is beautiful," I said, as I took in its surroundings. It was decorated in nautical style. The inside resembled that of a ship with port-holes for windows, and a miniature ship as a bar. Anchors hung from the knotty-pined walls and a huge shiny bell hung from the ceiling. The place was spotless! Rita showed me around and I just couldn't get over how beautiful this place was.

"Wow! This is really living," I'm totally impressed.

The kitchen or galley had plenty of food in the freezer and the bar was well stocked with beer and liquor.

"May I fix you a drink, Mr. Walewander," Rita asked.

"Yes, I'd like a Manhattan, if you don't mind."

"One Manhattan coming up," she replied as she disappeared behind the bar looking for the sweet vermouth.

"Are we going to go swimming today? I asked.

"Of course we are, silly!"

"Isn't the water awfully cold?

"It is, but you get used to it," she laughed.

"Well than you better make my drink a double!"

We took our drinks with us as we walked along the beach, hand in hand. Eventually we took off our shoes and waded into the water. It was cold but not unbearable.

"You want to go for a swim Gyrene?"

"I don't know it's pretty cold?

"Cluck! Cluck!" she clucked as she ran towards the beach house. I was right behind her and tackled her before she got very far.

We rolled around in the warm sand laughing and giggling like the two lovers that we were.

Rita and the Manhattan convinced me to take the plunge and so we went into the beach house to see what was there for us to wear. As Rita began to sift through a multitude of bathing suits, she would periodically hold one up to her and ask me if I liked it.

"How about this one," she asked, as she held up a white bathing suit next to her body.

"I like it! It goes with your red hair."

"Good ! Cause you're wearing white too," she smiled. Rita went into the master bedroom to change, while I changed in the den. I picked up a couple of beach towels, draped one around my neck, sat down and waited for Rita. I've never seen Rita in a bathing suit and I was eagerly awaiting her entrance. The door slowly opened. Rita stuck out her head and said, "Ready?"

"Ready!" I replied.

"Well, how do I look?" she asked, as she paraded herself in front of me.

I looked at her and she was just gorgeous. Her legs were smooth and shapely and her hips seemed to proportion her bust measurement. She possessed a slim waist line and as she turned to model the suit for me, I realized she was a perfect goddess.

"I think you're simply beautiful," I remarked, as I took her in my arms.

Rita was about two inches shorter than I, and as I leaned over to kiss her, I couldn't help but notice her well-rounded breasts. With every breath she took, her breasts seemed to be crying out for freedom. We were kissing passionately when I suddenly realized my hands were caressing her breasts.

What am I doing? I thought. I quickly grabbed Rita by the hand and ran out of the door with her clinging desperately to me. The cold water was the remedy!

Rita was a very good swimmer, much better than I was. We swam side by side and whenever I saw that Rita was beating me I grabbed one of her shapely gams and pulled her under the water. We kissed amongst the escaping air.

"Lee Walewander you're a poor sport," she said as she pushed my head under water. I went under but I took her along with me. We sunk to the sandy bottom, our arms about each other. Our lips met, we came up for air, and went back down again. With our arms around each other, we walked back to the beach house, as the sun began to disappear in the horizon.

"The New Year's Eve party should be fun," Rita said as she maneuvered the MG through the evening traffic.

"I'm sure it will be," I replied.

As we pulled into the driveway, June was there to greet us.

"How was your swim?" she asked.

"A little cold," Rita replied, "but it was fun and we had a great time."

"Very good, and now come with me I want Vance to meet your fiancé."

Van Stewart was a middle-aged gentleman in his late forties. He was tall, partly bald, and a little on the heavy side. His eyes were steel gray and the little hair he had left was quite gray. When he walked into a room there was an air of respectability about him.

"So you're Lee," he said as he shook my hand.

"Yes Sir," I replied, "and you must be Mr. Van Stewart."

"That I am son, but since I hear you're going to be my brother in law, I want you to call me Van."

"Yes Sir! I mean Van."

The guests were pouring into the Stewart household and Rita and I were lost in the shuffle.

June and Van were so busy meeting and greeting all of their guests that they completely forgot about us.

Every now and then Van would come along with a drink he concocted and offered it to us.

"Here you are Lee, drink up lad," he roared, as he handed me another drink. Whenever Van drank too much he became very boisterous and vociferous.

"Happy New Year," someone shouted.

The party was in full swing. The butlers brought out party hats which most everyone wore. Balloons were released into the room while the band was playing a melody of romantic songs. Rita and I loved to dance so we were on the floor most of the time. I think that all the drinks Van had me drink were taking effect. I was feeling romantic when Rita blurted out,

"Lee, let's go to the beach house"

"Won't they miss us?"

I doubt it and besides we'll be back before this party breaks up. I so want to be alone with you when the clock strikes twelve."

"I feel the same way. Let's go!"

We jumped into the MG and headed out for the beach house. It took us a few minutes to get there, so we still had about an hour before midnight. We turned on the radio and I made a fire in the fireplace while Rita fixed us a couple of drinks.

"Happy New Year darling," she smiled, as she handed me my drink.

We sat down on the white soft rug in front of the fire and made ourselves comfortable.

Rita kicked off her shoes and rested her back against the sofa that stood nearby. I rested my head in her lap, and gazed at the flickering dancing flames while I sipped my drink.

"Lee when will it be?"

"Any day now, in fact I'm almost certain that this is my last liberty before I ship out."

"Oh Lee what am I going to do without you?" she cried.

" Rita, don't cry! Please don't cry, I'll be back!"

"You better because if you don't I'll join you," she sobbed. Just then the radio announcer began to count down the seconds to the New Year.

"Ten, nine, eight, seven, ----------

I took Rita in my arms and kissed away her tears as the clock struck twelve.

"Happy New Year! I whispered as our lips met in a loving and caring way.

'Let's go for a midnight swim," Rita begged. "I want this to be a night I'll never forget," she pleaded.

We put on the white bathing suits, the one's we wore before, and ran out to the surf. The water wasn't as cold as it was this afternoon. As we dove into the waves they gently pushed us back to the shore. We did pretty much what we did in the afternoon and finally Rita cried out: "Last one in the beach house is a rotten egg!"

She had a head start but I was much faster than she was so I paced myself so I could be right behind her. I got in step right behind her and her every step was synchronized with mine. She laughed and giggled feeling my body behind hers. I was the rotten egg!

The fire was nice and warm. I rubbed Rita very briskly with a Turkish towel while she giggled and rolled around on the white rug. During our love play I accidentally loosened the top of her bathing suit

"Oh Rita, they're beautiful," I gasped as I gazed down at two perfectly sculptured breasts. They were soft, firm and slightly tilted upwards.

"Do you really think so darling?"

"Oh yes," I gulped in short hot breaths. Her pink nipples were so inviting that I couldn't control myself.

"Oh Lee, it feels, so wonderful," she groaned.

I then slipped off her bathing suit and I let nature take its course.

My heart was beating wildly and beads of perspiration coalesced on my brow.

My manly desires took over and the deep warmth of her body, raised my metabolism to a feverish crescendo. I quickly put on a condom as an uncontrollable pleasant sensation was building up, a sensation so gratifying that once experienced, man can never do without.

"Lee I feel so wonderful! Please hold me tighter!

All at once an indescribable feeling bolted through our activated bodies that left us glorifyingly relieved. The tenseness was no longer there. The white rug was stained with crimson tears. Our love for one another was now complete.

We showered, dressed and left for the Stewart estate. The party was still going strong. We entered through a side door, picked up a couple of drinks and sat down at a nearby sofa. As we sat there sipping our drinks, I couldn't help but wonder how a pretty girl like Rita evaded the clutches of all the sweet talking wolves in uniform. Maybe someone up there wanted us to be together. Nevertheless, I'm glad it happened !

"Lee do you think we should get married before you leave for oversea duty?"

"I don't know?" I remarked.

"I know every girl wants a church wedding with all the trimmings and if we did get married it would have to be by a Justice of the Peace.

If we really love each other there's no reason why we can't wait. Who knows you may find someone else and I'll be getting a Dear John letter from you."

"That would never happen! No one could ever take your place," she vowed.

Rita and I spent the rest of the evening dancing and when the last of the Stewart's friends left we were ready to go to bed.

I was happy, contended and exhausted. I slept in one of the guest rooms and Rita in another.

I don't know how long I slept but a gentle tapping on my door awakened me.

"Wake up sleepy head," Rita said, as she stuck her pretty head through the partially opened door.

I managed to open one eye, yawned and rolled over on my stomach. Rita meanwhile snuck up behind and started tickling me.

"Rita don't!" I squirmed.

"Why Lee, you're not ticklish are you?" She giggled.

"Yes I am!" And upon saying this I caught hold of her and began tickling her. I wasn't familiar with her ticklish zones but I soon found them.

"Are you ticklish Miss Shaw?" I asked, as I continued tickling her. To make matters worse, I held her closely and tightly, gently blowing my warm breath into her ears.

"Lee will you please stop! I give up! "

"Not until you kiss me!"

"Okay!"

I relinquished my grasp, she tore free, grabbed a pillow and began beating me with it. I wasn't sleepy any more, only playful! We fought, laughed and loved.

Rita and I came down for brunch and were greeted very warmly by the Stewarts.

"We heard all that ruckus in your bedroom so we figured you had a lover's quarrel," June remarked.

"Nope! Just a pillow fight," we smiled.

That evening the Stewarts went to the Opera and some night clubbing afterwards. Rita and I decided to spend the rest of the day at the beach house.

We went swimming again and afterwards snuggled up around the fire place.

"Rita promise me that you'll wait for me, no matter what." "I promise, I promise," she purred, kissing me after every promise.

"When people fall in love and are as happy as we are, why can't it always be this way. Why are there so many divorces?"

"I don't know, but I've never been happier in my whole life," she said, as we kissed each other lovingly and then passionately. What a wonderful feeling. After a delicious fish dinner, we packed and were ready to leave for San Diego. June drove us to the bus station and kissed us both goodbye.

"I'm so happy to have met you Lee, and you must be one heck of a guy because I've never seen Rita any happier than she is right now. Please take good care of yourself."

"I will, and the feeling is mutual. I've never been happier in my life than I am right now," I confessed, as I gently squeezed Rita's hand. The sisters hugged one another and I heard June tell her sister to call her every night and reverse the charges.

The long bus ride to San Diego enabled us to confirm our deep love for one another.

"Lee this was the most pleasant and wonderful weekend I've had. If I live to be a hundred I shall never forget it!

"Neither will I! You have made me the happiest man in the Marine Corps by accepting me as your life long companion. I hope I never disappoint you!"

When we arrived at San Diego, I didn't want to say good bye just good night. I had a premonition that this would be the last time I would see her.

Somehow I got enough courage to keep a stiff upper lip. As I held her tightly in my arms, I kissed her lips for maybe the last time in my life. I started to walk away, and did an about face and said,

"May I have one more kiss for the road?"

"You most certainly may Lee Walewander" she said, as tears trickled down her cheek. We kissed long and hard and when our lips parted—I departed!

Chapter 15

We were awakened before reveille.

"Everybody up! Get your asses out of those sacks, pack your gear and be ready to move out," shouted Ruff Tuff Donlon.

I didn't know what to do. How will Rita know that I shipped out? I quickly took some stationary out of my pack and scribbled the following message:

Dear Rita:

Our orders came through. By the time you get this message, I'll be gone! I'll let you know where to write me as soon as I can. I love you very much and I will think about you and the weekend we spent together, the entire time I'm out here.

> With all my love,
> Lee

"Hurry up Lee," Chuck said excitedly. Ruff Tuff will be all over you if you don't move it.

"I have to get this letter to Rita, so can you give me a hand and pack some of my gear for me," I pleaded.

"Sure Lee, Chuck replied as he got Sammy to help him.

Meanwhile, I addressed the envelope and printed "Special Delivery" across the top of it. I didn't know what the Special Delivery postage was so I pasted all the stamps I had in my bag onto the letter and stuck it in my pocket.

Chuck and Sammy had all of my gear packed and it wasn't a minute too soon. Ruff Tuff ordered us to fall out on the double. We were given last minute instructions, and then marched to the mess hall where special chow awaited us.

"Mail this for me will you Steve. It's urgent!" I said, as I handed him the letter.

"Sure Lee," he replied.

We ate a hearty breakfast, boarded the trucks awaiting us, and as the bugler blew reveille we were at the Pier in San Diego, California.

"Don't tell me that's the ship we're going to board," Sammy beefed, as he fidgeted with his pack.

Sure looks that way, doesn't it?" I remarked.

The ship we were going to board was a troop ship from World War I. It was called the S.S. President Tyler and was decommissioned to do the same job it did in World War I. As we waited in line to board her, I couldn't help but think of Rita and how unhappy she will be. Yesterday she was so happy, and today, all that will soon change.

S.S. President Tyler

"Man this pack is heavy," Porky blurted out, interrupting my thoughts. I wasn't conscious of the weight on my back, but now that I was reminded of it, my back began to ache.

Here's what we had to carry aboard ship. In addition to our dungarees, boondockers, leggings, and steel helmet, we also had a double pack with blanket roll strapped to our backs.

A cartridge belt, canteen, first aid kit, bayonet, rifle, gas mask, knife and entrenching tools were also a part of our ensemble. We were loaded to the hilt!

Pier 7 was crammed full of Marines. Twenty four hundred of us were boarding this one ship, and I for the life of me didn't know where we would all fit. Of these 2400 men leaving, only 100 were from our Replacement Squadron. The rest of the men were from Line companies from Camp Pendleton and Camp Ellington. In addition to all the men boarding this relic, huge cranes were lifting trucks and Jeeps and lowering them into various hatches.

With all of this equipment aboard plus the ammunition and troops, the S.S. President Tyler war riding very, very low in the water.

We called off our names, hobbled up the gang - plank and were ushered into a hold. One by one we descended down the narrow steel ladders until we were deep down in the ship's structure. "Place your packs against the bulkheads," a Swabby directed us.

"What bulkhead?" we asked. They were obscured by the hundreds of packs that were already there.

"I heard there are 2400 of us aboard this ship and I think they're all down here in this hold," I surmised.

"You're not kidding Lee, but I'd like to know where in the hell are all of us are going to sleep," Sammy grumbled.

We were located in the lowest part of the ship. The ship creaked annoyingly and it seemed that any minute it would split in two. A couple of drops of water found their way into our quarters; we wondered if more would follow. I felt like a sardine, in these cramped quarters.

We slept on canvas cots that were suspended by chains from the ship's girders. The cots were stacked five high with about two feet between each one.

If a heavyweight slept above you, the canvas would sag to such an extent that he was practically resting on top of you. To remedy this situation, we staggered our weights. Porky had the lowest cot because he was the heaviest. Sammy was next, followed by Chuck, then me, and the top cot went to Hillbilly, who was the tallest and the lightest.

It was so hot and humid down in our cramped quarters that we slept in our skivvies. There were no sheets, blankets or pillows. We used our life jackets as pillows. The canvas was usually soiled from previous occupants. If the previous occupant was of the same height, the dips in the canvas would fit the contours of your body perfectly. If they weren't, than you either had to sleep above or below this cavity. It was very uncomfortable.

Right next to us was another row of cots, five high. There was just enough room for one man to walk through the aisles, so if by chance, two of you meet going in opposite directions, one of you had to crawl in an unoccupied cot in order to let the other person pass. Any odor emitted by any one of us had to be enjoyed by all. "Yeah! Right! "

We placed some of our gear on our cots to make sure no one occupies them while we're topside. We had to wear our life jackets at all times, because we were in enemy waters and at any time we could be sunk by a Japanese submarine or attacked by Japanese planes. We had no escort, we were strictly on our own. Our only hope of not being sunk is if we're lucky enough not to be spotted. If we are, we're going to be sunk and we'll wind up dead or floating in the ocean as "hors d'oeuvres" for the hungry sharks.

As the S.S. President Tyler was pulling out of the harbor, the fog was lifting, the city was awakening, and 2400 Marines were sailing out into the vast Pacific Ocean without an escort. Destination Unknown!

The food aboard ship was as bad as our sleeping quarters. We ate our meals standing up in the ship's mess hall. With so many troops aboard, you ate and moved out!

The first day at sea was very calm. That night we ran into a storm and our ship creaked and rolled. As we lay on our cots it was like being on a roller coaster. The Swabbys meanwhile were busily involved in placing large garbage cans throughout the hold.

No sooner were the cans in position, they were quickly surrounded by sea sick Marines who began vomiting into them. It looked like a football huddle only the signals were nauseating. More cans were being hauled out as more and more of us were joining the huddles.

I didn't feel a bit sea sick and wondered how long would it be before I got sick, or would I? Porky was already in the huddle and Chuck was rushing to join him. The ship continued to "Rock and Roll." With all this activity going on it was impossible to sleep.

Whenever chow was ready in the Mess hall, a buzzer would sound and it was on a first come basis. If you didn't feel like eating, nobody cared.

"Let's go to chow men," I said, as I stretched my sleepless tired body. The word "chow" sent Hillbilly rushing to the huddle. Sam and I began to laugh. As I got up the room began to spin and my stomach was rising so quickly that I dropped my socks and headed for an open spot in a huddle. I dove into the huddle and began to spill my guts. Sammy was already there. There was so much vomit in that can that it came splashing back into my face. The odor was nauseating. You kept your eyes closed, for fear of vomit getting into them. When I was a complete vacuum, I lied down to die. As long as you lied still and on your back it wasn't very bad. The minute you got up, it hit you. So all that day, we laid in our cots, on our backs, eating dry crackers. This was about the only food that would stay down in our stomach.

We fared a little better the next day, but our stomachs were still queasy. We were able to hold a little of the food we ate, but not for long. We ate breakfast and dinner in the mess hall standing up. Our lunches were brought topside or on deck for us. Lt. Gordon and Sgt. Johnson carried a box of sandwiches and a crate of oranges up on deck for us to eat.

"As I call your name, step up and select a sandwich and an orange and move out. Is that clear?"

" Yeah," we sickly replied.

The first few men followed orders to a tee, but when it became evident that the choice sandwiches would be gone very shortly, a few eager hands dipped into the carton when the Lieutenant wasn't looking.

Others followed suit and before you knew it sandwiches and oranges were strewn all over the deck. I managed to grab about 4 slices of bread and traded with Sammy who had bologna but no bread. It was disgusting to see grown men fighting for food. The sandwich meat was cold and greasy and hard to swallow. We washed it down with water from our canteen, and ate our orange.

Just then an announcement came over the loudspeaker:

"Now hear this ! Now hear this!

"What the hell does he want us to hear?" Sammy remarked as he continued to deal the cards.

"Who knows?" I replied.

"Men we are in enemy waters without an escort. Our only hope of reaching our destination is to pray to God that we're not spotted. Every precaution has to be taken! Under no circumstances are you to throw anything over board! Many a ship has been sunk because the garbage it threw overboard left a trail for the enemy to follow. At night we'll have a complete black out! No smoking on deck, or you'll be shot by the sentry on duty. We're not going to sacrifice the lives of the people on this ship for one blundering idiot. That is all!"

"Well I guess he told us," Chuck remarked, as he looked at his hand. The rolling motion of the ship, obviously wasn't to our liking especially when Porky blurted out: "Deal me out!," and then making a bee line for the railing. Porky wasn't alone! The railing was crowded with retching Marines.

We soon learned the best way to get over sea sickness was to lie down and eat nothing but crackers and let your "innards" get accustomed to the ship's movement. This is what we did, but we were constantly being interrupted by the following announcement, which pissed us off.

"Now hear this! Now hear this! There will be a clean sweep down, fore and aft. That is all!"

Now what the clean sweep down involved is that everyone who was top side has to move their butt to the front of the ship. The Swabby's would then come with their brooms and hoses and clean that part of the ship. Now they have to clean the "aft" part of the ship and once more we have to move. This ritual takes place twice a day. It seemed that every time we found a good spot to play cards in, we had to move because of the clean sweep down. After the sweep downs there was a wild scramble for a choice location. Some of the Marines could be found in the same place every day; I wondered how they managed.

When I wasn't playing cards, I would look at Rita's wallet size picture and reminisce about the fun we had at the beach house. I wore her shock proof watch and I D bracelet all the time. They were my constant reminder of her.

That night I couldn't sleep. I vomited a few times and now began to feel sharp shooting pains in my stomach. I quickly dressed and double -timed it to the head that was located top side on this old troop ship. There were about twelve stools in this one head, six on each side. Every stool was occupied and as I waited by the door for someone to leave, a line began to form behind me. My pains were becoming unbearable!

"Hurry up! We shouted, "Shit and get off the pot!"

A couple of them took the hint and began wiping their butts and before one of them had a chance to button his fly, I was sitting down on his stool. It almost reminded me of musical chairs. My excretion was fluid, it literally poured out.

"Hurry up will you Mac," a fellow sufferer pleaded.

"One second!" I answered as another urge came upon.

"Can you move over a little," he pleaded, expecting me to share my stool with him.

I'm done!" I said, as I picked up the roll of paper that was being passed around.

I wiped quickly, got up, and moved out!

"Man that feels good!" he uttered as he sputtered.

The line outside the head was staggering! The toilet facilities highly inadequate! The ship reeked with "shit" as Gyrenes were straddling cans, railings, and rolls of coiled rope or just squatting on the deck eliminating their bowels. I almost broke my neck when I stepped into a mound of this crap, in the darkness.

"Five bucks for your stool!" someone shouted.

"I'll give you a sawbuck," was the next bid.

What a mess, I thought, as I headed for the shower room. My boon dockers were covered with excretion, they had to be washed off. The shower room was as crowded as the head, and it stunk just as badly!

Gyrenes were straddling the wash basins! It was impossible for me to get inside, so I decided to go back to sleep and clean my boondockers tomorrow.

All my buddies were gone and I knew where they were. As I laid there I wondered why we all got the runs and the Swabby's didn't! Did they slip a laxative into our meals? If this is their idea of a joke, it sucks!

When we arose the next morning, the Swabby's were already washing down the ship, fore and aft. They found excrement in the oddest places, they laughed hysterically when they found some on their five-inch gun. The ship was washed down and the stampede for squatting rights began.

This was our third day out at sea. I was still weak but slowly becoming acclimatized to the ship's movement.

"Man what a flush job that was!" Hillbilly chuckled, as he looked at his cards. "I was cleaned out at both ends!"

"It must have been the greasy sandwich meat we fought over," I cut in dryly. The others agreed with me and dropped the subject because it was one we wanted to forget.

The fourth day at sea found us all hale, hearty and dirty.

"Let's take a shower Chuck," I suggested. "I feel awfully dirty!"

"God idea! Let's go! "

We picked up our soap, towel and entered the shower room. We expected the shower room to be crowded, but it wasn't. There were eight shower stalls present and no showers'. With so many troops aboard we wondered why it was empty, but we soon found out. Our soap wouldn't lather in salt water, it spread on like grease.

"Wrong soap!" we grinned, as we picked up a special type of green soap which had the fragrance of pine needles. This soap didn't work any better, and consequently we were stuck with a lot of sticky soap on our bodies. The salt water rolled off the soap like water off a duck's back. My hair was glued together!

"God damn it!" Chuck bitched. "Everything seems to be happening to us. What the hell are we going to do now? "

"Take it easy Chuck! Let's rinse off our hair with our canteen water and get the hell out of here."

"Good idea!"

We rinsed off as best as we could with the small amount of water that was rationed to us, every day. This was the last shower we were going to take for some time to come.

The men aboard ship were letting their beards grow because water was at a premium and shaving without plenty of water was agonizing torture. I had a very light beard because of my age which was hardly noticeable. Sam's beard on the other hand was dark and bushy.

We stunk with body odor and were an unkempt lot indeed! Some of us would carefully tie our dirty clothes to a rope and toss the bundle overboard. After about an hour we hauled up our laundry, dried it in the sun, shake out the salt, and wear it. The clothes weren't very clean but they didn't reek with B.O.

After about a week out at sea, we were awakened in the middle of the night by an alert. Our radar picked up the presence of a submarine lurking nearby. We quickly put on our life jackets and went top side. If we were going to be torpedoed, the Captain wanted us topside, ready to abandon ship if necessary. There was only so much room top side, so most of us were deep down in the ship's belly. As we stood there, with our life jackets on, we prayed along with the chaplain that the submarine lurking was one of ours. The moon was very bright tonight, too bright for our own good. I guess everyone thought of their loved ones at this time, I did too! We all knew that if we were torpedoed there was no way for us to get out of this trap, and we were doomed to drown like rats.

Just then an announcement came forth –

"Now hear this! The submarine in question is ours! As you were!"

" Yeah ! we shouted, for the time being.

The lunches were as poorly organized as ever. Every day Lt. Gordon and Sgt. Johnson came forth with their box of sandwiches and crate of oranges, hoping that this would be the day when everything would work perfectly.

"Let's not be pigs!"he screamed. "One at a time, only today we're going to start with end of the alphabet. When you're name is called we're going to give you a sandwich and an orange. You don't have choice. If you don't like what we give you, make a trade. The reason you're given an orange every day, is so you don't come down with Scurvy.

"A short arm inspection in 15 minutes," Sgt. Johnson informed us.

Our detail of 100 men fell out as ordered and lined up in the passage way. One of the Navy Corpsman came forward and said-

"Line up alphabetically and as the Doc walks by skin it back and milk it forward. We're checking for "clap" he said. "You gyrenes might have picked up a dose before you left Diego, and we can't take a chance on any of you contaminating everyone aboard ship."

I wasn't worried, but for some reason Sammy was !

"What's wrong Sam ? You look nervous!"

" I may have what they're looking for !"

" What makes you think so?"

" Look how red it is!"

"Why didn't you go to sick bay?"

"I don't know!"

Just then the Doc approached, and the Corpsman told Sammy to skin it back and milk it forward.

"Looks like I have it Sir!" Sam answered peevishly.

"I'll say you have it! What the hell do you think this pus coming out is? Pea soup? Corpsman take this man's name and get him over to sick bay immediately."

"He did!"

Besides Sammy, about ten more Gyrenes were found to have gonorrhea. Sammy reported to sickbay and was put on antibiotics.

The days aboard ship were long and drawn out. Fights were constantly breaking out for one reason or another. Every now and then a Marine would disappear as if whisked away by a magic wand. Did he commit suicide? Was he tossed overboard?

No one knew, but I could see someone like Bulldog or Beer belly O'Shannon being tossed overboard, very easily.

"Now hear this! Now hear this!" the loudspeaker blared.

"We are approaching the equator and there's a little initiation that you people have to go through. If you're crossing the equator for the first time, you're a "Polywog. If you have crossed the equator before, you are a "Shell back" and entitled to all of the privileges befitting a Shell back. The Shell backs will take over and initiate the Poliwogs in the tradition of King Neptune and his court. That is all!"

We had quite a few Shell backs aboard ship. They had a meeting, we were identified and prepared us for the upcoming events. Practically all of the Swabbys were Shell backs and were eagerly awaiting a chance to give us Marine Polywogs a hard time.

As we approached the equator, the fun for the Shell backs was to begin. We were instructed to wear only our pants and our personal belongings were locked up for safe keeping.

As the five of us emerged from the hold, we were told to crawl on all fours, as two Swabbys watered us down with water. The stream of water had so much pressure behind it that it forced us back against the bulkheads.

We had to crawl forward against this stream of water while two other Swabbys were moving us along by swiping at us with straps. These swipes were stinging in nature, after all they were falling on wet buttocks.

The Polywog officers were also hit with straps, watered down, and then sent up to the crow's nest with a couple of coke bottles as binoculars. The chicken shit Polywog officers were really given a hard time.

A Polywog Captain was told to put on his dress uniform and report back on the double by a lowly Shell back Private. Upon his return, the Private asked him?

"Captain what do you think of the Shell backs? He asked, as he poured a bucket of water over him.

"They're all bastards!" the Captain shouted. Just then two burly Shell backs lifted the Captain and deposited him in a barrel of salt water, dress uniform and all.

"I didn't hear you Captain, now what was that you said about the Shell backs?

"They're a no good bunch of bastards, that's what I said."

More water was poured over him and then he was instructed to do push-ups while being asked the same old question?

"The Captain doesn't like Shell backs, so maybe a couple of sea bags on his back will change his opinion about us."

The Captain was asked one more time what he thought of the Shell backs?

"A miserable bunch of shit heads," he shouted.

Another sea bag was placed on his back and then still another. The Captain finally told the Shell backs that they were wonderful and so they left him to look for another Polywog officer they could torment.

The Shell backs also had an electric chair rigged up which each and every Polywog had to sit in and be shocked. Each and every one of us also had to stick their head in some kind of milky gooh.

Just then a Shell back shaved a strip of our hair right down the middle of our head. The finale' to our initiation was to approach a fat bellied King Neptune, who was sitting on a make shift throne, and kiss his bare stomach and also his dirty stinky feet. We passed our initiation and were now full -fledged Shell backs.

The only consolation we received from this ritual was that the next time we crossed the equator we would be Shellbacks and do the initiating. That is if we were lucky enough to have a next time.

The next day we were issued our shellback certification cards stating that we were duly initiated in the Solemn Mysteries of the Ancient Order of the Deep.

The days were passing by very slowly. We were playing cards incessantly. There was nothing else to do.

"I've got it all figured out," Sammy said as he put in his ante.

"Got what figured out?" Porky asked.

"Why the Marines are so terrific when it comes to taking beach heads. You see," he added, "They make life so God Damn miserable, aboard ship for them, that when they hit the beach they're so pissed off at everything and everyone that they're raving maniacs. God have mercy on any Jap that gets in their way."

"You know what Sam, you may be right!" we all snickered.

"Now hear this ! Now hear this! Will the officers please get back on duty and out of the Nurses' quarters. This is an order ! That is all!"

"Well I'll be a horse's ass," Chuck remarked. "Here we are living like pigs and the Officers are shack-shacking up with the Nurses.

If that's the Democracy I'm fighting for, than I'm for mutiny and those nurses."

"Mutiny!" we cried, "and those Nurses!"

We've been aboard the S. S. President Tyler for three weeks and still no sight of land. Constant alerts were making nervous wrecks out of all of us. We were becoming quite restless. We had rifle inspection from time to time, just to give us something to do.

We also sharpened our knives and bayonets until we could dry shave with them.

Fights were breaking out as we were getting on each other's nerves. Men were disappearing, and if we don't get off this scow pretty soon we'll have a battle aboard ship.

After the twenty-sixth day, we were told of our destination. We were to land in Noumea, New Caledonia. Noumea was the stopping off place for Marines who participated in a battle and now needed a little Rest and Recreation. We were their replacements and they would either be sent home or get liberty in Australia or New Zealand. This was called, R and R. Rest and Recreation..

The Line company Marines aboard our ship went on to Australia where the 1st Marine Division was recuperating from the Battle of Guadalcanal. It was here, where 1,044 Marines were killed, and 2,894 wounded. Our contingent of 100 men, were going to join a Marine Air Group in the Solomon Islands. We got off at Noumea, but before we did, we said goodbye to our new found friends as they stayed aboard ship and headed for Australia.

Noumea, New Caledonia was a French Province, and therefore French was spoken by its natives. We were amazed to see these dark skinned Polynesians with bright red bushy hair. This redness was due to the bleaching effect of the strong Naphtha soap they used.

We boarded trucks and were taken to the Marine Air Corps Transient area on the outskirts of town. Planes, pilots, and ground crew were constantly being eased into the combat areas, after spending a few weeks in Sydney Australia or Auckland New Zealand

The policy of the Marine Air Corps at this stage of the war was to keep a combat squadron in action for about six weeks and then give them a week of liberty in Australia or New Zealand.

The people of these countries were very hospitable, especially the damsels, that made us very happy to hear.

"Pick up your gear and get squared away in one of those tents," the Sergeant instructed, as we climbed down from the truck.

"Don't get too comfortable, you're leaving tomorrow for Bougainville which is an island next to Guadalcanal, where the Battle of the Perimeter is in progress. I want you to shower, shave, get haircuts, and wash your dirty clothes because this may be your last opportunity to do so, for some time to come.

Tomorrow morning, bright and early, you people will board an LST (Landing Ship Tank) and be taken to Guadalcanal and await further orders. Your new outfit is desperately in need of replacements, so we can't give you any liberty while you're in Noumea. It's too bad, but as they say in the Russian Marines, "Toughski Shitski !"

"Okay, fall out! Chow in fifteen minutes! The Sergeant informed us.

The five of us selected a nearby tent, which already had cots present. The first thing we did was double time it to the shower stalls to wash off 28 days of dirt, perspiration and stench.

We then went to chow and immediately afterwards went to the base barber shop to get the standard GI haircut.

We then took our dirty clothes to the wash racks and like in Boot camp we began to wash and scrub them. We then hung them up to dry and while they were drying we shaved and then crapped out on our soiled cots.

That evening, we hit the sack early as we haven't had a decent night's sleep in twenty eight days. Sleep came easily and pleasantly.

We bid Noumea, New Caledonia farewell, as we boarded the LST which was awaiting us. Our destination was Guadalcanal in the Solomon Islands about 800 nautical miles away. As far as we knew, Guadalcanal was secured; the only Japs on the island were either dead or hiding out in the hills.

LST –Landing Ship Tank

The living conditions aboard the L.S.T. were so much better than those we were subjected to on the S.S. President Tyler.

We squared away our gear and went topside. The L.S.T. was riding low as it too was loaded to the hilt with tanks and armaments. All of these landing crafts were constructed with shallow bottoms so that they can get right up on the beach, and dispose of their gear and personnel. A couple of destroyers escorted us to the Canal as we were in enemy waters.

The first few days aboard the L.S.T..were serene. Just before dusk, on the third day out, bedlam broke loose. A couple of Jap zeros came in low over the horizon and began strafing us. The destroyer's guns opened up but weren't even getting close to the very fast and maneuverable Zeros. They made two fast passes at us, killing four from our Replacement Squadron before they disappeared.

"They killed Joe!" They killed Joe! I shouted, as I gazed down at Pfc. Joseph Malek's bullet riddled body. The blood was still squirting out of his severed arteries. A bloody magazine was still in his grasp.

"He didn't have a chance!" I lamented.

"Those dirty bastards will pay for this," Chuck vowed.

"I agree! We owe them one!" I answered.

The sight of our buddies warm red blood, gushing out of his wounds, was too much for my nervous stomach to endure. I felt nauseous! I puked!

A few days later we arrived at Guadalcanal and were given our orders.

"You men are to remain on this beach until an L.C.I. (Landing Craft Infantry) picks you up. That should be in a couple of hours," the Captain informed us.

We disembarked, and crapped out on the warm sandy beach. We were prepared for battle. Every man's cartridge belt was loaded with clips of eight, and every man had bandoliers of "Ammo" slung from his shoulders. We also had grenades clipped to our belts and enough ammo was stacked on the beach to stem off an invasion.

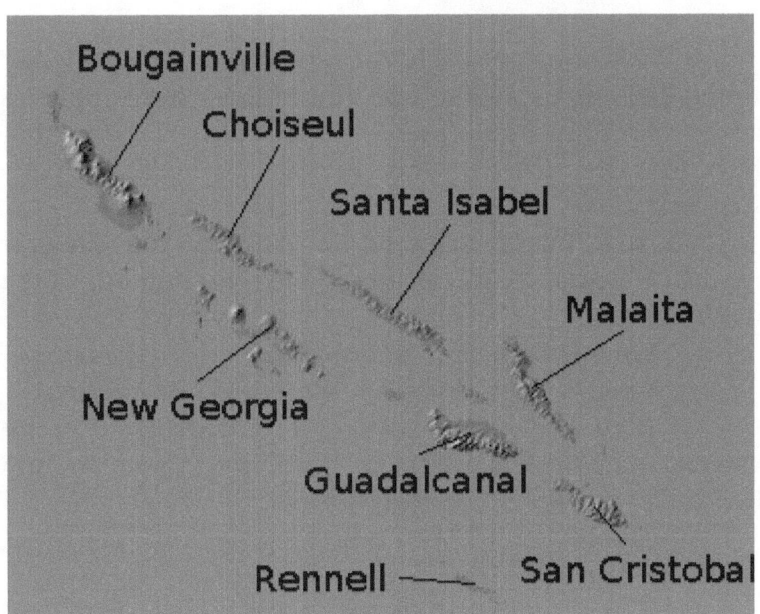

Solomon Islands

"I don't care if we never get picked up," Sammy reckoned, as he stretched out on the warm somewhat dirty sand.

"That's exactly how I feel," I yawned.

We dozed off for about an hour and after our siesta, we arose, refreshed but hungry. Since the Solomon's chief export was coconuts, we began to indulge. The husks were easily chopped off with our sharp bayonets, the eyes pierced, the milk drunk. The coconut meat was delicious, the chewing laborious. I ate so much, that I swore off coconuts for good.

We waited, waited and still no L.C.I. The Navy and the Army were in sole possession of this island. The 1st Marine Division was now in Australia, for Rest and Recreation. It wasn't too long before we accidentally walked into the abandoned, 1st Marine Division camp.

Rows of tents were still neatly aligned and the remnants of the 1st Marine Division was still prevalent. Luckily we found some cots, mattresses, and mosquito nettings in one of the nearby tents and proceeded to hit the sack.

We arose very early the next day as our growling stomachs kept us awake half the night. The Anopheles mosquitoes didn't help matters. They were so huge that they literally lifted your netting to get at your corpuscles.

I was busily engaged in rupturing a coconut when Pvt. Pedro Manuel Ortiz, came running out of the brush.

"Mucho Comida!" he shouted.

"What's he shouting? " We asked one another.

"Who the hell knows! Hey Pedro you're an American ! Speak English, or we'll ship your ass into the Mexican army," Chuck quipped.

"Chow!"

"Where?"

"Down the road about a mile," he answered breathlessly, as he dug frantically in his sea bag for his mess kit.

We quickly followed suit, and followed Pedro through the jungle. Very shortly afterwards, a large Acorn Naval Base loomed before us. The Swabby's were lining up for chow, so we joined them.

"Where the hell are these Gyrenes coming from?" we heard one of them ask.

"The Japs are on the next island!" some Swabby shouted.

"Don't tell me the Japs are going to invade us again?" another quip.

"Yes they are," we replied.

We're here to protect you and your chow! Mostly your chow! "we laughed.

They also laughed, but still had no idea why we were here.

We reported back to our abandoned camp area, packed our gear and headed out back to the beach. We once more crapped out on the sand while Lt. Werner and Sgt. Johnson went to see the Commanding Officer of the Acorn base.

They were gone about an hour and upon their return, they informed us that the L.C.I. that was to pick us up was sunk, along with our orders. Therefore we are to remain in the abandoned 1st Marine Division camp until they straighten out this mess. Meanwhile we are to eat our meals at the Navy mess hall.

We returned to our camp area, squared away our gear and went to chow. That afternoon, we went for a swim in the nearby Tenaru river. It was here that 900 Japanese soldiers of the Ichiki Detachment Division attacked and were slaughtered by the 1st Marine Division. The river was crystal clear now, but when you thought of all the men whose blood spilt into it, a faint red tint became evident.

We took off our clothes, except for our skivvies, and dove into the river, and began swimming to the other side. The water was refreshingly cool which was very much to our liking.The river at this point was about 100 yards wide and flowed lazily into the Pacific Ocean. We swam and frolicked for about an hour at which time we went back to our camp area to see if anything new developed while we were gone.

"No word as yet," Sgt. Johnson informed us, from under his mosquito netting. He was reading a Mickey Spillane murder mystery and didn't want to be disturbed. We let him be!

The natives of Guadalcanal were short, dark skinned, and possessing black kinky hair. They were affectionately called, "Gooks" by the Americans. They wore make-shift skirts around their waists, the material appearing very familiar at times. It was a very common sight indeed to see the man of the household leading the way with his spouse following close behind. If there was any firewood to be carried, it was tied in a bundle and placed on her back. The wife was the workhorse of the family, the man the King. From our standpoint it looked like a wonderful arrangement.

Natives of Guadalcanal 1944

Just then a native girl passed by with a load of firewood on her back. The women walked around topless on the Canal and if they were young their breasts were small and firm. As they got older their breasts hung down to their waists which affected the way they walked.

"Now's your chance Sam," I kiddingly quipped.

"I think I've learned my lesson," Sammy replied, referring of course to his bout with gonorrhea.

We all knew what he meant!

The next day, the five of us went swimming again, but picked a different location. We stumbled across a little pier made of bamboo logs. Alongside the pier and tied to it was a small boat that had a little outboard motor attached.

"I wonder whose boat this is?" I asked.

"Who cares, let's see if we can get it started," Sammy excitedly remarked.

"You think we can get it started?" Chuck wondered, as he checked to see if there was any gas in the tank.

"There's plenty of gas in it, but where's the cord to get it started?"

"I don't know, but I think I can get it started," I replied.

"How?"

"I'll show you guys how it's done."

I proceeded to pick up a thin vine that was growing near the shore. I stripped off the leaves and smaller branches, wrapped it around the disc and gave it a good yank. The motor sputtered momentarily and cut out. I tried it once more and this time the motor kicked over immediately. Chuck Sammy and I piled in and we were on our way. Since I started the motor, I was the Skipper, and so I headed for Porky and Hillbilly to see if they wanted to get in. They on the other hand thought I was going to run them over so they swam back to shore.

I turned the boat around and headed deeper into the jungle. It was like we were on a sight-seeing tour, waving at the natives, as we sputtered by. All of a sudden our little excursion was interrupted by rifle fire from a nearby hill.

"Duck!" I shouted, as a round splintered a board on the top of our boat. We dove into the water, and protected ourselves by hiding behind our boat, and got the hell out of there. When we were some distance down the river, we helped each other into the boat.

"Chuck, you've been hit!" Sammy noticed.

"I know! It's only a flesh wound," he calmly replied.

"I wonder who the hell is shooting at us? Sammy asked as he looked around.

"They say there are a handful of Japs still hiding out in the hills and jungles waiting for their brethren to return," I added.

"Well if that's the case, I think we should go Jap hunting. What do you say" Chuck replied, as he wiped the blood off his arm with his snot rag.

"Yeah! We all agreed! We have a score to settle with those yellow bellied bastards."

After a few days of deliberation and strategy we decided to go Jap hunting. Since Chuck was the one that was injured we decided that he was the acting Sergeant in charge. Immediately after breakfast, the following day, we prepared for our excursion into Japanese territory.

"We'll need a Jeep guys, it's a cinch we can't walk up there," Chuck surmised.

"Maybe we can borrow a Jeep from the Swabbys they'll never miss it!" Porky added.

"I agree, but one of us has to borrow it! Any volunteers?" Chuck asked.

Not a whisper!

"Since we don't have a volunteer, why don't we draw straws?" Billy added.

We all agreed but we drew cards instead. I was low with a four of spades and so I set out to get a Jeep. I walked over to Officers quarters where many Jeeps were parked and picked one out that had a full tank of gas and drove it back to the camp area. During wartime ignition keys were never used because if you're in a hurry to get away you can't go looking for your keys. As I pulled up behind our tent and got out, everyone was ready to go.

"Nice going Jim, any trouble? Chuck asked.

"Nah, piece of cake! I also made sure it had a full tank of gas."

"Good thinking! We may need it!"

We began to load the Jeep with our ammo, rifles and a B.A.R. (Browning Automatic

Rifle) that Sammy requisitioned

We finally got the Jeep loaded, piled in and drove off. It wasn't too long before we were bouncing along the river banks and on our way towards an unsuspecting enemy. I drove for about fifteen minutes up this hill when Chuck told me to stop.

"I think we better park the Jeep and walk the rest of the way," Chuck added. We agreed that the shots that were fired at us came from this location. After a short deliberation, we worked out our assignments. Sam was going to handle the B.A.R and Porky was going to carry the ammo for it. A "B.A.R" uses a lot of ammo quickly and so we couldn't take a chance on running out of it. Chuck and I were to move out first and do a little scouting. If we see any Japs, we will fall back and plan a mode of attack. If on the other hand were spotted and you hear rifle fire, you guys come to our rescue, on the double, but spread out when you do so.

"Roger!" They acknowledged.

The jungle was hot and humid and the mosquitoes were relentless.

The colorful parrots were screeching as if to tell the Japs that we were coming.

We moved very cautiously through the thick foliage when it happened. Before I knew what had happened a Jap dropped down on me and was about to slit my throat when Chuck placed a round right between his eyes. Death was instantaneous the hole was neatly formed. When I stopped shaking and trembling, I looked at Chuck and gaspingly said,

"Boy am I glad you shot expert ! I owe you! "

"Yeah! You're lucky Sammy didn't have to take that shot."

"Yeah right!"

"We better take cover, I don't think he was alone!" Chuck correctly surmised.

We scrambled back about twenty five yards, dropped behind a couple of logs and waited.

The parrots were quiet now, and all that was audible was our heavy breathing. A mosquito determined to land on my neck broke the silence. She sounded like a B25 when she buzzed my ear. Because I was afraid to move, she deftly landed on my neck and began to clean her proboscis before drilling through my skin. I was afraid to move for fear that a sniper might locate my hiding place. I looked through my peep site as two crouching figures approached. They were Japs! I felt like running, my stomach was one big knot, and that God damn mosquito kept drilling. They spotted their dead comrade and hit the deck. We heard them scream something in Niponese and a couple of more Japs appeared. They were plotting their strategy. The mosquito left, only the itch remained.

I felt like throwing a hand grenade in their midst but the dense jungle prevented my doing so. There were four of them now and Chuck and I must have had the same thought in mind when we opened fire. I picked off the one on the extreme left, Chuck the one on the extreme right.

As the two end Japs dropped, the two remaining had to hit the deck. Three down, and two to go.

As we peered from behind the log, we completely forgot about our buddies. They came up very suddenly!

"Hit the deck" I screamed, as Chuck and I poured round after round in the direction of the enemy. It was too late! Porky and Hillbilly were hit! Sam seeing his buddies drop beside him became a raving maniac.

"You dirty sons of bitches," he shouted, as he poured round after round into the brush. I caught a glimpse of one Jap getting up to retreat when Sam's B.A.R. practically took his head off. The other Jap threw up his hands to surrender but it was too late as 30 caliber bullets were cleaning out his intestines. When the smoke died down, there were five dead and two wounded. Luckily the dead were theirs. Pfc. Joseph Malek's death was avenged.

We placed Hillbilly and Porky into our Jeep and got the hell out of there. Porky was hit in the shoulder and Hillbilly got hit in the leg.

"Should we bury the dead?" Sammy asked.

"You're kidding aren't you? If you want to bury the dead be my guest but we're not sticking around. We have to get Porky and Billy to sick bay before they lose too much blood." Chuck snapped.

"Okay! I guess you're right! "Sammy replied.

Now here's what we have to do. We're going to hide all off the ammo, rifles and B.A.R. in the jungle and come back for it later on. When we get to the base hospital we can say that you guys were shot, while we were swimming, which we were. Who knows they may even award you guys Purple Hearts for your injuries."

"Yeah Right! Porky and Billy grimaced.

When we arrived at the base hospital, we took Porky and Billy inside where they were rushed to the operating room. One of the doctors interviewed us and when we told him what we were doing and where the shots came from he bought it.

"Yeah, we had other men shot at when they were swimming in that river."

Porky and Hillbilly were recuperating at the Naval Hospital while we bided our time. We went swimming ever day, as there was nothing else to do. If we weren't swimming, we were playing cards or reading Mystery novels, which we checked out of the Acorn library.

I was deeply engrossed in reading a Perry Mason thriller when I heard a lot of commotion outside our tent.

"Ride "em Pedro!," I heard someone shout.

I dashed outside, and in doing so, I almost got run over by a Navy Jeep.

"Jesus Christ! What the hell is happening?" I thought aloud.

It seems that Pedro Ortiz borrowed a Naval Jeep and was teaching himself how to drive. He was in first gear, the engine was racing madly and he looked panic stricken.

"Stomp her!," Sammy shouted.

Pedro responded and the Jeep bolted forward like a frightened fledgling. It was headed right for a nearby tent. The occupants were storming out of it like bats out of hell.

"Caramba!" Pedro screamed, as he furiously tried to stop the Jeep, but couldn't! The tent collapsed upon impact, trapping the Jeep and rider. The movement resembled that of a caterpillar under a leaf as it desperately tried to emerge. Before it had a chance to, a large coconut tree blocked its path.

"I can't look!" Chuck replied.

The crash was deafening, and as the shock waves traversed the island, the tree pummeled the Jeep and driver with coconuts.

"He must be killed!" Sammy bemoaned.

We double timed it to the scene and began to pull the tent off the Jeep.

Well I'll be, there to our amazement sat Pedro with a big shitting grin on his face.

"Muchas gracias ! he replied as he rubbed his head.

Pedro was very lucky because Lieutenant Werner and Sergeant Johnson weren't around to see this fiasco, otherwise he'd be spending the next six months in a Naval brig. All Pedro had to show for his clutch happiness was a welt on his noggin. We had to ditch another Jeep.

With all this time on our hands, we were constantly getting ourselves into mischief. One morning, while swimming, we took the boat out and accidentally sunk it.

"I wonder who this little boat belonged to?" I asked Chuck and Sammy.

"Who knows, and who cares," Sammy replied, as we swam back to shore.

It wasn't very long before we got our answer. A Catholic missionary appeared at the pier and beckoned me.

"Young man, have you seen my little boat anywhere?"

"Your boat Father?" I gulped.

"Yes, I keep it tied up to this pier. It's my means of transportation to the native villages," he added.

"It may have come loose and drifted out to the ocean," I lied.

"Oh my Lord! I hope not! What shall I do?" he lamented, as he clasped his hands and looked skyward.

I felt like a worm without a hole to crawl into.

"We'll find your boat, Father. It may be beached somewhere," I lied once more!

He slowly left the pier mumbling a prayer in Latin . He was a timid little man, I thought, as I swam out to where our group was swimming.

"Do you meat heads know who that was, that I was talking to?" I asked.

"The Pope!" Sammy laughed.

"No you idiot! That was a Catholic missionary and you know what he's looking for"

"To convert us to Christianity," Chuck laughingly replied.

"Go ahead and laugh, but that little boat we sunk belonged to him. He uses it as his means of transportation to the native villages. I told him we'll try to find it for him."

"I don't think we have to look very far to find it," Sammy added.

"Yeah but how in the hell are we going to get it out of the water? " I asked.

"Maybe we can pull it out, if we got a Jeep and tied a line to it," Chuck surmised.

"Since it was my fault that the boat sank, I'll go out and get us a Jeep and a coil of rope," he said, as he began to swim towards shore.

In about a half hour, Chuck was back. We dove under water and tied the rope to the outboard motor and slowly maneuvered the boat from under the water. We cleaned out the mud and debris, rinsed it out, tied it to the pier, and let the sunlight dry it.

When the Padre came back and found his boat tied up to the pier, he was so happy that he told us that he was going to say mass in our behalf.

"It would please your God, if you were present," he said. We promised to be there.

Early Sunday morning, after breakfast, we headed out to the Padre's little bamboo church. For all practical purposes the church was out in the open.

There was a little grass canopy over the make shift altar, that was all. We sat down on a log and waited for the services to start.

Needless to say not too many natives attended. Those that did attend were mostly women. The Padre came forth with his two little native altar boys. He wore his priestly robe while his altar boys were garbed in white. The Padre greeted us warmly, and promptly at 0900, one of the altar boys rang a bell and the services began.

The mass lasted about an hour. When Mass was completed, we complimented the Padre on his congregation and the prodigious task he had undertaken. We left very much refreshed and enlightened.

Our island paradise was the nuts. At times I felt like Robinson Crusoe.

One day when we were swimming, I got an idea. Since we couldn't use the Padre's little boat anymore why not build ourselves a raft. Everyone thought it was a good idea so we began to sketch how we could make it.

We used our bayonets to cut bamboo logs that were very plentiful. We tied the bamboo logs together with young tender vines and made our raft two logs deep. When completed the raft was about nine feet wide and fourteen feet long.

"Do you think it will float?" Sammy asked.

"We'll soon find out," I said.

"Don't you think we should christen it before we launch it?!" Chuck suggested.

"Yeah, let's give it a name," Sammy added.

"How about "Semper Fidelis" Pedro replied.

"Not bad! Only Semper Fidelis in the Marine Corps means "Hurray For Me and Fuck You," Chuck laughed.

"Fits perfectly!" we shouted.

We found an empty bottle, filled it with river water and presented it to Pedro.

"You christen it Pedro after all you suggested the name."

"Okay!" he said. "I christen thee "Semper Fidelis," as he smashed the bottle against one of the bamboo logs. The bottle didn't break but we didn't care. We slid the raft into the water, it sank momentarily, and then emerged as if gasping for air. "We did it! It floats" Pedro shrieked with joy.

We all smiled triumphantly, and began to board her. The raft sank under our combined weights but still managed to keep itself above water. We took a few poles along in case we hit a sand barge. We rafted all that afternoon and finally decided to let the river currents take us out to the Pacific Ocean.

The raft picked up speed as it approached the mouth of the river.

"Hold on to the vines, or you'll be flipped overboard," Chuck shouted over the sound of the crashing waves. The Semper Fidelis cried painfully as it lost a couple of its logs. Another wave hit us before we had a chance to recover from the first onslaught.

"Abandon ship!" I shouted, as the Semper Fidelis fell apart. The waves and the undertow were trying desperately to add us to their list of victims, but didn't succeed. One by one we helped each other onto the beach. We collapsed on the warm sand, completely spent.

Guadalcanal was secured as far as the Allies were concerned. During the peak of the war, the Japanese had over 36,000 troops on the island.

Of this total 14,800 were killed or missing, 9000 died of disease and 1,000 were taken prisoners. What happened to the rest of these troops no one knows. We could lessen this figure by five, but won't!

The Japanese stronghold in the Pacific was Rabaul, in the Bismarck Archipelago Group. It was located about 160 miles from Guadalcanal. At the time of the Japanese invasion, Australians, Melanesians, and Chinese traders inhabited Rabaul.

The great port of Rabaul was to become the center of activity in the Southwest Pacific. It became the headquarters for the Japanese fleet and its bastion, and totaled over 100,000 men at the peak of the war.

The Allies concentrated their efforts on Rabaul. The battles on Guadalcanal and Bougainville were only stepping stones to this fortress island. The recapture and neutralization of Rabaul was the objective of the Allied Forces.

Our nights on Guadalcanal, were interrupted by, an occasional nuisance raid. When these nuisance raids occurred it sent the island personnel scurrying into fox holes and dug outs. These solo raids were aimed at lowering the combat efficiency of our troops by loss of sleep and increase exposure to malaria. In addition to these nuisance raids, the mosquitoes gave us more trouble than these raids. We used to think that the common household mosquito, Culex Pipien, was bad, but not until we were introduced to the Anopheles quadrimaculatus on Guadalcanal.

This is the mosquito that carries the microscopic parasitic germ which killed over 9,000 Japanese soldiers on this island. These parasites are transmitted by the bite of an infected mosquito and so the mosquito was a bigger threat to us than the Japanese.

The symptoms of malaria are chills, fever and sweating. Six from our platoon came down with malaria and had to be rushed to sick bay. Once you're infected it takes anywhere from two to three weeks for complete recovery, assuming they have the right medication to kill these parasites.

To make sure we didn't come down with malaria we were ordered to take an Atabrine tablet with our meals every day. These yellow pills were very bitter and had a bad habit of dissolving almost instantaneously, when coming in contact with the saliva in one's mouth.

The trick was to swallow it very quickly, but if per chance it got stuck in your throat, the bitterness remained for the rest of the day. We hated taking these pills, but it was far better than coming down with malaria. These Atabrine tablets were so strong that we used them to dissolve the rust in our canteens.

"Look how yellow my skin is getting," Sammy noted. "My insides must be rusting out!" We all laughed, but we too were getting that Asian look.

Time waits for no one, even on an island like Guadalcanal. We were becoming quite accustomed to our island paradise and subconsciously were very happy with our lot. If our L.C.I. wasn't sunk and our orders lost, some of us would probably be six feet under by this time. We ate, played and slept. The two men in charge of our contingent were married men with families. They wanted to get out of this war alive, so consequently they weren't eager to leave this paradise and get their asses shot off by the Nips on Bougainville. Therefore, they left well enough alone. The Navy knew we were here and that's all that mattered.

We were entering our fifth week on Guadalcanal. The days were getting longer, perhaps because we were running out of things to do. One of our Gyrenes, caught a parrot a few weeks ago which he trained expertly. We marveled at "Squeakers" antics and were determined to catch a parrot for our quarters.

"How are we going to catch a parrot?" Sammy asked.

"I have no idea, but if we all think about it maybe one of us will come up with a plausible idea," I replied, as I put down the book I was reading.

Sam meanwhile thought so hard, that he fell asleep. I was about ready to wake him up when Chuck stopped me.

"Don't wake him up Lee, he'd probably want to shoot them down," he laughed.

"That's it!" Sammy shouted, as he bolted upright.

"Are you kidding Sam? One of our 30 caliber bullets would tear a parrot apart," Chuck replied.

"I agree," Sam responded, "that is if you hit it squarely, but if you were just to nick it, we could nurse it back to health. Just think how grateful the bird would be," Sam smiled.

"I think you've got rocks in your noggin Sam, but I'll go along with you, just to keep my trigger finger happy," he replied.

"How about you Lee?"

"Nah, count me out. There must be a better way." I surmised

"Well if you change your mind you'll know where to find us," they replied as they picked up their M1's and headed out for the jungle.

I must have fallen asleep, because I jumped about ten feet in the air when the firing started. I heard a burst of rifle fire followed by laughter, another burst of rifle fire, more laughter.

I couldn't stand it any longer so I picked up my ammo belt and M1 and headed out for the jungle. There they were laying flat on their backs shooting up at the parrots in the treetops.

"That one's a gonner," Chuck laughed, as a blue and white parrot plummeted to the ground."

I joined my buddies in this wild but enjoyable escapade. Pedro joined in too after he saw how much fun we were having. The parrots were screeching bloody murder and it was literally that.

Parrots were flying madly, never getting a chance to perch for more than a second before a round would singe their fathers. More and more of our coningent joined in, I even caught a glimpse of Sgt. Johnson blasting away.

Just then our fracas was interrupted by, a caravan of Jeeps that came storming into our camp area. An Army Colonel jumped out of the lead Jeep, a forty- five grasped firmly in his hand, as he approached us.

"What the hell are you men doing here?" he bellowed.

No one replied ! You could hear a pin drop.

"Who's in charge?" he shouted.

Lt. Werner stepped forward saluted the Colonel and said, "I am sir!"

"You still haven't answered my question. What the hell are these men doing here?"

"Our orders were lost, sir, and we're waiting for the Navy to find out where we were to be assigned."

"How long have you been here ?"

"Four weeks, Sir"

"FOUR WEEKS !" he screamed.

"Yes Sir!"

"My God!" the Colonel raved. "There's a raging battle going on in Bougainville and they're crying for replacements and where are their replacements? They're killing parrots instead of Japs on Guadalcanal.

Get your gear packed and be ready to ship out this afternoon. If I can't get a vessel to transport you to Bougainville, I'll row you over myself. Now get going!"

We double timed it to our tents and began to pack our gear.

"I guess the Army thought the Japs were invading the Canal again," Chuck laughed.

"Yeah, did you see that Colonel come storming down the road. I thought he was going to bust his gut!

Man was he "pissed" off. We kept packing!

That afternoon an L.C.M. (Landing Craft Mechanized) was waiting to take us to Bougainville. As we boarded the ship, we were greeted by Porky and Hillbilly. I guess the Navy thought they were well enough to be transferred back to our outfit. Needless to say we were very happy to see them.

LCM- Landing Craft Mechanized

"Did you guys get your Purple Hearts?" Chuck sarcastically asked?"

"Yeah! They said they'll mail them to us."

"Yeah right!" we all laughed.

We were now, pretty far out at sea, and when we looked back at Guadalcanal we had mixed emotions about leaving it.

Not only did we have fun and adventure on this island, but being lost here for almost a month, probably saved some of our lives. I wonder how much longer we would have remained on Guadalcanal if we didn't fire at those parrots. I guess we'll never know.

Chapter 17

As the L.C.M. churned its way towards Bougainville, a well-rested and somewhat perturbed group of Marines were eagerly awaiting their new assignment. All they knew is that they were assigned to Marine Air Group 24, which was now on Bougainville.

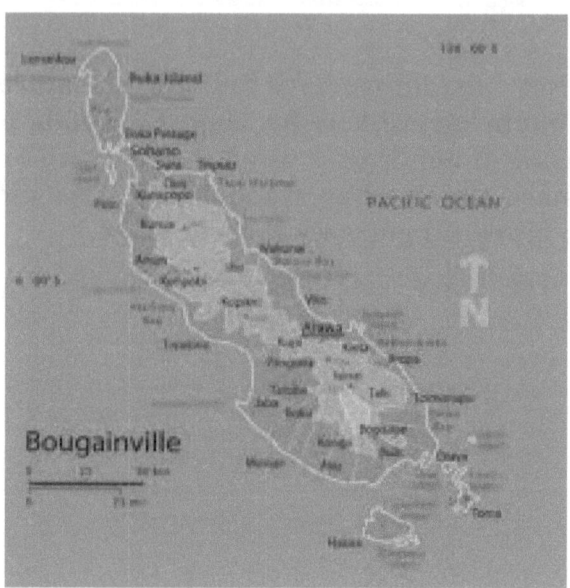

Bougainville – Solomon Islands

Bougainville was one of the islands that the allies had to occupy because it was so close to Rabaul, the headquarters of the Japanese Army in the South Pacific. The invasion of Bougainville was inevitable, as airfields closer to Rabaul were desperately needed. The only question confronting the Allied strategists at this time was where to strike. There were approximately 40,000 Japanese troops under the command of General Hyakutake. These troops were mainly concentrated at Buin and Shortland Islands in the south and at Buka in the north. The center of the slipper shaped island was inhabited by only a handful of Japanese soldiers.

To land in this area was hazardous as the beaches were very narrow and the waters poorly charted, and furthermore there weren't airfields in this area which the allies needed. The prize air strip on Bougainville was Kahili in the south but it was storming with Japanese troops.

After months of deliberation, it was agreed upon to land the 3rd Marine Division and the 2nd Raider Regiment at Cape Torokina in Empress Augusta Bay. They were to secure a beachhead approximately six by eight miles. The Naval C.B.s (Construction Battalion) were to follow the Marines with their construction equipment. They were assigned the gigantic task of building a temporary air strip as quickly as possible. From this strip, fighter planes as well as dive bombers would give close air support to the advancing Marines.

In order to confuse the Japanese, two preliminary invasions were scheduled for October 27, 1943. A small force of New Zealanders landed at Mono and Stirling Islands.

On midnight on the same day, the 2nd Parachute battalion landed at Choiseul Islands. The Japanese began preparations to send troops into these areas when they were caught flat footed by the unexpected Cape Torokima landing on Nov. 1, 1943. The beaches were bombed and strafed by our planes as our landing crafts headed for the narrow beachhead. The coral reefs tore off the bottoms of our landing crafts leaving about sixty of them stranded on the beach.

The Marines pushed onward under very adverse conditions. The dense jungle was reeking with mosquitoes, centipedes and enemy snipers. The Seabees meanwhile were working feverishly to complete the Torokima airfield. They were constantly harassed, by enemy planes and snipers. The native village nearby was called Piva, so the Seabees named the two air strips that they built Piva North and Piva South.

When General Hyakutake heard about these air strips that were being built at Cape Torokima, he realized that he was duped, so he had to save face. Having 40,000 troops at his disposal he knew these air strips had to be taken at any cost, because if they weren't, Rabaul would be constantly attacked by bombers operating from these air strips. Marine Air Group 24 was supposed to be operating from these air strips.

As we approached Bougainville, a couple of our destroyers were busily engaged in shelling the Torokima perimeter to make sure our debarkation was a safe one. A squadron of our Dive bombers flew overhead as our L.C.M. neared the beach. We quickly disembarked and were greeted by Master Sergeant Ryan. He looked as if he hadn't slept in days.

"All right playboys," he shouted, "better late than never! Get in those trucks and on the double!" he screamed.

We double-timed it to where the trucks were parked and began to board them.

The driver had the engine running, while his buddy scanned the skies. We quickly moved out!

As the trucks rumbled along, we couldn't help but notice a large wooden sign erected near the road. It was a rhymed tribute from the Marines to the Seabees. It read as follows:

"So when we reach the "Isle of Japan"
With our caps at a jaunty tilt
We'll enter the city of Tokyo
On the roads the Seabees built!"

Third Marine Division
2nd Raider Regiment

The Marines never got along with the Army or Navy but with the Seabees it was entirely different. These two outfits often fought side by side and each respected the others ability, be it fighting or constructing. You could always count on a Marine to come to the aid of a Seabee and vice versa.

The truck continued along its way, amidst the crack of rifle fire. An occasional big gun went off which shook the island. The guns as far as we knew belonged to the Army's 49th Coast Artillery Battalion and were used to keep the Japanese troops scattered. Every minute or so, one of these big babies went off! The noise was deafening, but after about ten salvos we were getting used to it.

The truck pulled into what looked like a camp area but we weren't too sure. The driver parked the truck under a large tree perhaps to conceal it from enemy planes. Sgt. Ryan jumped off the truck before it stopped and began to bark out orders.

"Get your butts out of that truck, find a tent and be out here with the following gear: Rifle, ammo, poncho, blanket, shovel, gas mask, change of underwear, and a couple of pairs of socks. Dismissed!"

We found a tent deeper in the jungle than the others and laid claim to it. The tent wasn't completely unoccupied. There was a rumpled sack with some gear on it situated near the entrance to a nearby foxhole.

"I wonder who our sack mate is?" Sammy asked as he looked at a picture of a gorgeous blond in a low cut dress.

"Maron! he drooled, in his best Italian style.

Because we were constantly being bombed, each person had to have a foxhole to jump into or sleep in when the alert was sounded. We were lucky in a sense, the former occupants dug them for us. The foxholes on Bougainville were constructed very sturdily. They were about five feet deep and were covered with heavy logs, canvas and earth.

There were two openings to every foxhole. One was for entering, the other for escaping gases. If a bomb exploded nearby, the concussion created by the rushing air would burst your ear drums, if this opening in the foxhole wasn't present. It also helped to circulate the stale air.

The cots were lined up in Boot camp style. Chuck, Sammy, Hillbilly, Porky, Pedro and myself placed our gear on each of the unoccupied cots in the tent, and then double timed it out with the gear Sgt. Ryan told us to bring.

"Hubba, Hubba," Sgt. Ryan bellowed, as we double-timed it to where he was standing. He was extremely nervous as he fidgeted with his Thompson Sub Machine gun. We couldn't help but notice that he had the type L drum attached; one that held 50 rounds of the 45 caliber ammo. He also had a 45 Caliber Automatic pistol slung from his hip. His stature was tall and lean similar to a poor man's, John Wayne. He looked haggard and beaten.

We waited for a few stragglers, and when everyone was present and accounted for Sgt. Ryan told us the bad news.

"Men, I don't know if you realize it but we've got a fight on our hands. The Japanese have thousands of troops massed someplace up in those hills which they are going to send down on us like a swarm of bees. The Army's XIV Corps and the 3rd Marine Defense Battalion are already dug in and waiting. The Army's Coast Artillery is blasting away at them intermittently. The Japanese are determined to knock out these air strips and drive us into the sea. Our job is to stop them!

There are thirteen miles of perimeter to cover and we have a part of that distance to protect. Before we move out there are a few things you have to know when you're in a combat zone. First of all you never congregate in groups. Secondly when you're moving through an open field or clearing you do so on the double.

Thirdly there is no saluting out here! We lost a good man to sniper fire because somebody saluted him. Don't wear shiny buttons or insignias unless you want to be picking daisies. Your rifle never leaves your side. Sleep with it! Eat with it! Crap with it! Nurse it! Baby it! It's your best friend and may save your life. Okay, let's move out!"

Marine Air Group 24 was organized into two infantry type battalions of four companies each. Since our group was expendable, we were taken to the front lines and told to dig in. The trained Marine Corps personnel who were needed to service the planes, were left to guard the air strips in case the Japanese got through the front lines.

"Hurry up and dig in," Sgt. Ryan ordered, as he scrambled from one group to another. We dug frantically!

"How deep do they want us to dig this hole?"Sammy asked breathlessly.

"I think big enough that the three of us can move around in, and sleep in, if we have to," I surmised

"Man that's going to take all day," Chuck added.

"Probably," I replied.

Well to our pleasant surprise, the ground was soft and sandy and easy to dig. It took us about two hours to dig a nice big foxhole and then we had to fill bags with the soil that we dug out and placed them around our fox hole. They were piled two high around the edges.

"That God Damn howitzer is going to rupture my eardrums," Sammy complained, as another projectile went hissing towards the enemy. The earth shook, the soil trickled back into our hole.

Porky, Hillbilly and Pedro were in another foxhole about fifteen yards to our left.

"How are you guys doing?"I shouted.

"Pretty good! How about you guys?" Porky asked.

"We're finished! We're resting now! " I replied.

"See any Japs yet?" Sammy jested.

"Not yet!" Hillbilly answered.

"You will!" Sergeant Ryan replied, as he crawled over to our fox hole.

"Nice hole, you got here! Any of you former grave diggers? he laughed.

"Yeah right! we sarcastically replied.

"The reason I'm here is to let you know what may happen at any time. The Japs will come running down that hill like raving maniacs. They'll be shouting and screaming, so don't let that scare you. We have barbed wire strung up out there to slow them down. If you see the enemy, you open fire, but don't waste your ammunition if you're not sure.

"How will we see them at night?" I asked.

"We're going to be shooting parachute flares into the air all night long,"Ryan remarked, "so don't worry about seeing the Japs, just don't let them get past you!"

"Where do we eat, sleep, go to the head and get extra ammo if we need it? Chuck wanted to know.

"We'll dump enough ration and ammo in your hole, to last you a couple of days. If you have to go to the head you dig a deep hole at the far end of your foxhole. If you have to sleep you have to do it in shifts. One person sleeps the other two are on watch. Got it? "

"Yes sir!" we replied.

"What if one of us gets shot, what do we do?" Sammy asked.

"Try to stop the bleeding, put a lot of Sulfur on the wound and shout for the Corpsman."

"What if we can't be heard, what then?"

"I don't know! Your guess is as good as mine," he answered, as he shook his head.

As we peered out of our foxhole, I couldn't help but think how much we resembled hunters in a blind waiting for the ducks to appear. The only difference is that these ducks shot back.

Just then it began to rain and our foxhole was getting wet.

"We better get a roof over our foxhole or we'll have our own swimming pool," Chuck remarked.

"Cover me guys while I get some branches," I said, as I crawled into the jungle looking for some sturdy branches. When I returned, I dropped the branches into our foxhole, where they were cut, trimmed and bent into a canopy. We then joined our ponchos together, placed them over the bent branches and lo and behold, we had ourselves a roof.

We soon found out, that on Bougainville it rained every afternoon. Not very long, but it rained.

It wasn't very long afterwards that the Japanese opened up with their artillery. They were dropping 75mm and 150 mm shells on our air strips.

Three F4U's and a one B24 bomber were destroyed and countless other planes damaged. The shells were hissing over our heads, landing in M.A.G. 24's camp area. Countless number of Gyrenes and Seabees were also killed by this barrage.

"You know what? I think we're safer here in this foxhole than back in the camp area?" Sammy surmised.

"Maybe you're right Sam, but I think they'll be dropping a few our way before the night is over don't you think?" I remarked.

"Yeah!" he replied.

No truer words were ever spoken!

As night fell, the first parachute flare was shot up into the air. When it reached a certain height it burst into a brilliant flame and slowly descended to the ground. When it hit the ground another flare was sent up. This went on all night long. After a few flares were sent up our eyes began to play tricks on us. We began to imagine that we saw something out there, when we really didn't. Out of the hundreds of men on the front line, all it took was for one individual to fire his rifle, and he was immediately joined by others. It took about 10 minutes for us to realize that no one was out there.

Meanwhile the warm damp jungle was teeming with mosquitoes. They were biting us unmercifully, which caused us to itch and scratch. Luckily we were taking Atabrine so we didn't have to worry about coming down with Malaria. To make matters even worse, the noise from our artillery was rocking our brains, against our skulls. There was no sense talking ! No one could hear you!

We waited nervously for the Japs to appear, but they didn't! Approximately 200 shells were dropped on our air strips before the night was over. We stayed awake all night waiting for an attack that never came. I fell asleep standing up with my rifle resting on a sand bag. The noise no longer bothered me. I just wanted to sleep. I was rudely awakened, from my deep sleep by Sammy.

"Here they come!" he shouted, as a swarm of Japanese soldiers came storming down the hill, screaming "Banzai ! Banzai !" whatever that meant?

"Don't shoot until they run into the barbed wire," Chuck reminded us. We didn't have to wait long before a fleet footed Jap got entangled in it.

"Now! Chuck shouted, and as we fired, we all must have aimed at this one poor soul because he went down onto the barbed wire like a sack of potatoes. The rest of the enemy slowed down a bit when they saw the barbed wire, but it was too late. They were caught in a crossfire and didn't have a chance.

We were picking "em" off like you would the toy soldiers at a County fair, only instead of an air rifle, we had the real thing. I caught a glimpse of a Jap about ready to throw a grenade our way, so I quickly placed a round into his neck. As he toppled backwards the grenade blew his hand off his arm.

Just then a grenade almost rolled into our foxhole.

"Hit the deck!" I shouted, as I saw a Jap throw a grenade our way.

It wasn't a second too soon. We quickly dropped to our knees and hugged the wall as the grenade exploded above our heads, tearing our roof to shreds and sending shrapnel in every direction.

"Man that was close!" we shakingly gasped.

The Japanese continued to come down the hill, shouting Banzai! My rifle bore was red hot, from all the rounds that went through it. Finally they stopped coming. Now they were lobbing mortar shells at our positions. I don't know how many men we lost from these mortars but by the movement of the Corpsmen, a lot. We were lucky, the six of us survived this first day of "The Battle of The Perimeter."

The skies meanwhile were filled with our dive bombing planes, flying sortie after sortie in an attempt to knock out their well concealed gun positions.

Sgt. Ryan asked for some air support when the Japanese were really getting close to breaking through our lines.

He asked for some bombs to be dropped on the enemy but because the front lines were so close together it was imperative that the pilots know exactly where the enemy was. To make it easy for the pilots we would shoot a white smoke flare above their positions and that's where the pilots dropped their bombs. The Japanese caught on to this tactic and began to shoot white smoke flares over our positions which confused our pilots. It has been known that many of our troops were killed by this procedure only in this case the bombs weren't dropped. It wasn't until we shot violet colored flares over the Jap positions that the planes silenced the mortar crews.

Close air support between the ground forces and air force really came into its own on Bougainville. The Japanese artillery was concealed behind steep hills which were designated by foot altitudes. The hills were numbered 111, 150, 250, 500, 501, 600, 1,000, 111, etc. The planes had to knock out "Pistol Pete" the Japanese artillery as he was called.

Our job was defensive. "Thou shalt not pass" was our motto.

The Marine Air Corps was given specific orders by the Commanding Officer to evacuate their planes for the night to Barakoma, Munda, and Green Islands. The Japanese knew that the planes didn't fly at night so they bombed the hell out of air strips knowing full well that they couldn't be protected.

Marston mats which covered Piva North and Piva South were bombed every night by the Japanese trying desperately to shut us down. Each morning the ground crew had to remove the mangled mats, fill the shell holes, and put in new mats before our planes could land. Each morning our planes would return to bomb and strafe the enemy before landing on the Piva air strips.

They flew their sorties from the Piva air strips continuously, trying desperately to knock out Pistol Pete.

Tons upon tons of bombs were dropped on gun positions around hills, 111,150,190,500 and 600. In the evening our planes left for Barakoma, Munda and Green Islands and Pistol Pete returned.

The Japanese would do most of their bombings by night because when they fired their canons during the day, with every salvo, there was a puff of smoke emitted. This smoke showed us where these canons were located and so we sent out our bombers to blow them off the mountain.

Since the Japanese didn't do very well with their early morning charge, our Sergeant told us that afternoon, to eat our K rations and get a little sleep because tonight they're going to throw everything at us including the kitchen sink.

We ate our dry crackers and opened up a can of Spam and washed it down with some water from our canteen. We slept that afternoon in shifts. One of us would sleep, the other two would be on guard duty.

The area in front of our fox holes was pretty wide open and without the early morning mist, we could see all the dead Japanese soldiers that were draped over the barbed wire fences.

Sammy and I were on guard duty while Chuck slept. The days on Bougainville were hot and humid and today was no exception. Mosquitoes thrived in this climate, and they especially liked damp foxholes with sleeping Marines. The mosquitoes didn't bother Chuck, the artillery did! With every blast from one of their large guns he groaned as if he were in pain.

I looked over the dead bodies in front of me, while Sam was going to the bathroom. Out of the corner of my eye I saw something moving. My eyes must be playing tricks on me I thought, as I tried to shake the cobwebs from my brain. I set my sights on the dead Jap and waited. He didn't move! I relaxed.

As I stood there looking through my peep site, thoughts of Rita and our last night together brought tears to my eyes.

I may never see her again, I thought, when all of a sudden I thought I saw that dead Jap move again. I must be cracking up! I rubbed my eyes and shook my head. I was determined, once and for all, to make certain that dead Jap was actually dead. I set my sight on him and waited. He didn't move! I waited! The Jap was lying on his stomach with his arms outstretched in front of him.

"He's dead!"I said, under my breath.

Just then I thought I caught a slight movement forward. Sure enough, the Jap moved! He was not dead! He was playing possum!

He was inching forward like an asp and must have traversed at least ten yards since I last looked at him. He held something in his right hand.

"It's a grenade!" I almost shouted aloud.

The Jap was too close for comfort. If I missed him with my first shot I may not get a another chance.

"Can't let him get any closer! I thought.

The Jap inched closer. I lined up my peep sight on his forehead and then remembering my rifle instructors, I took a deep breath, squeezed the trigger like I would a little 'ole tit and the next thing I knew the rifle fired; The Jap collapsed. The round entered the top of his skull killing him instantaneously. His grasp on the grenade weakened; the explosion blew the fingers off his hand.

"Sammy did you see that Jap I just blew away? He tried to throw a grenade into our fox hole" I shouted.

"Yeah right!" Sammy answered, as he continued to sit on the make shift commode we made for our fox hole. Chuck wasn't impressed either! He never woke up! The Battle of the Perimeter subsided for a few hours. The enemy hid their artillery in caves during the day, and dragged them out during the night. Our planes had trouble knocking out these guns because they were hidden so well.

It seems that the Marine Raiders will have to climb up there and use their flamethrowers and grenades to get them out of these caves. Very shortly afterwards, it was starting to get dark. When we couldn't see the dead bodies any more, The Army began shooting up the parachute flares. The Japanese countered with their cannons. Our planes were long gone, but the Japanese barrage on our strips was tearing up the Marston mats on Piva North and Piva South.

"It won't be long now!" Sammy shouted above the roar of the artillery, "they're probably getting ready to attack!"

"If I don't make it," Chuck shouted, "I wan't you to tell my familythat I love them and I'm not afraid to die."

"Knock it off Chuck, we're going to make it! Think positively!" I shouted. The mosquitoes were out in full force but the Japs weren't! Their mortar crews were getting too close for comfort.

After shelling us for about an hour, the Japanese made their move. They charged down and around the ridge like raving maniacs.

"Banzai! Banzai! They screamed.

The enemy blended in with their dead brethren. We were pumping lead into every torso out there; living or dead! My rifle was getting so hot I had to wrap my jacket around it. It was a good thing we had that barbed wire out there to stop them, otherwise I'm afraid to think what would have happened to us.

"Bastard Yankee! You die!" was the cry. We didn't want to! They kept coming! We kept shooting! The Japs finally stopped coming. I don't know if we killed them all or if they took off for the hills. I didn't care! I was a bundle of nerves! I felt dizzy, my hands were trembling, and I felt nauseous, I puked!

For all practical purposes "The Battle of the Perimeter" was over! We lost about 20 men from our contingent, mostly due to mortar fire. If one of these mortars fell into your foxhole, it would explode upon impact, killing everyone inside. We had some close calls but lucked out.

The Battle of the Perimeter cost General Hyakutake pretty close to 6000 troops as compared to 300 for the Allies. He had thousands of troops still present in the hills but in no condition to fight. Their rice rations fell from a high of 750 grams per day to a low of 200 during the battle. After the battle he could have surrendered but he decided to stay up in the hills with his troops, growing rice and vegetables, and plan for another offensive in May.

From the prisoners we captured, we acquired the following information. The canons that they used, had to be hauled piece by piece over grueling jungle trails.

It was a tremendous undertaking as more Japanese artillery was concentrated here than anyplace else in the South Pacific. Each 100 pound shell for example took two men four days to carry.

General Hyakutake's troops approached the perimeter from the North, Northwest and East. His ultimate objective was the Torokima airstrip located on the beach, but in order to do so, our two strips, Piva North and Piva South had to be taken first. He was determined to avenge the defeat of his troops on Guadalcanal. In fact, he was so certain of victory that the area of our surrender was already designated on captured maps. The General evidently wasn't familiar with the oft spoken proverb-
"Don't count your chickens until they're hatched!"
The Allies weren't concerned with driving the Japanese off the island. Their objective was to operate the existing airstrips for strikes on Rabaul. The enemy was beaten, hungry and scattered. We didn't expect any trouble from them as long as they remained this way.
To maintain this type of existence, our T.B.F's sprayed diesel oil and dropped "Napalm" petroleum bombs on their gardens every day. These sorties were called "Potato Runs" and the pilots hated these sorties because they were greeted with rifle fire as they approached. Needless to say, many a pilot and gunner were shot down.
As soon as the Battle of the Perimeter was over, a lot of our troops were killed, or injured because they went looking for souvenirs. Little did they know that there were a lot of unexploded grenades in the hands of these Japanese soldiers and when they turned them over to take their rifle or sword, the grenade exploded.
The Commanding Officer of our area issued an order. Any man going into war zone looking for souvenirs will be shot on the spot by the sentries on duty!

No questions asked! Even though the Japs were beaten, there were thousands of them still in the hills that we had to be concerned about. We didn't want to have our throats slit when we were sleeping. To prevent this from happening, the Army posted guards along this 13 mile perimeter.

The dead Japanese soldiers in this war zone, were beginning to decay and the stench was unbearable. Since no one wanted to go in there, for fear of some bomb going off, the Seabees came in with their bulldozers and dug a huge grave. The dead bodies were counted, dog tags removed and their dead bodies were deposited into this huge grave.

Even though we defeated the Japanese in the Battle of the Perimeter the war was far from over. With over 10,000 Japanese still up in the hills, and their canons and snipers still very active we could be picked off by a sniper at any time. Consequently no one walked !

Chapter 18

When the Allies were convinced that the Battle of the Perimeter was over, our contingent of Marines were relieved from the front lines by the Army. We were instructed by Sgt. Ryan to go back to our camp area and get some sleep.

Our camp area, during the Battle of the Perimeter, was shelled unmercifully. There were shell holes everywhere. Our tent was destroyed as well as all the cots that were in the tent, but our fox holes were intact.

As the six of us looked at the remains of our tent, we were startled by a disheveled figure emerging from one of the foxholes. I've never seen six faster rifles. We drew a bead on him before he took another step.

"Hi!" he greeted us.

"The bastards drunk!" Sammy noted.

"What are you doing here?" Chuck asked.

"What do you mean, what am I doing here?" he slurred.

"What are you guys doing here?" he mumbled.

"Oh you must be our tent mate," I said, as I extended my hand.

"The names Lee Walewander."

"Hi Lee, my names John Jarston, but my friends call me "Cookie"

"Don't tell me you're a cook," Porky replied, almost gleefully.

"Yeah, but since there was nothing for me to cook they stuck me in the front lines with you guys."

"Do you know you're drunk, John?" I informed him.

"I hope so! I want to forget what I went through."

"Where'd you get the booze?" Sammy asked. "I could use a shot right now!"

"Can you keep a secret?" Cookie asked.

" Sure!" we all replied.

"I make my own !" he boastfully replied.

"How?" We looked around to see if there was something here that we didn't see.

"Follow me!" He sheepishly beckoned to us.

We dropped into the foxhole he previously emerged from. It was a lot larger than we were accustomed to. In the center was a good-sized crate covered with canvas. A candle, a beat up deck of cards, and four empty boxes were present, but no booze. The disappointment was written all over our faces, but even though we didn't see any "gootch" the place smelled like a brewery.

Cookie lifted the canvas that covered one side of the wall and lo and behold another smaller foxhole was evident.

"Well frost my balls if he doesn't have a still in there! Hillbilly smiled, "Reminds me of home."

We soon learned that Cookie was a bootlegger in his youth and was supposed to have made the best bathroom gin this side of Brooklyn. Obviously, he learned his trade very well!

Being a cook, he had access to pots, pans and the necessary ingredients for making the best "booze" this side of the Canal. In one deep pan, which was hissing back at us, he had water, apple peelings, sugar and yeast. In another pan he had water, sugar, raisins and yeast.

"This is my favorite," he burped. His alcoholic breath rocked us back on our heels. I felt tipsy already.

"What'll it be gentleman?" Cookie asked, pretending to be a waiter.

"I'll have Scotch on the Rocks!" Sammy jested as he removed his canteen cup from its holster.

"Make mine a Manhattan!" I replied.

"Do you have Tequila?" Pedro asked.

"How about a Mint Julep?" Hillbilly asked

Porky ordered a shot of straight whiskey while Chuck wanted a Rob Roy.

Cookie dipped Sam's canteen cup into one of the pans and handed it to him. It was heaping full! "Enjoy!" Cookie grinned as he proceeded to fill each of our requests from the same container.

"Chug a lug Sam," we shouted.

Sammy was reluctant to do so, but he finally mustered enough nerve to sip a little bit of this elixir.

"Not bad!" he gasped, as he rolled his eyes and pounded his chest.

Meanwhile, Cookie was filling all of our canteen cups to capacity. I shut my eyes, held my nose and swallowed a mouthful. It was like I was drinking acid, it burned so much. The second mouthful didn't burn which made me continue to drink. I wanted to get drunk and forget what we went through the last three days. Maybe when I wake up, I'll wake up next to Rita and this was just a bad dream.

"Hey Cookie this stuff is pretty good! It tastes like wine!" Sammy exclaimed.

"Yeah, it's pretty darn good if I have to say so myself," Chuck replied as he licked his chops.

"Drink up guys, I want to get rid of this batch before the revenue agents come around," he laughed.

We sat down on some of the crates in the larger foxhole, lit a candle and began to drink, laugh, and sing :

> "Oh the biscuits that they serve us
> They say they're very fine
> One rolled off the table
> And killed a pal of mine
> Oh I don't want to _ _ _ _ _ _ _ etc."

The pots and pans were empty but for a few worms that squirmed amidst the apple peelings. The candle flickered and long since died while the seven of us passed out and were deep in the arms of Morpheus.

We were awakened not by a bugler, but by a 150mm bomb exploding nearby. The explosion rattled us to such an extent that, we forgot where we were.

I felt like shit! My head was throbbing like someone was in there, trying desperately to get out. I never experienced a hangover before and if this is what it's like I don't think I'll ever drink this much again, ever!

As we emerged from the fox hole we were informed by Master Sergeant Ryan that this afternoon we would get our new assignments.

"I hope they don't stick us in the front lines again" Porky pondered.

"No I don't think they will," I replied. "The Army took over that job and we'll have to do something around the air strips." I replied.

Well for a change, I was right. We were assigned to the Guard Company.

Captain Connors was the Commander of the Guard Company. He was sitting at a table when we entered his tent. We stood at attention, waiting for him to complete what he was doing.

"At ease men!" he said. "First of all let me congratulate you on the great job you did on the front lines. But now you have an even tougher job. As a guard you will be asked to guard and protect the property and personnel of Marine Air Group 24.

As you know there are a lot of unhappy Japanese soldiers up in those hills and they're going to try to booby trap our planes and kill the pilots and mechanics during the night. Every night someone is found dead in their foxholes or some fire breaks out on our base.

Some of you will also guard the few Japanese prisoners that we have and also protect the cooks and bakers during the night when they're baking bread."

As he spoke, his low guttural voice likened itself to a frog croaking for his mate. His eyes bulged out and watered profusely. He wiped them constantly! He was above average in height and weight. His hawk like nose and wispy hair added to his ruddy countenance.

"And one more thing, before I dismiss you. Don't salute any officers on this base, is that clear?"

"Yes Sir!" we shouted.

After being dismissed, the Corporal of the Guard assigned us various duties.

The Guard Detachment was located at the entrance to our camp. It consisted of five tents and a circular stockade or brig. The stockade was fenced in by a wire mesh and was about ten feet high. Two guards circled the enclosure, constantly.

Chuck and I, were escorted by the Corporal of the Guard, to the stockade, where we proceeded to relieve the two patrolling guards.

"Don't let those yellow bellied bastards talk to one another," The Cpl. of the Guard told us. "They're being interrogated by intelligence and we don't want them to get their stories straight."

"Roger!" we replied.

No sooner had we taken over when the Nips began to jabber.

"Knock it off," we shouted as we began to poke our bayonets into their butts.

The Japs jabbered even more, but this time is sounded like good old bitching.

"Zip your lips," we shouted again, only this time we demonstrated the motion.

There were ten of them in the stockade at this time and a few more on work detail. The prisoners were kept busy at all times. In addition to filling up the crater holes on our air strips, they were presently digging fox holes and latrines in Officers quarters.

As we patrolled the stockade, I noticed the prisoners looking toward the hills for salvation. This made me very uneasy.

"Hey Chuck, what's to prevent a sniper from taking us out?"

Chuck looked around and replied, "Nothing!"

"Well I don't know about you, but the way they keep looking up at the hills I think we may be in a snipers scope right now," I added.

"What do you think we should do?"

"Well let's not walk around the stockade. Let's keep the prisoners in front of us at all times, so the snipers can't get a good bead on us."

"Good idea, Lee !" We proceeded accordingly.

During daylight hours, Pistol Pete stayed in his cave and was well concealed. At night he would emerge like a nocturnal predator, delivering death and destruction everywhere. The Allies were depending on Air Power to knock out the Jap artillery, as it would be suicide to send the infantry up those hills. The Navy helped out on occasions by shelling the hills from their ships. It was just a matter of time before Pistol Pete was silenced for good. We bided our time.

The Marston mats which covered M.A.G.'s 24's air strips were damaged every night. Each morning ground crews had to remove the mangled mats, fill the shell holes, and put in new mats before our planes could land. At night we guarded the air fields, during the day we put our prisoners to work, to repair them.

Since this was going to be our home for some time to come, we were told that we could write a letter home to our loved ones. We couldn't say where we were, only that we were some place in the South Pacific area.

The letters we sent were all checked by certain officers whose job it was to read every letter and cut out or delete any message that would tell the Japanese our whereabouts and what we are doing.

I wrote two letters, one to my family and one to Rita. I didn't say much just that I was fine and the food was terrible!

Since our deposition on this fair island, many changes have taken place. With the help of the Seabees and prisoners, M.A.G. 24 now had a mess hall. It wasn't too large, but it did give the cooks a chance to bake some bread and heat up a few cans of Spam. The lower half of the mess hall was submerged underground, the upper half covered with logs and sandbags.

The first day the mess hall opened there wasn't a schedule prepared. A big line formed outside its door. A couple of Officers tried to disperse us but to no avail! The aroma of freshly baked bread filled the air; it was too much for our deprived vitals. A well placed mortar by the Japs could take out at least twenty of us. We all knew it! And we're willing to take this chance for a fresh slice of homemade bread.

The doors opened, the chow line was no longer orderly. The mob was trying desperately to enter when it happened. A couple of snipers picked off a couple of Marines and before long bedlam broke loose. There were mess kits strewn all over the area, as Marines began to fire into the tree tops. The results were gratifying! First a pair of binoculars fell out of the tree, followed by two rifles and two dead Japs.

Snipers usually come in pairs, so when two dropped out of the tree tops, we picked up our mess gear and double timed it to the mess hall. Our first warm meal consisted of two slices of bread, some warmed over Spam, dehydrated potatoes and peas. We washed it down with warm coffee. We ate our meal behind a large palm tree.

On the night of March 18, 1944, Hillbilly and I we're patrolling Officer's quarters. We didn't like this assignment because of some of the crap that we had to take from some of the officers.

Many of them insisted on smoking during the blackout or playing cards by lantern light. Most of the officers followed the rules but there were some that thought they were above the law. One Captain in particular was a real ass hole. He insisted on playing cards with his buddies, every night, by lantern light during the blackout. The reason we had a blackout was not to give the Japs a target to shoot at during the night. After all they still had canons and mortars at their disposal.

"Knock off the light in there!" I shouted.

"Get lost!" Was their reply.

A Smokey beam of light poured out from the foxhole. The card players were drinking, smoking and telling jokes.

"Lights out!" I shouted once more.

The same reply, "Get lost!"

"Dirty rotten bastards," I said under my breath. I should shoot that fuckin lantern but they'll bring me up on charges, I surmised. I disgustedly kicked some dirt into their fox hole and went on my way.

Then it happened, a couple of mortar shells came flying out of the jungle and exploded around their foxhole. I hit the deck when I heard the shells whistling above my head.

The explosions were too close for comfort and as I laid there for about a minute, I heard some groaning sounds coming from where their fox hole was located. I was sure that these assholes were hit, deservingly so. But when I got there they were still playing cards oblivious to the shells that exploded nearby. My next thought was Billy.

"Billy!" I shouted. "Are you all right?"

No answer!

"Billy! Are you hurt?"

No answer!

I frantically began searching for my buddy, when I heard a faint wail arising from behind a tree.

"Lee, I've been hit! He cried. "I hurt all over!"

I quickly fired three fast rounds into the air, waited a few seconds and fired three more. This was our signal for the Cpl. of the Guard to get his ass out here.

I reached down to help my stricken buddy when my hands felt his warm blood oozing out of his wounds. I took off my dungaree jacket, rolled it up in a ball and placed it under his head.

"Lee am I going to die?" he sobbed, as he asked me.

"No you're not! The Corpsman will be here in a minute. Hang in there!" I cried.

Tears were rolling down my cheeks like water pouring over falls.

"Look Lee, look how light it's getting. Isn't that a beautiful sight!"

I looked around to see if I were missing anything. I wasn't! It was pitch black"

"Oh look how beautiful it is up here! He said almost joyfully. Goodbye Lee, I'll be seeing you and don't forget to -------------------."

"Billy! Don't go! Don't leave me!" I cried.

I was still crying when the Cpl. of the Guard finally found us. I've never ever had any one die in my arms before and I didn't like it. We placed Hillbilly's body in the jeep to take him to sick bay. It was too late! Billy's war was over.

"Lee, I'll have a relief out here for you in a about ten minutes, so hang in there."

When the jeep pulled away I was so pissed off at those"Mother Fuckin Officers" that I felt like blowing their fuckin heads off. I walked over to the fox hole lifted the flap and said :

"Lights out gentlemen!" and proceeded to empty my clip into the lantern. It went out!

Hillbilly's funeral took place the next day. With all the casualties we had out here, the Seabees cleared some land so we could have our own cemetery. The five of us paid our last respects to our departed southern friend. A simple white cross was placed at the head of his grave.

"Pleasant sack time Billy," I said under my breath, as our jeep began to pull out of the consecrated area. "Sleep peacefully, until Gabriel blows reveille."

That afternoon I was told to escort a couple of Japanese prisoners to Intelligence Headquarters.

"All right let's move out! I gestured waving my 45 in front of their eyes. They looked frightened!

"Move out!" I shouted, as I nudged them along. I wasn't in the mood to be fucked with!

Whenever we escorted prisoners, whether it be to chow, work details or to the head, we did so on the double and remained about six feet behind them. We brandished our 45's, hoping at times that they would make a break for it.

Today was no exception, in fact after what happened last night, I was praying for one of them to have guts enough to run. My prayers were answered, but somewhat indirectly!

A squad of Line Company Marines were crapped out alongside the dusty road when I approached with my prisoners. I nonchalantly waved to them, when a short burst from a B.A.R. dropped my prisoners.

"Who fired those shots? I shouted as I looked down at my two dead prisoners.

"Sorry Mac!"a dirty, unshaven, haggard, Private replied, "My trigger finger slipped!

"Yeah Right!" I cut in angrily. "I'm responsible for these two dead bastards, so get your ass off the deck and come with me to the guard house unless you want to join them."

The Sergeant in charge of the squad stepped forward in defense of the Private.

"Don't get your balls in an uproar," The Sgt. remarked. "It's only a couple of dead Japs. The hills are filled with them! You want a couple of replacements?" he smirked.

"That's not the point! These two were officers and they were to be interrogated to see what the rest of them are up to."   -248-

"Sorry! We didn't know? Our motto is "The only good Jap is a dead Jap!""

I was really pissed off, but they finally complied with my orders. They picked up my dead prisoners and accompanied me back to the Guard Company. I reported the incident to the Cpl. of the Guard who in turn reported it to Captain (Frogy) Connors. He chewed them out, put them on report, and made them bury the dead.

Guard duty at night was especially dangerous. Since the Army patrolled the thirteen mile perimeter the Japanese Raiders would attack us from the sea which was unguarded.

They would use rafts to sneak into our camp area and slit the throats of pilots and airplane mechanics as they slept. Their purpose was to kill deftly and quietly. They often dropped live grenades into foxholes housing sleeping Marines. As guards our job was to protect our sleeping mates.

Tonight I wasn't patrolling the beach, I pulled guard duty in the enlisted men's area.

As I was making the rounds, I heard a hissing sound.

"Psst, hey Guard ! Psst, hey Guard!"

I cocked my rifle and took cover behind a tree.

"Psst, hey Guard ! Psst, hey Guard !"

I recognized one of our mechanics beckoning to me from his foxhole. I didn't know what the hell he wanted, as I carefully walked towards him.

"What is it?" I quietly asked.

"Would you like a pancake?" he whispered.

"Pancake?"

"Yeah, come on in. I've got a sea bag full of pancakes."

"Oh no!" I said to myself. Another victim, for the Psycho ward. As one can imagine seeing all the dead and your buddies being shot and blown up, a lot of these Marines crack up and lose their minds.

I reported him to the Cpl. of the Guard and the mechanic was surveyed, pancakes, seabag and all. He was sent back to the states to get Psychiatric help.

The following night I was to patrol the area around the mess hall. The moon was especially bright tonight, ideal conditions for snipers. The mess hall was out in the open, so it was easy to guard. After I was thoroughly convinced that the bakers weren't in immediate danger, I dropped down into a nearby fox hole and stood watch from there. Every half hour or so, I would scramble across the clearing to check on them.

"How's it going?"

"Pretty good Lee!" they replied as they removed crispy brown bread from a large oven. I guess the baker's knew, from the way I licked my chops, I was hoping they would offer me a slice or two. They didn't disappoint me! I took them back to my foxhole and indulged. Nights on Bougainville were very eerie. There were certain birds that screeched like new- born babies.

If one didn't know any better, he would swear that there were abandoned babies somewhere in the jungle.With the birds crying, mortar shells dropping and sniper fire made me extremely jittery. My post tonight was the entrance to Officer's Quarters. A wide dirt road ran alongside this entrance and my duty was to walk this road back and forth for about 100 yards. On one side of the road was where the officers slept and on the other side a dense jungle that was eyeing me suspiciously.

I walked up the road a piece and then darted into the shadows. I'll be damned, if I'm going to walk down that road in bright moonlight, I thought, "after all there's a pretty red head waiting for me in San Diego, so why press my luck."I looked around for a good vantage point and found one, up in a tree. My view was perfect! I could see everything in either direction clearly. I tried to make myself comfortable for what I assumed would be a long vigil.

Pistol Pete and the Army artillery were exchanging calling cards while I fidgeted for a better sitting position. I was in the process of descending when I caught a glimpse of a darting crouching figure. He double timed it across the road and disappeared into officer's quarters.

"Oh shit! Who the fuck was that? I better find him before he kills somebody," I thought, but how will I find him in the darkness. What if he sees me first? Should I challenge him or just shoot him? The password today was "Macy's Basement."

All these thoughts were racing through my mind as I moved out slowly and very cautiously! The bright moonlight helped me see, somewhat.

"He's around here somewhere," I thought when all of a sudden a figure appeared from behind a tree.

"Halt! Who goes there?"

"No answer!"

"Who goes there?" I shouted once more.

"Fliend!" was the sick reply.

"What's the password?"

"No answer!"

We were always told that once you ask someone for the password, and they don't answer immediately, start firing your rifle. Meanwhile my legs were shaking like two plucked guitar strings. I was afraid it could be one of our pilots or gunners so I didn't fire immediately. But before I could get a chance to see him, he jumped out towards me as I fired. The bullet stopped him.

I then fired three rounds into the air, waited a few seconds and fired three more. The Cpl. of the Guard and a few more guards were there in a matter of minutes.

"What's up Lee?"

"I think I just killed a Jap," I stammered.

The two guards flashed their flashlights on the suspect and murmured-

"You're right Lee it's a Jap!

"Joe why don't you take over for Lee, I think he could use a break"

When the word got around that I killed this Jap in Officer's quarters I had the next day off! No guard duty!

The following afternoon, Chuck, Sammy and I were cleaning our rifles when a Catholic chaplain entered our tent.

"Ten Shun! I shouted in true Boot Camp style.

"As you were," he remarked warmingly.

"My names Father Christafano. I was passing by your tent when I overheard you fellows beating your gums. I just had to drop in and give you this," he said, as he began passing out what looked like a business card. The message read:

Sympathy Chit

The recapitulation of your trials and tribulations touches me deeply. Your burdens are more than any human being should be forced to endure. I fear the combined concentration on your troubles will cause my morale to snap and my heart to break! I can't take it!

This sympathy chit, when presented to your Chaplain, will entitle you to one hour of Spiritual Consolation.

Father Christafano
Office Hours : Any old time !

Lt. Christafano was a Catholic chaplain assigned to M.A.G. 24. He was young, witty and extremely handsome. He looked more like a movie star than a priest. We wondered why a young man, like himself, would devote his life to the priesthood, especially someone like Father Christafano who seemed to have it all.

"I guess priests are like pilots," Chuck surmised. "It takes a special kind of man to fly planes and a special type of man to devote his life to God.

"Jesus Christ!! He can have it lopped off and it wouldn't make any difference to him, would it?" Sammy reckoned.

"Yeah!" we nodded affirmatively.

All of a sudden we heard someone shouting, "Mail Call! Mail Call!" We haven't had mail in over three months, so everyone was ecstatic!

Gyrenes were pouring out of their fox holes, mess hall, tents and even the latrines. Master Sergeant Ryan was reading off and passing out the mail. My take consisted of fourteen letters and two packages. I hurried to our tent, sorted out Rita's letters according to dates and began with the first.

My dearest Lee:

I don't know how to begin this letter, as I'm too broken hearted to think straight. I was happily working at the hospital when I received your Special Delivery letter. From the number of stamps on it, plus the fact that it was written hastily, I immediately knew what it was about.

Oh my darling, If you only knew how upset I became. I cried convulsively and any attempt to concentrate on my duties, was for naught. My superiors noted that I was a basket case so they told me to take the rest of the day off.

-        As I'm writing this letter, the moments we spent together all pass in review. Without you my dearest, life would not be worth living. If for one minute I thought that you wouldn't come back to me, I too would bid this world adieu.

My dearest Lee, I love you with all my heart and soul. I shall love you always and will wait for you eternally. Please be careful my darling and don't try to be a hero.   With all my love,

Rita

P.S. I'll try to write every day.

I re-read the first letter, before I opened the second. It was so refreshing to hear from Rita. After all there is nothing like a letter from your loved ones to bolster one's morale. For month's I thought that Rita was a figment of my imagination, but as I read her scented letters, I knew she was for real. I could smell the perfume she uses on her letter.

Just then Chuck came in off guard duty and wanted to know if there was any mail for him. I casually pointed to a stack of letters and a package that were on his cot and continued reading my mail.

Rita's first few letters were sorrowful and reminiscent. They progressively got more informative, telling me about her training as a Naval Nurse, and about her sister June, and her marriage to Van.

When I held her letter in my hand, I felt like she was there with me, perfume smell and all.

The letters from home were of the usual variety; be careful son! We're praying for you, etc. The packages I received contained cookies, a fruit cake, and some reading material. The cookies we're water logged, but the fruitcake was delicious. Porky ate most of it!

Chapter 19

The next few days were serene. The enemy was up to something! We haven't been shelled for a couple of days, nor were we attacked, by its ground forces. The scuttlebutt had it that the enemy was massing its troops for one last attack. General Hyakutake was either going to drive us into the sea or commit "Hara Kiri". The latter appealed to us.

On March 23, 1944, Sergeant Ryan broke out M.A.G. 24 for last minute instructions.

"Men he said, we have it on good authority that the Japanese will attack us tonight with all the force they can muster. We have to go back to the front lines and help out the Army. We have the same sector of the 13 mile perimeter to cover so you know what we expect you to do.

They are going to hit us with everything they have and if they don't succeed they'll probably surrender or commit suicide. We're going to leave here at 1400 hours except the following men. He began to read off the names of mechanics, radiomen, tinsmiths, etc., the guard company wasn't included.

"Looks like we're expendables again," Chuck remarked.

"Yeah, Let' em Die! should be our slogan," Sammy replied

"You know guys, we volunteered for oversea duty, so we have no one to blame but ourselves," I curtly replied.

"I guess you're right!" they nodded affirmatively.

We were driven to the front lines and took up our positions in a vacant fox hole. We realigned the sand bags to our liking. Chuck, Sammy and I were together once more only this time we had access to a B.A.R. We were also issued a First Aid kit and packs of Sulfur which we hoped we wouldn't use.

Sgt. Ryan and his entourage came around to each trench and dropped off K Rations and ammunition. We were as ready as we'll ever be!

As twilight faded, the Army began to shoot the parachute flares up into the air. They exploded with their usual brilliance enabling us to see the enemy when and if he decides to attack.

After a couple of hours of waiting, the big moment was here. It was around ten o'clock by our standards, when the first wave of Japanese soldiers came down from the hills, around the ridges and into our barb wire area. This time they cut the barbed wire and were getting too close for comfort. Their blood curdling screams and the battle cry of Banzai! were heard above the roar of the artillery.

Chuck was blasting away with the B.A.R. while Sammy and I were firing our now red hot M 1's. The enemy didn't have a chance! We were dug in, they weren't !

I was blasting away with my trusty M1 when Chuck spun around very suddenly. He grabbed his left arm at the biceps in an effort to stop the bleeding. The blood covered the lower extremities of his arm in a purple hue. He quickly removed his belt, applied a tourniquet above the wound and resumed firing.

"What guts!" I thought, as I dropped another of the enemy. The battle roared on!

A few hours after midnight, the first sign of the enemy weakening was noticeable. We encouraged it by pouring more lead their way. They stumbled over their fallen brethren, in some cases never getting the opportunity to regain their balance. Once started their retreat spread throughout the front lines.

As they began to retreat, we got out of our trenches and began chasing them before they got back into the hills. We shot, what was moving, chasing them deeper into the hills.

"Battle of the Perimeter" March 1944

We went as far as the barbed wire, and on the way back to our trenches I picked up a Japanese rifle as a memento of what had happened here. Sammy and Chuck did the same.

During the early hours, we took off our T shirts, because it was so hot and humid and began to look for any Japs that may be still alive. There were mangled bodies all over the place but nothing living as far as we could ascertain. Meanwhile the Marine infantry went up into the hills with their flame throwers to burn out the few Japanese soldiers that were still manning the canons in the caves.

So after about a month of constant bombing, Pistol Pete was silenced. We didn't have to sleep in our fox holes unless we had an air raid.

Meanwhile Chuck was recuperating at the base hospital. The brave idiot almost died! He had to have a couple of transfusions because he lost so much blood.

Once the enemy was subdued, Father Christifano paid us a visit.

"Hi men!" He greeted us upon entering our tent.

"Whatever it is you're selling, we're not buying," Sammy jested.

"Wait till you hear what I'm selling," he excitedly remarked.

"Give me that 'ole' time religion, Give me that 'ole' time religion ,etc." Porky sang exuberantly.

"Knock it off Pork!" "What is it Father?"

"How would you like to build a home for our Lord?"

"Come again?" Porky asked.

"I have permission to build a little Chapel, and all I need right now is the man power. How about it guys?"

The Padre was so excited about his project that we couldn't possibly refuse.

The four of us looked at each other and I said,

"What the Hell or I mean Heaven, it might be fun! When do we start?"

"I'll let you know very shortly. First of all I have to round up a few more Christians," he winked. With that he gingerly left us.

The next day, we began to clear an area deep in the jungle. Father Christafano wanted to get away from the hustle and bustle of our camp area proper. He was able to get the Seabees and the Camp Construction crews to help out with their tractors, bull dozers, tools and know how.

The first thing we had to do was to cut down the trees. After they were cut, by axe or saw they were then trimmed and dragged out by a tractor. The huge roots had to be removed and this was a job for the Seabees. They used a combination of tractor and bulldozer to uproot these monstrosities. After two days we got the area cleared. We helped out during our free time or when we weren't on guard duty.

The Chapel when completed was a thing of beauty. It was about fifteen yards wide and about twenty five yards long. It was constructed of logs, but for the straw that covered it's slanted roof. There were no walls, just railings. A wooden rail separated the aesthetic altar from the church proper. The pews consisted of peeled and sanded logs symmetrically aligned on either side, inside the church. A large wooden cross graced its top.

We completed the Chapel Saturday afternoon. Father Christafano was elated, as he was so looking forward to conducting Mass Sunday morning. Before we left, we knelt down in fervent prayer as Father Christafano blessed the structure. With our heads bowed in reverence, we suddenly became aware of a cool gust of wind that arose from nowhere. It whirled about us for a few seconds dissolving almost instantaneously. We felt peculiar, but strengthened.

Sunday morning, after chow, the three of us went to church. Pedro was on Guard duty. We stacked our rifles outside the edifice before entering. Mold covered prayer books were passed around by one the Gyrenes who was acting as an altar boy. My prayer book fell open to the "Litany To the Blessed Virgin Mary." Immediately, memories of attending Mass with my Mother and my three sisters became very vivid. I remember my sisters and I always got the giggles in church. I don't remember why, but this infuriated our mother.

"Now don't giggle in church," our Mother would say to us, before we entered.

"Yes mother," we replied, but once inside the seriousness of it all brought on the giggles once more. We were reprimanded for this behavior every Sunday.

The altar boy entered, rang a bell, and the services began. About mid-way through the mass, the crack of rifle fire descended upon us.

"Snipers!" someone shouted. We hit the deck !

Porky meanwhile let out a death defying scream.

"I'm hit! I can't move my legs!" He screamed hysterically.

He was lying on his stomach, a little hole in his back was emptying his blood.

"Oh my God! I hope his nerve cord wasn't injured," I gasped.

"Help me God! Please help me," he cried as he looked at the altar and then at Father Christafano. The Padre rushed over to where Porky was writhing in pain; knelt down beside him and began saying prayers in Latin. Porky meanwhile took hold of the Padre's wooden cross and began to kiss and caress it.

"Please God, Let me die! I don't want to be a cripple for the rest of my life" he cried convulsively. His stream of tears bathed our Saviors wounds.

The Padre continued to pray.

"Let's get those sacrilegious bastards," Sammy cryingly suggested.

Our Chapel

We scrambled out of the chapel, snatched a rifle and took cover. The two Jap snipers were in the process of descending when we spotted them. I pumped three fast rounds   into one of them before he hit the deck.

Everyone else, followed suit. The bodies were mutilated beyond recognition.

"That'll teach these heretics to fire into a chapel", Sammy rasped as he turned over one of them with his foot.

Porky meanwhile was rushed to the base hospital where his condition was listed as critical.

"I'm afraid he'll never walk again," the Medic informed us.

"Are you sure?" I asked.

"Positive. The bullet shattered his spinal cord.
 He has no feeling in his legs.

"Does he know?" Sammy wanted to know.

"I think so, but he has so much medication that he's out of it."

"May we visit him before he's shipped state side?" Sammy and I asked.

"Of course, why don't you drop in on him in a few days."

"Thanks Doc, we will!"

It's been two weeks now since Pistol Pete had been knocked out. But for an occasional air raid from Rabaul, our island was secure. We wanted the enemy to come down from the hills and surrender, but to our dismay they didn't! Most of them were busily engaged in growing food, but a handful still wanted to kill as many of us as they possibly could. These were the Japanese that we were concerned about and so we still had to protect and guard our air strips and living quarters.

While on Guard Duty at the air strip, I became acquainted with quite a few of the pilots. Whenever they returned from their strikes, the first thing they did was relax with a hot cup of coffee.   -

A young cocky S.B.D. (Scout Bomber Dive) pilot by the name of Lt. Ahlgren and I became very good friends. He was a former Minor League Baseball player and loved nothing better than to sit around and swap baseball yarns with me. He was tall, blond and twenty one.

One day during our bull sessions, I told him why I signed up for oversea duty and forsook a career as an aerial gunner. He also laughed when I told him how Beer Belly O'Shannon treated me when I went over his head to play ball for the Camp Miramar Marines.

"I think I would have done the same if I were in your shoes," he replied.

"By the way Lee would you like to accompany me tomorrow on my daily "Potato Run ?" he asked.

"What about your gunner, won't he object?"

"Are you kidding! He's been under the weather the last few days, and I'm sure he'd welcome a little more rest."

"I'd love too! I don't want to go through life thinking what it would have been like to be an aerial gunner." I excitedly replied.

"Good ! Be here at 0700.

"Roger!"

I couldn't sleep that night thinking about what I talked myself into. That morning, promptly at 0700, I met Lt. Ahlgren at Field Operations. I was issued some flight togs, parachute and a Mae West life jacket. Six planes were scheduled for this morning's sorty. Our plane was loaded with "Napalm," a petroleum jelly bomb, as were the others.

"Burn up their gardens!" was the order.

The SBD's sounded like overburdened wash machines as they waited to taxi out of the revetment areas. The pilot and gunner sat back to back in this dive bombing plane, the idea being that the gunner would protect the pilot from attacks from the rear.

A fifty-caliber machine gun was mounted in the rear cockpit, with its nose pointing upwards at a sixty-degree angle, so the rounds fired would avoid hitting its rudder.

Dauntless Dive Bombers

After a few minutes, the "Follow Me" Jeep led the first plane out of the revetment area. The rest of the planes followed the leader. One by one, we lined up at one end of the Piva North strip and waited. The noise created by these planes was deafening. Butterflies were buzzing in my stomach as we awaited the go ahead from the control tower. We finally got the green light, and one by one our planes raced down the runway. The sensation of rising with my back to the forward motion sent chills up and down my spine. I have never been up in a commercial plane before let alone a fighter plane.

"Keep your eyes open for Jap Zeros, Lee, and if you see any, don't be shy. Blast them out of the sky," he informed me, through his head phones.

"Yeah ! Right!" I replied.

After about five minutes in the air, Lt. Ahlgren announced:

"Hold on to your hat Lee, here we go!"

The plane swerved to the left and began to peel off. I felt like I was on a roller coaster ride but I was too embarrassed to scream. Before I knew what had happened, we were out of our dive and gaining altitude. My stomach was still trying to catch up with me when a cloud of smoke arose from below. I could see what looked like little ants scurrying for shelter. The petroleum jelly burned intensely. Dante's Inferno couldn't be any hotter, I said under my breath.

The Japanese soldiers were shooting at us with their machine guns and rifles. It's a good thing that's all they had! But for an occasional bullet hitting our plane, they were perfectly harmless.

As we prepared for another dive, I caught a glimpse of one of our planes strafing what looked like a cow.

Where the Japs got that cow, I have no idea. Perhaps they carried the cow up the hill the same way they carried up their canons.

As nauseous as I felt, I had to smile when I thought of the report the pilot would have to turn in: "Strike carried out! Gardens burned! Cow strafed!"

My thoughts were interrupted by Lt. Ahlgren's resounding voice piercing my ear drums.

"We're done Lee, How did you like it?"

"It's okay, but I don't think my stomach agrees with me,"

"Haw! Haw!" he laughed. "Well at least you won't go through life wondering what it would have been like to be an aerial gunner," he added.

"Yeah, I guess you're right," I replied.

In about ten minutes we approached our landing strip. Lt. Ahlgren set down our plane deftly and smoothly, a perfect three point landing. The "Follow Me" Jeep led us into a nearby revetment area where a truck was waiting to take the pilots and Gunners back to their camp area. I was relieved to be back on solid ground once more.

################

For the last week or so Sammy had been relentlessly scratching his crouch.

"Sam do you have the crabs? " I asked.

"Naw! Just mosquito bites," he replied.

"I don't know Sam, I'd report to sick bay if I were you."

"Come on, I'll go with you. I have to have the fungus growth on my shins treated."

"Aw, Okay," Sam replied.

The Navy Corpsman was working at his desk when we entered.

"What's up guys? He asked.

"I think I may have the crabs," Sammy blurted out.

"Crabs! Impossible! We haven't had a case of crabs on Bougainville yet."

"Well I think we made your day!" I laughed.
The Corpsman gave me a frown full look.

"Okay! Drop your pants and let's take a look."

He picked up a flashlight from a nearby drawer and with a tongue depressor began to search the dense growth.

"Well I'll be a horse's ass! You do have the crabs! And you now, also have the distinction of having the first reported case on this island.

"What an honor!" I laughed.

"Yeah right!" Sammy disgustedly replied.

"How do I get rid of them?" Sammy wanted to know.

"We can clear it up with D.D.T. or this pink ointment."

"Pink ointment! Isn't that what you treat my fungus with?" I asked.

"Yup! We swab throats and kill athlete's foot with it too," he grinned.

"So what's it going to be, DDT or the pink ointment."

"I'll try the DDT bomb," Sammy replied.

He went into the back room, emerging very shortly with the DDT bomb.

"Spray the loused area up area when it starts to itch and lay out in the sun whenever you can."

"Why the sun?" Sammy asked.

"The crabs will get sunburned and die," He smirked.

I had my shins swabbed with this pink ointment and we left. Fungus was actually a parasitic microscopic plant that grew on damp logs or the feet or legs of service men that had to wade through swamps, or dense moist jungles. It didn't need sunlight to grow. It also itched like hell. If I didn't put on this pink ointment, I would scratch my shins until they started to bleed.

When Pedro found out that Sam had the crabs he was extremely overjoyed.

"Hey Sammy, I have a sure cure for getting rid of your crabs?

"Yeah, you do? What is it?"

"Well you get your razor and ice pick. With your razor, you shave an area right down the middle and when the crabs try to cross this clearing, you jab them with the ice pick," Pedro laughed hysterically.

"I'll jab you with an ice pick," Sammy shouted as he chased Pedro out of the tent and around the stockade. Even our prisoners laughed, even though they didn't know what the hell was going on.

Chuck was released from the base hospital with only a scar to show for his heroism. Porky on the other hand was shipped stateside. He was an entirely different person. His eyes were sunken and had that sadness that one would see after a person cried a lot, and I'm sure he did! We tried to cheer him up, but we didn't succeed. He would have to be completely rehabilitated. What a rotten break!

With our daily "Potato Runs" the Japanese were getting hungrier by the hour. They were surrendering by the hundreds.

It got so bad, that at times we would find them in our chow lines waiting to be fed. Our small stockade couldn't hold all of these prisoners so they were shipped out to Guadalcanal.

One thing I can say about Guard Duty it is unpredictable. Last night I had to patrol and guard the entrance to Officers Quarters. I didn't like this duty because I had to walk up and down a long narrow road adjacent to the dense jungle. I was an easy prey for anyone lurking in that jungle so I decided to guard my post from a nearby tree.

As I sat on a heavy branch overlooking the road, I thought I heard voices coming out from the jungle. I knew that this part of the jungle was off limits to us, so anyone, who would be in there, would have to be the enemy.

There still were a lot of Japanese snipers that didn't want to admit that they were defeated nor were they going to surrender. So when I heard these voices, I became concerned.

I released the safety on my rifle and looked through my site at a couple of crouching figures. They looked like Japs, I thought, but I wasn't sure. I had the taller of the two in my sight and about ready to squeeze off a round, when a Jeep came barreling down the road. I didn't realize it at the time, but they were coming to relieve me. The Cpl. of the Guard brought his Jeep to a screeching halt when he saw the two figures emerge from the jungle.

"Who goes there?" he shouted, as the other guards in the Jeep aimed their rifles at these two Japs.

"Don't shoot!" they screamed were from the 49th Army Defense battalion.

"What the hell are you guys doing here?" he asked.

"We're lost we don't know where the hell we are!"

"Well you're in the Marine Air Group 24 Camp area.

"You guys are lucky you didn't get shot by one of our guards." he said, as I emerged from behind the tree.

"Yeah!" I replied if the Cpl. of the Guard didn't come around when he did you guys would be picking daisies." I was relieved of my duty, and we gave these two doughboys a ride back to their camp area. They never realized how close they came to being shot, or even dead.

The afternoons were usually very hot and humid. Today it was especially hot. Since we were scheduled for Guard duty tonight, we had the afternoon off.   "Let's go swimming," Sammy suggested.

"Great idea Sam!," Chuck acknowledged, from under his mosquito netting.

"I'm game," I replied, as I rolled over onto my side.

"Okay! let's go!" Pedro chimed in but no one was moving.

I finally made a motion to get up; everybody groaned, nobody moved. We finally managed to crawl out of our cots and walked over to the nearby ocean.

We did some swimming, as did other Marines, when we spotted someone using their mattress cover as a surfboard. Our mattress covers were made of cotton and impregnated with some kind of water repellant. Leave it up to American ingenuity, it was air tight.

It was a very simple procedure to fill them with air. All one did was to run down the beach with the open end forward, tying a large knot into it when filled. We then proceeded to walk out into the ocean with our billowy mattress covers carried high above our heads. When a huge wave approached, and at times it must have been at least ten feet high, we straddled our balloon like conveyance for an exciting, exhilarating ride back to the beach. The beach brought back pleasant memories, all that was missing was Rita and the beach house. The ocean was there!

Bougainville Beach 1944

While we were frolicking on Bougainville beach the Allied offensive against Rabaul reached its peak during the months of February and March. More sorties were flown from our air strips, Piva North and Piva South, during these months, than at any time during the war.

The Japanese on Rabaul, though cut off from Japan proper, were faring quite well on their island fortress. They were growing their own food, were issued monthly allotments of soap and toiletries and above all had brothels hosted by prostitutes that were imported at the beginning of the war. This is a lot more than we had!

The radar network used by the Japanese was so letter perfect that it was impossible to strike Rabaul without them knowing it. They knew we were coming at least a half hour in advance Obviously they broke our code and whatever we did, they knew immediately.

They also constructed miles of underground tunnels which they used to advantage every time our planes approached. Their losses were very small in contrast to the tonnage of bombs dropped.

A few nights later, I was guarding an area in the Quartermaster Depot, when an incident occurred which frightened the hell out of me. While walking my post, it started to rain, so I took shelter in a nearby tent. The tent was empty but for a few crates. I made myself comfortable on one of these crates, as the rain drummed a steady monotonous tune, which put me to sleep. I must have dozed off, when I heard a weird sound approaching me.

"What the hell is that?" I shouted aloud, as I jumped to my feet.

It sounded as if a horse was galloping towards me. I dropped my rifle in the process and was groping for it wildly when the thing crashed into the center pole of the tent.

The tent collapsed, trapping a frightened Marine and a screeching, snorting companion. I finally found my rifle and proceeded to empty a clip of ammo into it. It was quiet now!

I crawled from under the tent just in time. The rifle fire brought the Cpl. of the Guard and company to my rescue.

"What happened here Lee?" the Cpl of the Guard asked me, as he jumped out of his Jeep cradling a Thompson Sub Machine gun.

"I don't know!" I was walking my post when I heard this galloping sound approaching me. Before I knew what had happened, the tent was down and I emptied a clip into it.

"Do you know what's under this tarp?"

"Nope !"

"Well let's take a look! And for your sake Lee, I hope it isn't our Commanding Officer," he smiled.

"Yeah Right! That's all I need!"

We rolled back the tent, and were we ever surprised!

"It's a wild boar! The Cpl. of the Guard surmised.

"Yeah and look at the size of it and check out those large tusks."

"Looks like we'll have pork tomorrow," one of the guards rejoiced.

"Good hunting Lee!" they laughed as they put the boar into the Jeep and drove off to the mess hall. I didn't think it was funny, but everyone else did! We did have pork for dinner the next day!

The next night, I was assigned to guard the mess hall and the bakers. The bakers baked their bread at night, ready for early morning breakfast. As I walked my post I bumped into Sammy who was guarding the canned goods stored in one of the nearby tents.

"You know what Sam, I'm getting tired of being in the guard Company.

When shit was flying, it was pretty good duty, because we could do whatever we wanted to but now it's become too regimented.

When the uniform of the day was fatigues, now its khakis, and clean khakis to boot. When we never had rifle inspection, now we have it every day. When an occasional tent inspection was held, now Frogy practically lives with us.

"Do you think we should ask to be transferred to another department?"

"Doing what? Remember all we know how to do is kill Japs, we're expendable, did you forget?"

"Yeah, I did!"

Just then I heard a volley of three shots coming from my post. I double-timed it to my post and as I approached I could see orange yellow flames radiating towards the skies. Pedro was there and was ready to fire three more shots when I came upon him.

"What happened Ped? I excitedly asked.

"Beats me Lee. I heard a slight explosion and the next thing I saw was the mess hall was on fire. That's when I fired three shots into the air.

When I got here, the bakers were running down the road like two scared rabbits.

I quickly fired three more rounds into the air.

"Now Ped you have to help me out. If they ask you what happened, tell them that you came over to help me after you heard the first three shots, and then you fired three more. Don't tell them what you told me unless you want to see me rotting in the brig, Okay?"

"Sure Lee!"

Just then the Guard Company Jeep pulled up, followed by a fire fighting truck.

Frogy Connors hopped out of the Jeep in front of us."Whos's on duty here?"

"I am sir!"

"What happened Private Walewander?" he croaked.

"I really don't know Sir! I was walking my post when I heard what seemed to be an explosion and the next thing that I saw were the two bakers running down the road, while the mess hall began to burn. That's when I fired the three shots and then Private Ortis fired the next volley when he came to assist me.

The bakers told Frogy about the same story I told him.

"Nice work Private " Frogy finally said.

The fire was under control, and the Camp Construction crew now had to build us a new roof.

That afternoon, Sammy, Chuck and I decided to transfer out of the Guard Company when a flag pole was erected in front of Officer's quarters and a color guard was assigned the task of raising and lowering the flag every day. Three of us comprised the color guard and could look forward to this detail about twice a week. All this activity didn't fare too well with us. We wanted out!

"Let's stick it out for another month," I said, "and then we'll decide what we want to do" We agreed !

-

Chapter 20

Today was April the 14th, the opening day for most Major League baseball teams. I was restless and irritable.

"What's eating you Lee?" Chuck asked.

"Nothing! Why?"

"Nothing!

You've been pacing around here like a caged lion, so what's up?

"Oh, I don't know, maybe it's because it's the beginning of the baseball season back home that has me so upset.

"What's that got to do with it?"

"You wouldn't understand."

"Try me!"

"Okay I will. What comes to your mind when I mention spring?"

"Love! You know, the stuff a young man's fancy turns to." "That's what I figured you'd say"

"Isn't that normal?" Chuck smiled, winking at Sam who was in his usual position; flat on his back.

"Just as normal as can be," Sam grumbled almost on cue.

"Well when someone mentions spring to me, I immediately think of Spring Training and baseball."

"You do! You're nuts! " Chuck replied.

"Yeah, cause I associate with guys like you," I remarked.

Every morning, we would check the bulletin board in the mess hall to see what's going on in our camp area. This morning one of the following memos was tacked to the board.

"The personnel of this base will refrain from swimming in the nude as Army Nurses have now been assigned to M.A.G. 24. Any man not conforming to the above order will be disciplined.

Lt. Col. McHenry
Commanding Officer

-274--

"Women! Wowee! "Sammy shrieked with joy.

"What the hell are you so happy about Sam?

You won't get within five miles of them," Chuck remarked.

"Probably not! But if I were to become deathly ill and,"

"Yeah, hmm, now that you've mentioned it I do feel under the weather," I sickly replied.

"Hey Lee, have you seen this announcement?" Chuck asked.

"No what is it?"

"Read it!"

I went over to see what Chuck wanted me to read and all of a sudden I got as excited as Sammy did when he found out that there were women on our island.

"Baseball tryouts for Marine Air Group personnel. If interested sign up with Sgt. Carter of Motor Transport, today."

"Yahoo!"I bellowed out joyfully.

"Don't blow a gasket!" Chuck snickered.

"Yahoo!" I roared once more.

"Here Chuck, take my mess gear back to our tent for me. I think I'll go over and sign up right now."

"Sure Lee!"

As I approached the Motor Transport tent, a squatty curly headed Sergeant was pounding his fist into an old beat up catcher's mitt.

"Sergeant Carter?"

"That's me Mac. What can I do for you?"

"I'd like to try out for the baseball team."

"Sure thing. Sign your name, position you want to try out for, and your assignment on this base."

"Roger," I replied.

Before I left, I asked the Sergeant whom are we going to play?

Well if you make the team we're going to play various Army, Navy and the Seabee teams.

"The Doggies and Swabbys have challenged our CO (Commanding Officer) to some games. I guess there's going to be a lot of money wagered on these games along with bragging rights. If we don't come up with a good team, we're going to leave this island penniless.

"Where's the ball field going to be?"

"The Camp Construction crew will build one for us, but for the time being we will hold practice in one of our revetment areas. This is where we park our airplanes."

"What time?"

"Tomorrow at 0800."

"What about equipment ?"

"The Doggies and Swabbys are going to give us some of their extra bats and gloves."

"Sounds great! See you tomorrow morning Sarge."

"Good luck!" he responded.

As I left his tent, I bumped into three more prospective ball players on their way to sign up.

The next day, immediately after breakfast, I reported to revetment area four. A few ball players were already warming up.

"Hi ! Sarge, I greeted Carter.

"Hi !" he answered apathetically.

"Where can I get a glove?"

"In that truck," he pointed. Cpl. Pruit will issue you one."

"Roger," I replied.

I walked over to the truck and began sorting through the gloves. Most of them were used and I had one heck of a time picking out one that I thought was broken in properly. A Marty Marion model looked like the best bet.

"Is that the one you want to check out?" the Cpl. asked.

"Not especially, but it seems like the best of the lot."

"Sign here." I did!

The thud of the ball imbedding itself in my poorly padded glove made me wince.

"Don't they have any gloves with a little padding in them," I winced once more, as I caught a hard high one.

"Your hands a little tender?" one of the players asked.

"I'll say they are!" I winced as I snagged a low throw that practically curled my toes.

"Whew!"

I folded my snot rag and placed it inside my glove. I then spit in the pocket, rubbed it in, pounded my fist into it, and resumed warming up. It felt a lot better now, and after about ten minutes, I was throwing with a little more zip and accuracy.

"Take it easy son," a husky voice commanded.

I spun around almost knocking down Captain Northey who was standing behind me.

"What's your name son?"

"Private Lee Walewander," I replied.

"Oh you're one of the Pro players we have in our outfit."

"Yes Sir!" I grinned, feeling good about myself.

"How did you know I was a Pro ballplayer, Sir," I asked.

"When our CO told me to organize a baseball team to play the Army and Navy, I immediately went to our personnel files to see if we had any pro ball players in our outfit. Well I found out that we had four of them, and a lot of College players. I put Sgt. Carter in charge since he's also a pro and a catcher to boot."

"That's great sir," I replied."

Good luck Lee," and with that he blew his whistle for all of us to assemble.

We formed a semi circle around Captain Northey and Sgt. Carter.

"Sit down men, my dissertation may be quite lengthy," he quipped.

"First of all, you men may want to know why we're organizing a baseball team and secondly whom are we going to play once we're organized. Well to answer the first question, we're organizing a baseball team because all the other outfits are and furthermore the Army General challenged our CO to a few games.

It seems that the Army has a top notch team and hardly anyone to play. Some of the Marine Squadrons are also organizing teams as are the Seabees and a Naval Acorn outfit. There should be about seven or eight teams on this island, so we better be pretty good or we'll leave this island flat broke. At the end of the week, fifteen of you will be selected to represent Marine Air Group 24. It's going to be a very difficult task to pick this team as the turnout is much larger than we anticipated. Sgt. Carter and I will decide which of you in our opinion are the best ball players. God Luck to you all! Sgt. do you have anything to add?"

"No Sir! You covered it adequately."

"Fine! Now let's get those legs in shape. A couple of laps around the revetment area, to start out with. Hubba! Hubba!"

Sgt. Carter broke forth followed by a flock of eager players trying to impress their coaches. The pace was being set, by Sgt. Carter, and it was almost like a jog the first time around. On the second lap we were running a little faster and the last fifty yards we were flying. I was puffing like an old war horse when I crossed the finish line. I was out of shape!

When I caught my second wind, I started a pepper game. I always play a little pepper game before I take infield practice. Meanwhile Sgt. Carter and Captain Northey were laying out our temporary infield.

The bases were fastened to the ground and one of the trucks was being used as our backstop. We had a little batting practice before the Captain assembled us.

"Men, I want all of the infielders to go out to the position you'd like to try out for. I'm going to hit each of you five ground balls. What I want you to do is pretend a batter just hit this ball and he's racing down the line to try and beat it out. Field it as if it were in a game and fire it to first base."

"Okay, who's first?"

The infield was crowded with eager infielders. There were about five for each position. One of the shortstops that I was competing against looked like real competition. He could bobble a ground ball and still get his man because he had a canon for an arm. The others were just average ballplayers, so I knew I could beat them out. I knew Ken, as he was called, was going to be tough.

"Next! Captain Northey shouted.

I took my position at shortstop, took a deep breath and was ready for anything that he was going to be hit to me. The Captain drove a ball like a bullet to the right of me. It was a line drive, only it never got a foot above the ground. I broke to the right and instinctively dove at the ball. I snared it in the webbing of my glove but my momentum carried me another ten feet on my stomach.

"Atta boy, Walewander," Northey shouted.

I got up, shook the dirt out of my pants, while the Captain eyed me earnestly. I took up my position at short again and waited to see what he'll hit me next. This time it was a slow bounder which I charged, fielded it cleanly and while still in a crouched position fired a strike to first base. He hit me a few more ground balls, which I fielded cleanly and was happy with my tryout.

"Next !" Northey barked.

"Nice going Lee," Ken remarked, when I joined our group.

"Thanks Ken, you weren't bad either," I smiled.

After our infield, outfield, and catcher tryouts, we took about ten swings apiece and called it a day.

Being attached to the Guard Company was no picnic. The two airstrips had to be guarded and patrolled all the time, especially at night, so that the few Japanese still remaining on the island couldn't sabotage our planes.

Our tent was deserted when I entered. I figured Chuck and Sammy are probably swimming and Pedro must be on Guard duty. I undressed, wrapped a towel around my waist, slipped into my boondockers and trudged over to the shower stalls. Our fire truck was filling the suspended drums with water as I approached.

"Hey Jake, how about a little hot water today?" I shouted.

"Sure Lee" he shouted back, as he proceeded to take the hose out of the drums and aimed it at me. "Is this warm enough?" he laughed.

"Cut it out Jake," I shrieked, "This water is ice cold!"

He didn't! My towel was no longer around my waist. It lay at my feet, water logged and muddy. I picked it up and heaved it upwards which caught Jake right smack in the kisser. He lost his balance and jumped off the rafters. I was up on the rafter before he could recover. I grabbed the hose and began to give him the dousing he gave me.

"How do you like the water now Jake? Is it warm enough for you?" I laughed.

"It's just perfect!" he lied, as he tried to hide behind his truck.

Our "goofing around" was suddenly interrupted, by an exploding bomb.

"Hit the deck Lee! He screamed.

I dropped the hose and dove headlong, butt naked, into the brush.

I looked up at the planes above us and to my surprise they were SBD's.

"Those are our own planes, Jake, what the hell gives?"

"Well kiss my ass if they aren't!" he excitedly replied.

"Let's go and find out!"

I picked up my dirty towel, wrapped it around my waist and followed Jake through the brush. Marines were pouring into the area from everywhere. A siren was crying wildly a sound, we were very familiar with.

"What the hell happened?" I breathlessly asked one of the Corpsmen.

"One of our SBD's came back from bombing Rabaul with a hung bomb on their wing. He tried to shake it off over the ocean but it didn't budge. Since he was low on fuel he had no choice but to land. So in the process of landing, he had to fly over our camp area and for some unknown reason or other it came loose and killed three Marines who were in the process of going to Australia for some rest and recreation."

What a rotten break! It just doesn't figure. These guys were in a couple of battles on Guadalcanal and on Bougainville and they come through without a scratch and then to be killed by a bomb from your own plane, it just doesn't make any sense. They were so looking forward to rest and a little fun. I don't know about the fun part but they sure are going to get a lot of rest. The Medics meanwhile were carrying the remains of these three men to the ambulance. Father Christafano was walking alongside the stretcher bearers praying fervently. I bowed in reverence as they passed.

I left to take my shower; the water was ice cold, but I didn't even notice it. My mind was elsewhere.

I showered, returned to my tent only to find everyone gone. I wanted to talk to someone, but there was nobody about. I dressed and walked over to the deserted Chapel and began to pray.

I very often prayed to God but when something like this happens, what good is it? These men spent the better part of one year out here surviving battles on the Canal and again on Bougainville. Why torment these men for over a year and then take their lives so suddenly. I always believed that there was a superior being somewhere but now I have my doubts.

I guess I was voicing my opinions too loudly when Father Christifano interrupted me.

"I'm sorry to frighten you Lee, but I couldn't help overhear your conversation with the Lord."

"Well then you know exactly how I feel," I disgustedly replied.

"Yes I do Lee, but you should never doubt your Lord's actions.

"But it doesn't make sense!"

"Does this war we're in make any sense? Look at all the soldiers that were killed in the Battle of the Perimeter. And what about your friend Porky? He survived two battles with the Japanese and then he was shot while praying in my Chapel. How do you think I felt when God allowed these snipers to shoot him in my Chapel? I was devastated, but I didn't question his motive."

"I'm afraid you're not convincing me Father."

"I didn't think I was. You're looking for an answer that I don't have. I'm sorry to have to disappoint you Lee but that's the way it goes. Life is full of disappointments, but for every disappointment there are as many pleasant happy experiences."

"I guess you're right, Father," and with that I left the house of worship. It seems to me that life is like a crap game.

You have no control over the dice and whatever happens you either win or lose. The men that died on this island were the losers.

Every day the number of ball players reporting for practice was diminishing. A great number of them cut themselves, and the rest were cut by Captain Northey and Sgt. Carter. We were down to 20 players with only 5 more to cut.

One day during our practice sessions, Captain Northey called me over.

"Lee, have you ever played second base?

"Sure I played second for the Camp Miramar Marines while I was waiting to go to school," I replied.

"Good, cause I want you to play second base for us. I like the way you turn the double play, much better than Ken does."

"Captain, Sir, I don't care what position I play, I'm happy I'm playing ball again," I remarked.

"Good! I like your attitude Lee."

Ken now knew he beat me out at short, but didn't flaunt it. While we were working out in the revetment area, the Camp Construction crew was hacking out a ball field in the jungle. Bulldozers and steam rollers were leveling and smoothing out the infield. An outfield fence of empty oil drums was being rolled into place. The distance along the left and right field foul lines was about 350 feet. Center field was an even 400feet. Signs were being placed on top or directly behind the make-shift fence. One of them in deep center field read:

OVER THIS SIGN
AND
WIN AND A FREE CIGAR

Courtesy Buffalo Bayou
Water Co. Subsidiary of
Bougainville Utilities   Buy Bonds

Another sign in left field had the following message:

HIT THIS SIGN
AND
GET A NEW STRAW HAT

Compliments of
Camp Construction

A backstop was already up and a grandstand along the third base side was materializing as if by magic. If our ball team, was half as good as our ball diamond we were in for a winning season.

Our ball team was now set. It consisted of two catchers, four outfielders, five infielders and four pitchers. A couple of the outfielders could pitch if needed.

Well today was the opening day of the baseball season for Marine Air Group 24. Because I was on the ball club my duties as a member of the Guard Company changed somewhat. I would no longer pull guard duty during the afternoon, that time was reserved for baseball.

I ate lunch, and reported to our new ball diamond as instructed. Sgt. Carter was already present, as were most of the other ballplayers. We were issued white jerseys which had M.A.G. 24 Volunteers and a pair of wings stenciled across the front of them, and a baseball cap with a large "M" inscribed on it. That was our uniform.

We had batting practice, before our opposition arrived. We were playing the Army Engineer Corps and this was the undefeated team that our CO wanted so badly to beat. We were just about finished with infield practice when we heard a lot of shouting and screaming emanating from the road.

"Here they come!"One of our ball players shouted.

A caravan of Army semi's approached loaded to the hilt with howling screaming dogfaces. Our practice was momentarily halted as we were completely taken in by our opposition. They were drinking canned beer and singing their "Caisson" song. It sounded horrible! It couldn't compare with the Marine Corps Hymn.

The first and third base stands constructed by our Camp Construction crew were filled to capacity. The front row was reserved for the Officers.

The Army Engineers were on the first base side, along with their boisterous, drunken fans. The M.A.G. 24 Officers and fans were on the third base side. The players sat on a long bench in front of the Officers.

Before the game got under way, the Doggies began to taunt our fans.

"Hey Jar heads, we're going to give you a bet of 2 to 1 that our team will whip your ass," they shouted.

The Marines complied. Bets were being consummated everywhere. I glanced at our stand and I could see Chuck and Sammy betting with some loud mouthed Dog face. I even saw our Commanding Officer shaking hands with the Army General. I assumed they had a bet of some kind, taking place. I told Sammy to bet five bucks for me.

After the Army Engineers had their batting and infield practice, the infield was raked smooth and slightly watered. Our Commanding Officer threw out the first ball and we all stood at attention as our Color Guard hoisted "Old Glory" in deep center field.

"Play Ball!" The plate umpire shouted.

The first man up for the Army Engineers lined the first pitch into left center. He rounded first and continued onto second. Lt. Ahlgren the SBD pilot who took me along with him on one of his Potato Runs was our center fielder. He back handed the ball and rifled it to me at second base. It was a perfect peg, only a little on the third base side. I scooped up the ball and dove headlong towards the hook sliding runner. He slid under me, toppling me over on top of him.

"Safe!" the second base umpire bellowed.

"Safe! You must be kidding ? Ken shrieked.

Our Manager, Captain Northey came storming out onto the field.

"What are you trying to do, give them the ball game in the first inning" he screamed.

"Play ball"! the umpire roared, turning his back on a irate Captain.

The Captain as well as Sgt. Carter kept jawing away at the umpire, which stirred up our fans. They were jeering, hollering and throwing empty beer cans onto the playing field.

"Play ball!" the umpire shouted, "or forfeit the game."

He meant business, so we reluctantly went back to our positions. The beer cans were picked up and the game resumed. We had a big right hander on the mound by the name of Steve (Sneaky) Hughes. They called him sneaky because he was very slow and deliberate. He had pin point control and seldom walked anyone. When you least expected it he would sneak in a fast ball along with his junk. His first pitch, to the second man up, was bunted between the pitcher's mound and first base.

Sneaky Hughes charged the ball, slipped but still managed to throw the ball to me at first base. The man on second advanced to third. Man on third, one out. Their left fielder stepped up to the plate. He worked the count to two and two and then hit a blooper into right field. I took off after the ball as did our first baseman and right fielder.

"I got it! I shouted, trying desperately to make an over the shoulder catch. The ball hit the finger tips of my glove and dropped lazily to the ground. The runner on third scored, the batter wound up on second base.

"Error!" the official scorer attested.

There clean up hitter was up next, a big lanky, left-handed, first baseman. On a two and two pitch he drove a screaming ground ball down the first base line which our first baseman knocked down, and flipped to Sneaky who covered first base. The runner advanced to third base. Their next hitter hit a deep fly to center, which Lt. Ahlgren leaped up and speared. One run, one hit, one error.

Captain Northey decided to make me his leadoff man because I could bunt and I could run.

I stepped up to the plate and glanced over at Captain Northey who was coaching at third base. He went through his ritual of signs and finally signaled for me to lay down a bunt on the second pitch. The third baseman moved up on me almost as if he knew that I was going to bunt. I deliberately took a vicious cut at the first pitch thrown to me and missed the ball by a foot. I guess the third baseman changed his mind because he fell back to his normal position. On the next pitch I dropped one down the third base line, which caught him flat footed and I had myself a base hit. Our next hitter was Sgt. Burton our third baseman. I took a normal lead off at first and was almost picked off. The fact that he was a lefty helped his cause quite a bit. I figured the pitcher figured I was pretty fast because lead off men usually are.

I took a bigger lead off and once more drew a throw. Sgt. Burton meanwhile worked the count to 3 and 2 and now the hit and run was in progress. The next pitch was a fast ball because they knew I was going. The pitch was low and outside. I took a pretty good lead off and when the pitcher released the ball I was off and running. Sgt. Burton struck out and now I was on my own. As I approached second base I noticed that the throw was a little high and on the third base side. I instinctively hook slid on the outside to avoid his tag.

"Safe!" the second base umpire shouted, as he waved his arms to indicate that I was safe. The Dough boys thought differently and so they shouted profanities at the umpire.

The next man up was my keystone partner, Cpl. Ken Rafter. I glanced at Captain Northey to see what he wanted Ken to do. I was startled when he gave Ken the bunt sign. I figured with my speed I can score on any kind of a base hit. The play that Captain Northey wanted to pull off was for Ken to drop a bunt down the third base line.

When the third baseman comes in to field the ball I'm rounding third and on my way home.

I took a good lead off and took off on the next pitch as Ken squared away to bunt. The ball was inside, catching Ken in the ribs, sending him reeling to the ground. Captain Northey ran out to see how badly Ken was hurt and as he approached, Ken was already getting up waving our Skipper back indicating that he was all right. He rubbed his rib cage while slowly trotting to first base. I had to return to second base and now we had runners on first and second with only one out and our clean up hitter at bat.

Sgt. Carter was about 5'11' and had to weigh about 200 pounds. I've seen catchers with better arms but what he lacked in speed he made up with his accuracy and quickness. He was also a left hand hitter with a lot of power. The lefty on the mound toyed with the Sarge throwing him nothing decent to hit.

On the next pitch he tried to jam him on the inside but Carter being the Pro that he was pulled it down the first base line for a double. I easily scored and Ken took third while Carter wound up at second. With runners on second and third and only one out our center fielder and switch hitter, Lt. Ahlgren was up. I guess the Army didn't want any part of Ahlgren so they decided to walk him.

Our next batter was our left fielder Pfc. Sunny Watkins. Sunny wasn't very tall, I'd say about 5 '8' but built like a bull. He had excellent speed and was a good contact hitter. He worked the count to 3 and 2 an then with everyone moving he hit a screaming line drive to the second baseman who caught it and fired it quickly to first base doubling off Lt. Ahlgren who was trying desperately trying to get back to first base. So a golden opportunity was wasted and all we could do was tie the score at one a piece.

The two pitchers settled down and pitched brilliantly until the top of the 7th when the Army pushed across a run to take the lead by a 2 to 1 score.

Lee

Marine Air Group 24 Volunteers

Their first man up drilled a fast ball into the gap between Lt. Ahlgren and Sunny Wadkins for a double. Their shortstop was up next and he dropped one over short for a hit but not far enough for the runner to score from second. So with men on first and third and nobody out, Captain Northey called time to talk to the pitcher and try to settle him down. Meanwhile, our backup catcher got up, along with one of our relief pitchers and started to warm up in left field.

After Sgt. Carter convinced the Captain that Sneaky Hughes still had its stuff, he returned back to the bench. Our relief pitcher was still warming up.

Their second baseman was up next and he proceeded to work the count to 2 and 2 and then promptly hit a sharp grounder to Ken at short. Ken scooped up the ball, flipped it to me at second, I pivoted and fired it to first for a twin killing. Meanwhile the run scored and we were now down by a 2 to 1 score.

The next man hit a ground ball to Sgt. Burton at third which he fielded cleanly and threw him out. The ball game was now going into the last of the ninth and this was it, now or never. I was leading off and was swinging a couple of bats when I heard my buddy Sam shouting--

"If you get on Lee I'll give you five bucks."

"You're on Sam," I waved to him.

"Come on Lee, let's get it started."

I stepped up to the plate and took the first pitch for a strike. The next pitch was high and inside for a ball. I was hoping the third baseman would play me a little deeper but I guess he learned his lesson, he was playing me as if I were going to bunt. I was hoping the next pitch was in there so I could drive it down his throat but no such luck.

"Strike 2," the umpire bellowed.

With two strikes on me I couldn't be a looker, so anything around the plate I had to swing at.

The next pitch was right down the barrel and I was ready for it. I swung as hard as I could but unfortunately didn't get all of it and hit it in the hole between short and third. The shortstop backhanded the ball deep at short and tried desperately to throw me out, but didn't succeed!

Sgt. Burton was up next, and the Captain was playing it safe. He gave him the bunt sign. The first pitch he bunted foul, the next pitch was a pitch out which almost retired me at first base. Another quick throw to first kept me from taking a big lead off. The next pitch was right in there and he bunted it perfectly enabling me to advance to second base.

We were out of the double play and with Ken on board I figured I had a pretty good chance to score on any type of a hit. Ken was a right handed pull hitter and so I had to be sure that if he hit a ground ball it had to be through the infield or I'm a dead duck.

Ken jumped on the first pitch and lined it right at the third baseman. I was almost doubled off, but managed to dive back in the nick of time. It was up to Sgt. Carter to be a hero. If he hits a home run we win the game.

If he gets a base hit he ties the game. If he walks it'll be up to Lt. Ahlgren to decide the ball game. The Gyrenes were shouting words of encouragement while the Doggies were screaming for their pitcher to strike him out.

Sgt. Carter dug in and waited for the first pitch. With me on second the pitcher didn't take much of a windup as he fired the ball high and inside and backed the Sarge off the plate.

"Ball one!" The umpire shouted.

I kept jumping around second hoping the pitcher would balk, but he wouldn't buy it. The next pitch was on the outside but knee high which the umpire called a strike.

"Where are your glasses?" I overheard someone shout.

"Your seeing eye dog can call them better!"

The count was now 2 and 2 and I was ready. The next pitch was right in there and the Sarge drove it like a bullet to left field for a base hit. I took off like a shot and as I raced for third, Captain Northey was frantically waving me around. I rounded third without breaking my stride and headed for pay dirt. My legs were pumping rhythmically, my heart pounding wildly as I raced towards the plate. I knew it was going to be a close play at home because the left fielder had a good arm and the ball was hit very sharply.

The noise was deafening, louder with every step I took. The catcher was blocking the plate when I barreled into him. He bolted backwards and jack knifed a few times before arising with the ball still clenched in his hand.

"You're out!" the umpire shouted.

That did it! The Gyrenes poured out on the field, ready to crucify the umpire.

"Let's string him up," someone suggested.

"He was safe by a mile!"

When the Gyrenes poured out on the field, the Doggies did likewise. Tempers were flaring, and a free for all was in the making.

Fights were breaking out everywhere as some of the Marines refused to pay off their bets.

"Fuck you!" they shouted, "if you want your money come and get it!"

Come they did! The free for all was on. I had no intention of getting into it, but a jolt in the kisser changed all that. My two buddies, Chuck and Sammy saw me getting cold cocked from behind, came to my rescue. They joined me on the field, and back to back, boot camp style, we battled the Doggies. Our guard company was broken out and the riot was squelched.

That evening a memo was posted in the mess hall, which read:

"The conduct of the Marine Personnel at the baseball game today was inexcusable! Another outbreak of this kind and our baseball team will be disbanded!

Lt. Colonel McHenry

After our initial loss, we went on a rampage, winning our next six games. The Marines had recouped their losses and were betting heavily on every game. The betting wasn't only confined to the enlisted men, the officers were getting rich too. We were the pride and joy of our camp area.

In a few weeks we will play the Army Engineers again only this time it will be on their turf, and we were ready to kick ass and win our money back. They were still undefeated!

****

Chapter 21

Being a member of the Marine Air Group 24 baseball team, had many advantages. I was technically still a member of the Guard detachment but my duties were drastically changed. Sergeant Ryan called me into his tent one morning to tell me what my new duties would be.

"Lee let me congratulate you on making the baseball team. As you know, the personnel on this island look forward to your games and it helps the morale around here. Now they're talking about your team and the players and they don't gripe as much. So your participation on this team is very much appreciated by all of us and we want you guys to get even better.

As long as you're a member of the baseball team, you will have the afternoons off so that you can practice or play games. In the evening you will have guard duty like everyone else, is that clear?"

"Yes sir!" I replied.

I was pretty happy with my schedule. I was playing baseball again, and that's all that mattered to me. When we didn't have a game or practice I spent my afternoons surfing on my air filled mattress cover. I loved the beach because it brought back pleasant memories of Rita.

During the war, companies would donate food, drinks, reading material, etc. to the men overseas. Therefore, once a week we would get a ration of three packs of cigarettes (Usually Camels or Lucky Strike) and three cans of beer (Golden Glow). The beer was always warm so we used a CO_2 fire extinguisher to get the cans nice and cold. Since I didn't smoke, I traded my smokes for beer.

That afternoon, I received a package from Rita. It contained a fruit cake, cookies, candy, crackers and a large salami.

"Let's have a picnic, guys, what do you say?"

"Sounds good to me," Chuck replied.

"Me too!" Sammy added.

We just got our ration of cigarettes and beer and so we indulged. We sliced the salami, ate it with our crackers and washed it down with cold beer.

"That gal of yours is alright," Sammy said in between mouthfuls.

"She's a doll," Chuck cut in.

"Where's Pedro?" I asked.

"He got a letter from his wife that upset him," Chuck said.

I went inside the tent and Pedro was lying on his cot with a crumpled letter in his hand.

"Are you alright Ped? Why don't you come out and have some salami, crackers and beer before Sammy eats it all. What do you say?" He didn't answer.

Sammy and Chuck then walked into the tent to see what was wrong. We knew something was wrong because whenever food was involved, Pedro was always there.

"Pedro buddy, what's wrong?" Sammy asked.

Pedro didn't hear a word we said. He was lying on his back with his arm covering his eyes.

"Nothing! He sobbed, turning his back to us.

"Do you want to talk about it?" Chuck asked sympathetically.

"No, Just leave me alone!" he sobbed.

We reluctantly did, and resumed picnicking.

"I'll bet someone in his family died," I remarked.

"I wouldn't be a bit surprised," Chuck replied.

Just then we heard a pistol shot which froze us in our tracks.

We rushed into our tent but it was too late. Pedro was still on his cot, only the barrel of his 45 was stuck in his mouth. Blood was gushing out from the back of his head running down his neck and onto his T shirt. A crumpled letter lay at his side.

"Pedro why'd you do it?" Sammy shouted at Pedro, as if he could hear him.

"His wife wanted a divorce because she fell in love with someone else" Chuck replied disgustedly, tossing the letter back onto the bloody cot.

"Poor stupid bastard! What the hell did he solve by killing himself. All he did was give her a ten grand insurance policy as a wedding present, instead of a good belt in the mouth. Silly, stupid, shit head," he added, kicking the dirt angrily as he left the tent.

As I sat on my cot, sullen and dazed, the oft spoken slogan kept running through my mind:

"The Marine Corps Builds Men!"

How I wondered? Is it when we're physically and mentally brainwashed with discipline, that we are now considered to be men by the Marine Corps. Or do we have to be in so many battles, or kill so many Japs? Is Pedro a man now, because he had the guts to take his own life? All these thoughts were running through my mind when all of a sudden our tent was like Grand Central Station.

Frogy Connors was running around like a chicken with his head cut off. He read the letter over and over again not wanting to believe what had taken place. The Corpsmen were busy looking over the body to make sure it really was suicide that caused his death.

Pedro's funeral took place the next day. The three of us paid our last respects to our dear buddy whose cheerfulness, jokes and silly antics will be forever cherished.

A simple white cross placed over his grave only had this to say :

Pvt. Pedro Ortis
M.A.G. 24 – USMC
6/12/44

As we left the Bougainville cemetery, there had to be hundreds of graves out here, and I easily could be occupying one of them, but for some reason, I'm not!

Once our island was pretty secure the Commanding Officer informed the Construction Crew to build an outdoor theatre. It was built, on the order of a drive in theatre, only instead of sitting in your car to watch a movie, you sat on logs.

Chuck, Sammy and I were eagerly awaiting its premiere tonight. The movie we were going to see was "Billy The Kid." It featured Robert Taylor, Brian Donlevy, Gene Lockhart and Lon Chaney Jr. It was about a notorious outlaw who robbed banks and trains.

"Gee I haven't been to an outdoor movie in years," Sammy rejoiced.

"All that's missing is popcorn and a gorgeous blond," Chuck grinned.

"I disagree! Not with the popcorn, only I want a red head instead of a blond."

Just then the Cpl. of the Guard walked into our tent.

"I hate to do this mates but one of our guards is sick and one of you has to take his duty."

"Get lost Kemmington, I wouldn't miss this movie for anything," Chuck replied.

"Yeah, beat it!" Chuck grumbled.

"Who's sick?" Sammy asked.

"Private Stolski. He has an upset stomach."

"Bull shit, he just wants to see this movie!" Sammy replied.

"Look Bergoni, it wasn't my idea to ask you guys," Kemington remarked.

"Why us?"

"Cause you three have late shift's that's why, and by that time Ski should be feeling better."

"He'll be better right after the movie, you' wanna' bet?"

"Okay who's it going to be?"

"Why don't you get lost!" Chuck laughingly responded.

"Okay, I warned you guys," he said as he stormed out of our tent.

Before we could leave for the movie, Frogy Connors stopped us.

"Ten Shun !" I shouted.

"As you were," he croaked. His gait, bulgy eyes, and frogy voice brought back memories of Pedro imitating him. I must have had a smile on my kisser when Frogy approached me.

"I don't know what the hell you're smiling about Private Walewander, but as of this minute you have Private Stolski's post. Isn't that a scream Walewander? Laugh damn you!"

"Yes sir, it sure is," I replied, as I faked a feeble laugh.

"Now why did you people refuse to fill in for one of our guards when the Cpl. of the Guard asked you to?

"Because, Sir," Chuck replied. We think Ski isn't sick, he just wants to go to the movie this evening.

"Too bad! As of now, you three have guard duty at 1800 this evening. Is that clear?"

"Yes Sir!, we shouted, as loud as we could, in true boot camp style.

Frogy Connors jumped about two feet off the ground by our unexpected, vociferous acknowledgement. He eyed us suspectingly, wiped his eyes, croaked something under his breath and left.

"Well I've had it! Tomorrow morning, I'm going to ask Ryan to transfer me out of this chicken shit outfit. How about you guys?"

"I'm all for it," Chuck nodded.

"Same here!" Sammy added.

Promptly at 1800, Cpl. Kemington marched us over to our posts. Our duty was usually four hours long. My post was Officer's quarters, only a stone's throw from the outdoor theater.

Our Outdoor Theater

I was close enough to see the screen but not close enough to make out the scenes

If I only had my binoculars, I mused, I could still see this movie. This thought no sooner entered my mind when I bumped into Cookie Jarston on his way to the movie.

"Cookie, you're just the man I want to see."

"The booze is still fermenting," he said."

"It's not about your booze. I want you to do me a favor."

"Later Lee, I want to see the beginning of this movie."

"It'll only take a few minutes."

"Okay, what is it?"

"Go to my tent and get me my binoculars."

"Where are they?"

"In my seabag."

"Where's your seabag?"

"Next to my cot."

He hurried down the road and shortly returned with my binoculars.

"You know Jim, sound doesn't travel this far," he smiled.

"I know, but maybe I can read their lips."

"Yeah, right!" he replied.

The movie was about to begin. I looked around for a good vantage point where I'll be able to watch my post and the movie at the same time. Trucks parked on the road blocked my view; I could only see half of the screen.

I picked out a tall tree scaled it and made myself comfortable amidst its branches. I had a very clear view of the screen and after about a half hour I was getting pretty good at lip reading. The movie was much too long for my buttocks and arms to endure so I got down from my perch.

Early next morning, the three of us dropped in on Sgt. Ryan. Since we signed up for oversea duty, the Marine Corps wanted us to learn a trade so we wouldn't be expendable. After all, if they wanted us to fight, they would have put us in a Line Company.

"Good morning!" Sarg.

"What are our chances of getting transferred out of the Guard company?" we asked.

"Pretty good if you want mess duty for a month."

"Why do we have to get mess duty, can't it be something else?"

"No! Mess duty is usually given to Privates and PFC's. As long as you're a Private without some skill, you will always get one month of mess duty every year.

"That sucks!" Sammy replied.

"No it doesn't! When you think about it, you wouldn't take an airplane mechanic and have him scrubbing pots and pans for a month, would you?" Sgt Ryan asked.

"I guess not!" we replied

"That's why we have to pick personnel that are expendable and they're usually Privates. Once you people are taught a trade, you'll get promotions, and become exempt. Is that clear?"

"Yup!" we acknowledged.

"Well do you still want to get out of the Guard company?'

We looked at each other and nodded affirmatively.

"Okay then, at the beginning of the month you people will report to Mess Seargent Nixson."

"Roger!" we replied.

That afternoon it rained, in fact it rains almost every afternoon, not very long, but it does rain. Our baseball practice was cancelled, and so we had a skull session (Baseball strategy) as to signals, cut off plays, pick off plays, etc. which we use during our games.

Late that same day a shipment of frozen turkeys arrived from the states. The cooks were instructed to get them roasted for the following day. They were working late that night and I was assigned the pleasant task of guarding these birds after they were done.

It was still raining when I walked my post. The aroma was driving me out of my mind. I just had to get my hands on one of these bronzed gobblers. If this wasn't bad enough, the poncho I was wearing made me so hot, that I was soaking wet. A steam cabinet couldn't do a better job. The rain continued to fall, unceasingly.

While I was inside the mess hall talking to my friend "Cookie", he excused himself to go to the head. "

"Keep an eye on the place Jim," Cookie winked, "I have to hit the head."

"Sure!" I replied hungrily.

Now was my chance! It was now or never. Maybe Cookie read my mind and that's why he went to the head. Nevertheless, I clutched a bird off the rack and made it quickly disappear under my poncho, along with two of his friends.

"Thanks Lee," Cookie replied, as he entered.

"Just a part of my job," I said, my hands trembling under my poncho. I nonchalantly nudged open the screen door with my shoulder and left. I breathed a sigh of relief once outside.

Chuck and Sammy were snoring soundly when I entered our tent. I took one of the turkeys, lifted up Sammy's mosquito netting, and passed it back and forth under his nose. He mumbled something under his breath and before I knew what had happened, he was sitting upright in his sack, chewing wildly. I quietly woke up Chuck and dangled the fowl in front of his nose. He didn't say a word. He grabbed the gobbler out of my hand and took a big bite out of it. I sat down on my cot and also began to indulge.

"Do you think Sam is still asleep?" I asked.

"Well if he is, it's the most realistic dream he'll ever have.

"Yeah," I laughed.

We went back to sleep leaving the carcasses for the insects to enjoy.

Today was the day we've been looking forward to. We were playing the Army Engineers the only team that beat us. We were 6and 1, they were 7 and 0. The odds were no longer 2 to 1, it was even money now.

Today's game was going to be played at their field at 0100 hours. We had an early lunch and then met at our ball diamond where a lot of trucks were lined up to take us and our fans to Briggs Field.

The ballplayers, coaches and their gear were in one truck while our Commanding Officer and his entourage were leading this pack in their Command car.

We left our field at 1200 hours and as we pulled away we began to sing the Marine's Hymn. Those that were restricted to the base waved at us as we drove by shouting words of encouragement.

"Beat those Doggies !" they shouted.

It took us about twenty minutes to get there and to make sure the Doggies knew we were on our way, the Marine's Hymn was getting louder and louder. As we pulled into the reserved parking area designated for our trucks, the Dog faces were all over us.

"Hey Jar heads we're waiting to take your money!'

"Come on, put up or shut up!" they shouted.

As we took the field for some batting and infield practice we were ready to get even with these cocky doggies. They played the National Anthem followed by a rendition of their Caisson song. Chuck and Sammy were busily engaged in placing bets for personnel from our base that couldn't make this trip. We were ready and poised to go. The stands were full and the fans were vociferous.

"Play ball !" the umpire shouted.

I walked up to the plate and glanced at Captain Northey who gave me the hit sign. Usually he has me laying it down, but their third baseman was up the line quite a bit. This pitcher had a habit of getting the first pitch over the plate. He never wanted to get behind in his count. Knowing this, I was ready. He threw me a sharp breaking curve which I reached out for and drove it down the right field line for a triple.

Sgt. Burton our third baseman popped up bringing Ken to the plate. Ken worked the count to 2 and 2 and then hit a deep fly to center field, which I tagged up on and scored.

Sgt. Carter, our catcher and clean up hitter was next and he jumped on the first pitch driving it over the left field fence for a home run. Lt. Ahlgren ground out to the second baseman for the third out. The score was 2 to 0.

Our pitcher today was Sgt. Bill Donner, a hard throwing right hander. He won his last two starts and was ready to win another.

The first pitch was high and outside. The second pitch was down the pipe for a strike. On the next pitch our third baseman was caught flat footed by a perfectly placed bunt down the third base line. The next man up was probably going to bunt and he did. He bunted it down the first base line which was fielded by our first baseman who threw to Ken for a force at second.

A left hand hitter was up, so I played a little deeper than usual.

"Let's get two Ken," I shouted.

"Roger!" He acknowledged by tipping his cap.

"Come on Billy, let 'em' hit it on the ground, we'll get two for you," I chanted.

On the next pitch he took a vicious swing and missed.

"Come on Billy, he's swinging like an old barn gate," I yelled once more.

The lefty worked the count to three and two and everyone was on the move. The batter missed the high inside pitch; Sgt. Carter fired it to second base to double up the base runner. The throw was perfect! Ken was poised, lowered his glove so the runner would slide into it, but lo and behold the runner kicked the ball out of Ken's glove and sent Ken flying flat on his back.

"Safe1" the umpire bellowed.

I retrieved the ball and walked over to Ken who was in the process of brushing the dirt off his pants.

"You were asking for it Ken."

"What do you mean? That bastard kicked the ball out of my glove."

"Sure he did! And you'd do the same if given the chance."

"Right now let's get this last guy out and I'll show you a little trick they taught me in a baseball school I once attended."

"Okay!"

The next man up hit a fly ball to our right fielder, Bruce Logue.

Since the bottom of our order was coming up, I had a chance to tell Ken about the unwritten rule in baseball.

"Ken never let a runner slide into your glove. Sweep tag him, at all times. When the runner is racing down to second and you're waiting for the throw from your catcher, straddle the base, with your feet on either side of the base. Now what the umpire is looking for is to see if the ball gets there before the runner does, and if it does then he usually calls the runner out. The minute you get the ball you sweep it across the runner very quickly and even if you didn't tag him he was still out because the ball was there before he was. This is how the umpires call this play and it seems to work pretty well."

"Thanks Lee, that's good to know!"

We took an early 2to 0 lead but it didn't hold up for very long. The Army rallied in the bottom of the seventh to tie it up. The game was still tied after nine innings of play.

I came up in the top of the tenth inning and drew a walk. Our third baseman sacrificed me to second bringing Ken to the plate. The pitcher was concentrating so much on Ken that he must have forgotten about me. I took it upon myself to steal third because I had such a good lead. As I raced to third, the catcher now realized what was happening, got excited and threw wildly to third base.

The ball went over the third baseman's head and I scored easily on the error. It was good that I made it because Sgt. Carter and Lt. Ahlgren both struck out. We were now ahead 3 to 2, with the top of their order coming up.

In the bottom of the ninth inning, their first man up hit a sharp single into left field. He was promptly sacrificed to second. Bill got into a little trouble and walked the next man. Two men on and only one out. Captain Northey called time and we had a little Pow wow on the pitcher's mound.

Their cleanup hitter was up and he was hitting about 400, leading the league in Homers and RBI's.

"Should we walk this guy and then have a play at any base." the Captain asked us.

"I think we should, Captain ! Their next hitter hit two ground balls in this game already, I reminded him."

"I agree! Let's walk him!"

So now we had the bases loaded, the bottom of the tenth, and only one out. The Army now called time and put in a pinch batter for their right fielder. He was a good contact hitter who seldom struck out. Our pitcher knew that he had to keep the ball low, hoping for a ground ball. The next pitch was low inside which the batter drove in the hole. Our third baseman went to his left, fielded the ball cleanly and fired a perfect throw, waist high to me which I caught, pivoted and completed the double play.

Our fans came charging out of the stands. Sammy and Chuck lifted me on their shoulder and paraded me across the field. The Doggies began to throw empty beer cans at me which I was catching with my glove. Some of the Marines were stuffing five and tens in my pocket in deep appreciation for my part in the victory. We were rich and happy!

Chapter 22

When we were assigned to the Mess Hall, we had to move out of the Guard Detachment tents and move back to the camp area proper. "Cookie" Jarnston, our old drinking buddy invited us to move into his tent.

"Áre you sure you want us?" I asked.

"You must be kidding! I need a few drinking buddies to keep me company," he grinned.

Corporal Jarnston was about 5 '11' and built on the stocky side. His gray hair was cut very close. It looked as if he cut it himself.

"Okay! You talked us into it, but before we move in our gear, I think we should have a tent warming party," Sammy quipped.

"I agree, he replied, and with that disappeared into his fox hole emerging very shortly with a bottle of clear liquid.

"Don't tell me you're drinking water now," I laughed.

"Water ! What's that?" Cookie smiled.

" Isn't that water? It sure looks like water," I surmised.

"Taste it and find out."

"How do we know it's not poison," Chuck asked.

"Here take a swig."

"No! After you," I shook my head.

"You guys don't trust me," he laughed, as he placed the cork between his teeth and pulled. The cork came out with a loud pop. He wiped his mouth with the back of his hand before placing his concoction to his lips.

"Okay! Stop already! Remember you have company."

He did, and handed me the bottle I wiped my mouth in the same manner as Cookie did and took a fast swig. I started to cough and gasp for air.

"I've been poisoned!" I wheezed.

"Pretty good stuff, huh Lee?" Cookie grinned.

The alcohol Cookie made was of the highest purity. It was distilled and redistilled by Cookie's make shift still in order to get a concentration of almost 200 proof. I diluted mine with water from my canteen and added some sweet hard candy to it. It tasted pretty good now. We killed that bottle and two more before attempting to move in our gear. It was past midnight when we finally emerged from Cookies distillery.

It was pitch black outside; the moon was hiding behind an overcast sky. We started down the narrow jungle path, singing and stumbling as we moved along.

Trigger happy guards challenged us constantly and rather than have our heads blown off by some nervous cat, we gave up on the idea of moving our gear that night. We hit the sack instead.

The next day was our first day of Mess Hall duty and all of us were hung over. We knew we were late and the last thing we want to do is piss of our Mess Sergeant on our first day. A burly Mess Sergeant, sporting a crew cut, was addressing a group of Marines when we barged into the Mess hall.

"Aren't you people a trifle late?" as he looked at his wrist watch.

"We are?" Sammy responded looking at his watch.

"We over-slept Sir!" I politely replied.

'Well don't let it happen again, unless of course you want to peel spuds and scour pots and pans for the rest of the month."

"We won't!" we replied.

Sergeant Nixson, we soon learned, was a stickler for cleanliness. He was a former Bacteriology Major in college, before enlisting in the Corps. The Marine Corps for some reason or other thought he'd make a good cook and therefore proceeded to send him to the Cooks and Bakers School.

His knowledge of germs and their habitat put him on constant guard against these microbes.

We consequently had to clip our fingernails very short, get short haircuts and wear a clean white T-shirt when serving food.

Each morning we had to report to Germy Nixson for what he called a hand inspection.

"Bergoni do you think I would let you serve food with those filth laden hands?"

"They're clean Sarge! I just washed them! Sammy remarked, wiping them off once more across his white T shirt.

"They are like hell! You must be culturing a million pathogenic bacteria under those nails."

"Is that good or bad?" Sammy asked.

"What are you stupid or just trying to be cute! Of course they're bad!"

"Do you people know how bacteria grow and multiply?" he asked.

Nobody dared to say anything, for fear he'd jump all over them.

"Well for your information, bacteria are tiny microscopic plants that multiply by a process called cell division."

"Let me give you a simple example. Bergoni supposing you had an apple and cut it into two, how many would you now have?"

"Is this a trick question?" Sammy asked.

"No it isn't! Just answer the question?"

"Two !"

"Good, Now let us suppose that these two equal parts are cut in two again, how many would you now have?"

"Four !"

"Fine! Now what if each part is divided again in two equal parts ?"

"Eight!"

"Right !"

"Now what if these eight equal parts are divided in two equal parts again, you'd have sixteen parts, etc.

This process continues producing millions of apples or should I say bacteria in less than an hour."

"You're kidding aren't you?" Sammy remarked.

"No I'm dead serious and if you don't get those nails cleaned you may be too!"

"Okay," Sammy replied, holding his hands in an upright position simulating a surgeon, as he walked towards the sink.

Chuck and I were standing behind Sammy during this bacterial examination.

"I think Nixson's off his rocker," Chuck whispered.

"You're not kidding ! He's buggier than his imaginary bugs."

"Next !" Nixson called forth in his authentic medico lingo. I stepped forward with hands extended.

"You too Walewander! Dirty finger nails ! Scrub 'em'!

"Chuck didn't fare any better."

"That "goof ball" Nixson makes me feel like a dirty slob," Chuck bitched

"Well!"Sammy cut in dryly.

"Yeah, how about that Chuck," I laughed.

Our laughter brought an irate mess Sergeant into our midst.

"I don't know what the hell the big joke is about, but since you people are in such a good mood, I thought I'd inform you that you have a lot of spuds that you have to peel this afternoon."

"But Sergeant I have a ball game this afternoon," I informed him.

"Tough Shit! Walewander, you'll peel spuds if I have anything to say about it," and with that he went back into the mess hall.

I didn't argue with Nixson, just bided my time.

That afternoon, after our regular chores were completed, the three of us were escorted outside the Mess hall by Germy Nixson.

"There they are, gentlemen, just as I promised."

"Holy cow! I've never seen so many potatoes in my life," Sammy remarked.

"Yeah, and there's more where they came from," Germy smirked.

"This is going to take all day," Chuck added.

"So who gives a shit! Now get to it! I want that large kettle filled with peeled spuds every half hour or you'll get the same detail tomorrow. Is that clear?"

"Yeah!" we grumbled, as we made ourselves comfortable next to the kettle and amidst the sacks of spuds. I picked up a paring knife and began to pare a dirt covered spud.

"Who are you guys playing today?"Chuck asked.

"The Naval Acorn team," I replied.

"Are they any good?

"I don't know, we haven't played them as yet."

"Who's going to take your place at second base?" Sammy asked.

"Probably Cpl. Frank Miller our utility infielder."

As we sat there peeling spuds and bull shitting, I wondered what Captain Northey will do when he finds out that I'm not there. Perhaps it was mental telepathy because a Jeep came barreling down the road and braked in front of us.

"Lee, what the hell are you doing ? Don't you know we have a ball game today?"

"I do sir, but Sergeant Nixson won't let me go!"

"What do you mean he won't let you go ? We have a lot of money bet on this game."

Just then Sergeant Nixson came out of the mess hall. The Sergeant saluted the Captain and asked if there's anything he could do for him?

"Sergeant why are you keeping one of our ballplayers from playing ball?"

These three were wising off to me and so as a disciplinary measure I have them peeling spuds.

"Well he can peel spuds in the morning, but in the afternoon he is to report to the ball diamond. Is that clear?"

"By who's order Sir? "Sergeant Nixson asked.

"By your Commanding Officer's order, that's who!" Captain Northey barked.

"For your information Sergeant, your Commanding Officer at this very moment is wondering what happened to our second baseman as he's sitting in the stands waiting for this game to start. Do you want to tell him?"

"No Sir!" Germy Nixson replied.

"Good! Now hop in the Jeep Lee, we've got a ball game to play."

"Yes Sir! See you guys later," I replied, as I climbed into the back seat of the Jeep.

"Hey Lee here's fifty bucks to bet on your game," Sammy said, "Twenty five bucks for me and twenty five for Chuck."

"On what team?" I shouted as our Jeep bolted forward, leaving a cloud of dirt behind us and two peel paring Marines and an unhappy Mess Sergeant.

In a few minutes we arrived at the ball field. The fans were stomping their feet in a staccato frenzy.

"Let's play ball they shouted!"

I hurriedly put on my team sweatshirt, picked up my cap and glove and hustled out to second base.

"Hey second baseman, did you oversleep," the Naval bench jockeys chided.

I ignored them, learning some time ago to disregard them or you'll have a miserable afternoon.

Once they get on your back, they needle you unmercifully. This looked like my afternoon, all because I was late. We finished our infield practice and waited for the game to start. I had our bat- boy get our bets covered and waited for our Anthem to be played.

"Play Ball ! " the umpire shouted.

The game turned out to be an easy win for Sneaky, who picked up his fourth win.

Working in the mess hall was a drudge. The Mess Hall was quite large. It contained thirty wooden tables that could seat about ten men on each side. They were constructed like picnic tables only a little larger.

When the Marine personnel were done eating, they emptied what food they didn't eat into a couple of large oil drums set out for that purpose. Another drum, of hot soapy water, stood nearby, to clean and another one to rinse their mess kits.

When everyone was through eating, we washed the tables, swabbed the cement decks, scoured the pot and pans, emptied and cleaned out the large drums and policed the area. If this wasn't enough we then had to peel spuds, dice carrots, onions, etc., before getting a little time off for lunch.

Every morning we reported to the mess hall at 0530, and began to scrub our hands with a strong alkaline soap, which made our hands very clean but red. We then ate a hearty breakfast and then prepared to set out our trays on the table. Trays of powdered eggs, bacon, sausage, cereal, toast, milk and coffee were ready to be served. We had to wear clean white T shirts, be clean shaven and look like interns in a hospital.

The doors were opened promptly at 0630, at which time the Marines began to file in. They carried their own mess kits and cutlery. As they filed past us, we placed the food in their trays.

If your buddies came by, an extra egg or slice of bacon, somehow managed to get on their trays.

Germy Nixson blew his stack whenever he caught us. As long as there was a line, a chow hound couldn't come back for seconds. He had to wait till 0745, at which time we stopped serving and whatever food was left over they can have.

After about two weeks of Mess duty an incident occurred which Germy Nixson will never forget, nor will I, for that matter.

It seems that during a violent thunder storm a plane on its way to New Zealand made an unscheduled stop at our air strip. There were many officers and dignitaries aboard. Since the weather wasn't going to clear up for a couple of hours, they were driven to our Mess Hall to be guests of M.A.G. 24.

When Sgt. Nixson received the call informing him of his good tidings, he was extremely overjoyed. He appointed Chuck, Sammy and me to act as waiters because we had the cleanest hands and T shirts. He told us to wipe off the two end tables and set out the plates, cutlery, water and napkins for his guests. He then went into the jungle and came back with some flowers. He placed them in a pitcher which he displayed in the center of each table.

In a few minutes the guests arrived and were shown to their tables. We brought dishes of fried chicken, mashed potatoes, peas, salad, etc., to the tables. We stood by, one of us at each table, making sure they didn't run out of food. The dinner was going along as planned until we had an uninvited guest appear.

I was busily engaged in refilling water glasses when I spied what looked like a "cockroach" scampering across my table. I was hoping no one else saw it, but no such luck!

"I say old man, wasn't that a roach?" a General asked one of the dignitaries sitting alongside of him.

"A roach, General ! I didn't see a roach!" he replied.

"Yes, right here! he said, pushing his knife into a crack between the boards. The knife blade must have disturbed a nest of roaches underneath the table, because about ten of them emerged from the gap between the boards and began to scamper across the table.

I don't know who moved faster, the roaches or our guests, as chaos was in the making. The table was overturned in the process, and one dignitary in his haste stepped into a bowl of mashed potatoes and fell flat on his back. I was stunned as to what was happening, but when another dignitary slipped, I couldn't control my composure any more. I began to laugh hysterically and before long everyone else was laughing too. The General was laughing so hard, tears were streaming down his cheeks.

Meanwhile Sammy went to the aid of a fallen dignitary and in the process of righting him, he too slipped on the mashed potatoes. The place was up for grabs. I laughed so hard my sides began to hurt. If this wasn't enough, Sgt. Nixson came charging out of the kitchen and before he could stop, he was flat on his back with the fat dignitary and Sammy. I've had it! I couldn't laugh anymore, so I staggered out of the Mess Hall and collapsed on a bag of spuds.

The laugher was so loud, that before long, everyone in our camp area ran over to see what was happening. It took over a half hour for things to quiet down. I don't know if they were still hungry, when the dignitaries left, but I do know that most of them were still wiping the tears from their red swollen eyes.

Sgt. Nixson was in the dog house and he knew it! Here's a man who prided himself on cleanliness only to have a General and prominent dignitaries eat in his roach infested Mess Hall. I felt sorry for the man! I could see how embarrassed, disgusted and peeved he was.

When everyone cleared out, Sgt. Nixson called us together and informed us that every one of these God Damn roaches has to be killed by us tonight. I don't care how long it takes, we're not serving food in this roach infested Mess Hall.

"Sure Sarg! We understand."

"Okay, then, roll up your pants, get a broom, mop or club and let's get to it.

We'll pour boiling water in all the cracks and when they come running out we'll step or club them to death. Don't let any escape ! or it'll be your ass."

"Roger !"

We formed a human circle around one of the tables as Sgt. Nixson and Chuck stood by with a large pot of hot scalding water. The table was turned over, the boiling water poured into the cracks. Hoards of roaches dispersed in every direction. Those that didn't get scalded to death met their waterloo by a boondocker, broom or swab. More scalding water was poured into every crevice, making sure that any egg or brooding roach was exterminated. The table was then scrubbed with hot soapy water, rinsed off and sprayed with a germicide. Each table was wiped clean and then taken outside to dry. Once all the tables were outside to dry, the mess hall itself was scrubbed down and germicide sprayed in every crack. When we finally finished, our Mess Hall smelled antiseptically – like a hospital.

It was about 0200 in the morning when we finally finished. We were totally exhausted and when we hit the sack we fell asleep instantaneously.

The days on Bougainville flitted by very quickly. Before we knew it, our month of Mess duty was over. Sgt. Nixson, must have taken a liking to us because he asked us to stay on and become cooks. We thanked him for asking us, but we weren't interested. The only thing we'll miss about Mess Duty is that we were well fed.

We reported to Master Sergeant Ryan bright and early the next morning.

"Good morning men, how did you like mess hall duty"

"It's a little better than being in the front lines," we laughingly replied.

After a good laugh, he asked, "What would you guys like to try this month?"

"We have no idea. What would you suggest ? "

"Well here's a list of openings," he said, pushing a sheet of paper towards us. Chuck picked it up and the three of us went off to one side to study it. After a few minutes Sammy pointed to the words –Gas Truck Driver.

"That's what we should do!" Sammy suggested.

"Why?" I asked.

"Because it's a snap, that's why. All you have to do is keep a few planes filled with 100 Octane Aviation fuel. When the fuel tanks are filled, and the planes are out on a strike, you park your truck in a shady spot and crap out until they return. Not bad, huh?"

"I think Sammys right. I've watched these drivers sleep for hours at a time, and who knows, we may like it, and if that happens, we could stay on and get our Corporal ratings in no time."

"What do you say Lee?" Chuck asked.

"Count me out!"

"Why?"

"Because I've never driven a truck in my life, let alone a huge semi."

"What's so hard about driving a truck ? It's no different than the Naval Acorn Jeep you borrowed on the Canal," Chuck reminded me.

"Don't you have to double clutch these babies?"

"So?"

"So, I'll strip the gears in nothing flat!

"Who cares," Sammy laughed, "it's not like you don't have a warranty on it!"

"What the hell, at least I can catch up on my letter writing," I replied.

Sergeant Ryan was very pleased with our choice. For some reason or other the job of driving a Semi with 100 Octane Aviation fuel, wasn't too popular with the expendable Marines. In fact, two of the drivers we were replacing seemed quite happy to be transferred elsewhere.

We reported to Technical Sergeant Myers, our new boss.

"God morning gentlemen," he greeted us. "Sergeant Ryan just called me to tell me about your assignment here. You guys are replacing two gas truck drivers and one oil truck driver. You guys decide amongst yourselves what you want to drive. I personally don't give a shit."

"I'll drive the oil truck!" Sammy eagerly replied.

"Like hell you will! I'll flip you for it," Chuck said.

I couldn't see what difference it made, so I didn't butt in. I soon found out that driving an oil semi was a choice assignment. The planes didn't use much oil but they sure used a lot of gas. Chuck won the toss and was assigned to the oil semi.

The man whom I was replacing was instructed to stay with me for the rest of the day, to show me the ropes, so to speak.

"My names John Graff ,"

"Hi John, I'm Lee Walewander," I replied.

I know who you are! I've watched every one of your games. You're one hell of a ballplayer," he remarked

"Just average," I modestly replied.

"Let's get out of here and out in the open areas somewhere, so I can show you how to drive this rig.

I climbed in alongside of him and watched his every move. I was particularly watchful how he double clutched.

"Are you familiar with double clutching Lee?"

"No I'm not!"

"Well here's a schematic diagram on the dashboard to help you, if you need it."

"I probably will," I smiled.

"We'll see."

As we drove to a nearby revetment area, John explained the duties of a gas truck driver to me.

"Lee, when you come in the morning to pick up your rig, Tech Sergeant Myers will give you a list of the planes that have to be fueled and their location.

Your tank should be filled with gas, but regardless, you write down the amount of gas you have in your tank and keep accurate records of every gallon of gasoline you pump that day. When your tank is empty you drive over to the Fuel Depot and have it filled. You never handle the hose yourself all you have to do is drive the rig and keep track of the amount of gas that goes into every plane.

Chuck–Sammy-Lee

Under no circumstances are you to try and fuel a plane if the mechanic isn't around. Your job is to drive up close enough that your hose will reach the plane and the mechanics take over from there. And one more thing, do you smoke?"

"No I don't!"

"Well that's a plus!"

"Why is that?"

"Well I don't want to frighten you Jim, but the stuff you're hauling is extremely flammable. When they're fueling these planes you can smell gas all over the place. If you did smoke you can only do so if you're at least 50 yards from your rig."

"No wonder no one wants these jobs," I remarked.

One of our F4U fighter planes

"Yup, but there are a lot of perks that go along with this job. For one, this rig has a radio that you can listen to Tokyo Rose if you like.

She's the only one that plays American music and she usually tells us things about our outfit that even our CO doesn't know about. Secondly you'll have a lot of free time on your hands so you can catch up on your reading, letter writing or just snoozing. Before the day ended I was pretty good at double clutching and operating this rig as John calls it.

The next morning, the three of us reported to the Motor Transport to pick up our rigs and job sheets. Sergeant Myers was drinking coffee and sifting through a stack of papers he had on his desk.

"Good morning Sarge," we greeted him.

" Good morning men, have a cup of coffee and a sweet roll while you're waiting.

"Sounds like a good idea," I said.

The coffee was a little too strong, but it was passable.

"Do you have a ball game today Lee," Myers asked.

"Yes we do!" I replied as I swallowed some of the sweet role I was eating.

"Whom are you playing "

"The Seabees,"I replied.

"At home?"

"Yup !"

"Should be a good ball game," he remarked as he poured through his papers.

I was very fortunate that Sergeant Myers was crazy about baseball. He was present at every one of our games, betting heavily on each game. Everyone was making money, so they didn't object when the ballplayers were given certain privileges. I for one, worked only in the morning. The afternoons were spent playing, practicing, or surfing.

All I needed was for Rita to be out here with me, and I'd be extremely happy.

Besides our planes, we occasionally had to fuel planes from New Zealand and Australia. The planes were really ours, but were loaned to them, so they can help us defeat the Japanese. Consequently they were flying the colors of their nation. The "Limeys" as we affectionately called them, were also lend leased a gasoline semi and an oil semi, to oil and fuel their own planes.

They were a bunch of characters, and I loved their accent and company. I never knew anyone who enjoyed tea as much as they do. Probably similar to how Americans love their coffee.

Every morning about 1000 hours we would meet in a nearby revetment area and they would make tea and then we would sit around and drink and also swap a few yarns. Their tea was more like Boston coffee.

Life on Bougainville was becoming too stagnant. We haven't had an air raid in over a month and consequently our unoccupied foxholes were slowly becoming breeding sites for mosquitoes. Malaria was on the increase, so our Commanding Officer ordered Major Warten, our Medical Officer to inspect the foxholes in our camp area. Any neglected foxhole was to bring extra duty to its owners, so Sergeant Ryan informed us.

"Hey Cookie, what are we going to do with your brewery? Chuck asked as we dropped into our foxhole.

"Don't know Chuck, any suggestions?"

"Yeah, let's ditch this stuff or it'll be our ass."

"Like hell I will! I've got some good brew in the making and besides the Major won't know that we have another foxhole behind the canvas."

"Maybe so, but is it worth it?" Chuck asked.

"Damn right it is!" Sammy answered, "that's good brew!"

"What do you think Lee?"

"I'm indifferent!"

"Then let's vote on it," Chuck suggested.

"Okay but I'm not voting," I replied.

"I can take it or leave it, but however the vote turns out, I'll go along with it."

"Okay, Chuck how do you vote?"

"I say let's bury it!"

"Cookie I know you want your still so Sam you have the deciding vote.

"Keep it!" Sammy replied.

That afternoon we nervously awaited the inspecting party. Meanwhile Cookie got a bottle of vinegar and doused the inside of the foxhole to cover up the smell of our brew.

Cookie was perspiring profusely; he had the most at stake.

"Relax Cookie, we're all in it together," I said.

"Oh no you're not! Remember all these pots and pans and the ingredients are all from the Mess hall. You guys had nothing to do with it!"

"That's a crock of shit," Sammy cut in abruptly.

"We drink the booze, so we'll take credit for its presence.

"That's right John, just relax," I nervously said.

The inspecting party was getting closer, the lumps in our throats larger.

"Ten Shun!" Cookie shouted, as Major Warten and Sergeant Ryan approached.

"At ease men, as you were," the Major replied.

"Is your foxhole in good shape?" the Major asked.

"Yes sir!" we answered.

"We'll see." And with that he lowered himself into our foxhole, followed by Sergeant Ryan. We held our breath, crossed our fingers and prayed. They shortly emerged.

"Looks pretty good men," he said, "I especially like the idea of lining the walls with canvas." He smiled.

"Thank you sir," Cookie replied.

"The only objection I have is that your foxhole smells a little rancid."

"It's probably the canvas, sir," Cookie stammered.

"Perhaps! Maybe you guys should air it out," The Major suggested.

"Good Idea! Will do!"

When the inspecting party left, we were all a bundle of nerves.

"That was too close for comfort. I need a drink anyone want to join me"

"Not now Cookie, we've got planes to fuel and besides it's much too early in the day, for us to drink," I remarked.

This reason wasn't accepted by Cookie; he went down into the foxhole and poured himself a drink. There was no doubt about it. Cookie was an alcoholic.

But for this foxhole episode, life on Bougainville was becoming too civilized.

There were rumors flying about that MAG 24 was going on another mission. The Joint Chiefs of Staff were planning another invasion and our Marine Group was supposed to be a part of it.

Meanwhile our planes were bombing Rabaul, Truk and adjoining islands every day, which kept us very busy because these planes used up a lot of fuel.

A few days later, our camp area was rocked by what sounded like a five hundred bomb going off. I was writing a letter to Rita when it exploded. I tried to hit the deck but the steering wheel got in my way.

"Jesus Christ! Don't tell me the Japs are bombing us again!" I thought. The steering wheel didn't give, but I think my skull did! It hurt !

After the numbness subsided somewhat, I pulled out of the revetment area and followed an ambulance that roared past.

It soon turned into another revetment area where a crash truck crew was in the process of extinguishing an inferno of burning 100 Octane gas.

There was no sign of the truck or driver.
"Oh my God! I gasped, immediately thinking that it might be Sammy or Chuck.

"Who was it?" I asked one of the fire fighters.

"Don't know! The truck has been blown to pieces and the driver may be too, for as much as I know."

Just then Sammy's truck came upon the scene, followed by the others. The only truck that wasn't accounted for belonged to one of the Limeys.

"I wonder what caused the explosion?" Sammy asked one of our tea drinking buddy.

His Limey buddy said that Nigel smoked a lot.

"I'm afraid Nigel was too close to his truck when he took his last puff. Now I know why they call them coffin nails.

The Corpsmen mean while, were picking up parts of Nigel's body and placing them in a burlap bag. It was sickening to watch!

The month of July was in its final stages. I was seriously considering transferring to some other job because of the aforementioned incident. Chuck and Sammy felt the same way about it, and besides it was more fun to do something different every month. Our Commanding Officer approved of job transfers for the "Expendables" because you never know when we may be called upon to perform a certain task. When our month of "gassing around" terminated, we signed up for the Construction Crew.

Chapter 23

Being in Camp Construction had many advantages. First of all, you only worked half a day. There were two shifts; one from 0600 to 1200, and the other from 1200 to 1800. Because I was on the baseball team, I was given the early shift. Sergeant Russo also assigned Chuck and Sammy to the same detail because he knew we were inseparable. He approved of buddies sticking together, but warned us that if we "goofed off" he would split us up. We promised we wouldn't!

The Camp Construction unit had a variety of tasks to perform. We worked in crews with an experienced man at the helm. Our first job consisted of helping the New Zealanders construct a mess hall. I spent the entire morning tacking tar paper onto its roof and drinking tea.

A few days later we built a latrine in Officer's Quarters, and a few days after that found us repairing a washed out road. This is how diversified our jobs were. But for a few swollen thumbs, we were beginning to drive nails with authority.

I addition to these jobs, we also had to perform lumber jack duties. I was especially thrilled when Sergeant Russo informed us what we were going to do. We boarded a few trucks and drove out to the dense jungle. The trees that we had to chop down, were marked for us, by experienced loggers.

We stripped to our waists, grabbed a couple of sharp axes and began destroying what took hundreds of years to grow. Chuck and I straddled a huge tree and began chopping out big chunks of cambium layers with each swipe. Sammy stood by to relieve one of us if we got tired, or insert a wedge if needed. We soon realized that it was a lot easier to use a two man saw than an axe. Once the tree began to quiver or crack, we drove a wedge even deeper making certain that it fell in the direction designated.

"Timber!" we shouted, as the huge tree toppled to the ground. When the dust cleared up we pruned the branches, wrapped a chain around its trunk and dragged it out of the jungle with a tractor. We took turns dragging the logs to the saw mill where another group of Marines were sawing the trees into boards. The boards were then neatly stacked to dry. Working like this all morning, improved our appetites and we felt so much stronger and healthier. It felt good to work hard for a change.

I worked mornings and played ball in the afternoons. It was a perfect set up. Chuck and Sammy attended all of our games and were the bookies for our team. Everyone was making money because we had a good ball club. Out of the last ten games we won ten of them, the last three by shutouts. We were unbeatable. Sammy suggested we lose a couple of games to bring the odds down.

Whenever a ball game or practice was called off, the three of us would go swimming. One day we took a short cut through the jungle and stumbled across a water hole. We stood in complete amazement as we partook of its majestic beauty. The water was crystal clear and poured down from a fresh water stream above, forming a small water fall. The water fell into a pool surrounded by smoothened white rocks.

"I wonder how deep it is in the center?" Chuck asked.

"Beats me," I replied.

"Well there's only one way to find out" he said, as he began to undress. He waded into the water and before long he was up to his waist. He then submerged to do a little exploring.

Sammy and I not being very good swimmers stood by and watched.

In a few seconds Chuck's head emerged from under the water, with a great big shit "eatin" grin on his face.

"This water hole is perfect! Come on in!" Chuck shouted.

He was right. Not only was it clean and clear, but it was deep enough in the center for us to dive into if we wanted to.

"Last one in is a rotten egg," I said, as I hurriedly began to strip. I suddenly realized what I had said. Wasn't that Rita's favorite expression? I'll have to write her about this water hole we discovered, she'll get a big kick out of it. My meditations slowed me down to the extent that I was the rotten egg.

Chuck meanwhile, climbed to the top of the twenty foot waterfall and began to beat his chest and scream like "Tarzan."

"Look out below," he yelled as he executed a perfect swan dive into the center of the pool. We climbed up to the ridge and jumped in, feet first. It was such a relief to swim in fresh water once more. The ocean wasn't bad, but its salty water burned our eyes and glued our hair together. We vowed to keep, "Shangri-La" a top secret.

We reported back to our camp area, only to find out that an inspection of our 782 gear was scheduled for tomorrow. This came as a complete surprise to us, seeing that we had a general appearance inspection only last week. I never realized so many of us needed haircuts, until I saw the two block line at the barber shop.

This inspection was called the "Majors Inspection of 782 Gear." It consisted of placing all your belongings neatly and in true Marine Corps manner on your sack, for the Major to inspect. Any neglected or missing gear would be noted and some form of penalty would be assessed.

That evening the outdoor theatre was practically empty as most everyone was busily engaged in scrubbing packs, belts, canteen covers, etc., which jungle rot was claiming. Perhaps this was the reason for the inspection.

The next morning, Sammy and I had some missing gear and failed the Major's Inspection. We consequently were given the detail of cleaning the latrine's in Officer's quarters. Immediately after inspection, Sammy and I picked up the necessary gear to clean the latrines. This consisted of a broom, bucket of lye, a flit gun and a can of gasoline.

There were four latrines to be cleaned. Each one was constructed solely of wood, but for the cheese cloth that took place of a wire screen. There were no stools as such, only six circular holes cut out into a wide board; six on either side. The twelve seater was situated over a deep hole into which all the waste material was to drop.

In order to kill the spiders, mosquitoes, flies, lice, centipedes, etc., that may be present in this hole, we had to spread lye around the enclosure and in all the crevices. The inside was sprayed with a flit gun and the "Piece de Resistance" came when we poured gasoline down into the hole and ignited it. But for a few charred boards everything went according to Hoyle.

The next latrine we cleaned and were ready to throw a lighted match into it, Captain Huntley came running into the latrine. This was the same crap head that played cards during the blackout and who indirectly was responsible for Hillbilly's death.

"I'm sorry sir, this head is closed, please use one of the others," I politely informed him.

"Get lost! I'll use this head if I want to," he barked, pushing his way past me.

He proceeded to sit down and began to read a magazine he brought with him.

"I should have placed a round through him and not his lantern," I fumed.

"You're not kidding Lee. If we ever get into a combat zone again, I'll salute this bastard every time I see him. Maybe a sniper will take care of him for us."

"Yeah, I feel the same way about him," I disgustedly replied.

Just then Captain Huntley proceeded to take a cigarette out of his pack and light it! He was so engrossed in his magazine that he forgot that the gasoline was already present in the hole, or did we forget to mention that to the Captain.

"I can't look!" Sammy winced.

The Captain didn't disappoint us. He proceeded to flip the lit match into one of the seat holes. All of a sudden there was a big explosion with shooting flames coming out from every unoccupied hole.

The Captain let out a death defying scream as the flames engulfed his buttocks. He bolted out of the latrine with his pants still around his knees. He was fiery red, ass and all!

Sammy and I laughed hysterically!

"Couldn't happen to a nicer guy!" we screamed with delight! The Captain was treated for second degree burns, while we were interrogated by our Commanding Officer.

"Okay Private Walewander, tell me what happened?" the C O asked me. I told him my version of what happened and as we talked, he tried desperately not to laugh. Our CO was at all of our games and I knew he liked me. Obviously he didn't like Captain Huntley, who was at the base hospital, being treated for second degree burns. Even though he seemed elated over this incident, our actions couldn't go unheeded. We were ordered to clean the latrines for another week.

Before the month of August was over, Sgt. Russo called me into his office.

"How do you like what you're doing in Camp Construction, and do you guys intend to come back for another month?"

"Well we enjoy what we're doing, but we're not sure."

"Well if you do come back, I'll put you in charge of the ball diamond detail.

I've been getting a lot of complaints from Captain Northey about the miserable way we've been taking care of the infield.

He's always on my back about one thing or another. I would appreciate it, if you could get that ball field, in the shape you ballplayers want it in, and at the same time get him off my back."

"How much help would you give me?

"Five men, including yourself."

"Can I pick my men?"

"Sure, but remember, you're responsible for the upkeep of that ball field. If the Captain has any complaints, he should get on your back, not on mine."

"It's a deal, Sarge," I smiled.

"So starting next month, you and four others will work on the diamond every morning, rain or shine."

"You bet!"

The ball diamond detail turned out to be one of the best jobs, we've had. Instead of putting in the usual six hours, we found that if we work hard we can do it all in three hours and have the rest of the day off. The biggest job was filling in the infield after a heavy rain.

Once filled, we had to rake it, roll it, and then drag it. The batter's box and sidelines were marked with chalk, last of all. We then spent the rest of the day on the beach or in Shangri-La. If we had a ball game away from home, we didn't even bother to go out to the field. We only worked when a game or practice was to be held. We had it made, and knew it!

Our baseball team won twelve straight before we lost one to the VMF Fighter Squadron battalion, 7 to 6. I made a crucial error in the twelfth inning to let the winning run score. Everyone could see I wasn't taking this loss very well.

I felt miserable! Captain Northey knew how badly I felt and so he tried to console me.

"Lee, how long have you been playing ball?"

"All my life Sir, I guess"

"Well haven't you learned that you can't win them all! Sure you made an error today which cost us a ball game, so what! Look how many games you've won for us with your superb fielding and clutch hitting.

No one is infallible! I've seen the best of them make errors on ground balls that practically had handles on them. Forget about it! Tomorrows another day and now that we were beaten, the betting odds may drop somewhat," he laughed.

"Thanks Sir!"

I felt somewhat better, but ball players have a bad habit of reliving the bad plays even when they sleep. What a nightmare I had. I must have made the same error in my dreams at least twenty times.

The camp area was stirring. A USO (United Service Organization) group of celebrities were coming to our island to entertain and cheer up the troops. Bob Hope and company were scheduled to entertain us. The only trouble was that it was going to be held at an Army base here on the island. Along with Bob Hope, there was Jerry Colona, Frances Langford, Patti Thomas, Tony Romano and Barry Dean.

"Let's get there early!" Sammy suggested.

"We have to or we'll never get a seat," Chuck replied.

"Good idea," I said.

That evening, immediately after chow, we left for the Army camp area. We got there about four hours early. The outdoor theatre was rapidly filling up, as everyone anticipated a large turnout. Some of the men in the front rows were playing cards in order to pass the time away. We no sooner got comfortable when the rains came. It was a question of getting wet or losing our seats.

The former won out! The rain continued to beat down on us for the next few hours. When the show finally began, Bob Hope's opening remark was about the number of fish he's seen in the audience. He wasn't kidding either.

Luckily the stage had a roof over it or the show might not have gone on, regardless of their motto.

A shapely dancer by the name of Patti Thomas danced for us in a very skimpy outfit. The troops sat there drooling, and I couldn't help but wonder if this teasing didn't do more harm than good for the morale of the men. Nevertheless, the show was a huge success. It was worth getting soaked for.

Tropical storms or hurricanes are very common in the Southwest Pacific Ocean. When they strike, they do so with so much force that all our planes have to be tied down or be blown away. If I live to be a hundred I shall never forget the night of September 21, 1944.

It started out as a normal storm, but about 0200 a violent thunderstorm descended upon us. Where it came from we don't know but its violent winds began to break off branches from the huge trees that grew in the midst of our camp area. The larger branches plummeted to the ground, oft times striking a tent and its occupants. I wasn't sleeping in my foxhole, and being half awake, I sat up in my sack when I heard this rumbling noise. It sounded very familiar but I didn't have time to analyze where I heard it before, but it didn't matter. I had to get out of here.

As I bolted out of my sack I began to shout for my buddies to get up and get out. In the process I tore a hole in my mosquito netting as I moved out on the double. I was half asleep and frightened! The noise was deafening now and very familiar. This is when one of us would shout "Timber"!" All of a sudden the earth shook as if an earthquake had taken place.

When the tremor ceased, the agonizing screams and cries of mercy were clearly audible.

I was fully awake now and trembling. I began to run toward the whining, sobbing cries.

Oh my God, I prayed, I wonder if Chuck, Sammy and Cookie are okay? I was relieved that they were all right even though a part of the large tree wiped out a part of our tent.

As I stumbled in the dark, it was still raining and I couldn't see where I was going.

I was barefoot and the twigs and plants were cutting up my feet. To make matters worse, I kept hearing cries of help, which I tried to answer.

"Where are you?" I would ask as I groped around in the dark to see if I could find them. The Marines who had flash lights enabled us to see where our victims were pinned down.

The large tree was clearly visible now. Its trunk flattened three tents when it came crashing down. Some of the victims were crushed to death as they slept, others had their arms and legs broken as they tried to escape. When daylight came and the storm subsided, we were finally able to clear away most of the debris. There were three dead and six others were wounded. The ones that were wounded had broken arms and legs.

It seems like these accidents are constantly plaguing us. If it isn't bombs dropping on us from our own planes now it's the weather we have to be concerned about. It was a sickening ordeal to see these mangled bodies being put on stretchers and rushed to the base hospital.

I could never sleep peacefully again after what had happened. On many occasions, I found myself running down the road whenever I heard a twig snap. This may not seem strange, but if you're still asleep, it is.

During the month of September, our Commanding Officer initiated a Non-Commissioned Officer School. This school was open to all Non Coms and was to last approximately two weeks.

It was to consist of a series of lectures on Field Sanitation, First Aid, Military Courtesy, Close Order Drill, Interior Guard Duty, Map reading, Extended Order and the U.S. Rifle, caliber 30 Ml. I addition to the lectures you had to be able to drill a platoon expertly.

The purpose of the school was two- fold. First of all, the troops were getting restless during the lull in operations, and this would give them something to do.

Secondly, rates were frozen since June, so this was an ideal way to eliminate hundreds of Marines who otherwise thought they should be promoted.

The Non Coms receiving the highest scores would be promoted to their next highest rank.

"Let's sign up for it," I suggested.

"I'm all for it!"Chuck replied. "What have we got to lose?"

"Nothing but time, and we've got plenty of that," I remarked.

"How about you Sam?"

"Nah, I've had it with boring lectures, and what the hell do I need a higher rate for? I'm not a twenty year man. All I want to do is survive this war and resume my life back home in Chicago. You guys sign up and I'll take care of the ball diamond while you're studying.

"Okay Sam, but you may be sorry," we said.

"I don't know! You guys may work your butts off and they still won't promote you." Sammy replied.

"Well nothing ventured, nothing gained," I remarked.

Chuck and I signed up for the morning classes. We attended all the lectures, took notes and every evening reviewed them.

In the evenings, Chuck and I would study while Sammy and Cookie were attending the outdoor theater. Before we knew it the two weeks were up and the Final Examination was upon us. That night we reviewed till the wee hours in the morning.

"How do you feel this morning Lee," Chuck asked me.

"A little groggy. I think we stayed up a little too long."

"It'll pay off Lee, you wait and see.'"

"I sure hope so!"

We went to chow and then to the outdoor theatre where the test was to be given. The test was in four parts and took about three hours to complete.

When I finished the last of it, I felt like a wrung out sponge. I turned in my paper and left. Chuck was waiting for me.

"How'd you do Lee?"

"Pretty good, I think. How about yourself ?"

"I think I did alright!"

"When will we know?"

"Tomorrow morning, they'll post the grades in the Mess Hall.

"Good!"

The next morning a list of names of those qualifying for promotion was posted. Chuck's name and mine were way up there on the list. The studying paid off and we were assured that we would be promoted to Corporal. How soon? We didn't know!

The month of September was ending and so was our very successful baseball season. The scuttlebutt around the camp was that our outfit was scheduled to leave Bougainville and this would probably be our last game. We had over thirty wins and only two losses. Our last game this week end was against an Army Anti Aircraft team we previously beat. We beat them again 7 to 2.

After this game Captain Northey and Sgt. Carter threw a party for us in our Mess hall. We had a large cake which Cookie baked for us plus, crackers, cheese, pretzels and of course a lot of beer.

"Gentlemen! Gentlemen! May I have your attention," Captain Northey shouted.

"First of all I want to congratulate you all for being the greatest bunch of ball players and men that I have had the pleasure to manage and know. You not only brought entertainment to our troops you "kicked ass" and made them rich.

Here's hoping we can play ball again someday, only under different circumstances. Good luck and May God bless you all.

"Let's hear it for the Captain, Sergeant Carter shouted.

"For he's a jolly good fellow, For he's a jolly good fellow, For he's a jolly good fellow that no one can deny! The beer cans were raised and so were our voices. We toasted each other a few times over and when the beer was gone, so were we. I never slept better!

Because our baseball season was over, we lost our jobs taking care of the ball diamond. The next morning, we reported to Sergeant Ryan about a new job for the month of October.

"Can't you people stick with one job for awhile," he grumbled.

"Naw," Sammy answered, "we get bored and besides we like to see you at least once a month."

"Yeah ! Right!" he replied.

"How would you guys like to be assigned to Field Operations up on the air strip," he asked.

"Doing what? "

"How should I know! They have a variety of jobs out there. Sgt.Phelps will tell you about these jobs when you report to him this morning.

The Field Operations shack was located mid-way and alongside the Piva South Air Strip. When we entered, a tall, lithe, Sergeant approached us.

"Good morning men. You must be the replacements Sgt. Ryan phoned me about."

"Yes we are," we answered almost on cue.

After the usual round of introductions, we were informed of our duties. We were to be trained as Field Operation Clerks, Control Tower Operators, Follow Me Jeep drivers and at times double as chauffeurs.

As Field Operation clerks it was our job to keep an accurate record (log) of every pilot and plane that takes off and lands on our air strip.

The departure and arrival time, as well as the destination is to be recorded in the log book and on a large blackboard that stood at the rear of the office.

Besides working in the office, and control tower, we alternated driving the "Follow Me" Jeeps.

These Jeeps were so named because of a large "Follow Me" sign that was firmly bolted on to two tall beams at the rear of the vehicle. Surrounding this sign were many colored lights, plus a flood light which not only illuminated the sign but the adjoining area as well.

The job of the Follow Me driver was to escort planes to and from the air strip. If a transient plane landed on our air strip, we drove out to meet it and beckoned the pilot to Follow Me. Once the plane is parked, we double as chauffeurs, transporting its occupants to Officer's Quarters. We looked forward to this duty because at times we met a lot of celebrities.

Two days later, an incident occurred that still has us shaking in our boots. I was working in the Control Tower when a pilot radioed in to tell us of a hung bomb on his plane.

"Control Tower to S.B.D., Shake bomb over ocean. Avoid flying over camp area!"

"S.B.D. to Tower, Tried! But no can do! I'm running low on fuel! Must land!"

"Tower to S.B.D. –Stand by!

"Roger"

"Lee get on the phones and alert the Crash and Ordinance crews to stand by. Get the area cleared of all personnel," Sgt. Phelps ordered.

"Roger!" I answered excitedly.

Our Control Tower

In a matter of minutes, the alert was in full progress. The sirens were sounded and the crash truck and crew were standing by in readiness, as was the demolition crew.

"Control Tower to S.B.D. You may now land, only do it gently, please !" Sgt.. Phelps informed the pilot.

"Roger!" the pilot gulped.

Sgt. Phelps hurriedly put down the microphone.

"Okay, Lee, let's get out of here!"

Our control tower was about 50 feet in the air. In order to get to the top of it, you had to climb a ladder.

In case of an air raid, there was a rope hanging from the center of the tower which is used if you have to exit quickly.

We slid down the rope right into a bunker. Our quick descent burned my legs and hands somewhat.

The S.B.D. was in the flight pattern and about to land. We peered from over the sandbags as the plane approached the field. The 500 pound bomb looked like a miniature coffin hanging under his belly.

"Keep your fingers crossed! Sgt. Phelps said, as the plane's wheels began to touch the Marston mats.

"Easy now! Easy does it!" Sgt. Phelps mumbled under his breath.

The knowledge of a 500 pound hanging loosely under his plane was too much for the pilot to endure, and consequently the plane bounced a few times before settling down. This jarring set the bomb free and it began to slide in front of the plane. It was like a bowling ball heading for the pins.

"Hit the deck Lee, that baby is likely to go off!" Sgt. Phelps shouted.

The bomb skidded and bounced across the field before friction slowed it down at the far end of the runway. We waited for it to explode but to our surprise it didn't!

After we caught our second wind, Sgt. Phelps looked over the field with his binoculars.

"I'd sure hate to be the poor bastard who has to go out there and dismantle it!"

"I agree!" I nodded.

In a few minutes one of the crew from ordinance started his long trek towards this sleeping beauty. It looked perfectly harmless, like a coiled rattle snake, ready to strike if disturbed.

As he walked towards it, I couldn't help but think what guts it must take to even get near it, let alone dismantle it.

We held our breath as the lone figure draped himself over the bomb and carefully began to unscrew the detonator mechanism. One false move and 500 pounds of steel would tear his body to shreds. We knew it! And so did he!

The tension was so thick, you could cut it with a knife. No one said a word; we watched and waited. Suddenly the figure sprang up brandishing the nose mechanism in his hand, and almost simultaneously collapsing on his haunches.

"Gung Ho!" the Ordinance crew shouted, as they ran up to him and congratulated him on a job well done. We were so engrossed in what had happened we completely forgot that there were other planes still in the air waiting to land. What a day!

Even though our airstrip was closed for the night, two clerks and a control tower operator were on duty every night. This was in case an emergency arose and the field had to be opened up very quickly. It hasn't happened as of yet, but with our luck it probably will.

I didn't mind this duty, as it gave me a chance to write a few more letters to Rita and my family. We also had a powerful Hallicrafter receiver , which enabled us to receive programs from all over the world. Most of them weren't very clear except the one coming in from Tokyo, Japan.

This program featured a girl disc jockey who was appropriately named Tokyo Rose.

Rosie as we called her, not only played the latest records, but also commented about the various American outfits that were out here. Her objective was to break down our morale, and at times, I'm afraid she succeeded.

One night, as I was writing to Rita, I couldn't help but wonder if she went out on dates occasionally. After all, I've been away from her for some time and who knows she may find someone very charming and I'll be getting a dear John letter like Pedro received. While I was deep in thought, Rosie cut in by saying:

"Are you Yanks lonely tonight? Are you yearning for your wife or girl friend? Do you wonder what she's doing while you're rotting in the jungles? Well my womanly intuition tells me that she's patriotic. She's out dancing with a smooth talking, handsome, stateside officer. They're probably dancing to this beautiful ballad by Frank Sinatra.

The song is "I'll be Seeing You!" and she may at that! Hope you like it!

"No I don't!" and with that I turned off the radio forcefully.

"Don't listen to her Lee, that's exactly how she wants you to react," Chuck replied.

"I know it, but she may be right!"

"Don't be ridiculous! Rita's too much in love with you to go out with anyone else."

"Do you really think so?"

"Sure I do. Now finish your letter and get some sleep. I'll stand watch for awhile."

"Okay."

"And turn that radio back on, I'd like to hear some music."

"Surely"

I finished writing my letter and crapped out on the cot which we had in the rear of the office.

Chuck, meanwhile, poured himself a cup of coffee and sat down at the desk to write a few letters. The music was soothing. I soon fell asleep.

When we went to chow that morning, we found the camp personnel in a state of excitement. It was official now, Marine Air Group 24 was to start packing. Our mission was to provide air support for the Army infantry in the Philippine Islands. We were to do exactly what we did on Bougainville. Protect and run our own air strip.

For the next two months, Bougainville was to become a training school for Officers, Pilots, Gunners and certain Non-Commissioned Officers.

Needless to say, our Field Operation Group was very busy transporting Generals, Fleet Commanders, Colonels, and Captains from one meeting to another.

Field Operations Jeep

A series of forty lectures were scheduled. The instructors were very well versed in Close Air Ground support. They included veteran air liaison officers, army ground officers and intelligence officers from all over the Pacific.

In addition to our own group, officers from M.A.G. 32 and M.A.G. 14 as well as officers from various Army divisions, which we were going to support were included. The Navy was also represented. They sent their intelligence officers from their 7th fleet.

After the Battle of the Perimeter most everyone involved in this battle had a war souvenir or two that they intended to bring home with them.

Since we were scheduled to be leaving for the Philippines in a couple of months the higher echelon decided that each Marine could only send back one item the others they had to leave behind.

We were going into a battle zone and there's no way we can carry our souvenirs with us.

Chuck, Sammy and I decided to keep our Japanese rifles instead of the bayonets, holsters, pistols, etc. that we had in our possession.

We went over to our base Post Office and to our pleasant surprise the Camp Construction personnel built us wooden crates, to protect our Jap 25 rifles from any damage during their trip back to the states.

Sammy was very unhappy because he had a locker box full of war memorabilia. He began selling some of these items to the Marines who weren't around during the Battle of the Perimeter.

During the Battle of the Perimeter, a few cases were reported where our pilots dropped their bombs on our own troops. So this wouldn't happen again, the Ground Support Officers were working diligently to solve this problem.

Another problem was the length of time it took before Air support would come to help out a squad or Platoon that was pinned down by enemy fire.

UNITED STATES MARINE CORPS
HEADQUARTERS SQUADRON-24, MARINE AIRCRAFT GROUP-24
FIRST MARINE AIRCRAFT WING, FLEET MARINE FORCE,
c/o FLEET POST OFFICE, SAN FRANCISCO, CALIFORNIA.

8 November, 1944.

From: The Commanding Officer.
To: The Group Mail Officer, Marine Aircraft
             Group-24.

Subject: Package, inspection of, case of
             Leo J. WALEWANDER, PFC, USMC.

    1.   I certify that no government property is
enclosed in this package.

    2.   This package will not be handled as official
matter.

    3.   I have inspected this package this date and
find the contents in order.

                              L. L. Jacobs
                         L. L. JACOBS

- -

        HEADQUARTERS SQUADRON TWENTY FOUR

    " I HEREBY CERTIFY THAT I AM A MEMBER OF THE ARMED FORCES
OF THE UNITED STATES, ON DUTY OUTSIDE THE CONTINENTAL LIMITS
OF THE UNITED STATES AND THAT THE ENCLOSED SHIPMENT IS SENT
AS A GIFT PURSUANT TO PUBLIC LAW # 790, AND THAT ITS VALUE IS
$50. OR LESS. (UNITED STATES CURRENCY).

                    DATED THIS 8th DAY OF November, 1944.

                         Leo J. Walewander
                              SIGNATURE

- -

    "MAY BE OPENED FOR CUSTOMS PURPOSES BEFORE DELIVERY TO THE
ADDRESSEE."

- -

-345-

In the past, a request for air support had to be cleared through the Air Support Controller back at headquarters. Sometimes this took a few hours, and at times too late to do any good. To remedy this situation, a new air support program was initiated. It was agreed upon that communication between pilot and air liaison patrolmen should be direct, without any middle man to stifle procedures.

During the next two months, simulated attacks on pill- boxes and enemy positions was practiced very diligently by the 37th Army infantry division and the Marine pilots. The maneuverability and accuracy of our S.B.D.'s and F4U's amazed the foot soldier to no end. The confidence that was so lacking during the Battle of the Perimeter, was now on the upgrade. Before this training period was to end, the Marines and the soldiers were to become the best of friends; trusting, cooperating and respecting each other's fighting ability.

This training period didn't interfere with our duties at the air strip. If anything, the traffic increased quite a bit making our job as "Follow Me" drivers and chauffeurs more demanding. We had to check out another Command Jeep from the motor pool to handle this overflow.

Tokyo Rose was very informative. Last night she interrupted a hot jam session to bring us the following announcement:

"To all personnel of Marine Air Group 24.

We know you people are in the process of leaving your island paradise, but I wonder if you know where you're going?

We do, and we'll have a warm reception waiting for you when you get here.

"I'll bet you will!" Chuck sneered, "but Rosie we're going to be ready too, right Lee?"

"Right!" I replied.

To be perfectly honest, I didn't particularly want to get into another battle. All I wanted to do was to play ball again. Why press my luck, I had a lot of close calls and I don't want anymore.

Chuck on the other hand just couldn't wait to get into combat again. I don't know how many times we talked him out of going up into the hills, and do a little Jap hunting, as we did on the Canal. Sammy was more like me. If we had to fight, we would.

But after the Battle of the Perimeter we realized how easy it was to be killed and we didn't want any part of that. We had too much to live for.

During this training period, the defense of the island was slowly being turned over to the Australians and New Zealanders. The American army was already relieved of its perimeter duty and now we were told that the New Zealanders would relieve us of our air strips. We were happy to oblige. A couple of weeks later, Sgt. Phelps called a meeting of all Field Operation personnel.

"Men," he said, "D day is finally here. Tomorrow the New Zealander's take over our two airstrips. This means that most of you will be assigned to other duties.

"Yeah, shit details !" Sammy whispered.

"When we get another air strip in the Philippines, I expect all of you to be back at your old job. But until then, this is it men. Tomorrow morning you are to report to the outdoor theater for further instructions. Good luck!"

The next morning we reported to the outdoor theater as instructed. Master Sergeant Ryan was already present with what looked like the camp roster in his hand.

"I wonder how many of us are here?" I asked.

"I'd say at least two hundred," Chuck replied.

"Closer to three," Sammy cut in knowingly.

Sgt. Ryan, meanwhile began to call roll and when he finished, there were 283 of us present. He handed the clip -board to one of 6is aides and looked around to see if any stragglers were coming, before he spoke.

"As you very well know, we are scheduled to leave Bougainville very shortly. Our destination is the Philippine Islands. Because you are expendables, you are going to fight alongside the Army infantry on "D" day or thereabouts.

This is going to be a big show and every available man will be given an opportunity to fight and maybe die for his country.

"He means expendable man," I whispered to Chuck.

"Yeah, aren't we the lucky ones."

"Once the beachhead is secured, you people will put down your arms and with the help of the Seabees and Army engineers you will help build an air strip for our Marine Air Groups.

During the next two weeks you are going to think you're in Boot camp again. You're going to bitch, sweat, call me an SOB and sweat some more. But when it's over with, you'll be in shape again, fighting shape that is. After all, you people are Marines, first and foremost, the best God Damn fighting force in the world, and don't you ever forget it!"

The expendables roared in uproarious approval when Sgt. Ryan finished his electrifying speech. It reminded me of the Knute Rockne picture when Pat O'Brien gave his memorable half time pep talk to his players.

We felt the same way! Bring on the tortuous training! We were ready!

Chapter 24

The expendables of our group were scheduled to leave Bougainville two weeks in advance of the main contingent. This meant that the 14 selected Officers and a good number of Non Commissioned Officers had to get us in fighting shape in two weeks.

The first few days we spent exercising and running. We gradually worked our way into calisthenics, judo, and bayonet fighting. An obstacle course was hacked out of the jungle and its itinerary consisted of hills to climb, rivers to cross, and dense mosquito infested jungles to fight in. In addition to these drills, we also got permission to use the Army's firing range.

Once the Battle of the Perimeter was over, we had a lot of replacements come in from the Aviation Replacement Squadron in Camp Miramar. They signed up for over sea duty rather than go to school and be trained in some capacity. There was no doubt about it, some of these Marines looked like kids, and were very naïve, pretty much like we were when we first came over.

After a couple of weeks, they performed like combat veterans, following our orders to a tee. How they will react under fire only time would tell and ours just about ran out. In less than a week we were scheduled to ship out.

"This morning you men have to be inoculated for certain diseases that are present in the Philippine Islands," Sgt. Ryan informed us.

"Not again!" Sammy began to gripe.

"Are you going to join us Sarg?" Chuck wanted to know.

"Sure I'll be there to straighten out the needles," he laughed.

"He's kidding," Sam, "Everyone going overseas has to take these shots."

"I know that!, but I enjoy pulling Ryan's chain from time to time."

"After you people get these shots you won't be in any condition to work out so you're going to listen to Captain Parsen. He's an authority on the Philippine Islands. Our Commanding Officer wants you people to become familiar with its people, culture, and flora and fauna," Sgt. Ryan told us.

"Hey, Sarg, who's Flora and Fauna?" Sammy asked. "Sounds like two popular chicks our C.O. wants us to make out with," Sammy laughed.

Sgt. Ryan didn't say a word, he just laughed.

After all of us got our shots, we marched over to the outdoor theater where we were ushered into a section that was reserved for us.

"Good morning men! My name is Captain Parsen and I'm here to enlighten you on the island you're going to visit."

We soon learned that the Philippines were the largest Archipelago in the world. They contained over two thousand islands, the largest being Luzon in the Northern sector. Manila, the capital of the Philippines Islands was located here. The islands are of volcanic origin. They are mountainous, and almost, half of them, are covered by dense forests and jungles. The climate on the Philippines is of two types. It's either wet or dry. In the summer and fall it rains; winter and spring are the dry seasons.

"You men can at least be thankful you're not hitting the beach during the rainy season. Just picture yourselves fighting in mud up to your ass holes," the Captain remarked. "The temperature is always around eighty degree, varying very little during the year.

We also learned that the majority of the Filipinos worshipped Catholicism although Mohammedism, Budhism and Paganism were still very much in prominence.

The language, natural resources, wild life, crops, etc. were scheduled for another day.

"I wonder if they'll give us a lecture on how to fraternize with these Filipino chicks,"Sammy remarked, as we left the outdoor theater

"I don't see why not!" I replied. "They're telling us everything else about them."

The training and lectures continued. We were in tip top shape not only physically but mentally as well. We knew more about the Philippines than we probably know about our own towns. We were eager to get going. That evening I wrote Rita a couple of letters one to Rita and one to my family.

December 23, 1944

Dear Rita:

I receive your letters and as usual I am very delighted to hear from you. I don't know if you realize it or not, but your letters are all I look forward to. Nothing else matters! I think I could endure any hardship, just as long as my reward is a letter from the future Mrs. Walewander.

I often wonder how your Naval Nurse's training is coming along. Who knows you may get assigned to the Pacific area and we can go for a swim together. Wouldn't that be great!

At the present time we're leaving our island and going elsewhere. If you don't hear from me for awhile, don't panic. Keep writing your letters and they'll forward them to me.

I love you very much and think of you constantly. When I go to sleep, I try to keep you in my mind so that I can dream about you. Sometimes it works and we're together having a wonderful time. Do you ever dream about me?

I love you,
Lee

P.S. Have a very Merry Christmas and a very Happy New Year!

Give my love and regards to June and Val.

Early next morning, we dropped off our stenciled seabags at the Quartermaster Depot. Chances are we won't see our seabags for at least a month or so. We were told to place our personal belongings in our backpacks.

We fell out in full battle attire and awaited further orders. After last minute instructions, we proceeded to march out of the camp area proper amidst the yells and cheers of our camp personnel, who hopefully will see us all in two weeks.

"Save a few Japs for us," they shouted.

"Virgins too!"

"We were still smiling when we boarded the trucks.

"Gung Ho! See you guys the Philippines," we shouted.

The trucks moved out and in about ten minutes we were approaching the beach.

Just then a couple of landing barges approached the beach and inched up onto the sand. "Okay men, off the trucks and into the barges, Sgt. Ryan ordered, "an on the double."

With our rifles at port arms, we double-timed it across the hot sand, hitting the wet ramp in stride and practically catapulting ourselves into the barge. When it was filled with perspiring Marines, the ramp was raised, blocking any last minute attempt for anyone to change their minds, like it would matter.

The landing barge we were crammed into was trying desperately to keep us on this island, but the powerful Naval engines thought differently. The propeller blades kept churning up the water into a white foam; the barge lost its vise like grip and slowly began to slide backwards.

We were clear of the sand and for that matter an island that was our home for over 10 months.

Our barge moved swiftly across the water. Cool fine sprays of the salty Pacific Ocean cooled us off somewhat, whenever we hit a wave. The ship was now in plain view. Its name was now S.S. President Polk

S.S. President Polk

We drifted towards the center of the ship where rope ladders were draped over the side of the ship.

"Up and at 'em', Sgt. Ryan ordered. "Let's show these Doggies how to climb up these ladders."

"Roger !" we gulped.

It was hard enough to climb these ladders without your gear, but shouldering your rifle and back pack, it was a bitch!

Chuck, the show off, that he was, took a hold of a rung and before any of us could get started he was half way up the ladder. We quickly followed.

The Army infantry was already aboard and watching us with great delight. They lined the railings egging us on as we weaved our way upward. But for an occasional helmet or canteen dropping back into the barge, we fared pretty well.

We were ushered into a hold and down a number of steel ladders before we reached our quarters.

"Pick out a hanging cot, square away your gear and report top side for Guard Duty," Sgt. Ryan ordered.

"Guard duty? I thought this was going to be a pleasure cruise? Sammy bemoaned.

"Bergoni, get off my back! If you have any gripes see the Padre. He has a seabag full of T.S. (Tough shit) slips.

We soon found out that we were sharing Guard Duty with the Army. It seems that Guards or M.P.'s (Military Police) were necessary because of all the troops aboard this ship. Fights were always breaking out mostly between the Army and Marines. So what else is new!

Once top side we were informed that the Army would stand guard, over their own men, and the Marines over theirs. The main concern is to stop the fights that may break out between the services. This is harder to do especially when there are so many troops aboard.Another important function of a guard was to enforce the blackout code. Even though we were protected by Destroyer escorts, we couldn't take a chance on a Japanese submarine sneaking through and sending us to Davy Jones's locker.

We left Bougainville, on December 23 ,1944 for the Philippine Islands. Which of the 2000 islands we were to invade we didn't know but we figured it was Luzon the largest and most likely to be hit at this time. Besides, Tokyo Rose said it would be Luzon and she was usually right.

The next day out, we ran into choppy seas. Our destroyer escorts dipped their bows beneath the white tipped waves in horrible unison. This didn't help our nervous stomachs any, but being "old salts" we knew how to relax and ride with the waves. This is what is called having your sea legs. Mine were a little wobbly

Tomorrow was Christmas, so consequently the Catholic troops wanted to receive Holy Communion at midnight mass. Father Christafano and another catholic chaplain held confessions all that day.

Since I was a Catholic, I needed to get absolution, for the number of lives I've taken, before I could receive Holy Communion, at midnight mass. I knew Father Christifano would give me absolution, because I only did what they told me to do. Kill or be killed.

Whatever faults the Catholic religion may have the confessionary is not one of them. It was a poor man's form of psychoanalysis and did wonders for the morale of troops going into combat. I for one felt so relieved when Father Christifano convinced me that I didn't do anything wrong.

Midnight mass was held in the mess hall and beyond. It was so crowded that it was impossible to kneel down. We stood the entire service. I prayed fervently and soon went forth to receive the Blessed Host. At that moment I felt like I could die right now and go to heaven. It was such an exhilarating feeling.

After a few days at sea we landed in the Admiralties on Christmas day and so we spent a few days of Rest and Relaxation on Manus Island. Meanwhile, other ships were joining our convoy from all parts of the Pacific theater of war. We toured the island and while touring we came across a whorehouse, which had a line of service men about a block long.

"Let's get laid!" Sammy excitedly suggested.

"I'm all for it," Chuck replied. "How about you Lee?"

"As much as I'd like to, I promised Rita that I would be faithful. You guys go ahead and enjoy it, I wouldn't. I'm going to go back to the ship and write her a letter."

"Okay Lee we understand." and with that they fell in line to get laid!

After a few days, there were so many ships in the harbor that we couldn't count them all. We spotted a battleship, cruisers, aircraft carriers, troop ships, tankers, destroyers, landing crafts, and even a submarine.

"I wonder what the hell they're waiting for? Chuck snapped, "Let's get this show on the road.

"Take it easy Chuck," I calmly said. "Maybe they're waiting for a few more ships to join us."

"More ships! If any more show up we could invade Japan right now!"

"You never know what they're up to," I remarked.

The delay was nerve wrecking. It was December the 31st and we were still anchored in the bay.

"I wish Cookie were here with his bathroom gin, boy would I get stoned tonight," Chuck remarked.

As I laid there on my sack I thought about last year's New Years Eve. What a difference a year makes. Last year at this time I was at the beach house with Rita, enjoying life to its fullest. Now only a year later, I'm on an island in the Pacific, that I never heard of, waiting to go into battle from which I may not return. I felt like shit !

Sammy meanwhile heard Chuck talking about Cookies gin, when all of a sudden he jumps off his cot and starts rifling through his seabag. He brought forth a canteen.

"Look here guys, I requisitioned some alcohol from sick bay when I was on guard duty. Who wants to take the first swig?"

"How do you know it's not wood alcohol or rubbing alcohol?" I asked.

"Beats me! All I know is that it was in a fancy bottle, smelled like alcohol, so I filled my canteen with it."

"Did you drink any of it?" Chuck asked.

"Naw, I was saving it!"

"You know we could be poisoned or blinded by this stuff if it isn't grain alcohol I added, as I smelled its contents.

"You know it smells like that 200 proof alcohol Cookie made for us that one day," Sammy added.

"Sure does! But how can we test it," Chuck wondered.

"I got it!" Sammy cried in delight. "Let's invite "Hands" O'Malley, he'll drink anything. If nothing happens to him than we can drink the rest."

"Are you crazy Sam, You want to kill the guy?" I replied.

While Sammy was holding the canteen in his hand, "Hands" O'Malley approached us. He was called "Hands" because he had a bad habit of touching the person he was talking to.

"What's up guys, what's with the canteen?" he asked as he placed his hand on Sammy's shoulder.

"Well it's like this Hands. We have alcohol in this canteen but we don't know----

Before Sammy could finish the sentence, Hands grabbed the canteen out of his hands and began to drink. We quickly grabbed it back, but it was too late. He drank about a half of cup.

"Boy that's good stuff!" he remarked as he wiped his lips and did the Irish jig.

We waited for him to keel over and die but he didn't.

We laughed hysterically as we passed the canteen around. The alcohol was 200 proof and so it didn't take much to get us drunk.

We sang "Auld Lang Syne" song over and over again until we fell asleep. It was a New Years Eve I shall never forget!

We finally left the Admiralties on January the 2nd, 1945. The number of ships in this contingent was stupendous, and more were joining us every day. Before this invasion was to take place, over 800 ships would be involved. This would make it the largest Armada ever.

Part of the 800 ship armada

As we approached the Philippines via the Sulu Sea, a part of the Naval Task Force blasted Okinawa, Ryukus and Formosa in an attempt to knock out Japanese planes that were being flown out to intercept us. Clark Field near Manila, was bombed by carrier based planes in order to knock out as many Japanese planes as possible.

The Japanese Air Force at this time was only a remnant of its once powerful self. Its Aces have long since hit the silk and only a handful remained. To remedy this situation and perhaps change the course of the war, the Japanese incorporated the "Kamikaze" plan.

It consisted of brain washing or indoctrinating men to willingly die for their Emperor by crash diving their bomb-laden planes into troop ships, carriers, battleships, etc.

The reasoning was simple enough; sacrifice one man, one plane in an attempt to kill hundreds of the enemy not counting the ship that may be sunk or put out of commission.

It was a formidable weapon and one we feared very much as we steamed through the Mindanao Straits and into the South China Sea.

One night, as we approached Lingayen Gulf, an air alert was sounded. Japanese bombers were heading our way. The decks were cleared of all personnel except those operating the anti aircraft guns.

As we stood below in our life jackets, I wondered what the odds were on our ship being selected by the enemy. 100 to 1, 200 to 1, I didn't know, but I felt they weren't great enough.

Kamikazee's in action – Lingayen Harbor Jan. 1945

The Japanese wanted to bomb our troop ships because they knew that these are the men that are going to invade their homeland. So with one good hit they can take out hundreds of lives. The lights were out, and all that was audible at this time was the heavy breathing of men who were waiting! Waiting for what? Maybe death!

The Japanese bombers were overhead, the steady hum of their engines could be heard below deck. I said the Lord's prayer over and over again in the darkened crowded hold.

"I'm frightened! "someone cried convulsively.

"Knock it off !"

"Another cry!" Followed by what sounded like a slap on the face.

It was quiet once more, but only for a minute. The Naval anti aircraft guns suddenly opened up. My prayers were jumbled, I didn't know what I was murmuring anymore.

We were sitting ducks, no way to defend ourselves. Strictly in God's hands. A nearby explosion rocked our ship, more men crying. Father Christifano's voice was clearly heard above the exploding bombs.

"Men let us pray!" He shouted.

"Our Father, who arth in Heaven, Hallowed be thy name, etc.

We prayed aloud, hoping to drown out the death and destruction that was trying to claim us. Our prayers were answered; we were trembling but unscathed for the ordeal. A great number of ships were hit and hundreds of lives were lost. We were the lucky ones, so far. The Kamikaze attacks increased in tempo as we approached Lingayen Gulf.

We waited below during these attacks, praying each time that it wasn't our ship that was going to be blown out of the water today.

One of the first ships to be sunk at this time was the Air Craft carrier, "Ommaney Bay." Other ships soon met similar fates. Our luck was still holding out!

The morning of January the 9th, 1945 was designated as "D" (Debarkation Day) We ate an early breakfast, got our battle gear together and waited. The Schedule called for the Army infantry to hit four beaches simultaneously.

There were no Line Company Marines involved in this invasion only a handful of expendable Marines from M.A.G. 24, M.A.G. 32 and M.A.G.14. This was an all Army invasion, something General McArthur wanted.

The 6th and 43rd Infantry Divisions of the XIV Corps were the outfits slated to move in first. If they ran into trouble, the Army had in reserve the 25th Infantry Division, the 13th Armored Group, the 6th Ranger Battalion and a handful of expendable Marines from the various MAG Groups.

As the doughboys scampered down the side of the ship and into the barges, the beachheads were pounded by Naval guns and planes for the last time. Meanwhile the Japanese Kamikaze pilots came over like a flight of ducks. They were up pretty high so that the anti aircraft guns wouldn't reach them. They all had their targets picked out and as they began to peel off each plane headed for one of our ships. Every Naval gun on each of the 800 ships opened fire. It was so loud that we stuck our fingers in our ears and kept our mouths open to prevent our ears from bursting.

Meanwhile the Army infantrymen were hitting the beaches wave after wave. Once the landing craft or barge hit the beach, the infantrymen got out on the double and the landing craft went back to pick up another group of infantrymen. We were waiting our turn to hit the beaches, while the suicidal Japanese planes came over like ducks during the migrating season.

Their planes were clearly visible now, rolling and dodging through the canopy of flack.

"Clear the decks!" the loudspeaker blared.

We tried, but there was nowhere to go. The entrances to the holds were jam packed with Marines. I hit the deck behind some crates and waited. My view was perfect! The noise deafening!

"Oh my God!" I gasped, as a Jap zero dove towards us. It's meat ball insignia was fiery red!

As he dove his guns were strafing us like rain drops in an inverted bucket.

"Hit the Son of a Bitch," someone screamed, as the plane plunged towards us. The Naval gunners were getting close and luckily they nailed him. His plane exploded in a fiery ball in front of our ship. It disintegrated so quickly, that the image of the plane was still retained by our visual ganglia.

After the dead and wounded were tended to, the Army resumed its disembarking.

We were lucky, once more! No one from M.A.G. 24 was hit! When the first wave hit the beach, they dug in, and waited. Not a shot was fired! No sign of the enemy anywhere. The beachhead was quickly expanded. The infantrymen moved inland. Nearby towns and villages were taken with very little resistance.

The Japanese were playing it cozy. They knew our ships and planes would pound the beaches unmercifully and therefore they dug in miles inward. The only people killed during this softening up process were the flag waving Filipinos who ran out to the beaches to greet us. Poor Patriotic Souls!

Our outfit, meanwhile, was still standing by.

"What the hell are they waiting for?" Chuck griped, as we scampered below in lieu of another attack.

"Beats me Chuck, it looks like the Army wants to get its troops ashore first. Remember this is an Army invasion, we're here primarily to build an air strip for M.A.G. 24, not to fight, unless we have to."

It was late in the afternoon when the order was issued for the Marines to disembark.

"Man it's about time," Sammy sneered, "If there were any women or children aboard they'd probably get off before we did!"

We climbed down the rope ladders with hardly any mishaps. A stepped on hand, or a kicked helmet was the extent of it. We dropped into the landing craft and moved back to make room for the others.

When it was fully loaded, the landing craft pulled away from the S.S. President Polk and sped towards the beach.

Sgt. Ryan, meanwhile, was up front and looking skywards. A couple of Jap zeros, fully loaded with bombs, were dodging and rolling through a barrage of flak trying desperately to hit their targets.

"Men," Sgt. Ryan said, "When we hit the beach, skirmish to the left and right and dig in. Those bastards may want to strafe us."

"Roger !" we acknowledged.

Shortly the beach loomed before us. The thud of the barge sliding across the sand informed us that our destination was reached. The ramp dropped open, and the first Marines to set foot on Luzon hit the beach.

Hitting the beach on Luzon –January 1945

We double timed it out of our conveyance and across the hot sand.

"Let's get out a ways!" Chuck yelled out to me and Sammy, as we darted from one unsavory location to another.

When a suitable site was found, we dug in awaited further orders.

"Man look at all the stuff on the beach," Sammy gawked, "I wonder if there's any chow in those crates?"

"Could be," Chuck replied. "Let's take a look!"

They disappeared behind some crates and after a few minutes returned.

"What's in the crates?" I asked.

"Most of it is ammo, but there is some fruit cocktail, Spam, soap, T shirts and dungarees in some of those crates," Chuck replied.

"You know what, we should reacquisition a few crates of this stuff, just in case we want to trade with the natives,' I suggested.

"Good idea Lee," Sammy remarked, "but where are we going to hide these crates?'

"How about up in those woods up ahead, I suggested."

"Isn't that a little too far?" Sammy noted.

"So what !" Chuck cut in, "It may be worth it!"

"Let's go then, times a wasting."

We picked a site about one hundred yards from where we were dug in.

No one noticed what we were doing, because we were far enough away from our contingent, and they were more concerned about the Jap zeros than what we were doing.

The site we picked was perfect! The dense foliage would hide our cache until we were ready to pick it up.

The task of hauling these crates was back breaking and also very risky. Luckily we were off by ourselves, just close enough to our outfit to keep tabs on it and yet far enough away so as not to be spotted by our superiors.

We were so engrossed with what we were doing we didn't see the landing barge approach us.

"Hey you Gyrenes, get your butts over here and unload this barge," an Army Captain ordered.

"Sorry sir, but we're waiting for our outfit to move out," I politely answered.

"I don't give a damn! This barge is loaded with ammo and has to be unloaded immediately. Get to it! I'll tell your Sergeant what you're doing."

"Yes Sir!" we disgustedly replied.

The Captain also ordered a few more Gyrenes from our outfit to help out.

We stripped to our waists, rolled up our dungarees, and took off our boondockers. We had to wade through a foot of water because the barge got stuck on the beach.

The sun was beginning to set; its golden rays danced and sparkled amidst a background of white fleecy clouds.   -

The skies were clear of flak now, and serenity prevailed so we thought. Pvt. Jack Trimble and I were deep in the barge wrestling with a crate of ammo when all hell broke loose. A Jap zero came in low over the horizon, strafing and bombing the beachhead.

"Get that barge off the beach," the Captain shouted as he took a flying leap into a mound of sand.

The Swabby reared up its engines and before Jack and I could exit, the ramp came up trapping us like a couple of wet rats.

"Let's get the hell out of here," Jack shouted, as he dove overboard. I was about to do the same, but chickened out at the last second. The fact that I wasn't a very good swimmer, plus the fact that the undertow was very great out here, I didn't take a chance on swimming back to the beach. I jumped back into the barge and hid behind a crate of ammunition.

"Oh my God! Have mercy on my soul! Please God spare me! I cried, I don't want to die!" I prayed.

Rat tat tat tat the Jap gun answered, spitting bullets across the empty part of the barge. I held my breath and prayed. My whole life raced before me as I expected at any second to be torn into shreds by the exploding ammo.

I was shaking like a leaf when the Navy boatsman backed up the barge and headed for open sea. The noise was increasing in tempo. It sounded as if every ship in the harbor was firing away. The Jap plane circled in the sky and now decided to plunge his plane into a nearby cruiser. He never reached it!

"All clear!" The Swabby, boatsman shouted.

"Thank God!"I shakily replied, "Now what are my chances of getting back to shore?"

"I'll get you there before you know it, mate!"

The Navy boatsman started to turn around the barge when all of a sudden the engine began to sputter and stop.

"What's wrong?"

"I don't know ! It just died!"

"Maybe you ran out of gas."

"I don't think so! I filled it up the tank this morning."

"We'll try to get it started, it's getting dark and I'm beginning to freeze."

"Look mate, if I don't get this engine started you'll have more than darkness and coldness to worry about."

"What do you mean?"

"Haven't you heard?"

"No ! what?"

Well at night the Japanese load up anything that floats with ammo and under the cover of darkness they ram the ships out here.

"Oh shit! Just my luck. A Kamikaze on water."

"Exactly, and if I don't get this engine started, we may be mistaken for one of these Kamikaze boats and be blown out of the water by our own ships or patrol boats."

"I see what you mean."

"Well here goes nothing," he said, "keep your fingers crossed."

The engine gave out a sickening growl, but did not kick over.

"I think we've had it mate."

"Now what?"

"Nothing! We sit tight and pray."

Oh shit, I thought. It seems all I'm doing lately is praying. I think I prayed more in my short stint as a Marine than I have in my entire life. Why didn't I dive overboard when I had the chance. Now I'm up shit creak without a paddle. If the Japs don't bump into us, our patrol boats might or I'll catch pneumonia.

"Hey Neil do you have a blanket or extra jacket, I'm really cold?"

"Sorry Lee, all I have is what I'm wearing."

"That's great ! Just great !"

The nights in the Philippines got very cold, probably in the low fifties. My flesh was covered with goose pimples and my teeth chattered uncontrollably.

"Hey Lee, why don't you sit next to the engine, it may be still warm."

I went down into the bilge and sat down next to the engine as Neil suggested. The engine was still warm but the odor of the oil nauseated me to such an extent that I had to leave.

It looks like we have a cold, miserable and frightening night ahead of us.

My associate was a Nebraskan by the name of Neil Varden. He saw how miserable I was so he took off his shoes and let me wear his socks. He then gave me his T shirt while he wore his jacket. I was a little warmer now, but still pretty cold. Now we were both freezing, but at least we were friendly.

"You know Neil, time can be so deceiving."

"In what way, Lee?"

"Well when you're with someone you adore, hours flit by like seconds and yet when you're miserable, like we are, seconds creep by like hours."

"That's so true Lee. The pleasant things in life never last very long!"

Our small talk was interrupted by what sounded like a boat approaching us.

"Shhhh Jim," Neil whispered, This could be trouble!

He then opened up one of the crates that was still in our barge which contained grenades.

"How did you know we had grenades aboard?" I whispered.

"Because I helped load this barge."

"Okay"

"Have you ever thrown one of these babies," Neil asked very quietly.

"Yes I have, on Bougainville," I whispered.

"Good because if this is a Jap boat we may have to defend ourselves.

The sound of an engine was clearly audible.

"Doesn't sound like ours?"

"Are you sure ?"

"Pretty sure Lee. Get those grenades ready.

The sound of their engine cut on and off intermittently.

"Maybe it's one of our patrol boats."

"Perhaps, but I doubt it!"

Neil's doubt was confirmed when the North breeze blew some Niponese dialogue our way.

We didn't move for fear of being detected. My heart was pounding crazily in its thoracic cage. The moon was frightened too; it was hiding behind a cloud. I crouched in readiness, the cold no longer bothered me.

As soon as the frightened moon emerged from behind the clouds we were able to see a silhouette of what looked like a small cabin cruiser.

"Now!" Neil shouted, as he heaved a grenade towards the small cruiser. I quickly followed suit and was ready to throw another when one of our grenades exploded followed by a huge explosion and fire which blew parts of their boat into our barge.

The fire brought our patrol boats to the scene. Neil being in charge told the Captain what had happened.

"You men are really lucky," the Captain informed us.

We boarded their patrol boat and were taken to an aircraft carrier where I took a hot shower and put on some clean clothes that they gave me.

We were then given some chicken soup and a hamburger to eat. Boy that hit the spot! I was told that I was to sleep on the carrier tonight and tomorrow morning after breakfast, they would transport me back to my outfit.

I had a hard time falling asleep, because of the number of announcements and alerts that were constantly interrupting my sleep.

What a night !

Chapter 25

Sunrise brought me warmth, the G.I. runs, and the Kamikazes. Four Jap planes were trying desperately to get through the flack and sink our carrier. They were maneuvering with artistic deftness but to no avail. By this time our Naval gunners had so much practice that they had little trouble knocking these Zeros out of the sky.

I went to breakfast and ate my first full meal on an air craft carrier. Everyone always told me that the best meals served, were on our carriers. They were right! I had orange juice, scrambled eggs, sausage, toast and coffee.

I was transported back to my outfit by Neil in a different barge.

"See you in L.A. Neil," I shouted as I made my way towards the beach.

"I'll try to make it Lee, good luck to you!"

"You too, Neil!"

I trudged across the sand and up on the beach where a group of Marines were huddling around a fire, brewing some coffee.

"Hey look! It's Lee!" someone shouted.

"Lee! Sammy screamed," Is it really you?"

"Sure it's me! Whom did you expect?"

"We thought you were dead!" Chuck cut in excitedly,

"In fact you're considered M.I.A. (Missing in Action)."

"What gave you guys that idea?"

"Don't you know?"

"Know what?"

"Jack's body was washed ashore last night, by the tide," Chuck sorrowfully replied.

"Oh no! Did he drown?"

"No that Jap plane got him. He died instantaneously though, a round passed right through his head."

"Dirty S.O.B.'s " I sadly replied.

"Where's Ryan?"I asked.

"He's resting right there," Sammy pointed to a makeshift nearby foxhole.

I walked over to where Sgt. Ryan was snoring and kicked a little sand on his dungarees to wake him up. He shot up like a shot, ready to blow my brains out!

"Hi Sarg !" I sheepishly greeted him.

"Walewander! What the fuck happened to you ? We looked everywhere for you.We thought you were dead. In fact we have you Missing In Action."

I proceeded to tell him what had happened.

"Lee, you must have a horseshoe up your ass."

"Have you eaten?"

"Yup !"and I told him what I had for breakfast.

"Boy what I wouldn't give for a breakfast like that," he remarked, shaking his head.

I walked over to my buddies and asked, "What did you guys do last night?"

"We pulled Guard duty," Chuck replied. "Ryan broke us up into squads and had us patrol the beach. The scuttlebutt had it that the Japs were going to sneak in a raiding party in an attempt to attack the Doggies from the rear.

"Did they?"

"Naw, the only excitement we had, was a huge explosion that occurred in the harbor, and also when we caught a couple of Filipinos trying to pour sand into the crankcase of one of our trucks.

"Filipinos?" I asked.

"Yeah, some of them are Pro Japanese, you know."

"No I didn't! Now what are we going to do?"

"Beats me, but I think Ryan said we're going to help the 308th Army Wing build an air strip near the town of Lingayen," Chuck added.

"That sounds like fun!" I smirked.

"Yeah right!" Chuck laughed.

That afternoon it became official. Our small group of men were to help in the construction of an Army air strip near the town of Lingayen. Chuck was right !

We moved out, boarded a truck and after about ten minutes, we arrived at a large clearing where activity was in full progress. Bulldozers were up front, clearing and leveling the land while in the dusty background men were scurrying around like ants sprayed with an insecticide.

Our duties were simple enough. We had to unload a truck full of Marston steel mats which were about 15 feet long and about 2 feet wide with baseball size perforations. They had prongs on one side and prong openings on the other. Our job was to carry and join these mats to one another on a level area of ground. When locked together these mats were stable and secure. It took two of us to lift, carry and lay these mats on the air strip.

We worked all that day and well into the night. Flood lights were set up, so that the work could continue. General MacArthur was scheduled to land here, as soon as the airstrip was completed. His was to be the first American plane to land on Luzon since the Japanese occupation. We were looking to Mac's visit.

The Japanese Air Force didn't like the idea of our constructing an air strip in their backyard. They retaliated by sending Bettys and Sallys (Bombers) to disrupt proceedings. We hid in our foxholes until they were finished bombing us!

After the all clear was sounded, we replaced the mangled mats, filled the craters and then put new mats in their place.

But for a couple of these bombings the work progressed on schedule. When the last of the steel mats were laid down, we congratulated each other on a job well done. Now we were told that General MacArthur was on his way!

"Do you think I could get his autograph?" Sammy asked.

"You won't be able to get within 50 yards of him," I remarked.

"Just think Lee," Chuck smiled, "Someday you can tell your kids you helped build the first airstrip that General MacArthur landed on during World War II."

"Yeah I'm sure that would impress them," I laughed.

Just then Hands O'Malley, shouted, "Here he comes!"

"Where?" We asked.

We scanned the skies and lo and behold a small observation plane came into view. Its wings dipped and fluttered before leveling out. We lined the strip waving and shouting as the plane landed. The "Old Man" emerged, pipe and all, waved to us and was immediately escorted into a Command Jeep.

"Man that was quick," Sammy remarked, "No speech or anything!"

"Are we sure that was MacArthur ?"

"Beats me! Could have been Tojo," Chuck replied.

We kidded around but deep down inside felt a little disappointed. Nevertheless, we were later informed that a Commendation by Lt. General Walter Krueger, Commanding General of the 6th Army was bestowed upon us for building this air strip while subjected to enemy fire.

The airstrip we helped build was to be used by the Army which meant that now we have to build another air strip for M.A.G. 24 somewhere else.

Our Commanding Officer had the impossible task of selecting the site for our new air strip. After looking over many locations, a rice paddy near the town of Mangaldan was selected. Mangaldan was about twenty miles from Lingayen and midway between the towns of San Fabian and Dagupan.

Normally a rice paddy would be the last place in the world on which you would want to build an air strip, but our C.O. knew better. Being an old Philippine campaigner he was familiar with the climate. He knew that if the rice hills were leveled, without destroying the roots, they would make a firm enough area on which planes could land. To keep the soil from blowing away, the airstrip was to be oiled and covered with the Marston mats. We were in the Philippines during the dry season which meant at least three good months of rain free operations.

Once the Lingayen airstrip was completed, we moved to Mangaldan. The Army engineers were already leveling out the rice paddy as we descended from the truck. We spent the rest of the afternoon clearing an area, near the airstrip, and set up our tent.

That night, after our gear and tent was all in place, we decided to go to the beach and pick up the crates that we hid in the jungle. We requisitioned an Army truck and headed out for the beach and our cache. An air raid was in progress, but it was second nature to us now. We hardly noticed it!

"You think our stuff is still there? Sammy asked, as he maneuvered the vehicle along the moonlit road.

"Yeah, but if you come across well fed Filipinos wearing our T shirts and dungarees you'll know what happened," I jokingly remarked.

"Man I hope you're wrong! This stuff is priceless. We could get anything from the natives for it," Chuck added.

"Yeah man," Sammy laughed.

It wasn't very long before we arrived at the beach.

"It's still here!" Sammy shouted with glee.

"Quiet Sam," Chuck whispered. "You want us to get our heads blown off by some trigger happy dogface."

We quietly loaded the truck and drove off. In addition to the night being chilly it was teeming with undernourished mosquitoes. They were relentless as they engorged on our sweaty arms and neck. American blood must be a delicacy out here seeing how these sucking irritating bugs were having a Smorgasbord. Nevertheless our mission was accomplished!

Early that morning, we dug a new larger foxhole in the dense jungle. It was located about 20 feet from our tent, and covered it with branches and leaves. No one knew about this cache but us and hopefully it would remain that way.

That morning, we were put to work on the airstrip. In addition to the strip itself, a control tower and field operations shack had to be constructed. This was the job for the Camp Construction Crew. At the rate we were going, it would probably take a couple of weeks before the first plane could land. To speed up the process, hundreds of Filipino laborers were put to work under our supervision. They worked hard and long for the few pesos they were to receive. Nevertheless, this was a hundred percent better than what the Japs would have given them.

The airstrip was called "MAGSDAGUPAN" with headquarters set up in a little school house. Although the strip was far from being completed, it shortly was to become the busiest airport in the Western Pacific.

Those of us assigned to Field Operations were to live away from the camp area proper and near the airstrip.

"Clear this area and set up your tent and foxhole right here," Sgt. Ryan ordered," and don't forget to dig your foxholes good and deep."

"Yeah," we grumbled, knowing full well we were in Harms way. When the Japs start bombing us they'll try to knock out our air strip, which means were liable to be hit."

"Hey Lee, let's see if we can hire some of the natives to do our work for us, Chuck asked.

We knew, from our lectures, that of the forty three native dialects spoken in the Philippines, the one most spoken was English.

Sammy volunteered to make a deal with them, because he said, he had a lot of practice dealing with the vendors on Maxwell Street in Chicago.

After about ten minutes the deal was consummated. The four natives were to clear an area in the jungle, put up our tent, dig our foxholes and build us a shower stall. All this for a few T shirts, soap and rations.

That afternoon, the work, Ryan expected us to do was coming along splendidly, so we noted from our supine position. We took turns in supervising the work, and also guarding the ones sleeping from Japs and Sgt. Ryan. Our siesta was interrupted by Hands O'Malley one of our patrolling guards.

"I'm telling you Lee, I saw fish jumping out the water in this rice paddy," he said as one of his hands pushed my shoulder.

"You're cracking up O'Malley! If you said the ocean maybe I'd believe you."

"Come on get off of it, I'm as sane as you are!"

"Probably saner," Chuck cynically replied.

"Look Sam, you believe me don't you?"

'Sure O'Malley, I believe you. Flying fish weren't they?"

"Screw you guys!" O'Malley disgustedly said, as he left.

"Come on let's go over and see what the hell he saw that looked like a fish," Chuck suggested.

"Okay, let's get Bentley to watch our workers," I remarked. "We have to keep an eye out for Ryan."

"Hey Bentley, remember, if you see Ryan coming shag the workers into the jungle"

"Will do!" he replied.

We left Bentley in charge, picked up our rifles and ammo and followed O'Malley to the aforementioned rice paddy.

"Well I'll be dipped," Sammy exclaimed. "There are fish in there!"

"See ! What did I tell you guys!"

"Okay O'Malley, so you haven't cracked up, but that still doesn't explain what the hell these fish are doing in here," I said.

"Don't fight it Jim,"Chuck added, "figure out a way we can catch a few. I haven't had a good fish dinner in months."

"You and me both, but how?"

"I've got it!" Sammy beamed, "Why don't we form a daisy line across the rice paddy and stampede the fish into the far end of the paddy."

"Then what?"

"Then we catch them as they try to get past us."

"Sounds like it may work, and even if it doesn't it may be a lot of fun corralling these fish," I laughed.

We took off our boondockers and socks; rolled up our pants and waded into the warm muddy water. Like cowpunchers, we herded the fish into one of the corners.

"Ya hoo! Ki Yi Yippe ! Ya hoo," we screamed in our best mid western style.

The fish didn't know what the hell was happening. It was either crawling up on the shore or get past screaming, howling Gyrenes. They chose the latter.

We beat the water furiously with our hands, crowding them into a smaller and smaller area. Before we knew what was happening, fish were jumping out of the water trying to escape from the human coral that was encircling them.

"I caught one!" Sammy screamed, as he held a good sized fish in his hands.

"Me too!" I shouted.

Fish were sailing through the air and so were we. We were having a ball when suddenly our frolicking was interrupted by a pistol shot.

"What the hell was that!"

We looked around and there at the far end of the rice paddy, next to our gear was Sgt. Ryan brandishing a 45 in his hand.

"Get the hell out of there!" he bellowed.

We slowly began to saunter out, fish and all. As we approached we could see he was really pissed off at us.

"Put those fish back into the rice paddy or I'll blow your heads off," he screamed.

"What's the big deal! There are enough fish in here for everyone," Chuck replied.

"Don't you guys get it! To these people we are liberators, not thieves. You're stealing the fish they have been raising to supplement their meager rations. Not only that but you're uprooting their rice crop.

"We're sorry Sarg. We didn't know," I quickly replied.

"You may be sorry Walewander, but what about your buddies?"

"They're sorry too!"

"What are they mutes? Let' hear an apology or you go on report."

"We're sorry!" they answered almost simultaneously.

"Okay, now get your butts out of there and get back to digging your foxhole. I'm sure Betty and Sally (Japanese Bombers) will pay us a visit tonight."

We quickly dressed and double timed it back to our jungle homestead. The Filipino laborers were far from being finished so we recruited four more to finish the job, same scale.

That night, Betty and Sally came over and pasted us but good. Luckily our fox holes were good and deep and covered with heavy logs.

In addition to these air raids, we were constantly on the alert for Japs sneaking into our camp area and while were asleep, slit out throats, just as they did on Bougainville. Most of us were issued 45's, in addition to our rifles, which we kept under our pillows when we slept.

One night, I almost blew Sam's head off when he got up in the middle of the night.

"Who goes there?" I shouted, grabbing my 45 from under my pillow.

"Take it easy Lee, It's only me, Sam"

"What the hell are you doing walking around in the dark?"

"I had to take a piss! Do you mind?"

"Yeah, I mind! Piss before you hit the sack, then you won't have to get up in the middle of the night. You don't know how close you came to having your head blown off. Whew! It's a good thing you don't stutter."

"Can I take a leak now?" Sammy indignantly asked.

"Yeah, but not too close to the tent. You know how the wind changes around here."

"We must have wakened Chuck because he asked us how long are we going to have this conversation?

"Do I have to shoot both of you to get a little sleep around here? Knock it off!"

Sammy continued out of the tent, stumbling over my boondockers in the process. He sounded like a horse!

During the next few days we had the tent up, foxholes dug, a bamboo shower stall, installed and a bamboo floor. All that was needed was someone to wash our clothes and tidy up around here.

Our prayers were answered when a young Filipino peasant girl approached our tent. She wasn't alone, a young toddler was at her side clutching her dress. Our crap game for Japanese pesos ceased momentarily as we sized her up. She was about five feet tall, had dark hair and eyes and sparkling white teeth. She was barefoot and underneath her torn but clean print dress her well proportioned body was blossoming forth. She was quite pretty!

"What's up baby?" Sammy asked in his best Damon Runyon style.

"Do you have work for Nina?"

"Come again?"

"Nina work hard! Wash clothes, iron, sew for little peso."

"Baby, you can take care of me anytime," Sammy growled wolfishly.

"Nina no understand!"

"Come wiz me to the Kasbah," Sammy purred, taking her by the hand and escorting her into our tent. The toddler never let go of her mother's dress.

"Mates, this little chick wants to work for us?"

"Doing what?"I asked.

"She wants to do our wash, iron our clothes and clean up around here."

"Who sent this angel to us?" I asked, as I looked towards the sky.

"Sounds great!" Chuck beamed. "We'll be the cleanest Gyrenes in the Philippines."

We agreed.

Nina our tent-keeper

Nina was nineteen years old, married and the proud mother of the little toddler that was clinging so desperately to her dress and a seven year old little son. Her husband joined the guerrillas shortly after the Japanese attacked his homeland. He hasn't been heard from since. During this time, Nina moved in with her parents who owned a small parcel of land about a half mile from our airstrip. She helped farm it.

The arrangements we worked out with Nina was advantageous to both sides. She picked up our dirty clothes, every morning, as we slept, and brought them back in the afternoon washed and ironed. We were the only Gyrenes in the camp area that had a crease on our dungarees.

Nina was paid a dollar a day, plus some canned goods and a bar of soap. She was very happy working for us and was extremely fond of Sammy. We suspected Sam was wining and dining her with our canned goods, seeing as to how our cache was slowly getting smaller. We didn't object. We adored Nina and as long as she was happy that's all that counted.

The camp area was stirring. The ground echelons of M.A.G. 24 and 32 were to arrive in a few days. Meantime, we were working feverishly to complete the airstrip on schedule. The first planes were to arrive on January the 25th just sixteen days since "D" day.

During this time, two airstrips would have been constructed and the drive to Manila was to begin. The 37th Infantry Division was to strike from the west, the Army's XI Corps from the south, and the 1st Cavalry Division was to support them. Our groups were to lend close air support when needed.

This morning Sgt. Ryan paid us a visit.

"Men when Sgt. Phelps arrives, I want you to get him squared away as quickly as possible.

Fill him in on what has taken place and do whatever he wants you to do.

He's your boss and don't you forget it! Just because he didn't get here when you people did, doesn't make him inferior. He has a big job on his hands and will need the cooperation of every man assigned to Field Operations. If he doesn't get it, I'll transfer every last one of you back to the Guard Company. Am I making myself clear?

"We dig you Sarg," Sammy replied.

"Good!"

That afternoon, Sgt. Phelps arrived and after a hot meal at our make shift mess hall he was driven to his new quarters. He liked our set up but was more interested in getting to work.

"Let's get out to the airstrip men, we have a lot of work to do." We did !

The next day, the Dauntless Dive Bombers of Squadron VMSB 133 and 241 began to land. We were ready! We logged forty six of them that morning, with more to come.

In addition to our planes, the Army Air Force was landing a few of their own. Eventually they had more planes operating from the Mangaldan airfield than from anywhere else. There were P47's, P51's, A20's, B24's, C47's and PBY's to mention only a few. It was quite an aggregate, the Wright Brothers would have been proud of their brain child.

Before the final drive to Manila was to begin, the role of the dive bombers had to be ascertained. Close air support was still frowned upon by many Army Divisions, especially those that didn't see the "Diving Devil Dogs" in action on Bougainville. If they did, they wouldn't have waited so long before calling for close air support. Nonetheless, seven Marines; three Captains, three Sergeants, and a Private First Class were attached to the Army.

They were the Air-Liason party and their job was to direct the SBD's to their targets.

Chuck tried to get in with this group but failed. He along with the rest of us had to be content with running the airstrip.

On February the 1st, 1945, the 1st Cavalry Division moved out of Giumba and the final drive to Manila began. Their orders were simple enough; take Manila as quickly as possible and free the American held prisoners at Santo Tomas University.

As the infantrymen trudged onwards, their flanks were protected from Japanese counter attacks by our patrolling dive bombers. Nine SBD's were constantly in the air, seeking out the enemy and lending close air support when ever needed.

The very next day, the advancing columns ran into a Japanese battalion, well concealed and on high ground. The doughboys called for air support when mortar fire sent them scurrying in all directions. Very shortly angels appeared in the skies, bomb laden and eager, and amidst the cheers of the G.I.'s completely annihilated the enemy.

Dauntless Dive Bombers in action

The Bougainville training paid off; the infantry routed the remnants of the Jap Battalion and the push towards Manila continued on schedule.

The advancing columns had to cross the Novaliches bridge before they entered Manila. It was feared that the Japanese would blow up the bridge in an effort to slow down our progress. SBD's were ordered to safe guard it at any cost. They strafed and bombed the enemy patrols as they hurriedly approached the bridge. Nevertheless, a couple of Japs did make it, and proceeded to mine the bridge.

A Navy mine disposal officer rushed onto the bridge and dismantled the mine amidst a rain of enemy fire. The bridge was saved !

The officer commended! The push continued.

Before the city of Manila was to be invaded, it was deemed necessary to capture the water reservoir and filter plant. It was feared that that the enemy would either contaminate the water or deprive the inhabitants of this elixir, and so it had to be captured. Patrols of the 1st Cavalry Division, along with one of the Marine Air Liason jeeps were sent out ahead to capture this vital outpost.

After a short but bitter battle, the water reservoir was taken. The Japanese retreated, but came back that night in full force to retake this strategic outpost. They hit the stubborn GI with everything in the book but couldn't dislodge him. The morning brought the "Angels of Mercy" to the rescue, and once more the day was saved.

It took two and a half days for the Cavalrymen to reach Manila from Giumba. The drive was so rapid and successful, thanks to the "Diving Devildogs" that thousands of Japanese soldiers were trapped in the city. It would take some time to get them out.

Chapter 26

When Sammy heard that when the Army infantrymen entered the city of Manila and freed all of the Americans and Filipinos that were imprisoned there, he got an idea.

"Hey guys, let's go to Manila and trade off some of our cache for whiskey and women. What do you say? We need a little excitement, and from what I hear, the city is up for grabs. They say that the parties and celebrations that are going on are pretty wild.

"Good idea Sam, but how can we get away, without getting caught," I asked.

"Well the only one that keeps track of us and gives us our duties is Sgt. Phelps."Chuck replied. "If we can con him, in some way, we can do it!" Chuck added.

"But how?" we pondered.

Just then Sgt. Phelps came busting into our tent ranting and raving.

"Have you people heard the latest?"

"No! What?"

The GI's have entered Manila and have freed the American held prisoners at Santo Tomas."

"That's great!"

"They say there are a lot of parties going on and whiskey is supposed to be flowing like water. Boy would I love to get my hands on a couple of bottles of it." he said as he licked his lips.

We looked at each other dumb-foundedly, but the wheels already began to turn.

"You can Sarg!" Chuck quickly replied.

"Come again?"

"Well supposing the three of us were to go to Manila and try to get some of this Whiskey. I hear the people are starving so maybe we can trade them rations and perhaps some clothing for it."

"Sounds like a good idea but what if something should happen to you guys? It would mean my stripes."

"No it wouldn't Sarg. If we don't come back within a certain time you could report us A.W.O.L"

"Naw, it's too risky."

"That whiskey is supposed to be American made," Chuck winked.

"Is that right?"

"Yeah man," Sammy grinned.

"You say its American whiskey"

"That's right! Schenley, Seagrams, Jim Bean, Four roses, etc.,"

"Okay already! You guys can go. But I know nothing what so ever about it. You also have to get Pvt. Bentley and O'Malley in on it, because they have to take over your duties, is that clear?"

"Yes sir !" we gleefully replied.

We had no trouble getting Pvt. Bentley and Hands O'Malley to go along with us. We promised them a couple of fifths of whiskey for their part in our venture.

Since there were very few Marines in Manila, we covered up the MAG 24 stenciled name on one of our Field Operations smaller trucks with some mud, and set out on our quest for whiskey and woman. We loaded our small truck with K rations, T shirts, soap, canned goods, etc., and while most everyone slept, we hurriedly drove off.

Manila was about an hour's drive from our airstrip and our plan was to get our whiskey and maybe some sex and get back that night.

Chuck was driving, Sammy and I were in the back of the truck with our cache. The sun was beginning to emerge as we barreled down the road to Manila. Farmers waved to us as they prepared to work their fields. We occasionally waved back.

As we approached the city, thousands of its citizens were leaving, because of the heavy house-to-house fighting that was in progress.

Both sides of the road were crowded with haggard, frightened little people pulling carts, wagons or just carrying their worldly possessions on their backs.

During this mass evacuation, it was a common sight indeed to see the elders resting alongside the road, too weak to keep up with the rapid pace that was being set by its younger generation. Nevertheless, they moved along, slowly but steadily.

As our truck moved past these people, Sammy guarded the left side of our truck while I watched the right. We didn't want to take a chance on getting shot or have a grenade tossed into our truck by Japanese disguised as Filipino evacuees. It was a very tense and nerve wrecking situation. We were extremely overjoyed to see the Novaliches bridge.

Since we didn't have a road map to follow, we kept to the main thoroughfares as much as possible. Once in awhile we would see a sign telling us which way to go to Manila.

Manila was slowly undergoing a change, all for the worse. Bombed out homes and buildings were very much in evidence. It was disheartening to see such a charming city ruined. Obviously, war has no boundaries.

We were driving past the Manila Jockey Club when our sightseeing tour was suddenly interrupted by rifle fire. A couple of rounds shattered our windshield which made us take cover behind our truck.

The rifle fire was coming from a two story wooden structure from across the street. A window was partly open and the unmistakable barrel of a rifle was seen resting on the window ledge and pointing towards us.

A soft breeze wafted the curtain long enough for us to see the enemy. There were two of them, at least!

"There they are!" Chuck shouted, pointing towards the window.

"Yeah, I see them," I cringed as another round bounced off the hood of our truck.

Chuck meanwhile, removed two grenades he had clipped to his jacket.

"Cover me gang, I'm going after them."

Before we could stop him, Chuck was on his way. Sammy and I blasted away at the open window as our mad crazed colleague double-timed it towards the structure. As he approached the building, he pulled the cotter pin and heaved the grenade into the open window. The blast removed the rest of the window and collapsed a part of the roof.

Chuck then whipped out his 45, shot out the lock on the door, and disappeared inside, before we had a chance to join him. The sound of two more shots frightened us as we ran up the stairs. Sammy spotted a Jap running down the back stairs and quickly cut him down with his 45. He tumbled the rest of the way.

We searched the rest of the house before we left. We double-timed it back to our truck hoping our cache wasn't stolen. It wasn't!

Chuck and Sammy were still shaking, so I took over driving. Not a word was said only our heavy breathing was audible. After about ten minutes Sammy broke the silence.

"Pull over somewhere Lee, I'm getting hungry.

"Me too!" Chuck added.

I was happy that they were hungry, this meant that they put what had just happened behind them. I parked the truck near the abandoned "Cine" (Movie theater) called the Rajah. We broke open a few boxes of rations, opened up a couple of cans of fruit cocktail and began to indulge.

Lee   Sammy   Chuck

Manila, Philippine Islands 1945

Our noisy mastication attracted youngsters into our midst. Before we knew it, there were about ten undernourished, unkempt urchins watching us eat.

We tried to get rid of them by giving them some food, but before we realized it, people were approaching us from all directions. They were reaching out us, hungry and ill clad.

"Now what? I asked"

"Let's get the hell out of here, that's what," Chuck snapped.

"Wait not so fast. Let's find out if they have any whiskey in their homes"

"Good idea!"

Sammy proceeded to get up on the truck and began to pantomime drinking.

"Wheeskey," he said as he placed an imaginary bottle to his lips.

"Si Senor!" they replied, as they took off down the road. They returned very shortly with bottles of American whiskey. We traded off our wares for bourbon, scotch, gin, vodka, etc. When we were finished we had 32 bottles of alcohol in our truck. We still had a few T shirts and boxes of rations left, but the canned goods and dungarees were gone.

"Boy what a haul," Sammy beamed.

"We're rich!" Chuck rejoiced.

"Yeah, at fifty bucks a fifth that should come to about 1600 dollars," Sammy added.

"Not quite Sam, remember we have to pay off Phelps, Bentley and O'Malley." I reminded him.

"Aw balls! I forgot about them.

We placed our alcohol in some empty crates and covered them with a tarpaulin and drove off.

"Let's find ourselves some women," Sammy suggested.

"Why? Isn't Nina putting out? Chuck kiddingly asked.

"What difference does that make? I'm not a one woman man and besides variety is the spice of life. Right Lee"

"I wouldn't know Sam, is it really?"

"Of course it is! Don't tell me you'd be happy with the same piece, night after night?"

"If I thought enough about the girl to marry her, Yes, I would be! Why look for variety when you know you have the best."

"Bullshit!" Sam replied. "I have a friend back home in Chicago who married a living doll. Maron, this gal was stacked if you know what I mean. Well this jerk is never at home, he's always promoting with some babe. You figure a guy that supposedly has the best wouldn't cheat on her and here he is night after night going out with pigs. Just doesn't figure."

"Sounds to me like she could be frigid and he doesn't know how to thaw her out," Chuck laughed, as he turned down one of the side streets.

Our discussion of frigid women came to a sudden halt when we spotted a couple of scantily dressed damsels waving at us from a doorway. The Japanese must have really enjoyed their sex, seeing that there were so many whore houses in Manila.

"Stop Chuck! This looks like it," Sammy grinned.

Chuck pulled in next to the house and parked the truck. We looked around and since there was no one around, we left our rifles in the cab of the truck, only taking our 45's with us.

A little frail Filipino, wearing a white shirt greeted us at the door.

"Welcome Yanks! Your wish is my command," he answered in perfect English.

"What is this place?" Sammy asked as we looked around.

"It's a House of Pleasure," He replied.

"It is huh?"

"Yes kind sir," he bowed slightly, a real Japanese mannerism.

As Sammy and the whore-master conversed, Chuck and I searched the house for Japs. There were none to be found. The only people in the house were the nine Filipino prostitutes, the whore -master and us.

This house of ill repute was comparable to the worst Madison street flop house in Chicago. Instead of rooms it had countless number of cubicles just large enough for a small bamboo cot and a wash stand. These tiny rooms were separated from one another by a thin bamboo wall. There were no doors as such, only drapes. It appeared that this place really flourished during the Japanese occupation.

"All right get all your girls out here on the double," Sammy ordered the whore master.

"He bowed politely, and slapped his hands as if he were applauding, and all the girls immediately ran into the room. They were well trained. There was a long wooden bench on which they sat down, while in their smocks.

When all nine of them were seated, and smiling, Sammy looked them over carefully. I think he was trying to impress us as he pinched a few cheeks and felt a few breasts.

"Let's take three apiece! Do you think you guys are man enough to handle three broads?"Sammy laughed.

"I think I can if I get the first three picks," Chuck pondered, as he looked over the bevy of so called beauties.

The girls were all in their teens and each one was built differently. Some were big breasted others weren't. Some were fat, others weren't, etc. So whatever turned the customer on the whore master tried to have.

"Okay let's flip a coin. Odd man gets the first, fourth and seventh pick.

The second pick will have the second, fifth and eight, pick and the third, sixth and ninth pick will go to the loser."

As we stood there matching coins these poor girls didn't know what the hell was happening. They just sat there smiling.

I felt positively guilty. I promised Rita that I'd be true to her no matter what and obviously this is "no matter what". To make matters worse, I'm going to try to have sex with three girls not just one.

"You're the odd man Lee so you get the first pick," Sammy reminded me.

Odd man, isn't that the God's truth, I thought to myself as my buddies continued matching for the next pick. Here I have the opportunity to get laid without any strings attached and I'm still apprehensive. Why can't I let my manly desires control my emotions? Is sex only animalistic, or does one have to love someone deeply in order to enjoy it? These girls must have had sex with hundreds of men, including the enemy. Do I want to travel this route? Didn't the doctor tell us that Syphilis can be carried in our blood stream for years and when you least expect it, it can be transmitted to your offspring. How could I tell my son that he was born blind or maimed, and can't play baseball because his father shacked up with prostitutes in the Philippines? I would rather die first!

"Go ahead Lee, take your pick," Sammy told me.

Since I had no intention of having sex with these girls, I picked the homeliest and sickest looking girl as my first pick. I figured at least my buddies will have the cream of the crop to fuck, before they come down with a dose.

After each of us made our selections, Sammy couldn't keep a straight face anymore.

"You sure know how to pick them Lee," he smiled.

"Who's going to keep an eye on our truck while were up here getting laid? Should we flip a coin again?"Chuck asked.

"No! Since I got the first pick, I'll watch the truck."

"Okay, if you insist," they smirked.

Sammy took his three girls upstairs, while Chuck remained below. I left my three beauties sitting on the bench with their pimp.

I stepped outside to get some fresh air and check the truck. Everything was ship shape. I returned, only to find the whore master gone, the girls still sitting and talking. They stopped talking when I walked in, and just looked at me. I ignored them.

It was very quiet when all of a sudden I heard one of the prostitutes wailing out-

"Keese me like Clark Gable!"

"That'll be the day!" Chuck tersely replied, his voice clearly audible through the paper thin walls.

I had to laugh, which also brought smiles to my wholesome beauties. They began to get up, but I quickly motioned for them to sit down. I began to browse through a Japanese magazine when a death defying scream filled the air. I whipped out my 45 and double timed it upstairs. The screams were getting louder and I couldn't tell from which cubicle they were coming from.

"Sam!" I shouted , "where are you?"

He didn't answer, but the prostitute's screams directed me to him. I pushed aside the bamboo drape and came across a sight that I shall never forget. There in a pool of blood, Sammy had the whore master draped over the cot and was choking him to death. A large knife was buried in Sam's back. I didn't know if the whore master was choking to death or drowning in Sam's blood.

Meanwhile the prostitutes ran out of the room, nude and hysterical.

"Sam let go of him," I screamed. "Stop choking him so I can blow his brains out," I shouted.

Sammy didn't hear me. He was exerting the last bit of pressure before the whore master gave out one last gasp and succumbed.

His eyes bugged out like two cue balls: his tongue unusually long and fiery red.

Chuck meanwhile was right behind me. He was stark naked and brandishing his 45.

"Take it easy Sam" I stammered as I gently and carefully removed the large knife imbedded in his back. I then took one of the clean towels that I found near the wash stand and jammed it into the wound to stop his blood from gushing out. I then wrapped a bed sheet around the towel good and tight. Luckily the blood wasn't gushing out which indicated that no major arteries were cut.

The girls amazed us. They washed the blood off Sam's body before we slipped a pair of pants on him. We placed a blanket on the stretcher we found in the Whore House and placed Sammy on it, face down. We carried him out and gently lifted him in the back of our truck. We took along a couple of blankets just in case Sam went into shock.

"How do you feel Sam?" I asked.

"I felt better!" he winced.

"Let's go Chuck we have to get him to a hospital."

"No hospital ! Take me back with you. I can make it! If you take me in, we'll all be court martialled; our whiskey will be taken away from us and Sgt. Phelps will lose his stripes.

"No can do Sam! Your life is at stake, Chuck said.

"He's right Sam, we don't have a choice."

"I can make it!" he groaned.

"No dice Sam, you've had it! Chuck sternly answered.

Sam raised himself off the cot and before we knew what had happened he grasped my 45 out of my holster and pointed it at us.

"Take me back with you, now, or I'll blow your heads off. I still have enough strength to squeeze this trigger."

"What if you die along the way?" Chuck asked.

"Dump me out and keep going."

"You're crazy Sam, you don't know what you're saying."

"Get going we're wasting time," he coughed.

"You drive Chuck, I'll sit back here with Sam in case he needs anything. "Okay, but hang on because I'm really going to barrel this baby."

Chuck quickly pulled out and took off down the road. Before long we were rolling across the Novalches bridge and homeward bound. Dusk was upon us, so we tried to get as much daylight between us and Manila. Sam, meanwhile winced with every bump we hit, but never complained.

"Sam do you want a shot of Morphine?" I asked noting the pain on Sam's face.

"No Lee, just keep talking to me."

I knew he was in pain, but at least he wasn't bleeding very much. "I'm sorry Lee?"

"For what!"

"For letting that Jap lover knife me. You never got a chance to fuck those broads, did you?"

"Sure I did Sam," I lied. "Chuck relieved me."

"I'm glad."

"Don't talk Sam, just rest."

The journey back seemed so much longer. It appeared as if everyone and everything was slowing us down. Then we got lucky, in a sense.

The Japanese decided to bomb our area and automatically all vehicles on the road are to stop.

The occupants are to take cover wherever they can. With the air raid in progress, the road was clear and Chuck was literally flying.

I could see Sammy was getting weaker by the minute. The engine in our truck was whining wildly, it was an eerie sound, almost like a death serenade.

"Please God, don't let Sammy die," I begged as I prayed.

Just then my prayers were interrupted by Chuck's excited cry-

"We're almost there Lee!"

"Great ! Drive right to the hospital."

It was past taps when Chuck pulled in next to the hospital. The plan was for Chuck to drive off as soon as Sam was taken inside. He was to hide the whiskey and return the truck approximately where we requisitioned it. He was then to tell Sgt. Phelps and the rest of the crew what happened and the story we concocted. He along with Sgt. Phelps were to meet me at the hospital.

As soon as the truck came to a stop, I ran inside and got a couple of Corpsmen to carry Sammy inside. A doctor was summoned and rushed to the hospital.

"This man needs a transfusion!" he excitedly shouted to the staff.

"I'll donate my blood sir," I replied.

"What's your blood type ?"

" Type O , Rh positive."

"Great!

I laid down on a bed alongside Sammy as one of the medics hooked up the apparatus for a direct transfusion.

"What are his chances Sir?"

"It's hard to say until we get him on the operating table. That knife blade may have injured one of his kidneys. It's touch and go!

During the operation, Sgt. Phelps and Chuck pulled up in a Jeep.

They were on the way to see Sgt. Ryan to make sure that our stories were the same.

"Jim here's the story we're going to tell Sgt. Ryan. Sam was knifed from behind by an unknown assailant while returning from the airstrip. When he didn't show up for a couple of hours we made inquiries as to his whereabouts. It wasn't until hours later that we found him in the brush, bloody and delirious. We administered first aid and rushed him to the hospital. Is that it?

"It has to be! That's the story, Sam's going to give, if he recovers.

"Pretty shaky, but I guess we're stuck with it. Now get back to the tent and put on an academy performance.

"Good!"

When we told Sgt. Ryan what had happened, he was a little suspicious, but swallowed our story. If Phelps weren't in with us, I'm sure he wouldn't believe us.

We returned to our tent and immediately hid the whiskey deeper in the jungle. Phelps was promised five bottles of his choice while O'Malley and Bentley each got a bottle. This left us with twenty six bottles to the good. It would be some time before we attempted to sell any of it. When Nina was told that Sammy was critically injured, she fainted. When brought to, she cried hysterically and asked one of us to take her to see him. We obliged, but Sammy was in no condition to talk or see anyone.

A few days later, Sammy was flown back to the states for better care, as his condition was listed as critical. We didn't get a chance to say goodbye to our Boot camp buddy; the move was so sudden.

"Now we'll never know if Sam makes it or not," I mournfully said.

"Maybe it's better this way Lee, If he doesn't make it I don't want to know about it."

"Yeah, maybe you're right."

Nina wasn't around for about a week. She spent all her time in the chapel, praying and burning vigil candles in Sammy's behalf.

For the next two weeks Chuck and I performed our duties as clerks, Follow Me drivers and chauffeurs to the best of our abilities. We dared not step out of line, for fear of being crucified by Sgt. Ryan.

Meanwhile our airstrip was plagued with activity; it was the busiest in the South Pacific. Our planes alone dropped over a million pounds of bombs during the drive to Manila and surrounding areas. Now they were assigned the gigantic task of bombing the twenty five mile mountainous Shimbu sector. This sector was well caved, had pill boxes and housed over 75,000 Japanese troops. General Yamashita was preparing to retake Manila and our planes were to keep his troops dispersed, and in caves, until the Army had enough troops present to wipe them out.

In addition to bombing the various sectors, our Marine flyers were asked to give close air support to the ill clad, poorly equipped Filipino guerrillas that were roaming the hills of Central Luzon, attacking and ambushing unsuspecting Japanese soldiers. We were happy to oblige.

A few days later, I was involved in a high stake poker game, in our camp area, when frenzied screams filled the air.

"I can't see! I can't see!" Cookie Jarnston was screaming maniacally. He was running down the road, bumping into trees and stumbling over fallen logs. His face was a bloody mess.

"I'm blind! Oh my God, I'm blind!" he cried.

Cookie was rushed to the hospital under restraint. It appears that he traded some food for a bottle of whiskey from one of the Filipino natives. Evidently the natives didn't know the difference between Grain alcohol, Wood alcohol or Rubbing alcohol.

To them alcohol was alcohol and so they mixed whatever they had on hand without thinking that it would hurt anyone. Cookie had no one to blame but himself. He should have known better.

The effects of wood alcohol are disastrous if taken in large quantities. If death doesn't occur, the optic nerve may be permanently damaged, leaving the victim blinded for life. Smaller amounts cause temporary blindness but the anxiety of waiting, is maddening.

Once hospitalized, Cookie was deprived of alcohol. He was experiencing an agonizing episode in his drinking career; blindness and the D. T.s (Delirium tremens).

"Can you get me some "Tuba" Jim? Cookie pleaded. "I'm getting the shakes!"

Tuba was to the Philippines as Saki is to Japan. It was a coconut fermented concoction of pretty good potency.

"Sure Cookie," I replied, only instead of Tuba we filled a canteen with the best Scotch we had. Nothing was too good for our drinking buddy.

In a few days Cookie was scheduled to be flown stateside. His eyesight was still impaired and only proper rest and treatment would bring it back to normal again.

We bid our drinking buddy adieu, slipped him a canteen of scotch and departed !

The scuttlebutt around our camp area is that M.A.G. 24 was expecting replacements from the Aviation Replacement Squadron in a few weeks.

All personnel who have been overseas for 15 months will be replaced unless they want to stay on. They would be shipped stateside, get a 30 days furlough, and then be shipped out here again or be assigned to a Marine Air Force base somewhere in the United States.

So much for rumors.

****

Chapter 27

They say East is East and West is West and
never the twain shall meet, but In Sgt. Phelp's case this
saying didn't apply. He fell in love with a beautiful
Filipino girl called Rosalinda Perez, while attending
mass in the town of Dagupan. She dropped her parasol,
which he retrieved and handed back to her. Their eyes
met, she smiled, and cupid sent his love dipped arrow
into a defenseless Marine. He had it!

Rosalinda was an extremely beautiful girl and
very well educated. She was the only daughter of Senor
Henrique Perez, a well known statesman. She was
attending the University of Santo Tomas when the
Japanese attacked their homeland. She fled Manila,
returning to Dagupan where she and her family lived in
the hills with the guerrilla soldiers. She was still hopeful
of resuming her studies in Child Psychology.

Sgt. Phelps was getting nowhere fast with his
new found love, as her "Duenna" (Chaperone) was
constantly at her side. It wasn't until he began to bring
canned goods was he welcomed in her home or to even
talk to her.

Since most of the people in the Philippines were
on meager rations, a can of hash, or fruit cocktail was a
delicacy to these people. Sgt. Phelps had it made as long
as he could bribe Rosalinda's parents with our cache.
We told him about our cache only after he backed up
our story about what happened to Sam. The food that
Phelps was so liberal with belonged to just the two of us
now.

"Hey Lee, let's give the rest of this food to Nina.
I'm sure Sammy would want us to," Chuck said.

"What about Phelps? Rosies parents will kick
him out if he comes empty handed.

"Tough shit! It's our food isn't it? If he wants to make out with her, let him steal his own food." Chuck angrily replied.

"He saved our skins, remember?"

"Sure he did, but we paid him off many times over. I hate black- mailers and I think it's about time we stopped." That afternoon we carted off the food to Nina's home. She was extremely overjoyed with the food. We told her it was from Sammy and he sends her his love. This made her even happier.

That evening, after sprucing up, Sgt. Phelps gingerly skipped into the jungle to pick up a few cans of "goodies." We waited patiently for the outburst that was sure to come.

"We've been robbed! We've been robbed! Phelps shouted as he ran towards us.

"Who's been robbed?" we excitedly asked.

"The canned goods that we had in the jungle! Everything is gone!" he almost cried.

"You're kidding aren't you? Chuck asked.

"No ! I'm not ! It's all gone ! Go look for yourselves."

Chuck and I double timed it to where our cache was hidden and in our best Academy Award Performances, we put on an act that we almost believed.

"How can I go to Rosalinda's home without something to give her? They won't let me in their house."

"Don't tell me they won't accept you without food?" Chuck asked, knowing full well what the arrangements were. He was rubbing salt into an already festering wound.

"I don't know," he stammered irritably.

"I guess you'll have to talk to our Mess Sergeant and see if you can buy some canned goods from him or better yet steal some from the stockade when they're not looking."

"Well there's no way I'm going to approach Germy Nixson with this proposal," Phelps replied,

"I guess you'll have to go out and steal some," Chuck added.

"What a Sergeant stealing?"

"Why not! Love has no boundaries," Chuck continued to bug Phelps.

"Get off my back O'Leary! I have enough trouble with you guys and now you're suggesting I get into more."

"Just trying to be helpful Sarg."

"Bull crap! he added once more, and with that stormed out of our tent and drove off. We had ourselves a good laugh, but afterwards, we began to feel sorry for him. It was too late, the damage was already done.

That night Phelps returned quite early.

"Hey Lee, how would you like to meet Rosalinda's girl friend?"

"Not interested Sarg. I have a gorgeous doll waiting for me back in the states."

"How about you Chuck?"

" How pretty is she?"

"Some would say she's prettier than Rosalinda."

"Hey Sarg, we're interested," O'Malley and Bently shouted.

"Okay, but you'll need some canned goods as openers."

"How many?"

"The girls I have in mind will cost you guys about five cans apiece."

"How about mine?" Chuck wanted to know.

"Yours is a ten canner!" Phelps grinned.

"Ten cans to meet a chick, man that's highway robbery."

"Not if you saw her!"

"Okay it's a deal. My curiosity is worth that much to me alone."

"How about you guys?"

"Got any ten canners?" Bentley asked.

"Don't push your luck!" Phelps remarked.

The next day, immediately after breakfast, Chuck and Bently checked out the area where Germy Nixson stored his extra food.

"How does it look?" Phelps asked upon their return,

"Not so good! The canned goods are easy enough to get at, but it's pretty well guarded."

"How many guards?"

"Two."

"Well that takes care of that." Phelps disgustedly replied.

"Not quite Sarg," Chuck added. "I noticed that their foxhole was about 50 yards from the stockade, so there may be a possibility of raiding the place during an air raid."

"Are you sure?"

"Of course were sure, when we case a joint, we case it. No farting around."

"Sounds like it may work, but pretty God damn risky, if you ask me?"

"We are Sarg," Chuck asked. "It's up to you."

"If it weren't for Rosalinda, I'd say go scratch your ass, but I'm so much in love with her that I don't know what to do !"

"Well what's it going to be?" Chuck wanted to know.

"I guess I have no choice, do I?

Whoever would have thought that I'd be willing to lose these three lovely chevrons for a girl whose parents only let me see her, because of the food I bring them. Oh what the hell! How about you Lee, are you in?"

"Go scratch your ass, Sarg, if I may quote you."

"You serious Lee?"

"Damn right I am ! I'm scheduled to be rotated stateside in a couple of weeks so why should I take a chance on getting my head blown off by a trigger happy guard or better yet, get killed by an exploding bomb."

"Okay Lee, but if we have a big party you won't be invited," Chuck winked.

I caught the wink, but as far as I'm concerned, I didn't give a hoot for parties or girls at this stage of the game. All I wanted to do was to keep my nose clean and get off this island safely. I've seen too many men go through hell for over fourteen months only to be killed accidentally a few weeks before their time is up.

Nonetheless, my buddies prepared for the auspicious occasion. Since air raids are unannounced, they were like firemen waiting for a fire, only in this case it was an air raid. A jeep was parked outside our tent, along with a ladder, rope, empty sea bags and a first aid kit.

A few nights later an air raid sounded at about 0200 hours. Chuck, O'Malley and Bentlley quickly hopped into the Jeep. Sgt. Phelps was going to meet them there. I dropped down into my foxhole and waited for the bombers to appear. The skies were filled with search lights and very shortly afterwards, the Army's anti aircraft guns opened up.

The night was chilly, the mosquitoes fierce. I wrapped the blanket tighter around my body so the mosquitoes wouldn't bite me; it didn't help. In about twenty minutes the all clear sounded. I was back in my sack before the last shrill notes dissipated.

The next sound I heard was that of a Jeep approaching.

"Hey Lee get your ass out here and see what canned goods we have", Chuck nudged me.

They had four sea bags loaded with canned goods.

"What'd you guys get?" I asked.

"How the hell should we know? Do you think we visited a Super Market," Phelps wittingly replied. "We grabbed a little of whatever was in sight and got the hell out of there. They'll never miss what we took."

Chuck meanwhile got a flashlight and began to examine a few cans. There was hash, frankfurters, Spam, corned beef, peas, carrots, beets, peaches, pears and fruit cocktail.

"Looks like we're going to have ourselves quite a party," Bentley rejoiced.

We all pitched in and carried the canned goods back to where our cache used to be.

I for one was very happy they succeeded. Who knows they may have enough canned goods to get laid.

Sgt. Phelps had no trouble convincing the Perez household that a party would be most enjoyable to all. Senor Perez agreed only went one step further. He said he was going to make it a formal ball similar to the ones they had before the Japanese occupation. He invited his relatives and friends and promised to supply the whiskey and girls if we supplied the food. He also told us there would be a small orchestra that would play music that we can dance to. He also told Sgt. Phelps to make sure that the Marines he invites should be clean shaven, and wear their khaki uniforms which included a field scarf.

The day of the formal party, Sgt. Phelps, loaded the Follow Me Jeep with the canned goods and drove out to the Perez household. When Senor Perez saw all the food that he brought, he invited him inside to have a drink and they talked about his relationship with his daughter.

Since I didn't help in the appropriation of the canned goods, I didn't go even though I was invited. From what I hear the band played a lot of American songs that Sgt. Phelps and friends could dance to.

Sgt. Phelps danced with his new found love, while Chuck, Bently and O'Malley would dance a few numbers and then sneak off the dance floor to get a little air.

"Yeah, Right !

The party lasted till the wee hours of the morning and so I took Chuck's shift at the Control tower because he was really hung over.

That night we had an air raid that left us partially paralyzed, as three five hundred pound bombs hit the far end of our landing strip and failed to go off. We didn't know if they were duds or timed to go off later. We made no attempt to find out.

The area was roped off, and "OFF LIMIT" signs were posted and the planes instructed to take off and land in only one direction, regardless of the wind currents.

A few days later, Sgt. Phelps came busting into our tent.

"I just got the word men, we'll be shoving off pretty soon."

"Where to, Japan ? Chuck excitedly asked.

"No ! Mindanao in the Southern Philippines."

"Mindanao?' Bentley gulped, "Isn't that the home of the Head hunters?"

"Sure it is but the Moros hate the Japanese as much as we do, so we shouldn't have too much trouble with them unless we piss them off, in some way."

"Let's hope not, those bolo knives can behead a man with one swish."

"Yeah right!" I replied.

"So when are we moving out?" Bentley asked.

"I don't know but M.A.G. 32 was told to start packing."

"How about that Lee, we're moving out," Chuck rejoiced.

"Yeah, and I thought this was going to be our last campaign before we're rotated state side"

"Don't fret buddy boy, I wouldn't miss this campaign for anything. Who knows we may even see a little action."

"That's what I'm afraid of."

Sgt. Phelps was right. We were moving out but not just yet. The ground echelons of MAG 32 were scheduled to move out on February the 23rd, 1945, leaving its planes and pilots to continue flying their sorties along with ours, for a couple of weeks. This meant that our workload doubled. We were busier than the proverbial bee.

When Nina found out that our outfit was moving out she was heart-broken. She's been picking up all of our dirty clothes in the morning, and bringing them back in the afternoon washed and ironed, for all these months. We were like her family.

Nina knew that eventually we were going to leave, but not this soon. One day when she returned our clothes she asked –

"Nina would like to know, if you boys, would come to her house for dinner tomorrow tonight?"

We looked at her and smiled.

"It would be our pleasure Nina," we replied.

"Do you like feesh?"

"We sure do! Chuck smiled, "we haven't had a good feesh dinner in months."

"Good ! Nina expect you at six oclock."

"We'll be there."

The next day we had forsaken chow because of our invitation. It was a few minutes before six when our Follow Me Jeep pulled up next to the bamboo shack.

Because of the long rainy season, most of the peasant homes were built on stilts high above the ground. Nina's shack was no different. As we waited for our hostess to come to the door, the sight of two little boys peeing in what looked like a well, made us laugh.

"They must be working for the water department," Chuck remarked.

"Good evening boys," she politely addressed us. We didn't mind being called boys because we knew it was a term of endearment.

"Good evening Nina, we greeted her as we filed inside. Chuck meanwhile presented her with a box of canned goods.

Nina's home was built almost entirely of bamboo, including the furniture. Colorful straw mats lined the walls and floors. It was quite cozy.

We sat down on the straw mats while Nina began to fill our water cups.

"Boy am I thirsty," Bentley announced as he gulped his down.

"Nina, where do you get your water?" I asked.

"From the well Lee, why do you ask?"

Just then Bentley who was on his second cup of water, almost threw up. His countenance turned a sickening green color as he excused himself. The three of us laughed hysterically which puzzled our hostess.

"What's wrong?"

"Nothing Nina, nothing we roared, the tears rolling down our cheeks.

"She joined us in our uproarious laughter even though she didn't know why. Quite the hostess !

"Drink up boys," she said.

We looked at each other and once more broke out laughing. It wasn't until Nina left the room that we had a chance to empty our cups. I poured my water into a flower pot. Chuck poured his into a crack in the floor, while Hands O'Malley flung his out the window.

We screamed hilariously when Nina's little boy came in wet and crying. Oh what a calamity !

The feesh dinner was excellent, the hostess congenial and the water incident unforgettable. I don't remember when I laughed this much and for so long; Unforgetable !

With the possibility of moving out at any time, Chuck and I agreed that it was about time we got rid of our whiskey.

We passed the word around that it was available at fifty bucks a fifth. Before too long a constant stream of buyers visited our tent and in less than an hour we had them all sold except for a couple that we saved for ourselves.

We came back from Manila with 32 bottles. We gave 5 to Sgt. Phelps and one each to Bentley and O'Malley. We also filled up Cookies canteen with two bottles which meant that we sold 21 fifths of whiskey. We made 1050 dollars which we were going to split three ways.

"Where do we send Sammy his money? Chuck asked.

"You know I thought about that! What if we gave Nina his money, because as far as we know he may be dead. And besides 350 dollars to Sammy is probably nothing. He could lose that or win that in one poker hand.

"I agree Lee, but let's give her an even $500 and you and I split the other $550 what do you say?

"Why not! She's a sweet, charming hard working young girl.

That evening Chuck and I went to visit Nina's home and told her Sammy wanted her to have his money if anything happened to him. She began to cry when Sammy's name was mentioned and after she calmed down a bit she said she was going to buy a wash tub, with a wringer, some clothes for her family and a new dress and shoes for herself.

Seeing her so happy was something we'll always remember.

That night, March the 2nd, 1945 the inevitable happened. Four Japanese bombers attacked the Mangaldan air strip, plastering us with anti personnel bombs. They must have been kicking them out by the bushel baskets because the next morning over 200 craters were counted in our camp area alone.

Four men were killed, and over eighty slightly injured, including our Commanding Officer. In addition to these craters, and the dead and injured, many of our planes were put out of commission; our mess hall was set ablaze and countless tents damaged.

Our small group of Field Operational Personnel fared much better. Only Hands O'Malley got hit by flying shrapnel. A piece of steel imbedded itself, in all places, in one of his oversized mitts. What a day for Purple Hearts!

A few days later, a plane load of replacements arrived from the states. This meant that Chuck and I would be rotated stateside, if we wanted to go.

"Chuck, We made it!" I howled, "We made it!"

"I'm not going back Lee!"

"Are you out of your mind! Haven't you killed enough Japs already? What are you trying to prove?

"Perhaps I have Lee, but I'm not leaving until I see Japan, and besides you have baseball and a girl to come home to, I don't!"

"Does Sgt. Ryan know what you intend to do?"

"Yes he does, he isn't going back either. He and I joined the Marine Corps to fight and that's what we intend to do. Remember Lee when we were on that train going to boot camp and I told you I would sign up for twenty years if I like the Corps."

"Yeah !"

"Well I love it! Do you know what I liked doing most of all?"

"No, what?"

"Being in the Battle of The Perimeter. I just loved killing those Japs on Bougainville," he smiled.

"Really ?

"Yes Really !"

"Well Chuck good luck to you! I'm really going to miss you, and I'm sure that I shall never forget you! You have been a true friend!

When the war is over maybe we can get together and reminisce about our Marine Corps experiences."

"I'd like that."

That afternoon, I said goodbye to all of my friends as I boarded the DC6 which was taking those of us that survived 15 months of hell back to the states. As the plane roared down the runway, tears filled my eyes. I felt like crying, but who ever saw a marine cry?

"Yeah Right!"

Our itinerary home took longer than I anticipated. The DC6 cargo plane flew us only as far as Peleiu in the Palaus islands. From there we boarded a troop ship, carrying the sick and wounded back to the states.

We arrived at Manus Islands in the Admiralties to pick up a few more ambulatory cases. It was heart breaking to see the cream of American youth coming home physically incapacitated. A cold sweat crept over me when I thought how close I came to being amongst them.

During our leisurely cruise home, I had plenty of time to reflect on passing events. It seemed incredible that so much of life could be experienced in fifteen short months. Yet it did!

About a week later our ship sailed into Pearl Harbor, Hawaii. We were given a couple of days of shore leave before boarding the aircraft carrier "Nassau" for our trip back to the states. While in Hawaii, I wired Rita a corsage and then picked up a few souvenirs for Rita, my mother and my three sisters.

The next day we pulled out of the harbor and headed for San Diego. I was very happy to be coming home, but extremely harassed. I know the 15 months I spent oversea had taken their toll. For one thing, I haven't had a decent night's sleep in months. It was rare for me not to get up in the middle of the night, choking a pillow, screaming, cowering or rolling off my bed into an imaginary foxhole.

The worst nightmare of all was the sight of a Japanese soldier standing over me, while I slept, ready to shoot me. How long would these bizarre nightmares continue? Will I ever outlive them? I had no idea !

I wasn't particularly worried for myself, only for Rita. Would she understand? Was our love strong enough to overcome this subconscious brain washing? Only time will tell.

After a few days at sea, the Nassau was finally snuggling up close to the pier.

USS Nassau

All of us were happily waving to the throngs below, when I saw her. She was attired in her Naval uniform and wearing the corsage I wired her. The band meanwhile began to play the Marine's Hymn.

As I walked down the narrow stairs I heard Rita's angelic voice calling me.

"Lee! Lee ! Over here." she waved frantically.

I dropped my sea bag, off to one side, and fought my way through the crowd.

"Rita !" I shouted.

"Lee !"

"Oh Lee! If you only knew how much I missed you! " she happily cried.

I closed my eyes and kissed her warm sweet lips, lovingly and wantingly. It seemed for a split second as if I had never left.

"Shall we go to Papa Igors for dinner?" I asked.

"Guess what? I figured you would like to go there, so I made a reservation for us and then we can go for a swim at the beach house.

"Will the last one in, be a rotten egg?"

"Of course," she purred, as her lips met mine once more.

As we walked to her car, I was deliriously and excitingly happy!

"Lee, have you ever wondered what happened to Sammy?"

"Yes I have ! Did he make it?"

"Yes he did! When he was shipped stateside, they brought him to our hospital. His kidney was in bad shape, but he recovered.

"Where is he now?"

"He's somewhere in Texas. I have his address and phone number in my purse."

"Great ! I'll have to give him a call."

"By the way did he mention to you how he got hurt?"

"Yes, somebody stabbed him from behind, when he was coming back from the air strip."

"Yeah right!" I laughed.

Epilogue

Chuck never returned from the Philippines. He was listed as Missing In Action. (M.I.A.)

Sammy was back in action. The last I heard from him, he was part owner of a casino in Las Vegas.

I never went back to playing Professional baseball. I took advantage of the veteran's GI Bill and enrolled at the University of Illinois where I received my Bachelor and Master's Degrees in the Teaching of High School Science.

Rita and I never got married. I was stationed in Congaree, South Carolina, she was stationed in Honolulu, Hawaii. She wanted to stay in the service, while I wanted to go to College. Little by little we slowly drifted apart.

Before long I met and fell in love with Peggy Morrison. I've been happily married for over 55 years and I'm the proud father of 4 children and now 7 grandchildren.

Even though I never fulfilled my dream of becoming a Major League ballplayer, one of my sons did make it to the Major Leagues.

Lee James Walewander

Books written by the author:

Civil Rights Activists
Grandpa's Animal Stories
Grandpa's Book of Rhymes
Grandpa's Christmas Stories
Grandpa's Fairy Tales
Grandpa's Holiday Stories
He Runs Like Hell !
Historical Heroes
Hypnotic Cops
Run and Gun
Starlita
Thumbs Up!

If you're interested in previewing or purchasing any of the above books go on line to -

http://www.grandpastories.com